LEGON ASCENSION
LEGON
BOOK TWO

NICHOLAS TAYLOR

SOMNIUM

Legon Ascension

Book Two in the Legon Series

Text copyright © 2011, 2025 Nicholas Taylor. Third Edition.

Somnium Press, LLC

This is a work of fiction. Names, places, characters and events portrayed in this book are fictitious and are a product of the author's imagination. Any similarity to persons living or dead is coincidental and not intended by the author.

ISBN-13: 978-1-938387-04-3

www.NicholasTaylor.co

CONTENTS

PROLOGUE
TAKEN

"No matter how hard we try to ignore it, the world we don't recognize is still there."
— The Exiled Captain (Author Unknown)

Rachel made her way home. She'd spent a lovely day with Timothy, her one true love—or at least that's what her sixteen-year-old heart told her he was. She trotted home, letting her dress swirl around her and waved as she passed her best friend Pamela's house. Pamela was more of a tomboy with her tough attitude and sturdy frame, but Rachel thought she was wonderful.

Dinner was normal. Rachel daydreamed while her mother and father tried to talk to her, but, like most teenagers, she wasn't much for sharing. The night was cool when she went to bed, so she closed her window and settled into a dream of Timothy. She sighed in contentment.

A sound woke her... what was it? It sounded like screams from outside. Still half asleep, Rachel went to open the window when her father burst into the room.

"Rachel, Rachel honey, come on, we need to leave!" he said frantically.

Why did they need to leave? With a snap of her father's fingers, she thought of everyone in town talking about the Iumenta that had been watching them. Feeling scared, she moved with her father to the living room. There was yelling and more screaming outside. Her mother was downstairs putting food in a bag. The door of the house burst open, and Rachel's father shoved her into a closet as four black-armored figures entered the house.

She heard her mother scream and her dad yell, "Get off my wife!" Then there was a thud, the sound of something being dragged, and her mother screaming, "NO!" Rachel, her heart pounding, knelt, looking out of the crack at the bottom of the door. A pool of blood oozed under the door, and she saw just a glimpse of brown hair that matched her father's. She moved to the wall, clamping her eyes shut. "No, no, no, no, no!" she whispered.

There was a sound from upstairs. What was it? Another cry that sounded like her mother... was she still alive? Fear and the need to stay alive finally won out. As she opened the door of the closet and confirmed her father's death and her mother's absence, she bolted for the door.

Shame filled her as she left her mother to whatever fate she was enduring, but Rachel had to run. The streets were in pandemonium. Black-armored figures were hacking people to death. The bodies of men, women, and children littered the streets. She slammed into one of the black figures and screamed as he raised a war hammer to hit her. Then, with a crunch, the man fell to the side, revealing Pamela with a skillet.

"Come on, we need to get to the town center to make a stand!" Pamela was a fighter.

They ran as fast as they could to the town center, where a small band of men and women were making a last stand. Pamela joined the fight, swinging her skillet with as much force as she could muster. Rachel, watching the slaughter, sank to the ground. Finally, the majority of the townspeople were lost, and those who were left were injured or had given up. Counting Rachel and Pamela, there were maybe ten people left.

The black figures surrounded them, and Rachel was sure that she was going to die or be dragged off like the other people she had seen. The figures parted, and an Iumenta walked up to the survivors, his gray skin fading in the moonlight and his yellow eyes boring into Rachel's.

CHAPTER 1
PLANS

"Reality is a matter of perspective; loss, gain, sorrow, joy—they depend on where you are sitting. By altering perspective, one can change the world."
— Diary of the Perfectos Compatioa

There was a glint of metal as the fenrra cut flesh and bone. Kovos' head detached in slow motion, turning in the air to bounce on the ground. As his face turned, his eyes bore into hers, and he whispered, "Emma."

Sasha woke with a start, straightening up in bed. She was covered in sweat, her breathing ragged. *Dream, Sasha, dream!* she told herself. She tasted for bile, but there was none. *Another night free,* she thought. Since the battle at the precipice, Sasha's episodes had been coming on once or twice a day, but for the last two days, she had been fine. Her dreams were normally about the battle: seeing lines of color streak the sky as dragons fought, the roars of familiars, and the screams of men. But last night was different—a nightmare, yes, but not of the battle. Instead, she watched as Kovos died. His disembodied head spoke to her, saying the name of the girl he intended to marry back in their hometown of Salmont. This made her think of her own loved ones back home. Both she and Legon thought of them often, but for now, there wasn't anything they could do to contact them.

Her mind reached out to the dragon dome's room controls, and the room was bathed in soft honey tones. She pushed back her sheets, which were wet with her nightmare's sweat, swung her legs off the side of the bed, and planted her feet on the warm wooden floor. Mornings were her time of remembrance, or at least they had become that since the battle and her episodes increased. Every morning she would replay the last few months: their escape from Salmont and journey to Salkay, being attacked by the royal guard, finding Sara, Kovos dying, Legon turning into an Elf. Eventually, her mind would stop after she replayed memories of coming to the dragon dome and the battle.

She made her way to the bathroom of her apartment. She was in a different one since her arrival at the dragon dome. Sara and Keither were now staying in the Human barracks, and Sasha and Legon shared an apartment. Her mind reached out to his room, where he still slept. She disrobed and stepped into the shower, her own piece of paradise, letting its steam and heat clear her mind. This morning, however, all she could see when her eyelids closed was Kovos, and she was thankful for the hot water that washed away her tears.

LEGON WOKE FROM A DREAMLESS SLEEP, HIS MIND FEELING Sasha dwelling on Kovos and their family as she got ready for her day. He blocked his mind, not wanting to think about either. His stress levels were high enough without thinking about that which he could not help at the moment. Instead, his eyes shifted over to a leather-bound book on his nightstand, the title in Elvish and the contents about the one thing Legon feared more than any foe—public speaking. This too he pushed from his mind as he rose to get ready for the day.

Brushing one's teeth was common in the Empire, but not like this. The brushes in the dragon dome were attached to the walls with thin vines, and when you put them in your mouth, they vibrated quickly, cleaning your teeth. He liked it now, but at first, he hadn't. When he was done, his teeth felt... well, slimy, and it took him a while to figure out that's how teeth were supposed to feel—not slimy, but smooth and polished.

Like Sasha, Legon loved the shower. He stepped inside, sliding his finger over the little ridge that controlled the water. As steam built, his mind drifted off, and time slowed with each breath of the thick air. The hot water ran down Legon's body, taking with it the stress and worries of the last few weeks. Most of those worries consisted of how he was supposed to be a leader and what to do about the war between the free lands and the Cona and Impa Empires. Also, he was now a public figure, one that would be expected to address his people and that of a nation. How was he to do that? Legon knew he was a man of action; he woke up, went to work, maybe got in a fight, and he would do whatever it took to protect those around him. But inspire and lead them? That was something entirely foreign to him. The water of the shower only gave a temporary reprieve, but a welcome one nonetheless. Once he was done and dressed, Legon stepped into the main room. Sydin was there waiting for him and Sasha and didn't seem to notice Legon as he entered. Sydin's eyes were unfocused. Legon figured he was in a meeting or something. Sydin wouldn't care if Legon looked in his head to see what he was doing, but Legon didn't want to pry. If it was important, then Sydin would tell him.

In truth, Legon didn't want any attention at the moment. The shower's temporary reprieve from stress and cares was over. Legon's mind was once again filled to the point of overflowing. Presently, Sasha joined them in the common room, carrying her shoes in her right hand. They were a sparkly silver that matched her dress. Sasha plopped herself down on one of the cushy white couches and put them on.

"Are you two ready?" she asked.

Sydin shook his head. "Oh, sorry, I was talking to Telunone of House Paldin."

House Paldin was one of the great houses of the Elvin Empire, or Pawdin Empire, to be correct. House Paldin was the house that gathered all of the great Elvin houses together in order to meet the Iumenta threat that would someday turn into the War of Generations. When the first council gathered all the leaders of the other houses, they found it

fit to name their new country the Pawdin Empire after House Paldin.
Sydin told Legon and Sasha that in the early days of the newly formed
Pawdin Empire, the members of House Paldin were flattered and a little
overwhelmed by the new country's name being in their honor. They
feared that in time the other great houses would see it as Paldin trying to
place it above the others. They didn't want to cause the first-ever Elf
conflict. Legon found it interesting that over the thousands of years
that the Elves were separate countries, there had never been war
between them, and like today, people moved from region to region
regardless of what house controlled it. This hadn't been the case for the
Iumenta's Impa Empire. Before they formed into one cohesive unit,
they were separate countries similar to city-states, and they fought
often. The pre-Impa era was one of constant battle for the Iumenta—a
time of killing, but also a time of hardening, the time that gave them the
strength for the War of Generations. Legon shook these thoughts from
his mind.

"Is he going to be taking over for Evindass when we leave?" Legon
asked.

"Yes, he's the blue dragon you saw the day you came in," Sydin said.

Sasha's face turned bright at the memory. "I remember him; he's
friendly."

Sydin turned and spoke to her. "Yes, I like Telunone. He's a
respectable man; I've known him for the better part of four thousand
years."

Sasha's head shook. "So, Sydin, what was it like when the world was
created?"

They loved to pick on Sydin for his age, which was a very Human
thing to do, as Elves don't age. To them, being thousands of years old
was just another part of life. Sasha picked a bad day to taunt him. Sydin
merely smiled at her.

Sasha reminded Sydin of his one and only daughter, of whom he
thought the world. Sydin was a father of twelve, eleven of whom were
boys. When Sasha would give someone—usually Legon or Barnin—a
dirty or reproachful look, Sydin said it reminded him of when his
daughter was a little girl and she would get mad at him for taking away a
toy. He didn't find her looks menacing or frightening, not that anyone

did, but rather cute and funny. So Sydin laughed harder, and Sasha's face softened.

"It's a good thing I like you," she said more lightheartedly than before.

"Can we eat, please? I'm hungry," Legon added.

Sasha rolled her eyes. "When aren't you? Ok, let's go eat."

As they made their way to the dining hall, Legon was thinking about breakfast, though there were more pressing matters at hand. He was in this war now and in it for the long haul, in it for the Humans and Elves who would not walk the land for centuries to come. So what was he to do now to ensure their future? Ideas had been rolling around in his head since he arrived at the dome, but now Legon was hungry and couldn't focus. The soft rhythmic sound of shoes and boots hitting the floor as the group walked seemed to help put things in perspective. That was it, wasn't it? Perspective. All this time, the filth had ruled by keeping people relatively happy, keeping them just content enough to not hate their owners, for lack of a better word. If people knew what their lives had become, what they would turn into if they stayed under the Iumenta? Would they be able to fight back? Would they want to? Yes, Legon decided they would fight back if there was a future better than the one they lived in now... but how to do that? War was not a better immediate future for anyone in Airmelia. All sides would suffer. The Elves would fight because those alive today would see that brighter future, but many, if not most, of Humanity would not live to see that future.

They were at the dining hall now. Legon found himself seated and waiting for Sydin, who ran off to get food. Sasha looked at Legon concernedly.

"What are you thinking?" she asked.

"Aren't you paying attention?"

"No, you blocked your mind. What's going on?"

Legon didn't want to talk about it now. "I'll tell you in a bit when I figure it out."

Sasha arched an eyebrow. "You could just let down your defenses, and then I could find out now," she tried in a persuasive tone.

He smiled wryly. "I could, but that wouldn't be as much fun."

Sasha stuck her tongue out at him but didn't push the subject. She would get her answers—they both knew that. Sydin returned with three plates of food. The scent of eggs, cheese, and something sweet instantly pushed the thoughts of the war from Legon's mind. Sydin sat after handing everyone a plate. He bowed his head, folding his arms. Legon hadn't noticed it at first, but the Elves were rather religious, something uncommon in the Cona Empire where he had grown up. But they weren't overt about their beliefs. It had taken Legon days to figure out that at meals when Elves bowed their heads, they were praying—something he found rather odd. Even Ise did it. They all prayed to the White Dragon, but neither Legon nor Sasha had pressed the subject with anyone. It felt awkward to them. Legon noticed Sasha eyeing Sydin's plate.

"You have chocolate here?" Sasha pointed when Sydin opened his eyes.

Sasha, like all girls, seemed to love this incredibly rare treat. Chocolate came from cacao or cocoa beans, but it grew in the south and was hard to acquire. It shouldn't have been a surprise that Legon's people had it; after all, they were the ones who controlled the south. Still, it was rare, so rare in fact that most people in the Cona Empire only got it once every few years, at best. Legon's mother said she was given a piece on her wedding day and then another when Sasha was born, but that was the extent of it. Arkin, of course, seemed to come upon it fairly often, so Sasha got a piece every year for her birthday. They never could figure out how he got a hold of the stuff, but it made sense now.

Two of the plates Sydin carried had eggs, cheese, bacon, and other normal breakfast items. The third had a small pastry on it that looked to be covered in chocolate, which dripped off the side. Legon felt his mouth fall open. The treat before his eyes would be a week's pay back home.

"Sydin, that had to cost you a fortune! What's the occasion?" Sasha said.

Sydin looked confused. "You've had this for breakfast every day; I don't under..." his voice trailed off.

"Sash, would you like to try this?" Sydin asked.

She sat back, waving the food away. "Oh no, it's yours, but it looks good."

Sydin pressed on, saying, "Do you want me to get you one?"

Sasha looked a little overwhelmed. "That's nice of you, but..."

Legon became aware of a familiar THUMP THUMP of boots behind him, and it was no surprise to hear Arkin's voice.

"Sydin, you forget that in the Empire, chocolate is worth more than a pound of gold."

"It's not here?" Legon asked.

Sydin explained. "Not in the least bit. It grows abundantly in the Elf lands. You know that hot drink you've been having every morning?"

Legon thought about it. They did have a hot drink every morning. It was bitter but exceptionally good, and it seemed to wake him up.

"Socolata?" Legon said.

Sydin nodded. "Yes, it's ground and brewed cocoa beans."

Sasha gasped. "We've been drinking chocolate every day? Shouldn't it be sweeter?"

"We can make it that way, yes. Elves and Humans in the south drink and eat a lot of chocolate. In fact, it's relatively worthless down here," Sydin said.

Sasha shook her head, and Legon sensed her disgust once again at their former home—not the people or the land, but the people's situation. Chocolate was worthless to the Humans here as well as the Elves, meaning the only reason it wasn't to Sasha and her family was that it was a banned substance in the Empire. Well, having it wasn't banned, but trading with the Elves was.

Sydin looked sad. "Sasha, I'm sorry, it's just..."

Sasha huffed and spoke. "I'm not sad about the silly pastry; I'm happy about getting those now. It's just another straw on the pile, you know what I mean?"

Legon did; they all did. It was funny how insignificant something could be and still mess up your day. New thoughts bubbled in Legon's head, and a smile pulled itself across his face. He dug into the eggs, not caring in the least about the little sweet next to him that would fetch the price of a horse back home. When they were done, Legon excused himself and Sasha, who got up without complaint but still morose.

As they walked down one of the many passages of the dome, Legon realized he was moving a little fast, and he eased back, locking one of his arms with Sasha. She looked up at him, confused but curious.

"So, are you going to tell me what you're thinking now?" she asked.

"Yep."

Sasha waited as Legon stuck his hand in his pocket, pulling out a small round piece of chocolate that Sydin had slipped him at the table. He handed it to her.

"Did I make that big of a scene?" she asked.

Sasha plopped it in her mouth, and her eyes widened. "It's got a cherry in it!" she said, amazed.

"Wow, that's neat," Legon said.

Sasha's sour mood returned. "Ok, spill it. Wasn't I an idiot?"

Legon didn't hesitate in his answer. "No, Sash, everyone knew what you meant... truth be told, you said it in a much kinder way than any of us would have, but you also solved the war," he said, beaming at her.

"Chocolate?" she asked.

"Exactly."

Sasha stopped and turned Legon to face her. The look on her face was one he'd seen a thousand times; it was the "did you hurt yourself or something" look.

Legon took a second to compose his thoughts. "I'm fine. Think about it. The Iumenta stay in control by making people think they are happy with material things, right?"

"Yes, I guess so," Sasha responded.

"But people really don't have that much now, do they?"

She thought for a moment. "No, but they don't know that."

"Ah yes, but we do, and I would be willing to bet that there are a lot of other things that people don't know. A lot of stuff that people outside the Empire enjoy that people in the Empire don't," Legon said.

"Ok, I think I see where you're going with this. If people knew their lot, they might not be so willing to support the Iumenta. And, once they see that they are slaves, they will rebel. So what is your plan?"

Legon started walking again and explained. "I'm going to send Arkin into the Empire to gather information and start spreading the word that the Iumenta aren't as wonderful as many people seem to think. I was going to have him gather information for us anyway, but now I think we can put him to more use."

"What about the dragons? With them influencing the minds of the people, they have such a strong hold there's no way it will work."

"Only if they are in an area to influence it," Legon pointed out.

"Ok, so that's what, every major city and then some patrols in areas with a lot of towns?" Sasha speculated.

"But not enough to keep thoughts in check for people in smaller, spread-out areas like co-ops and small towns—the food source of the Empire," Legon explained.

It clicked home with Sasha now. "You're going to sow resentment in the rural areas and then, in effect, the cities."

"Basically, my goal is to keep the Iumenta Dragons focused on the cities. Think about it: as the Iumenta's control over the minds of the rural areas weakens and as the people's animosity grows, they will hate their government. So, when our forces inevitably move into an area, the surrounding people will welcome us, cutting off the cities from supply. Thus, by doing this, discord in the cities will rise, and the Iumenta will be forced to put more and more effort and resources into controlling the population in the cities."

"And with farming communities cutting off food supplies, it will make it easy to put cities under siege; just wait it out with a secured countryside," she nodded, impressed.

Legon went on, "...and if we up raids on the borders, the Iumenta will have to send more dragons down to help."

Sasha finished for him, saying, "...taking them away from the cities. Good thinking; it could take years, but why not? It worked for the Iumenta. That's how they took over the Cona lands to begin with, so why not us?"

Legon smiled. Sasha was on board with this, and that was a good thing. Now he needed to get Sydin and Iselin in on it as well. Plus, he was going to need to have people attacking the Empire's supply trains, and Legon knew just the group to do it.

For the most part, the Precipice and its forces were commanded by the Elves. It was labeled as a joint affair between the Pawdin Empire and the Cona Republic, but with the constant influx of refugees from the

Cona Empire and planning raiding parties, the Human staff was overwhelmed. There would be no issue procuring a special unit to wreak havoc on the Empire, but he still would need to talk to Telunone about it. After all, in a few days, Telunone would be in charge of this dome. House Evindass was scheduled to meet with Telunone in the afternoon, so it shouldn't be a problem.

When it was time for the meeting with Telunone, Sydin and Iselin were all in the loop and in agreement with Legon and Sasha. They all walked into a command room of the dome. This room used to be Sydin's command center, complete with House Evindass banners, but now they were greeted with the gold on white of Paldin, hanging from the ceiling of the far wall. The banner was ivory, and in the center was a large dot that represented the sun, with waves rising from the dot to symbolize the sea. All of this was woven in thread that looked like gold—and it probably was. The sun and sea shimmered as the banner slowly moved from the constant movement in the room. Off to the left side of the room was a doorway, out of which a harassed-looking, raven-haired Elf strode. He ran his hand across his face and through his short hair. His firm jawline was set in a look of agitation, but despite that, he still looked friendly enough. He turned a set of large green eyes at them, which sparkled with sapphire blue flecks.

"Bad time, Telunone?" Sydin asked.

Telunone responded, frowning. "Are you sure you don't want to stay here, Sydin? I mean, House Evindass has done such a fantastic job with this place; I don't want to mess up a good thing."

Sydin laughed heartily. "Not on your life. This place has been a pain since it was built, and it's impossible to supply."

Telunone ran his hand through his hair in exasperation. "Yes, I can see that a storm hit last night in those horrid mountains. Of course, that's when all our belongings were heading through there, and well, now you can guess what."

Sydin chuckled again and patted Telunone on the shoulder. "So I take it that's where most of your staff is?"

"Oh yes, and my wife—her favorite painting flew off. Sorry, those aren't your problems. Let's find a place where we can talk more privately. Sorry, Un Prosa and Un Prose, my name is Telunone; it's an honor," he said, extending a hand to Legon and then Sasha.

Sasha looked confused at his words. "Sorry, what did you call me?"

Sydin broke in, speaking to Telunone. "Forgive me, it has been busy. They don't know all of the formalities and etiquette yet."

Telunone seemed to understand. "Un Prose is the feminine of Prosa. You are a lady of a great house. It's like when the Humans say 'my lady,' for example."

Sasha hesitated and nodded. "Oh, ok, thank you; you can just call me Sasha if you like."

Telunone laughed softly. "Of course, Sasha; now come; let us talk."

Telunone led them to a small room with a domed ceiling like their apartments. As they walked around a large table in the center of the room, Legon noticed the table's natural beauty; it was quite unlike anything he had seen before. It was round, but the edges rippled out as if it was once a giant stump now propped on legs. The top was shiny, like glass, and when he looked down on it, he could see that it got its shine from layer upon layer of some sort of clear coating. The wood looked like it was torn from the tree with large chunks missing. The clear coating made the table look submerged, like you could dip your finger in the liquid surface and touch the tortured wood below. Legon placed his palms on the table, leaning slightly against it, and the shining top held solid. The rest of the room was nice as well, with the same rough eloquence of the table. Telunone strolled over to a mini bar, over which hung Paldin's banner. He began fiddling with decanters, filling several glasses with the deep amber Poti that the Elves preferred. Legon took a glass, sipped the liquid, and resumed admiring the table.

Something about the room felt awkward to Legon, and he looked around. "Where are the chairs?"

Telunone grimaced at this. "As I said, it has been a hard move."

"Oh, sorry."

"Don't be; it's not your fault. Now, Sydin, I got all of your reports for me, so I think I'm up to speed. Is there something else?"

Sydin stepped up to the table, and everyone looked a little awkward standing at it, but no one brought that up.

"We know that House Paldin is going to be running this dome, but

House Evindass would like to continue to use some of the Human units here, if you are agreeable with that. We would like to coordinate through you."

Telunone looked at Legon. "Of course, that's fine. May I ask what you had in mind?"

SASHA LOOKED AT TELUNONE'S GLITTERING EYES NOW FIXED on her brother. She could see no resentment in them; Telunone honestly didn't mind. If House Evindass needed something, then it would be provided without question. Telunone was simply curious. She knew this would have never happened in any of the Human governments, and she wondered how long it took the Elves to get to this level of trust.

Legon spoke. "We are planning on disrupting the inner workings of the Cona Empire with raiding parties and a propaganda campaign."

Telunone inclined his head, indicating for Legon to continue.

"I'm trying to think of how to explain this correctly," he paused. "We want to make people in the Empire think twice about their current government. We will do this by sowing discord throughout the land."

Telunone looked confused. "You want to polarize the land?"

Legon pressed on. "Yes, and then take advantage of that."

"Well, it won't be easy with the Iumenta Dragons spread throughout the Empire like they are. You may be able to sway a few small towns and co-ops, but I'm not sure what good that will do."

Sydin started to talk. "Well, there is more than that. If you remember, that's how the Iumenta took over in the first place."

Telunone thought for a moment before responding. "Yes, so won't they see that coming then?"

Sydin smiled and explained. "Ah, you forget; when the Iumenta took over, we had no dragons in the Human lands swaying people's thoughts. That is the only way they stay in control."

Now Sasha could see the wheels turning in Telunone's head. "So, if we can weaken that, then we could have a chance of turning the people against them, making the fight simpler. Yes, I see where you are going with this…" He looked down at the table, deep in thought. "We will also need to pull as many dragons away from the cities and towns as possible."

Sasha couldn't help herself. "But how?"

"Easy, my dear; we are a bigger threat than a bunch of angry farmers. If we increase the presence of our Ascended along the borders, they will in turn send more of their own. In fact, they will be forced to send most of their military to the borders, which will cause quite a fuss if we don't attack."

Iselin chimed in. "If we keep feinting, then they won't be able to justify pulling their forces back. But conversely, they won't be able to justify the cost of matching our numbers in the sky. They must be stretching themselves thin trying to control the bulk of the Cona lands as it is. And that's not even counting those Ascended that keep Impa air safe."

"Yes, that's a good point too," Telunone said.

Sasha was getting part of the Elves' overall strategy now. The Elves were slowly working to kill off as many dragons as possible. If they upped those efforts by agitating the Iumenta, then there would be fewer dragons in the rest of the Empire to keep the unstable population under control and then…

Legon finished Sasha's thought aloud. "Civil war." She heard the bitterness in his tone, but there was also resignation to what needed to be done.

"Maybe not… the Iumenta will try to hold the cities, but the rest of the land will be out of their control. When we do invade, we shouldn't encounter much resistance. In fact, if done right, we will receive aid," Telunone said, smiling. "Legon, House Evindass truly is lucky to have you as its head. You are like your father."

Legon looked a little uneasy at the compliment but happy at the same time. Sasha noticed that Iselin was suppressing a smile. She reached out with her mind. "What are you smiling at?"

Iselin responded in Sasha's mind, "Isn't it obvious? If this works, then we may have a chance of winning without having to wipe out all of Humanity in the Empire."

"Was that an option?" Sasha asked.

Iselin answered, "Eventually, yes, it would have been. Well, maybe not all of Humanity... the resistance, of course, would have been saved, but if the Iumenta hold up with us in the number of dragons, then it would have turned into the War of Generations all over again."

"And now what's different?" Sasha asked.

"If this works, they will only have enough dragons to hold their own lands, and it won't be nearly as bad."

"I don't understand." And she didn't. This wasn't making sense to her. Sasha knew dragons were important, but just how important?

"You will, don't worry," was all Iselin would say.

Sasha went back to paying attention to the meeting, but it looked like it was over. Telunone couldn't do anything without contacting his head of house, and the other houses would need to be in on this as well. It was going to take a concentrated effort. As for Barnin's unit, they had it. Enrich wouldn't care about one unit. Telunone wouldn't even have to pull any strings to get them. As the conversation slipped into trivial and non-important things, Sasha found herself wondering what the Elf capital was going to be like and what her parents were doing right now. Did they know about the royal guard? Did they think they were dead? Sasha wondered if Arkin could get a message to them, then pushed the thought away. It wasn't worth the risk. What if it got intercepted? What would she say anyway? "Hey mother, hey father, I'm a lady of a great Elvin house now. Hope all is well, love and kisses." She shook her head, chuckling at the thought. It didn't take much longer for them to leave, and when they did, she felt an unexpected surge of excitement; they were doing it, this was actually happening...

———

LEGON MADE HIS WAY TO ISELIN'S APARTMENT, FEELING excited. Since their arrival at the dome a few weeks ago, Iselin spent time in the afternoons working with Legon and Sasha. Now that Telunone was running the dragon dome, Sydin had time to work with Legon and Sasha. Most days, Sasha went with Sydin for one-on-one training and Legon with Iselin.

Iselin answered the door, and Legon's heart gave a slight skip. Her ears easily being able to hear the sound, she smiled.

"Good to see you too; come on in," Iselin said warmly.

He was past feeling awkward whenever she noticed something like this; it was just part of being an Elf. It also helped that every time he saw her, he was able to see her cheeks flush a bit when she heard his heart, so he thought he was fine. Iselin's loose white skirt wafted as she dashed into her bedroom. She was back a moment later and seemed a bit shorter to him than normal. He cocked an eyebrow.

"Oh, I'm not wearing heels. We are going for a walk in the valley today, hence the skirt. The normal ones just aren't as comfortable for sitting in a field," Iselin said, playing with the white pleats.

"So what are we going to be doing today?" Legon asked.

Iselin smiled widely. "We are going to make you a proper Elf." She winked at him.

Legon smiled. "Oh wow, already? Should I have brought a bottle of Poti?"

It took Iselin a moment before she smacked his arm and laughed. "No, not like that, you deviant. You're going to learn how to make plants grow."

They made their way out of the dome and down its side, moving toward the far end of the valley, away from the Humans and Elves. Legon was starting to get used to the heat, and the sun felt good as they traipsed across the valley to a small hill. Iselin sat down on the top of the hill. He did the same, sitting next to her. Legon couldn't help but wonder at how graceful Iselin was, even when plopping down on the ground. She stretched out her legs and ran her hand over the grass. As she did this, little pink and white wildflowers burst into bloom. Legon marveled at how little effort the gesture seemed to take.

Iselin spoke. "All Venefica can make plant life grow, but not to the same level that we Elves can, and not so easily. Also, all Elves can do this whether or not they can use magic." She placed her hand on the ground, and a little shoot of grass grew and widened into the shape of a cup that she then picked up. "But altering plants is not as easy. It takes time to learn, and only Elves are capable of truly mastering it. Iumenta have dedicated centuries to the task but cannot attain the same level you will within a few months."

"Why is that? I thought the Iumenta didn't want to control plants like we do," Legon said.

"They don't, but after they lost the ability over time, they found that there are times when they need it. For example, you know that the dragon dome makes energy and that's what powers the crystals, right?"

Legon nodded his head.

Iselin went on. "Well, the Iumenta domes are stone and ceramic, like all their buildings. The crystals in these buildings need energy, so they grow a kind of algae that they can harness energy from to charge the crystals." Iselin placed her hand on the ground again, and this time a little green tube formed that spilled water into the cup. She took a sip. "You see now the many practical uses for this ability, and it takes little effort. Indeed, children can do what I just did."

Legon was amazed and said so. "That's incredible. Is it hard to learn?" he asked.

Iselin paused for another sip. "For you, it will be a little because things like this are easier to learn when you're young, but we will start with the basics. Like just making a plant grow in its natural form, and then we'll move on to altering it to what you want."

And with that, Legon started learning how to make plants grow to his will.

CHAPTER 2
EXECUTION

"The power of security, even if only a falsehood, should never be underestimated. Nations have fallen from less."
— The Exiled Captain (Author Unknown)

B arnin stepped into the old stable-turned-briefing-room. As he walked, little plumes of dust erupted where he stepped, adding to the twirling bits of cobweb and debris playing in the shafts of midday light making their way through the gaps in the ceiling. He sucked in a breath of rain-moistened air, letting the mustiness of the room fill him. Barnin always liked this room; it was dark, dank, and dingy, yet somehow relaxing—the perfect setting for preparing oneself for the chaos of battle. The men were standing around, waiting for Barnin to arrive and tell them what to do. This made Barnin feel good. He liked being in charge, and he was good at it. He took his place at the front of the room with Ankle on his right, crossing his arms. This was Ankle's standard "it's time to be quiet and listen to mommy and daddy" stance. The men stopped what they were doing and looked at Barnin, a few in the front kneeling. *You really need to get some chairs for this place... maybe Legon...* Barnin thought and dismissed it right away. It was his turn to give to House Evindass, not the other way around.

"Listen up, our command has been transferred. We're now directly under the command of Telunone of House Paldin."

Barnin waited for a moment. The men weren't mad. Everyone wanted to be under Elvin command. Sydin was the best commander any had seen, and Telunone wasn't bound to disappoint either. "We were recommended by House Evindass," Barnin added.

There were happy nods now. Everyone liked their new armor, and after Legon and his guard wiped out the imperial cavalry in front of Barnin's unit, Evindass earned a lot of loyalty and respect.

Barnin went on. "We are going to be doing some raiding of supply trains. We all know that this is not the safest work to do, but we're the best, got it?"

One of the new boys from Manton huffed, obviously not convinced that raiding supply routes would be unsafe.

Ankle was on it. "You there—Josher, right?" The boy nodded.

The kid couldn't be over seventeen. His round face still looked like it had baby fat. His brown eyes bore into Ankle; he looked haughty and overly confident. He would have a hard time.

Ankle pressed on. "Is there something you would like to add?"

Josher's tone was petulant when he answered. "I just didn't," he sighed, "sign up to go make someone's dinner late, if you know what I mean. I think I'm a bit more skilled than that."

Yep, this kid would have a hard time. When Josher spoke, he looked at the other men, expecting them to agree with him and look up to him for his boldness. Some of the other new guys looked a little like they agreed with him, but most looked down. All of the vets shook their heads in disappointment; it was always trying to break in new people and required extra work to keep them alive long enough for them to be of any help.

Ankle didn't miss a beat. "So you think that this is going to be easy, do ya?" He didn't wait for Josher to respond. "Have you ever been outside the Cornis Mountains? Have you seen the wide-open plains out there? Sure, we can see trains coming from miles off, but so can the trains and their guards. Did you think of that? Did you know that supply trains are what keeps an army afloat, and therefore something to be heavily guarded? No, I bet not, and while we're out in those plains behind enemy lines, do you think the grass will hide you from dragon eyes?"

This got Josher's attention. Ah yes, how quickly people forgot about dragons. It was easy to do, really. The Elvin dragons were a benefit to society and friendly, but the Iumenta ones that would be hunting them were not.

Josher spoke again with a bit more respect. "The dragons will be looking for us? I thought they just went after the Elvin dragons."

"Yeah, they just ignore enemy units as they fly overhead. Good point, great thinking, kid. I don't even know why I'm explaining this. You've got it figured out; sorry, Sir, go on with your briefing," Ankle retorted.

Barnin held in a smile. The seed was planted in the new ones' minds. They would have their eyes on the sky all the time now. In truth, dragons were a threat, but not a large one. They would definitely relay information back to their command, but if you protected your mind and hid your weapons, they normally wouldn't investigate too much. Still, if dragons were close, that was a bad thing. If they suspected anything was amiss, they could cast spells that gave you away, and then they might just decide to take care of you themselves. That happened a lot more than people wanted to think about. The only real comfort was that the deeper you got into enemy territory, Iumenta dragons were more concerned about dealing with Elvin dragons and didn't pay as strict attention to the ground. Rumor had it that over the last few years, the Elves had been stepping up their air presence along their own borders in addition to the one separating the Cona Republic and Cona Empire. Barnin hoped that tonight the Iumenta would be busy.

Barnin resumed his briefing. "Thank you for that waste of time. We're going to be hitting small targets, nothing large. They shouldn't be protected, or if they are, it will be light. We're not going to be taking anything; just hit 'em, kill 'em, and burn the supplies. We need to move fast; hitting as much as we can before the Empire gets wise and sends out help." The men looked confused.

"I know you have questions, and I know what you're thinking—the

Empire will just consolidate its supply routes and our little adventure will be done. I know, and I agree, but at least in this case, I think that Telunone has something he's planning. I would also bet a month's worth of pay that Legon, Sasha, and Sydin have something to do with it too, so stay sharp."

With that, Barnin walked out of the room. They would wait for night before leaving. He heard heavy footsteps behind him. Barnin turned to Ankle, who was at a slight jog.

"What?" Barnin asked.

"Where you heading?" Ankle asked.

"Blacksmith. I have my sword in getting worked on. It's pretty dinged up right now."

Ankle shook his head and spoke. "Sir, why don't you get a new sword? That one is older than you, and you got it at training."

Barnin huffed. "I know that, but it fits me, so what do you actually want?"

"What do you want me to do about the new guys? This is the most we've had, and I don't want to get killed tonight when they mess up, ya know what I mean?"

Barnin thought about it. "I don't think it's going to be a problem. We're not going into anything all that bad for the next few days. They should be all right." He hoped.

"Ok."

With that, Ankle left him to his thoughts. That was one of the things he liked about Ankle—when you earned his trust, you had it. There was no need to continue proving yourself. If Barnin said he didn't think it was going to be bad, then that was fine with Ankle.

———

Legon walked across the large chamber that held the dragon hangars. Everything looked like it always did, running smoothly, and other than the new banners, there was no sign that the dome had changed hands. He loved the consistency among his people. There also weren't any petty disputes or houses jockeying for position. Everyone played his role. This wasn't due to some supernatural goodness built into the Elves; no, it was the result of thousands of years of experience. Long lives and memories made life less complicated. Society didn't need to learn from its mistakes every generation. Legon was almost to Sydin's hangar, which looked empty. Most of his things were already on their way back to his house in the capital city of Seeon. Iselin wouldn't be sailing with them, but she was going to meet them there when they arrived. Thinking about her gave Legon a weird sensation in his gut. *Cut that out. Don't get all hopeful. She probably just said yes to be polite to you,* he chided himself.

"No, she likes you," Sasha's voice rang in his head.

"You're not supposed to pay attention to things like that; cut it out."

"Can you sense it when I roll my eyes at your stupidity, or is that something you need to be here for?" Sasha asked.

Legon ignored her as he was at Sydin's hangar, with its high brown ceilings curving above his head and lines of little lights on the top glowing down at the floor. The hangar was all but empty—just one large smooth floor. He didn't want to think about Iselin right now. He wanted Ise to like him, but he also didn't want to get swept away in daydreams that, if he wasn't careful, Sasha would see... again... or infinitely worse; if Ise joined his mind and she saw them! No, it was better for him not to think that he had a chance with her. Oddly, thinking this helped keep his nerves in line.

"Legon, what can I do for you?" Sydin said, coming out of a storage room built into the wall of the hangar.

"Hello, Sydin. If I can, I would like your opinion on something," Legon said.

"Shoot."

Legon took a moment to organize his thoughts. "Ok, Arkin has been in the Empire for some time now and has never been detected. He has contacts and assets there as well. I was thinking that he would be perfect for heading a large-scale intelligence agency in the Empire."

Sydin looked thoughtful. "An intelligence agency?"

Legon explained. "Yes, an organization whose sole purpose is covert operations. We have spies, and the Human resistance has a few small organizations, but nothing like what I'm thinking."

"Ok, I'm listening," Sydin said.

"Alright, what if Arkin were able to put together a group of highly trained spies and assassins, many of whom should be Venefica, and give them ranks and the whole bit? Now, if they are all Humans, they can infiltrate all parts of the Empire. Think of the information we could get, along with always having people on the inside should we need to do anything. If we are to sow discord in the Empire, we will need a way of doing it. This group could be that tool."

Sydin rubbed his chin. "It's a good idea. As you said, these organizations already exist, but from the sound of it, you want something more. Most spy networks today answer to some lord or commander and don't have more than five or six people max, most fairly untrained and more disposable, if you will. If you had a wider network and they were as trained as Arkin, then that could be of use. Who would this organization answer to?"

"House Evindass, of course, and they would have our resources at their disposal. It's a model that will work; look at how effective Arkin was with Sasha and me."

Sydin spoke. "He did do well. So how big do you think this organization will end up being?"

"Large, but that's what I'm not sure about. We have resources, but the spies will need to be able to get a lot of things on their own. I mean, can you imagine smuggling supplies into Bailaya?" Legon said.

"No, you're right, that would be a bad idea. Maybe they could set up businesses as fronts. Arkin did that as a cover in Salmont, and it was also effective. Legon, I'm sorry I don't know more about this, but espionage is relatively new. Iumenta and Elves have always used magic. We look so different; there's no hiding in plain sight. But as far as Humans go, they've only truly needed it for about fifty years, and even then they've only started to actively spy in the last ten."

"I know," Legon said. Sydin thought it was a good idea, but how were they going to do it? As Sydin said, this was new, or at least it was new on a large scale. In the War of Generations, Elves and Iumenta crossed enemy lines, but they didn't become part of the enemy society. As for Arkin, he had a small network for relaying messages and keeping an eye out. Most of his contacts were those loyal to the resistance. It wasn't all that organized, just a haphazard collection of people to create a link. Assassins weren't all that new either, but once again, never living in society. The problem wasn't that the Elves couldn't figure this out, but rather that they never had a reason to. The downfall of being around for thousands of years was that you didn't do anything new. Legon knew this was where he would need to live—not in the old established tactics but in coming up with strategies the filth or Elves hadn't seen—things a Human would come up with.

"Talk to Arkin. He has more real-world experience with this than possibly anyone in history," Sydin suggested.

"I will. Besides, if he's going to be heading this thing up, he should have a role in deciding how it works."

ARKIN MADE HIS WAY UP THE SIDE OF THE DOME. IT FELT good to be moving around again. The medical staff wasn't letting him up much. In his opinion, he hadn't even been hurt all that badly. It was dusk now, and the nighttime flowers that bloomed on the dome were opening up before his eyes. The side of the structure was painted in whites, reds, and blues, along with a half dozen other colors. As the flowers' fragrances mixed, the air smelled sweet and soft. The sky matched this as well, with the clouds a pink that was almost orange, mixed with swirls of purple-black and midnight blue. The mountains became a black silhouette on the horizon, the jagged Cornis peaks cutting the sky like knives and daggers. Separating the soft clouds and tattered mountains was a line of the purest periwinkle blue. As it darkened, soon the faint lights of stars would be seen.

It was dark when he reached the top of the dome. A giant emerald dragon burst from the opening, its scales refracting the pillar of light emanating from inside the brightly lit structure and contrasting sharply with the darkened sky above. The dissimilarity of the dark sky, the vibrant dome, and dragons never failed to amaze Arkin. He had a hard time thinking of anything more beautiful than a sparkling dragon leaving the soft green dome. Conversely, there was nothing that inspired more respect for the danger and power in both the dome and dragon.

Like everything about this enchanting race, Elves were a careful balance of grace and death, ease and precision. Arkin thought about this as he made his way into the depths of the dome and down to Sasha and Legon's apartment.

"Come in," came Sasha's muffled voice after he knocked on the door.

Arkin entered. "Hello, Sasha, how are you today? Are you looking forward to leaving soon?"

Sasha smiled at him, but it didn't touch her eyes; she didn't want to leave her friends behind, and Arkin suspected that the dome was beginning to feel like home to her. "Yes and no. I've never seen the ocean before, and Sydin said that he and Iselin will be flying us to Manton."

Arkin chuckled. "Scared of heights?"

Sasha winced. "No, just falling from them."

Legon spoke. "You're not going to fall, Sash. Honestly, do you think Sydin would drop you? And even if he did, it's not like you couldn't be stopped with magic. Heck, you could even keep yourself from getting hurt," Legon said with a little agitation. It was obvious Sasha had been worrying about this for a little while.

She rolled her eyes at him. "Oh, I'm so comforted now, thank you, brother. Maybe they can catch me in their mouths," she said tartly.

It was good to see them back to normal. "I'm sure you taste great, Sash. I'll tell Sydin," Legon said.

Sasha looked at him and smiled genuinely this time and stuck her tongue out. "You guys are something else," Arkin said.

They were both serious now as Legon spoke. "Arkin, we have asked you here tonight because we need your help with something."

"Of course."

He listened as Legon outlined what he wanted to do. Arkin gave his views on the matter and how he thought it would best work, and indeed he did think it would work rather well. Lists of things ran through Arkin's head as he tried to figure out what he needed to do to pull this together. The concept was straightforward enough, provided the filth weren't planning the same thing. Even if they were, that was just one more thing Arkin would gladly take out. When they were done, he was feeling even better. It was good to have direction again in life, and soon he would be back on his way.

Sasha poured them some tea. "Will you stay awhile? I don't think we will be seeing you again for some time."

"Certainly, dear. So, what are you going to be doing while Legon is on his date?" Arkin said, winking at Legon.

Legon fidgeted. He was nervous, and he should be. Sasha looked thoughtful for a moment. "I think that Sydin is going to take me around town."

"That will be fun. He does like you, doesn't he?"

She smiled. "Yes, he does, and he says he can't wait for his wife to meet me. She's seen me in his head and agrees that I'm just like their daughter. And since his daughter doesn't live in Seeon anymore, I think I'm her replacement."

"He loves that girl to death. He wouldn't let her move out of the city for three hundred years; drove her husband nuts."

They all laughed, and Legon spoke. "I bet that did, but I don't blame him; you're never moving away, Sash."

She rolled her eyes again. "I know I'm stuck with you... I like Ise though, so it won't be bad."

Legon snorted. "Sash, we haven't even gone on a date yet. Don't start planning the wedding, ok?"

"What? I have a good feeling," she said, rubbing her temples.

"You've had good feelings about everyone I've gone out with," Legon pointed out.

She thought, "Not everyone. Well, if it doesn't work out, there's..."

"Not Sara!"

It was amusing seeing them give each other a hard time again. Arkin knew they were happiest this way, but at the same time, he was sad. What would happen to Sasha in the Pawdin Empire? They would see what a truly virtuous person she was, and of course, they would adore her, but would she end up alone for the rest of her life? Elves almost never picked Humans, and why would they? Why fall in love with someone just to have them torn away from you after sixty or seventy years? Yes, when you lived for millennia, you needed to be careful with whom you gave your heart. Eventually, it would be hard for Legon too, because someday, even with all the Elves' power, Sasha would pass away. Would Legon survive that? The connection between them was already strong, and decades from now, how powerful would it be? It didn't matter now, anyway. That was unavoidable and hopefully far in the future, so Arkin contented himself with listening to the playful bickering.

THE BLACKENED LANDSCAPE RUSHED BY AS BARNIN RODE across the plains that separated the two principal powers in Airmelia. There was the sound of a dragon flying in the distance, but it was behind them, so Barnin knew it was an Elf. There was an almost tangible shift in the air when they crossed the border. A subtle but steady stream of mental nudges assaulted his mind. The nudges, like so many fiery darts, sank their way into his consciousness, making him uneasy. The Iumenta dragons influenced the people in the area a lot, and Barnin could feel it. The air seemed crisp as they rode, but he knew that it was also only in his head. He hissed an order back to his men, telling them to guard their minds. Barnin did the same himself, and the feeling of unease settled a bit. He tucked his head under his arm and looked at Josher, away from the Elvin dragon's influence. He wasn't so cocky; his face was drained of all color, as were the faces of the other new guys.

"Is this how everyone feels in the Empire?" Josher asked a little hoarsely.

Barnin answered, just loud enough to be heard, "No, most feel content. This is just a welcome for those crossing the border. When we get farther in, it will get better, but it will always be like this when you cross the line. This is why you guard your mind. They want you to be afraid and turn around or at least make a mistake."

Josher shook his head and looked forward, creasing his eyebrows in concentration. Under normal circumstances, Barnin would have laughed if it wasn't for his first memory of crossing this exact line. The men stayed silent as they moved deeper into the Cona lands. Only the rhythmic thumping of Poisson and the other horses' hooves could be heard. The horses seemed to know when they crossed the line as well; they too tensed and seemed to make less sound.

Up ahead was one of the dense islands of trees that dotted these plains. *This is as good a spot as any to rest for the night,* Barnin thought. It would be light in a few hours, and that would make things more difficult. Not that dragons and Iumenta didn't have phenomenal night vision—no; they were in trouble if they met one of those patrols night or day—but it was the Human patrols that were most likely to find them.

Barnin's unit entered the grove of trees and was getting ready to dismount when he smelled it. Barnin turned to the one magic user in his group, whose name was Heath. Heath wasn't a powerful Venefica, only a class one, but he was useful in battle. He could usually keep enemy Venefica off them long enough to do whatever it was they needed to, but he wasn't a medic, and he wasn't a swordsman.

Heath lowered the hood of his brown robe, revealing shaggy red hair and way too many freckles. He looked around and sniffed.

"Heath, do you smell that?" Barnin asked, watching Heath's nose crinkle with the scent of doused campfires.

Heath answered, "Yes, Sir, I do. I will check the area."

Heath's eyes went out of focus for only a moment, and then they snapped wide. "There are people here hiding, no Venefica, maybe thirty."

That there weren't any magic users was a good thing. Even if this was an ambush of some sort, if Barnin and his unit played their cards right, they could walk away without any casualties. Heath's face scrunched a bit, and Barnin knew he was getting ready to use magic. With a breath, even a class one like Heath could take out dozens of people. Barnin gestured, giving a command to his men.

There was the immediate sound of swords being drawn and horses darting in all directions. For all the motion of it, there was surprisingly little sound. Barnin lurched forward with Heath at his side. Heath spoke a few words in the Elves' tongue, and little dots of yellow light appeared around them in the trees. Each dot was someone not of their group. The dots began to move now, obviously aware they'd been discovered, but it was too late. These groves were small, and by the time whoever this was figured out they'd been found and started to move, Barnin's men had the grove surrounded.

"You're surrounded, and you can't hide, as I'm sure you've figured out. Now come out!" Barnin ordered.

There wasn't any movement for a few moments, and then, slowly, tattered-looking people started to make their way out of the brambles and brush, some climbing down from trees. It was an assortment of men, women, and children, all dirty and frail.

Barnin huffed. This was why they didn't attack first. "Stand down, they're only refugees," he ordered.

The refugees were gathered in the middle of the grove, all huddled together in fear. Mothers clasped their children while husbands tried vainly to shield their entire families with their bedraggled bodies. Barnin felt his throat tighten as it always did when they found these types.

Barnin waited. He knew when all the refugees were gathered together because Heath released the magic, and the yellow dots vanished from over the people, who still looked terrified. How was he supposed to introduce himself? Normally, he was under Human command, but now they were under Elves.

Barnin did his best and tried to come off the way an Elvin emissary should. "My name is Barnin, and I represent the Great Elvin House Paldin. You have nothing to fear from us."

A thin, dirty man in the front stepped forward, his clothes over-sized, showing that he hadn't eaten much for the last few weeks or maybe even months. He looked a little suspicious. "You're an Elf?" he asked.

"No, my unit is currently under Elvin command. Normally we are under the command of House Posein, a Human house..." Barnin trailed off, realizing that these people probably had no clue what House Paldin or Posein were, and they most likely were hungry and didn't care.

"So you're not going to arrest us?" the man asked.

He looked happier now, and the other refugees were relaxing a bit too. Barnin spoke. "No, we're not here for you. We are here to let Hoelaria know how much the Elves and Humans care about her," he smiled at the end, and there was a chuckle from his men.

The man who was talking to them was now openly smiling. "Well, please give her our compliments too."

Barnin swallowed a smile. "We will, but you'll need to get a move on as soon as the sun sets tomorrow. There doesn't appear to be any patrols or anything in this area now, but there will be soon."

The tension was back in the group as they nodded their heads. "Should we leave now?" the man asked.

Barnin responded quickly, not wanting the people to start moving. "No, it will be light soon. There was a battle not too long ago just southwest of here, so there are both dragons and a big military presence in the area. If you wait until we tell you to go, most of your enemies will be trying to kill us and shouldn't notice you. That said; get to the Cornis Mountains as fast as you can. Once there, you're safe."

There wasn't much talking the rest of the night and throughout the next day. Barnin wished he could escort the refugees back to the Precipice where they could get food and medical attention, but orders were orders. He tried to sleep during the day; it was surprisingly easy to do by this point. When Barnin first signed on, he never slept in the day, but now he could sleep anytime. Experience taught his body to take rest when it could get it.

He woke as the last of the sun's rays were fading behind the mountains. Most of the rest of his men were getting up too, Heath among them.

"How are you doing? You look a little tense," Barnin asked Heath.

Heath looked down. It was in these moments that Barnin realized just how young the kid was.

Heath's voice was etched with concern and resolution. "I don't know, Sir. I know we're going in deep this time, and I don't like that much. You know I'm not good at concealment; I'm just a class one."

Barnin needed to keep Heath from doubting himself. Heath needed to be at the top of his game. "You don't need to be good at hiding us; we're too big. We would have to rely on our own abilities anyway. Besides, you're good to have around in a fight, or even like last night: being able to see where the enemy is hiding is useful. I haven't always had someone there to show me where to swing. Plus, even if it's just refugees, they could still attack us if they don't know we're friendly."

"I know what you're saying, Sir, and I'm not trying to sound whiny or anything; it's just that if we're going in deep and ruffling feathers, then that might mean we encounter Iumenta. If that happens, I won't be able to keep them off us long enough to get out."

This was not a point lost on Barnin. They were going to cause problems. He thought back to Legon's story about his encounter with the Iumenta and his friend's death. There was a time in Barnin's life when he would have said, "That won't happen to me," but that time was long gone. Kovos was a better swordsman than he was any day of the week, and even with two Venefica, they still had to run without his body. Barnin put the thoughts out of his mind. He would cross that bridge when and if they came to it.

Barnin could tell Heath had more to say. "What's on your mind? Spit it out."

"Have you talked to the refugees, Sir?" Heath asked.

"A little, but not much. Why?"

"They said something is going on, Sir. Things have gotten... well, odd. This lot is all the way from Impoto Province, a northern village."

Barnin's ears perked up. The Impoto Province was the northernmost province in the Cona Empire, bordering the Impa Empire. It was also the province that Bailaya was in. "Are you sure? People up there never venture this far down. The Iumenta have it too tied up. Everyone up there thinks Hoelaria is the greatest thing in history."

Heath waved over the man Barnin spoke with the night before. "Tell him what you told me."

The man nodded. "Well, we had to leave. It just wasn't safe up there anymore. I mean, it's always been tense with more and more Iumenta-only cities starting up in Impoto. It just wasn't safe anymore; too much stuff going on."

Barnin gestured for the man to continue.

"Troop movements up there, which aren't much, they have always been Iumenta. But we were seeing Human troops. Plus, people were vanishing. There was a census done last winter, and then come spring, young girls started to disappear. There were young men vanishing too, but mostly it was the girls."

Barnin interrupted. "What did the census have to do with it?"

"Well, they were all the same type of people that went missing. That's when we connected the disappearances to the census. I know that sounds odd, but they all were the same age and some in the same trades. In short, it was all things the census asked that scared the daylight out of the rest of us. Then we started noticing Iumenta troops just standing and looking at the village at night. Not all the time though; just part of it. Well, we heard a few rumors about things like this happening to other villages close to the border that up and vanished. So this lot you see here, well, we went to the woods nearby just trying to get a breather from town, ya know. Things were so tense there. Here's the thing: when we came back later that week, it was empty."

"Empty?" Barnin asked.

"Yeah, everyone was gone, some signs of a struggle. Anyway, we knew it was the Iumenta. They never liked having us that close to them. So we figured we would tell our regent, and he told us we had made it up."

"And that was it?" Barnin asked.

"Yes, we knew that if the Regent didn't care, it was sanctioned by the Queen. Nothing happens up there without her go-ahead. So we left. What else could we do? On our way, we saw plenty of reasons to hate the Empire, I might add."

Barnin thanked the man and sent him on his way. "Well, that's some story, isn't it?" Heath asked.

"I don't know. Iumenta hate crimes aren't new, but it seems extreme. It's one thing to harass a few people, but another to wipe out a village. I don't see Hoelaria going for it. We'll tell the Elves, just to be on the safe side," Barnin said.

As Barnin mounted, his men followed suit, knowing the drill, and the refugees caught on quickly. Barnin gave them a few instructions on how to get to safety, and they were on their way. He could see the boy Josher watching the people go, and he was glad to see the conflict on the boy's face. That was good. You needed to keep your mind on what you were fighting for in this job.

They made their way farther north. Most small supply trains met at depots or crossroads and then turned into larger, better-guarded trains the closer they got to the border. Usually, raiding parties didn't go too far into the Empire. It just wasn't safe or smart, but that's what they were doing now. It was a two-week assignment, and Barnin suspected that other units were doing the same. These first few nights would be easy. They were past the main patrols and wouldn't be bothered by anyone. Plus, the supply trains wouldn't have much in the way of protection this deep in. Their orders were clear: hit the train, kill the soldiers, and burn whatever wasn't needed to refit their unit. Sounded simple, right? And it would be until the Empire figured out what was going on.

CHAPTER 3
CLASS

"One oftentimes must wonder where the will to learn comes from, and what power, if any, that will has on the rest of life."
— Conversations in the Garden

Blue sky and cotton clouds made themselves visible as the craggy Cornis peaks gave way to the fjord where Manton lay. Sara felt herself automatically lean back in Ghost's saddle as they began the slight descent into Manton.

Before her was a city made from the cold gray stone of the Cornis Mountains. The buildings stood out with their whitewashed facades, a far different look from her last home of Salez. For one thing, Manton wasn't as large, and there was no real city wall to speak of. Manton sat nestled at the base of a long fjord, whose water was turquoise in the center. As the water got closer to the walls of the fjord, it turned dark. Sara knew the little white dots circling the water in the distance were seagulls, a name that had never made sense to her. After all, she saw them in Salmont, which was nowhere near the sea. She refocused on the city. The architecture was beautiful; Iselin had called it gothic. Buildings stood out with decoration. Every building had gargoyles carved with extraordinary detail on the roofs. Colored fabric hung from buttresses and balconies, giving what would have been an otherwise intimidating city a warm, home-like feel. The breeze carried with it the smell of salt, giving the air a sharp but not unpleasant taste. Entering the city, Sara realized just how close together the buildings were, which was also different from Salez, with its endless plains to fill.

Sara was happy Ghost was content following the horse in front of her, as she was not paying any attention. Instead, she was looking at all of the ships in the fjord, which made for a perfect harbor.

Okay, Sara, enough. You have stuff to do. You can sightsee later. She did have stuff to do. Legon and House Evindass were providing her and Keither with an apartment here in Manton while Sara went to school to be a healer and Keither began his training. Keither would be arriving in about two days, and she wanted to have a place by then. If she waited for Keither to help, they would still be looking a year from now.

The training center was on the south side of town, so Sara headed in that direction. She didn't want to have to ride Ghost every day to the training house, so that meant finding a place within walking distance. She decided to check in with the training house, just so they knew she was in town, and maybe they would be able to help her pick out a place to stay.

The training house wasn't hard to find. It was one of the finest-looking buildings in the city, and of course it would be—the Elves built it. It was a joint operation with the Pawdin Empire, meaning that most of the staff was Elvin, as most of the skilled Humans were badly needed elsewhere.

Sara rode to a long, tall wall made of polished stone with a gap for an entrance. She suspected the wall was more for privacy than protection. Past the wall was a large lawn that surrounded a two-story building made entirely of stone, keeping with Manton's theme. She had expected it to be like the dome. Though this building was still beautiful, she felt a tingle run down her spine, once again remembering Salez. The Iumenta constructed buildings there, and they too were breathtaking, but the ones in Salez were built with far more detail and skill than the Elvin structure. The memory was a sad reminder that while the Elves seemed all-powerful, to her the Iumenta were their equals, and stone was their specialty.

On either side of the entrance were banners of red hanging from the top of the structure. The rest of the wall was broken up by long vertical lines of windows. Sara dismounted Ghost, and not knowing where to take her, she pulled a tent spike from her bag. She used magic to drive it into the ground and tied Ghost to it. She walked to the building hesitantly. She didn't think that the people who ran the place would be thrilled about a horse being tied to the ground in their front yard.

"Well, that's what they get for not leaving directions," she sniffed aloud.

It was a good thing Sasha wasn't here either. She wouldn't have gone for being so rude. Sara walked to a set of large oak doors and pushed. They moved with soundless ease, and she stood in an entry bathed with the Elves' magical lights. A Human woman was standing behind a counter reading something. She looked up at the sound of Sara's footsteps. Her sable hair came loose from behind her ear, falling across her olive cheeks. She put the hair back in place, revealing green eyes and a warm face that looked to be no older than Sara's.

"Hello, how may I help you?" Her voice was friendly.

"My name is Sara, I was sent by Legon and Sasha of House Evindass."

The woman's smile didn't waver. "Welcome! Is Mr. Keither with you?"

Mr? Sara thought, but this place did look formal, so Mr. worked.

"No, he's arriving in a few days. I need to get an apartment, but I don't know my way around."

She looked thoughtful. Sara recognized that look. This woman was more than a receptionist—she knew how to communicate with her mind.

After a moment, she spoke. "Yes, sorry, an Iselin picked a place out for you in the Elves' building..." her eyes slid out of focus again. "...Two-bedroom, view of the sea. Does that work? Or would you like to look elsewhere? I would be more than happy to show you a few places."

Sara felt a weight drop off her chest. Of course, if Evindass was paying for the accommodations, they would put them with the Elves.

"Thank you; is it okay for us to stay in the Elves' housing?"

The woman didn't answer but looked thoughtful again. Then she smiled, "Do you have a white horse?"

"Yes; why?"

She dropped the formality this time. "I'm going to like you, I can tell, but I don't think the groundskeeper will..."

Sara winced. "The spike in the ground?"

"Umm, yeah, he'll get over it. Good for you getting an Elf apartment. They're nice, and you'll be close. Are you hungry?" she asked.

"Yes, a little. I'm sorry, what's your name?"

"Oh, I'm sorry, my name is Samantha, but I grew up with four brothers, so you can call me Sam—everyone else does."

Sara was going to like her too. "Okay, Sam, it's good to meet you."

Sam flashed Sara a bright smile. "I could go for some lunch too, and I know just the place. Come on, I'll send someone to take care of your horse. The stables will keep her fat and happy for you."

"Oh, okay, and my things?" Sara asked.

"We'll get them after lunch, and I'll show you around."

With that, they left the building to go to who knows where, but Sara felt herself relaxing more and more. It was so good to be out of the Empire.

KEITHER HUFFED AND PLOPPED DOWN ON HIS LARGE behind. He was committed to becoming a man now, but did Legon have to insist that he learn the Jezeer? Keither had tried it a bit when they were on the road—well, he didn't try all that hard, and by the time he was committed to doing the right thing, they were running for their lives. To make things worse, Legon was having Elves teach him, of course. If it were Humans, maybe he wouldn't look so pathetic; but no, one of the Elvin spotters jumped on the opportunity to teach him.

Right now, Pada's turquoise eyes bore into him. Like all the Elves, she looked young, but could have been ten thousand for all Keither knew. Her hair was silver and long, her face thin and delicate. Her thin lips were pursed, but the look on her face wasn't one of irritation. It had the look of someone trying to solve a difficult puzzle.

Her voice was light and patient. "Are you okay?"

"Yes, just lost my balance," Keither said.

She looked thoughtful. "Hmmm, that does seem to be a problem, hmmm."

"So what do we do?" he asked.

She sighed. "I honestly don't know; you just need to keep trying. You'll get it, I'm sure..." but she didn't sound all that sure.

Pada certainly didn't look sure either. That was fine with Keither. He didn't honestly feel all that sure himself about the Jezeer. He thought maybe if he lost some weight, he might be able to do it. They continued to work for a while, but he didn't make any progress, and Keither was pretty sure that he was soon to break Pada's perfect patience. He didn't want to do that, but at least then he would have accomplished something. He was doing poorly, but not for lack of trying. In all his life, he had never put energy into learning something like he was doing now. Pada could see that, and he suspected that's why she wasn't losing her composure. Finally, she called an end to it.

"I'm sorry, Pada, I am trying. Am I the worst at this you've seen?" Keither asked.

"That's okay; I can see that you're trying. We won't do anything else until you're settled in Manton, then we'll start with some of the less physical things and work on perception, voice stuff like that."

She didn't answer the question entirely, which in effect was an answer. "So am I the worst, then?"

Pada laughed kindly. "I'm sorry, but yes, you are. Please forgive me, this is rude; you are trying."

Keither couldn't help but smile. So many of the Elves were overly polite, as Pada was most of the time. Another question came to mind. "You said when we are in Manton?"

She answered, "Yes, my husband and I are planning on heading home. Our son is about to have a baby, so we want to be there for that. We'll be in Manton for about a month before we catch a ship home to Seeon."

If they were here for another month, then why go to Manton?

"Why aren't you staying here then?"

Pada smiled again. "Most of the students you're working with will be further along in most things than you. I will continue to tutor you unless you find that unpleasant?"

Keither was taken aback by her dedication. "No; thanks, that's nice of you."

Legon's voice sounded in his head. "Are you done with Pada?"

"Yes," he thought back.

"Okay, good, come up to the dome for dinner. We're leaving soon. Ask Pada to come too."

Sasha spoke into his mind, and she sounded irritated. "Sorry, please come up to dinner, Keither." It was followed by a quick, "Don't be rude, Legon."

"I'm not being rude; I don't want to interrupt him if he is busy. Now we are being rude," Legon snapped.

"I'll see if she would like to come," Keither said, and shook his head to block out their bickering.

Pada looked interested.

"Would you like to have dinner with Legon and Sasha? I'm going, and they wanted me to invite you," he said.

She seemed to stiffen in surprise. "Prosa, Legon would like me to attend dinner?"

"Yeah, you can bring your husband if you want. I think he wants to make up for how hard I am to teach," he explained.

"Oh, you're not hard to teach; I doubt it was that. But yes, we would love to. Well, I would, I should say. My husband is out on patrol."

Legon was asking her to dinner because Keither wasn't just hard to teach; he was a nightmare. He wasn't depressed about it. He liked to think he was born with mental agility as opposed to physical.

"Okay, well, let's go then; I'm starving."

Pada fidgeted. "Oh, I think I should change, I mean..."

It was hard for Keither to remember that Legon and Sasha were different to the rest of the world than they were to him.

"This will be low-key; don't worry. Besides, how could anyone not find you gorgeous?" *No, he didn't say that.*

Pada smiled, and then smiled wider as his cheeks reddened. "Thank you. Don't be embarrassed," she said kindly. Keither decided to keep his mouth shut for a while.

They left the Human fort and headed up the side of the dome. His breathing increased, and he heard his footsteps get heavier, but never once was there any sound from Pada next to him. The Elves were silent and graceful, never faltering. He wondered if that was the Jezeer or their nature? It would be nice to be that confident. He looked over at Pada, her periwinkle blue dress playing in the breeze. It was the same kind he always saw Ise wearing and now Sasha. As the breeze caught the fabric, he saw the slight outline of the Faloon on her left side.

He appreciated these moments. They were reminders to him that even something beautiful can be dangerous. Pada looked happy and content with her silver hair drifting in the air and curling around her face, but she could draw the Faloon and slit his throat before he knew what was coming. He knew she wouldn't, but she could, and so could her counterpart in the Iumenta.

He must not have been paying attention. "What is on your mind, Keither?" Pada asked.

Should he say what was on his mind? He didn't know her all that well, but she was kind, and she was trained in the Jezeer, so he couldn't lie to her. "I was just thinking about you walking over there. You're a kind person, and you look so thin and fragile, and beautiful like your entire race, but you could kill me without missing a step."

She nodded her head in agreement. "Yes, I could, but I wouldn't."

"I know, I know, but Elves and Iumenta are kind of equal physically, right? I mean, I know that you can make plants grow, which is something I would like to see, by the way..." he trailed off.

She understood. "The Iumenta can live in harsher environments than we can. Cold, hot, dry, wet; you name it. They can live in extremes where we cannot. But as you said, we can make plants grow, and while they can live in more places than we can, they don't seem to like the sea. We always have the advantage there. As for magic; yes, we are equals. They are better with crystals, but we can use plants. In the end, we are well matched. Why do you ask? Are you afraid?"

"I don't get it; how did we end up being such a large race? And how can we even hope to defeat either of you? Not that we'd ever want to defeat the Elves," he added quickly.

Pada was silent, and they entered the dome. "It's true, we are stronger and more powerful, but you are just as intelligent as we are, and your race is incredibly resourceful and adaptive."

"But still..." he pressed.

Pada went on. "You also have overwhelming numbers. That alone would guarantee your success if you ever became a cohesive force."

"But we won't..."

"No, probably not. There is more on your mind, isn't there?"

He smiled. "Maybe."

"You never run out of questions, but that's a good thing. Ask away," she said.

Keither asked the question that had bugged him the most. "How did we take over so much of the land?"

Pada stopped, and it took him a second to follow suit. "I'm sorry, did I...?"

"No, you're fine." Her eyes filled with ancient sadness. "There was a time when the land was filled with mostly Iumenta and Elves. Humans were in the wings, so to speak, but not a big player. Your kind didn't have government or anything close to organization. You lived in the Cornis Mountains' caves. The Iumenta would have removed you like vermin, but you were mostly in our land, and we didn't care about you."

She looked guilty, and he could tell that she was one of the ones who hadn't "cared" about Humans; it was a sign of her age.

She went on. "We lost over seventy percent of our population in the War of Generations, as did the Iumenta. Both sides had no choice but to collapse far within their own borders. We abandoned entire cities, leaving everything. There were so few of us. Humans started to move into those areas, and your kind breeds quickly. You have three or four children in a six- to seven-year period, whereas we and the Iumenta have one child only every one or two hundred years."

Every one or two hundred years? The thought boggled Keither's mind. "You only have children every few hundred years?"

"Correct. We live forever; why rush? Anyway, neither side bred as much after the war. We needed to put ourselves back together. Even today, we are not half of what we were. That is how your race became a dominant player. Does that answer your question?"

"Yes, thank you."

They didn't talk the rest of the way to the mess hall, nor as they entered the private dining room where they were to meet Legon and Sasha. Keither missed Sara a little bit, not just because he had a thing for her, but also because she was another Human. She was someone who wasn't caught up in the world of dragons or family members living for thousands of years. He was beginning to understand why the Humans and the Elves were separate. At first glance, the two races looked almost the same, but they really couldn't be more different. He wondered if this was the same for the Iumenta and the Elves, if that was why they hated each other so much.

The dining room wasn't extremely large, just large enough to fit fifteen or so. From the dome ceiling hung a chandelier that sparkled with a thousand tiny faceted crystals, gold chains wound through each piece, and soft light refracted to create little rainbows on the walls and ceiling. The table was oval, growing right out from the floor, and in the center of it sat dinner. It looked like an assortment of food tonight, all small dishes. These dinners were for the benefit of the Everser Vald and his sister, a way to introduce them to the different foods of the Empire. It was enjoyable for Keither too, and most of the foods seemed to be pretty good.

"Hello, Keither, how was your training today?" Sasha's voice inquired. He looked to his right to see her making her way over to them.

She gave him a hug and then looked to Pada.

Sasha gave a slight bow. "Hello, you must be Pada. I'm Sasha. We've heard so much about you. Thank you for joining us tonight."

Pada looked taken aback. It was not standard for the higher member of society to speak first in an initial greeting, but Sasha was new. Pada recovered. "Thank you, Un Prose, it is an honor to meet you."

Legon was there now, and he too didn't seem to know or care about social procedures. "I'm Legon; it's so good to meet you. I hope we aren't taking you away from anything?"

"Oh no, you're not. Thank you for inviting me, Un Prosa."

Legon chuckled. "Please, call us Legon and Sasha."

Pada looked a little uncomfortable with that, but she nodded. Sydin, Iselin, and Telunone were present as well, as was Telunone's wife, an auburn-haired Elf whose name Keither knew he had heard somewhere but couldn't remember for the life of him. Of course, when she greeted him, she knew his name. She didn't say her own. Pada seemed to know her too. They probably met five hundred years ago or something. This wasn't supposed to be a big dinner, although there was a lot of food... but Legon was here. Anything with the head of house was a big event for the Elves, but for Keither, it was pretty normal.

The meal was incredible, of course. Keither sat next to Pada with Sydin on his other side. Despite the attendees, the dinner was relaxed. Sydin and Telunone shared stories, and to his amazement, Telunone's wife poked fun at Legon's appetite. Pada was relaxed now too, but she still seemed to hang on each word that anyone said. Though she had met every Elf in the room, she seemed the most interested in Sasha. How could she not be? The girl was fitting in with the Elves perfectly, and for the first time, she seemed to be where she belonged. Dessert was fabulous. Earlier, Sasha had discovered that chocolate was not an expensive commodity outside of the Empire, and she asked the cooks to prepare a "death by chocolate" lineup.

Pada leaned in close to him. "Is something wrong?"

She must have been reading the look on his face. "I know that chocolate here is all but worthless and it's only at a premium in the Empire because it's from the south, but this dessert," he gestured with his hand at the many cakes and truffles now littering the table, "this could nearly pay for a two-room house in Salmont."

Pada pursed her lips. "Yes, it could; you're right. Does it bother you that we're eating it?"

"No. As I said, it's all but worthless here. It's just messing with me a little, not in a bad way, but it gives perspective, you know?"

Pada nodded, and he dug in with everyone else.

The next day was more of the tedium of schooling, but this time it was with Sydin. He was going over the basics of the Mahann. This would be the tool Keither would use the most for the rest of his life, or at least his time in the resistance. The Mahann was something he could understand; it was all in your head. Thinking in pure logic was difficult for most people. Not due to any lack of intellect, but rather that most people were social, thus they expressed more emotion than someone who spent his whole life in his room playing with puzzles. It turns out that the mind has to do a lot of work to feel emotions. Sydin was explaining to him how the mind worked.

"You see, Keither, your brain is just a bunch of cells, as you know, but think about how that works for a moment," Sydin said.

Keither sat trying to figure out the mechanics of thought. He was at a loss and shrugged.

Sydin didn't look surprised. "Well, it's basically signals. To put it simply, when a brain cell receives an impulse from another cell, then let's call it on, or maybe active is the best term. If there is no signal, then the cell is inactive or off."

"Okay, like a one or a zero. I think that may be easier for me to think of," Keither said.

"Okay, yes; a one or a zero. It's these ones and zeroes that make up a thought."

He wasn't getting it. He got the gist that every emotion was in essence a math problem—a chemical reaction in the brain, reactions that formed behavior and how someone thought. He needed to be able to make his mind think or react in new ways when he wanted. It was easier said than done, but he was making progress.

"Sydin, why are you working with me on this? Isn't it the Jezeer I'm behind in?"

Sydin answered, "You're not behind in anything. We just think you should know the basics of the Jezeer. As for the Mahann, Arkin taught you a lot on the road, and your mind seems to be ahead of the curve in it. When you go to Manton, you will be in an advanced class. I want to make sure you're ready for that class."

He was going to be in an advanced class? Keither? Town moron always getting himself into trouble because he couldn't think? No, that wasn't correct. He could think; he just didn't have common sense. A thought popped into his head.

"Do most of the students there learn the Jezeer?"

Sydin paused. "Well, they learn the exercises for health, but mostly no."

"Then why am I in it?"

Sydin sidestepped the question. "It should be taught to them all, but only the most advanced units know it. Now let's go on."

Why wouldn't he tell him?

"Is it because I can't stand on my own?"

Sydin's shoulders fell just a bit. "Maybe with the Jezeer you won't be as apt to hurt yourself in combat, or..."

"Or what, in life? Just day-to-day activity?" Keither asked angrily and got up and stalked out of the room.

Sara loved Sam, and she hadn't even known her for more than a day. Sara was a little nervous about starting medical training in the morning, but Sam told her she would do fine. It didn't help.

"Come on, you're sharp, and let's face it, you have real-world experience. It's not like you're going for the full training either, just enough to help the healers and keep people from dying," Sam said, trying to calm her.

"I know," Sara responded.

"So what is it then?" Sam asked.

Sara knew what it was, but didn't want to say. Sam prodded her some more, and Sara caved. "I miss them..."

"Them?" Sam asked, perplexed, and then said, "Oh, Keither will be here soon, is that who you mean?"

Sara shook her head.

"Well then, who, Sara?"

"Sasha and Legon." It was more the latter, and this surprised her.

Something in her tone gave away too much information. "Legon, huh? Is there something I should know?" Sam was wearing a wry smile.

Why not miss Legon the most? Sasha was her best friend and always would be, but Legon was her protector. She hated to think that she needed a protector. No, she didn't need one.

"No, there's nothing there."

Sam wasn't going to let it drop. "Well, there has to be something."

Sara paused. Why should she tell this girl she didn't know at all her most sacred moments, even if most of the Elves and Human command knew them?

Sure, why not, a voice in her head said.

"I assume you know a little bit about me since you work at the training house?" Sara asked.

"Yes, I read a bit of your file. Sorry, I was bored," Sam responded.

Sara wasn't upset. If it had been her, she probably wouldn't have only read just a bit.

"Do you know when I started traveling with Legon?"

"In Salez, right?" Sam confirmed.

"Yes, do you know why I was in Salez?"

"No, that wasn't in there," Sam said.

That was a big detail to leave out, but then the Elves had more discretion than Humans did, so of course the bit about her forced prostitution wasn't there for the whole of Airmelia to see.

Sara started her story from the beginning, from when she was collected from Salmont, her journey to Salez, and her eventual sale. She told her about what she did for her master, glossing over some of the unpleasantness of her first few days. Then she thought about it; if she wanted Sam to understand, then she couldn't hold as much back. She revisited her training, not holding back much in the department of detail. Maybe it was too much; Sam was crying now. Sara moved ahead to the best day of her life, the day when she was walking to the city wall. She liked to walk along the top. Of course, it was off-limits to anyone who wasn't military, but this rule didn't apply to her. When it came down to it, she could break a lot of rules in Salez—all her co-workers could. Not all of their patrons were military by any stretch, but if she was willing to walk long enough, she could usually find a customer and get up on the wall. Sometimes she would wonder what would happen if she jumped. It wasn't far, but maybe if she pointed her head down...

Sam was looking more uncomfortable now, and Sara went on, "Sorry, that day I was walking to the wall, I wasn't going to hurl myself over the edge or anything like that."

Only because you would just break your leg, the voice in her head spoke again.

"Anyways, as I was walking by a tavern, Sasha came out. They were passing through, and she brought me in. To make a long story short, Legon was moved by my story, and when he touched my arm, I felt his feelings, and then the mark on my neck was gone."

Sam looked incredulous and impressed. "He used magic? That was so dangerous; he could have been caught."

"That event was his first time using magic. He didn't even know that he had it. I knew, of course," Sara said.

She smiled to herself and touched the spot on her arm. Sam had a look of admiration on her face.

"You're stronger than I thought, Sara. And wow, the first one the Everser Vald used magic on?"

Sara nodded. That's what she missed. Not some protector; she missed her Everser Vald. No, not hers, or was it something else? He did more for her too. He took her pain, but that memory she wouldn't share, not today, maybe not ever. No, he was much more than the town butcher, now wasn't he? Sam could see that the conversation was over, and she changed the subject, back to the trivial and mundane.

CHAPTER 4
I DON'T DESERVE THIS

"Life is emotion. With it we can scale mountains, or conversely destroy them. Of course, that depends on whether you see yourself as a mountain or not."
— Excerpts from The Diary of the Adopted Sister

E mma fell into the empty bed, praying for sleep to come before the tears started. A breeze from the window cooled a line of moisture on her cheek, and she knew that she wasn't in luck tonight. She lay still, waiting for the onslaught. The house creaked, and her sorrow was momentarily interrupted by fear. Was someone in the house? *Maybe, maybe he's back*, she thought.

"If he was back, he wouldn't break in the house in the middle of the night," she said aloud.

No, he would climb up the side of the house and in her window while she bit her nails, hoping the idiot didn't fall. She smiled to herself and wondered how her Kovos was doing. Was he still waiting for the coast to be clear? Probably. It hadn't been that long, after all. She hoped that he was okay. She thought back to when he left, running off with

Legon and Sasha. She hoped they were all okay. She wasn't thinking about the sounds of the house anymore, and the tears were starting to come on stronger now that she was thinking about them all. Not just her love and his friends; no, she had lost so much more in the last few months. Her parents died when their wagon rolled over, both gone and leaving her with no one.

Now Emma slept in her parents' house night after night, crying herself to sleep. If it weren't for Laura and Edis, she didn't know how she would make it. This made her cry more. They were so kind to her. Kovos' family was nice too, but not in the same way. She needed a job. The Empire took so much when her parents passed that all she had was the house, and it was mostly empty. Emma wouldn't go into the care; she wouldn't do it. Laura let her work for her part-time, and so did Edis; now that they didn't have their old helpers, they needed a new one. When all of her friends failed and when most of the town went back to life as usual, they were still there, encouraging her, making her stay for dinner every night. She couldn't count how many times she soaked Edis' shirts with tears. The same went for Laura too. It wasn't like they didn't have their own problems, but they took her in like a daughter; they even offered her a room.

This was about the time every night when she went from depression to self-loathing. Laura and Edis offered her Sasha's old room. This thought almost drove Emma over the edge every time. She didn't deserve these people, not after the way she had treated their daughter— their sick daughter—no less. She was such a monster to that girl growing up. All of her friends were; well, the whole town was, but that didn't excuse it. She thought back to the little girl. She always shared with everyone, of course. She just wanted friends. She was so trusting and forgiving. That didn't stop Emma and the others from being horrible to her by throwing things at her and telling her she was going to end up a slave and that no one wanted a demon. But Sasha would still help people. Oh, how Emma took advantage of that by asking Sasha to come over and help out with this or that and then telling her to leave before anyone saw her there. Even right before Sasha left, she was there for her, talking about Kovos. The girls in town were the worst. Not that the boys liked Sasha more, even though she truly was a pretty girl; but more that Legon, Barnin, and Kovos would beat them to a pulp if they spoke out against Sasha.

Emma tasted acid thinking about it. She would make it up to Sasha if she saw her again. She understood now. She saw her mistakes. More tears came as she hoped she would get the chance to undo this sin of hers. They had to be alive. About a week after Kovos left, some people found remains on the road, all male and with royal guard armor. The bodies were robbed, but that didn't mean anything. Arkin followed them, and Legon and Kovos were a force to be reckoned with. Sasha was fine. They all were. These were the thoughts that finally let Emma sleep.

EDIS SWORE SOFTLY AND PUT HIS THUMB IN HIS MOUTH. "Idiot."

The door clinked shut, and he saw Emma eye him. She looked like she had been crying all night; no surprise there, but she also looked concerned.

"Morning, Emma," he said.

"Morning—did you cut yourself?"

"It's no big thing. I just wanted to see if the knife was sharp; did it on purpose."

She smiled wryly at him. "You cut yourself on purpose?"

She didn't buy it, but he wanted to make her smile; the poor thing had been through a lot. "The back needs to be mopped," he said gruffly.

"Yes, sir," she said, and gave him a slight curtsy.

As soon as she was out of sight, he sucked his bleeding finger again. It really did hurt. Maybe Laura would need to clean it or something. He knew it wasn't that bad of a cut, but Laura would treat it like a major injury. She always doted on him like that, and he had to admit he liked it, even to the point of hamming it up a lot of the time. He shook the thought from his head before Emma saw him.

"How did ya sleep? You look tired," he yelled toward the back of the shop. She didn't look up. "Fine, and you?"

"Now Emma, don't lie to me. I know you better than that. What's got you bothered? Are you afraid of being alone in that place? You know we'd love to have you with us. Just hold on to that place for the tax collectors and..."

"No, it's not the house, well, not all the time..."

"So what is it then?"

She'd been through quite a bit, but she needed to snap out of it. She needed to breathe again.

Laura stepped into the shop from the back door and smiled warmly at Emma. This seemed to break the girl. Tears brimmed in her eyes, and Edis felt himself instinctually move to her. Laura looked to be thinking the same thing. As they moved toward Emma, she stepped back.

"What's wrong, dear?" Laura said soothingly.

"I don't deserve this! You're too kind to me, and I can't take it anymore!" Emma threw down the mop and ran out the back. Edis looked at his wife.

"What did you say to her?" Laura asked.

"Nothing, I asked what was wrong."

"Are you going to go talk to her?"

"I suppose she probably went to the hill overlooking the town."

Laura looked curious. "What makes you say that?"

He was already taking off his apron and moving to the door. "That's where everyone goes unless they're my age."

Laura's concern cracked for a moment. "And where do people your age go?" she asked, raising an eyebrow.

"Not up hills, that's where," Edis said gruffly.

She laughed. It was the place he always found Emma when she ran off or when she wanted to be on her own. Sometimes in her wanderings, it would take her a bit to get there, but that's where it ended. Legon liked that place too, and so did Sasha. His throat tightened a bit at the thought of his children.

Thankfully, the day was mild. The trees wouldn't turn for another month at least, but the air was starting to cool, which was nice when you tried to follow someone half your age up a steep hill. He wound his way through the familiar trees, his increasingly heavier breathing and twigs snapping underfoot the only sounds.

When he got to the top, there she was, of course; sitting on the ground, covering her pale blue dress in grass and dirt. Her sable hair caught the breeze, a few strands twirling around her head. She made no move to put the renegades back in place; she didn't even seem to hear him. She must have been hurting badly today if she didn't hear him. He heard himself, and every animal in the forest heard him too. It wasn't just his breathing and heavy steps they heard. He was willing to bet most of the valley heard him stub his toe on the root of a tree.

He plopped down next to her and wrapped his right arm around her. She tried to shy away, but he pulled her into a half bear hug. He didn't talk; he just waited. That seemed to work best for women—just wait; don't fix it. If you try to fix it, you get in trouble. It went against his better judgment to do this, but he fought the urge to talk. This was how it was when Sasha was upset too. *Just give her time, Edis; she knows you're here and you care,* he thought.

"Is your toe okay?" Emma asked after a bit.

He winced. "Heard that, did ya?"

"I think everyone heard that."

"I know I'm too old to come up hiking like that anymore. I'm not like you children."

She was silent again. What was on her mind?

"Edis, you don't want to comfort me," she said, dejected.

"Really? Wish you'd said something before I walked up here. I would have sent Laura instead."

"She doesn't want to comfort me either, or she shouldn't."

"And why is that?"

He thought he knew where this was headed.

Her words came out in a rush. "I was horrible to your daughter and made her suffer so much. I used her, made fun of her; I even told her she was going to be made into a whore once, but I don't know if she heard me."

He felt himself tense. Was he ready for this conversation?

She went on. "So you see; I don't deserve your love or anything from you. If anything, you should hate me."

"She heard you," Edis said soberly, remembering that time on the hill too.

Emma seemed to collapse in on herself when he said it.

"I'm so, so sorry, Edis. I didn't—I didn't think about..." she trailed off.

He felt the air in his lungs leave in a breath. "Look, kid, you weren't any different than anyone else. If you can believe it, you were pretty nice, comparably speaking, and we know everything people did to her. You aren't the first person I've tried to console up here." He wasn't trying to be mean, but he wasn't going to sugarcoat it either. His daughter should not have been treated the way she was.

Emma sobbed. "I was one of the good ones?"

"Yes, you were," there was flint in his voice now.

She looked at him. The dust from the trail was separated by tear tracks on her face like rivers on a map—a face not unlike his Sasha's. Memories of his hurt daughter assaulted him, and he felt his heart begin to break.

"Look, Sasha would have and did forgive everyone, frankly, and so will I. You've grown up, so to speak, and I don't see you treating anyone badly now, am I right?"

She nodded vigorously. "So you don't hate me?"

"No, I don't, and neither does my wife. We like you a lot, kid. Also, it's not like it's all your fault, either."

She looked confused. "What do you mean?"

Did he want to tell her this?

As he spoke, he felt uneasy—not for what Emma would think, but for the subject matter. "Arkin told me a bit of how the Queen stays in control, something about dragons and stuff I don't know or don't want to know, but she's the one behind all this."

That was a lie. Sure, the Queen was behind a lot of it, but so were the people. They didn't have to let themselves be cruel, but Emma didn't need to hear that now.

"How did Arkin know that?"

He paused. "I don't think he was from here. I think..."

"You think what?"

"I think he was here on assignment. He never said so, but he left when Legon did, and he looked after that boy. Sasha too—never saw anything like it before. Sometimes it bothered me, but he was devoted to

Sasha, and he gave Legon the skills to defend her, so..." he trailed off again, not knowing where this was going.

"You must think I'm a bad father for letting my kid learn from someone just so he could hurt people."

"Not at all. Sasha needed that, and he would have done it anyway. I can see what you mean. The Royal Guard was looking for Legon, and they were all killed. Do you think it was Arkin who did that?"

"Maybe; I don't know, just so long as those young ones weren't involved. That's all that matters to me."

She was leaning into him now. "Edis."

"Yeah?"

"Thank you. I won't be so gloomy anymore."

"Okay, kid, you better not. Do you want that room we offered? So long as you own a house, you won't get taxed for living with us."

She looked thoughtful. "You know what? I will take it. Thank you." She smiled widely at him, and he gave her a squeeze. "Emma?"

"Yes?"

"Today when you mop, make sure you get the corners of the room."

She leaned away from him and hit his arm. "Oh, slave driver!" She was still smiling as she got up.

"Do you need help, old man?"

"Old?" he paused. "Yeah, I could use a hand."

Laura waited patiently for Emma and Edis to come home. It would take Edis a little while to get up the hill and then to talk to Emma. Laura was making her way to her bedroom. It was the largest bedroom in the house, with a window looking out the back. Her eyes moved to the left side of the room where the bookshelf sat. It was one of Arkin's, and it took up the whole wall. It was actually more like three bookshelves. Laura wasn't a reader, per se. These were mostly out-of-date medical books, ones that she should really get rid of, but then the wall would be so bare. Some were not books, but logs of things she'd tried as a healer and things she thought might work in the future. One whole shelf was covered with her logs for the Empire. Every person she treated, barring her family, was in these, including every treatment in detail, dated with the cost, the amount she charged, everything. These logs were audited at random, and she needed to keep only the last ten years' worth, but she kept them all. Hers was a compliant industry, as was the butcher's shop. Edis had logs as well, though not quite the same. Most of his audits involved cleanliness and procedures. He was audited every six months. She was only saved this because, unlike butchers, healers needed to be certified.

The back door opened downstairs, and she quickly grabbed the book she wanted. She moved to the railing, looking down into the small living space. Emma was with Edis, which was a good thing. He was jubilant, and his face looked like it would crack from the smile he gave her.

"Honey, she finally caved!" he called to Laura.

Now her face hurt with a much-too-large smile. "Good! We have so much to do!"

Edis looked a little confused. "What do we have to do? She needs to keep her house looking like it's hers for taxes, remember? She can't move too much stuff over. It will take us maybe an hour."

She was heading down the stairs now and sidled up to Emma, placing her arm around the girl's shoulders. "Emma, you asked me once if it was hard to become a healer."

Emma nodded.

"If you want, you can become my apprentice. You know most of the herbs I use, and I need to go to Salkay in a week or so to stock up on things. You could come."

"You'll really teach me?" Emma said, overwhelmed.

"Yes. I need the help more than Edis does, and once the weather gets cold, I'll get busy."

Emma looked astonished. Laura knew what she was offering her, and it was a big deal. It would take her some time, and eventually, she would need to go to Salez or some other large city to finish her training and get certified, but this gave her a future.

Being a healer was a great advantage. When the Iumenta took over, they didn't improve much on Humanity; if anything, they tried to hinder them. There were a few things they did improve on, and one was medicine. They needed a healthy workforce, a workforce that wouldn't get upset because they were sick, so healers went from having only the training their fathers or mothers gave them to being certified and schooled by the Empire. It was hard to get into medical school if you weren't an apprentice of a healer before you came, but if you were and you could pass the basic test, you were accepted.

This had been Laura's hope for Sasha, why she trained her from the time she could remember anything. In truth, Sasha was just as capable as Laura, if not even a little bit better, though Laura would never tell her that. One of the many perks of being an apprentice was that if you were taken into the care, you weren't really mistreated. You were sent to one of the schools and were then given a recommendation of towns to live in. You didn't have to go to one if you didn't want to, but you had a choice. Also, when being taken into the care, you wouldn't be treated harshly. It was more that you were just getting a ride to the training house. You received tax credits, more so if you could use magic. Sasha could have made a wonderful life for herself if it weren't for her episodes. Those alone condemned her to a life of misery. That wasn't the case for Emma. If she came on as an apprentice now, she would get a half tax status, and Laura, now able to claim a valid apprentice, would get a full tax credit. The beauty was that Salmont was large enough to justify one and a half healers.

"I would love to do that, Laura. Are you sure?"

"Very. I need the help, and when Kovos comes back for you, then maybe you can stick around for a while and get to the point where you can go to a training house. That would mean you could live just about anywhere you want." With Kovos' trade, they would have an exceptionally good life indeed. Even the most hostile of enemies needed both smiths and healers, making them all but immune to being victimized.

EMMA FELT HER EYES WATER AGAIN. WELL, THEY STUNG LIKE they were tearing up, but she was pretty sure she was out of tears, at least for today. She didn't answer Laura but hugged her instead. She couldn't believe this—yet more that she didn't deserve—but she would be more dedicated than anyone. She would earn this. She would earn her new adopted family. That's what she was now—family. Just like Legon had been brought in when he was a baby, she was being brought in now. She wouldn't let her new brother and sister down either; even if she never saw them again, she was going to do her best.

Their trip to Salkay was pushed up a bit because Edis couldn't leave his shop for a week, and Brack needed some tools that she didn't know the name of. A year ago, the two women would have made the trip on their own, but not now that the royal guard had been found dead. Not that Brack would be able to help them all that much. Emma didn't know much about the military, but she knew the Royal Guard was supposed to be tough, and if something took them out, their little three-some wouldn't stand a chance, but it was still nice having him there.

She felt better when the journey to Salkay was completely uneventful. It had been about three years since she had been to this town, and it looked like it was growing. They now had a sanitizer, which was something for water, she thought. They found an inn to stay in, and the people were friendly enough, but something seemed off to her. She couldn't figure it out.

They were downstairs eating dinner, and she noticed a short man resembling a bear looking intently at Brack. The man came over to them.

"The name's Bear," the man who looked like a bear said. Emma suppressed a giggle.

"Brack." He looked apprehensive.

"Where are you lot from?" Bear asked.

"Salmont; why?"

The man's face brightened. "I thought you looked familiar. You have a boy who's a smith?"

Brack almost fell out of his seat. "Yes, his name is Kovos."

Bear looked thoughtful. "Can't remember his name, but he was good, I'll tell you that...did some shooing for me."

Emma couldn't help herself. "When did you see him?"

Bear considered. "I don't know, a few months back. He and his party were just passing through though."

"His party?"

"Yeah, there was kind of a plump one like me, but taller, an average height man who looked like he was one big muscle, a very good-looking young woman who looked a lot like you, ma'am," he gestured to Laura. Sasha was a spitting image of her mother. "And then a long-haired gentleman with a great sense of humor." Arkin. Arkin was with them, and they made it to Salkay. They were alive. Emma knew it.

"Yes, the girl was my daughter, and the muscular one my son, but good sense of humor?" Laura asked.

Bear laughed. "Well yeah, you could say he didn't want my noise where it didn't belong. They came into town with way too many horses; the long-haired guy said they killed a bunch of Royal Guard to get them; can you believe it?" He got serious. "Drove a hard bargain, I'll say that."

It looked like Bear was going to say more, but a severe-looking woman across the room called his name, and he seemed to crumple. "Sorry, I'm late getting home. It was good meeting you. Tell that boy of yours he can still have a job if he wants one."

Bear walked off, and they all looked at each other. Emma noticed herself leaning in with Laura and Brack. Both looked like their hearts stopped.

Laura was the one who broke the silence. "Arkin's with them; they're okay."

Brack went next. "Laura, they killed what, ten royal guards? Isn't that the same number of bodies we found? I thought there was more to Arkin than he let on. And Kovos and Legon are well..."

They kept talking in low voices, but she didn't hear them. He was alive. Her chest seemed to get lighter and swell all at once. He was alive, of course. If they did kill those men, which wasn't a big surprise; Legon was wanted. Kovos wouldn't be back for a while to claim her. She could look for him, but where to look? No, she would stay in Salmont. That's where he would go, and then they would be together. By the time she got word from him, she might almost be done with her training.

The rest of the trip was a haze. All she could think of was being ready to welcome her love home. Nothing could ruin this for her, nothing.

CHAPTER 5
NIGHT ON THE TOWN

"What is love? Is it an emotional tie or merely an impulse in the mind? Is it a noun or a verb? In my time I have found it in all these forms but never stronger than when a noun becomes a verb."
— *Tales of the Traveler*

L egon took one last inventory of the apartment. He and Sasha hadn't brought that many things, so it wasn't that hard to do, and it was more out of habit that he double- or triple-checked everything. Sasha was doing the same. Everything was already on its way to Manton, if it wasn't already there waiting for them; but still, it felt right to check.

He walked into the common room the same time Sasha did. Today she wasn't in a dress. She was wearing brown leather pants and boots suited for being on a dragon's back. The cream button-up shirt and leather vest looked odd on her after so many weeks in Elvin attire. The vest and pants weren't leather, strictly speaking. It was something the Elves grew, but it looked and felt like leather, so as far as Legon was concerned, it was leather.

He donned a similar outfit. They would be flying on Sydin and Iselin today. Sasha looked out of place in the pants. He felt her looking at herself through his eyes.

"I look..." she turned, and he averted his gaze.

"You know I hate it when you do that," Legon said.

"Oh come on, you're the best mirror there is. And besides, even if I did use the mirror, your eyes are much better than mine," she said teasingly.

"Come on, let's go," he said, rolling his eyes.

She hesitated but then joined him. They didn't talk on the way to the hangar. Legon knew Sasha was terrified of flying on a dragon, but he couldn't empathize with her. After spending time in the minds of birds, he couldn't wait to get off the ground and feel the air on his body and on his skin, not the feathers of some other creature.

As they entered the hangar, Sydin and Ise were standing in the middle, already in their ascended forms. Legon's heart fluttered as Ise winked one giant pink eye at him. That reminded him they had a date later that evening.

SASHA BEGAN TO HYPERVENTILATE. LEGON WAS NO HELP AT all. He was ogling over Ise, as he should. It was stupid for Sasha to feel fear. Both the dragons seemed to be glittering in the hangar, and she felt calming waves coming from both. It didn't escape her that they were only trying to calm *her* down, not her brother.

Legon was beaming at Ise. "Hey Ise, I can't wait to ride you!" he said, like an idiot.

Sasha heard rocks grinding together as the two dragons chuckled, and Iselin's voice boomed in their heads. "Yeah, I bet." She winked at him.

Sasha suppressed a grin as she saw her brother's face turn a lovely shade of scarlet. Ise turned and made a "come on" gesture with her head. Legon leaped onto her back with ease, his unnatural strength still surprising Sasha. Sydin lowered his head to her level, and one of his giant eyes locked on her.

"Now, try not to freak out, okay? I won't let you get hurt; I think you know that," he said.

She tried to speak, but all she heard was a squeaking sound.

Ise rolled her eyes. "Sash, honestly, this isn't a big deal. It's not like we're horses or anything. We aren't going to get spooked and buck you off."

"Are you two sure? I mean, like you said, you're not horses..." Sasha tried vainly to come up with an argument.

"Enough. Every Elf has ridden on dragons; it's not a big deal. It's fun for us, like giving a little kid a piggyback ride," Ise said, exasperated.

"But we're not children and AHHHH!"

She screamed as Sydin's head came around behind her, bit down on the top of her vest, and lifted her effortlessly into the air, settling her on the base of his neck. She felt a sticking spell securing her in place. She looked around, mortified to see that most, if not all, of the Elves in the hangar were either laughing or trying not to laugh at her. There was a flicker of black as Sydin placed a spell that would keep the wind out of her eyes.

Iselin was turning around, her wings unfurling. She crouched like a cat about to spring, looking up into the angry sky. Legon looked like he was going to burst with excitement.

"Ready?" Ise asked.

Legon didn't respond; he just leaned forward on her neck. Sasha saw powerful muscles in Iselin's legs bunch and release as she hurled herself into space. She cleared the lip of the dome, and her wings thrust down, sending a torrent of air into the hangar. Sasha heard Legon whoop. She was aware that Sydin was now taking Ise's place, and his wings were extending too. Her stomach came up into her throat as the great black dragon coiled up to jump. She was being tilted up, and she clung for dear life to one of his ivory neck spikes.

Iselin and Legon were getting smaller as they ascended. Sasha's stomach went from her throat to somewhere on the hangar floor as Sydin rushed up past the opening of the dome. She couldn't make a sound. The wind buffeted her, whipping her hair around and tugging at her shirt, but not her eyes. They hovered for just a moment as the movement from Sydin's initial jump faded, and for a time slowed. They were just above the opening, and she could see that Elvin woman Pada standing at the lip, looking up at them serenely. THUD! His wings came down, and they jolted up, now thirty feet above the dome, and oh, it was high! THUD! Sixty feet, THUD! The buildings were looking small now, THUD! The wind was so strong. She looked at Sydin's neck, not taking her eyes off two shiny scales. She felt them getting higher and higher. Soon they were going more forward than up, and pink light glinted off one of the scales. She turned her head to see Legon and Ise next to them. She forgot where she was when she took in the look of pure happiness on Legon's face. Her grip on the neck spike slackened, and she looked at their surroundings. They were above the peaks of the Cornis Mountains now; when did they get so beautiful?

Below her, the peaks reached toward the sky, dotted with scrub brush and roaming goats and sheep. The ice-capped tops gleamed, looking peaceful, almost welcoming. She started to relax a bit, leaning into Sydin's neck. As she relaxed, she became aware of a mind trying to talk to her.

"Sasha? Sasha, are you calmed down yet?" Sydin was asking.

"Yes, sorry Sydin, I'm fine now, I think. I know you wouldn't drop me," she said, feeling embarrassed.

It was natural now to talk to people in her head, something she thought she would never get used to, so it didn't bother her when Legon and Ise joined their thoughts.

"So Sy, do you want to play catch?" Iselin asked wryly.

She didn't like Ise's tone. "Catch?"

"Yes; catch—not with you—but if Legon wants to..."

"Iselin, he is the head of a great house; I don't know if..." Sydin started.

"If this is going where I think it is, then you guys are playing catch. Sasha can take over for me. Not like it's going to matter anyway... I can stop myself before I hit the ground," Legon said exuberantly.

"This is not a good idea," Sydin said again, but without conviction.

"Oh come on, Sydin, he's going to have to learn it someday anyway," Ise poked.

"Learn what?" Sasha asked.

Sydin answered. "At times, Venefica and other units will ride on dragons over enemy lines. We can fly high above the clouds and carry about ten people with ease. When over a target or drop zone, as they're called, the Elves on the dragon let go and drop to their target. Magic stops them before they hit the ground. What Ise is talking about is when being trained for this position; dragons take Elves up and drop them to other dragons so the trainee can learn what it's like to fall and how to maneuver when in a fall."

"Okay, so you're going to drop me, then?" Legon said, still sounding happy but not as excited as before.

"No, we're going to have more fun with it than that. This is very uncommon, so don't expect it to happen again in the near future," Ise said.

Sasha was beginning to wonder something. "Sydin, have you done this before?"

"Yes, in training, of course."

There was more; she knew it. "But that's not the only time, is it?"

She felt him huff under her, and a plume of smoke whizzed by her head. "No, my children used to love it when I took them up. It's no different than when a father tosses a toddler above his head and catches them."

Iselin barked out a laugh. "You tossed your children around? What did your wife think of that?"

"Just because we're connected doesn't mean we don't all have our little secrets. This is one of mine that I would greatly appreciate you keeping. If she knew..."

Sasha patted Sydin's neck, and she felt them starting to go up, higher and higher until the mountains looked like little more than hills. Legon's excitement was almost tangible, and so was Iselin's and Sydin's. Sasha, however, placed a sticking spell of her own on Sydin's back, just in case he got the idea in his head that she was going to be participating in this nonsense.

She looked to Legon, who was now unstuck and sidling down Ise's sparkling back to her massive tail. At the tip, he rolled to the bottom of her tail, and she saw the glint of pink that said there was another spell in place. Sydin and Ise made a small gap between them, which she thought was just maneuvering room. Iselin rolled in the air, swinging her tail up.

There was another flick of light as Legon rocketed up in the sky, screaming in fright—or was he happy? She couldn't tell. He soared above them as she watched Ise move far away. The dot in the sky that was her brother was getting bigger as he came closer toward them. At the last second, Sydin flipped over and caught him with a spell.

"How was that?" Sydin asked.

"AMAZING! I WAS FLIPPING AND TURNING ALL OVER THE PLACE!" he gushed.

Sydin relayed a few instructions to help guide him in the sky and then barrel-rolled, flinging him to a waiting Iselin. He traveled in a long arc, and this time Sasha could see that he was able to control himself a bit. As he approached Ise, a pink ball of magic formed around him, and instead of catching him, Iselin swung her tail, hitting him like a kid might a rock with a stick. Just like a rock and stick, there was a *thwack* as the magic hit her tail, and Legon shot through space. Sydin chuckled and dove to intercept. Sasha screamed, but with the wind, she was supremely confident that he didn't hear her. In fact, she was sure he wasn't aware of her presence at all. They passed and hit him back and forth most of the way to Manton, only stopping when they were in sight of the city.

"That was great!" Legon crowed.

"Speak for yourself," Sasha said to him alone.

Iselin took the lead, with Sydin just behind her right wing. It took a moment for Sasha to figure out why Iselin was the lead—she had Legon, the head of a house. While to her and her brother they were just with friends, this was a big deal to Sydin and Iselin. They were their guard, and now she understood why Sydin was hesitant to toss Legon through the air.

They passed over the white city to the docks, where they landed and dismounted. Sydin and Iselin took their Elf forms again, and they walked to a peculiar-looking ship. It was obviously Elvin. One large mass with two smaller, silk-like sails rolled high above. It was one solid piece of wood, as she knew it would be, sleek and fast-looking. Her name was the Propero, and the bow looked to be made of silver, a half-moon of metal that was one large piece reaching into the water and cupping forward. The forward edge looked sharp, not like a knife, but maybe an unsharpened axe. The aft looked the same, and there was no rudder visible.

"Sydin, what is that?" she said, pointing to the bow.

"The bow and stern are made of metal—mostly platinum, because it resists corrosion—but it's an alloy to give it strength."

Platinum was rare and expensive. "Are all our ships like this?"

"Yes, all of the warships are."

The ships behind her were creaking as the wood rubbed against itself. The Propero made no sound. Midway along the dock, there was a ramp leading to the deck of the Propero. They went up it until they were on a slightly curved deck. The ship was a dark wood, and the deck was no different. It didn't feel gritty, but almost sticky. Sydin told her this was so you didn't slip and fall when it was wet. The masts rose from the deck seamlessly, all being one. The riggings shone in the sun and looked far thinner than those on the Human ships. The thread was like that of a spider's web. Knowing that, she knew each cord was stronger than if it had been made of iron. The sails would be the same. All Elvin fabric and rope was this same material. Ballistae covered in heavy cloth were placed along the rail. The bow's rail was the platinum alloy that seemed to turn on its own accord into the wooden deck. They made their way to the back, where there was an extra level that rose above the main deck, where the wheel would be found. In front of them was a door that led below. There were surprisingly few Elves on board the vessel. Up to this point, they had only seen two or three. While more cramped than the Dragon dome, the interior of the ship was just as elegant. She could hardly believe that this vessel was for war. She and Legon had their own cabins, with all of their belongings already there. Sydin stood in the door.

"So, do you two like it?"

"It's very nice, Sydin, thank you," Legon said.

"Well, Legon, you should shower and get ready for tonight. You too, Sasha. We have lots to see." Then he left.

IT DIDN'T TAKE LEGON TOO LONG TO GET READY. THE shower was tight in the ship, and they didn't have a whole lot of room to move around in the cabins. He didn't have any choice of what to wear because Sasha made the decision several days back—black slacks, a white shirt, and a long black coat. It was all lightweight, so he wouldn't be hot, but he still placed a few choice spells that Sydin recommended. One was to make his heart not so dang loud; he didn't want Ise to hear it race. Then there was one to make sure he didn't sweat and another to keep his hands from getting clammy. Last, he placed one that made his breath smell like cinnamon. All of these spells would have been handy to know over the last few years, but better late than never. Sasha fussed with his hair, and he could tell she was more nervous about his date than he was. She had on one of the Elf dresses, this one crimson, which left her shoulders uncovered. It was form-fitting, like all of them were, looking like a single sheet of fabric wrapped around her body. Her hair looked like she spent hours on it. Sasha was enjoying magic as well. From her neck hung the ruby crystal that protected her, which the dress and her lips matched. Her eyelashes were oiled, and real rubies hung from her ears. All in all, Legon had to admit she looked stunning. For a moment, he thought about telling her that she wasn't going out looking like that, not without him there to keep any low-lifes away, but he didn't. She was going to be with a class seven dragon who thought of her as a daughter, and of course, half of his guard following close behind. Maybe a few more guards might be in order...

They made their way on deck and then to the pier. As they moved closer to the end, he caught sight of people looking at Sasha. One man at the end of the pier was gathering a sack, with presumably his wife standing next to him. The man was a little older and was either over the stage of not wanting to irritate his wife or Sasha just looked that good. At any rate, he was ignoring the woman who was now starting to turn red, so he could stare at Sasha. The woman hit him on the head, and he turned to her, enraged, until he figured out who had hit him. Most of the time, Legon wouldn't go for people ogling his sister, but looking the woman over and seeing the fear in the man's eyes, he almost felt sorry for him.

At the end of the pier, Sydin stood waiting for them, and next to him was Ise. She was not wearing one of the standard Elvin dresses Legon was used to. No, this one looked like it was painted on her body. As she turned to face them, he thought his heart stopped, and he wondered why he placed spells to keep it quiet. It didn't need spells to make it silent; it needed spells to keep it beating. Her dress was gold and glittered with a thousand tiny faceted jewels. Her hair shone, seemingly of its own accord, little crystals refracting the light in it. Her lips were a wet, glossy red, and her eyelashes seemed to be longer and oiled. The skin on her face, exposed arms, and shoulders looked soft and smooth even from a distance. Diamonds hung from her ears, and another large diamond was displayed on a necklace. When he was next to her, she smiled, and it went to her eyes as the little pink flecks glowed. He hadn't realized before just how lovely she smelled. His heart kicked back into gear, pounding so hard that he actually felt the tug of energy from his silencing spell as it vainly tried to not give him away. He should say something... but what? You're beautiful? No, that was a lie. She was far more than that...

"I told you he would be speechless. You look lovely too, Sasha," Sydin said, beaming at Sasha and glancing at Iselin.

"You look good, Legon; nice work, Sash," Iselin added, patting Sasha's shoulder.

"Thank you, and wow, Ise, you look incredible. Did you put crystals in your hair? I can only see their light."

"Oh yes, I don't do it most of the time because when I ascend, they never look right when I come back down." She frowned.

The couple from the pier had caught up to them, and this time both stared.

The woman spoke silently to her husband when they got closer, trying not to be heard, but it was still easy for his Elvin eyes. "Oh, they're Elves! Well, no wonder you were so taken, dear; sorry I got mad with you. The men do look good too, now that I think about it. Hmmm, a treat for us both, I guess."

"She thinks I'm an Elf?" Sasha asked, enjoying the link that allowed her to hear all that Legon did.

Ise answered, "Of course they do, dear. You are more one of us than you think."

"No, they were looking at you; I'm just guilty by association," she said and winked at Iselin. "The way you look, I bet you took ten years off that poor man's life."

Iselin laughed. "Sash, I wasn't the one that he was looking at the most."

Sasha looked confused. "But who then? Not Legon or Sydin!"

Sydin hooked her arm in his, beginning to lead her away. "No dear, it was you. Humans find us attractive, but we aren't their own—you are. And you can easily hold your own with any Elvin woman."

They left, and Legon felt Sasha close her mind to him with an encouraging thought... she wasn't going to help him tonight? He looked at his date, now almost regretting asking her. He could sense the five members of his guard who would be with them tonight and decided he wanted privacy. A flick of his mind, and they went to escort Sasha and Sydin. Not like they needed the protection... Sydin was a class seven and already had five members of the guard. No, it was to protect Legon and what little pride he had left.

In the moment he did this, he felt an unimaginably soft hand take his. "Privacy is good," Iselin's voice said closely, too closely.

The spell she was using on her breath made it smell like strawberries —of course, his favorite. That was Sasha if he ever saw it. He would get her back later, but for now, he needed to concentrate on the present.

"Ise, I have no idea what I'm doing when it comes to Elvin courtship..." the words tumbled out of his mouth.

She smiled. "I know. Well, you need to ask yourself, 'Is this just a nice night out, or do I think I might want something more?'"

"Okay, then what?"

"Well, what is your answer?"

He thought it was a little early for this conversation, so he tried to dodge it. "Don't people, I don't know, talk for a while before they decide that?"

"Yes, but we know each other, so it's different. You don't have to decide now, nor do I. I don't want this to be uncomfortable for you." She sounded sincere.

Once again, without thinking, he said, "No, I want to see where this goes." What happened to that little filter in his head that kept him from saying stupid things?

She smiled. "Good; so do I." She started to lead him into the city. "You don't mind if I take the lead? I don't think you know where you're going."

"No, that's fine; you know the town. So now that we've answered that question, what's so different?"

She took her time trying to figure out something that to her was common knowledge, as it would have been for him if he had grown up in the Pawdin Empire. "Let down your mental defenses, not the ones that tell me what you want to say, but rather the ones guarding your emotions. That will be new for you, I know."

"People know how I feel all the time; that shouldn't be hard."

"No, people know what your conscious mind wants them to know, and even then only strong emotions are shared with all but Sasha. Try to sense what I'm feeling—not my words; don't listen to those in my mind, not yet—just emotions."

"Okay."

It was harder than he thought it would have been. But as they walked, he began to feel her emotions in her head. They were patient. They cared for him, which felt odd, somehow like he was prying. He pulled away from the contact; his own defenses were down. He felt her consciousness there hovering, reading them with seeming ease. He felt truly naked for the first time. This was so much more intimate than he thought it would be.

She squeezed his hand in response. "It is easier for me, but not by too much. We are like this with our families and close friends. You only have it with your sister, but the bond there is far deeper than even I have with my sisters."

"Why do you think that is?"

He felt her mind again, and the emotions were running wild, which wasn't bad. It was no different than with Sasha or even in his own head. There was confusion, concern, and wonder all flashing rapidly.

Finally, she spoke. "I don't know, but I'm happy for you two. She needed your strength, and you needed her light." There was the slightest hint of agitation and once again concern in her thoughts, but he didn't want to know more, not right now.

"I noticed you didn't bring a Faloon. Are you that confident in me?" he asked, smiling.

She rolled her eyes. "Yes, it's you that I'm confident in."

"I thought so; I mean, after I took out that dragon..."

She bumped into him lightly, and their emotions for a moment were one. He reached down and took her slight hand as if it was the most natural thing to do, and in a way, it was. She wanted him to do it, and he did, too. *Maybe this connection thing could be kind of nice*, he thought. From her mind, he could see what direction they were headed in, but other than that, he wasn't paying any attention to his surroundings. He was far more interested in how Ise felt about everything, from the architecture of the city to the smell and taste of the air. The sun was setting behind them, casting the city in a fiery light that painted the ornate buildings in various shades of orange. The shadows in the street lengthened and grew in power, putting everything into sharp contrast.

They came to a restaurant with a green awning. This was the place that Ankle's family owned. As they approached the door, Ise faded back just slightly so he could open it for her. He placed his hand on the small of her back, and they entered. The inside was dim, giving it a romantic edge. Candles lit the tables, and the smell of garlic met them. A small woman with shoulder-length white hair bobbed up to them.

"You must be Master Legon and Iselin; my name is Marietta. You know my William, but I think you know him as Ankle." Marietta's voice was light and bouncy.

Legon gave her a slightly skeptical look. "You're Ankle's mother?"

"He gets his height from his father. Why the man became a chef is beyond me. With how often he hits his head indoors, you would think he would be a farmer or something. Never mind about that; let me take you to your seat." She made her way through the restaurant, weaving in between tables with ease.

Both Elves found themselves having a bit of a hard time keeping up with her, which was saying something. Legon let go of Ise's hand. They wound their way to the back corner, and he noticed with some pleasure that this section of the restaurant was deserted.

"There you go, dears, a nice quiet spot for you. We serve food here that I doubt either of you will have had experience with, so if you would like, I can order for you. Ankle told me a bit about what you like."

"That would be lovely, thank you," Ise said. He could feel her amusement; she thought Marietta was cute. He never understood women's use of the word 'cute,' and even now, feeling Iselin's emotions, he very much doubted he ever would.

Up to this point, neither had said much out loud, but that wasn't to say that they weren't learning volumes about each other.

Once Marietta had left, Legon asked, "So do you do this much? I mean, is it common for our people?"

She considered this. "Well, the connection seems to be easy with you, but it depends on the person. Some try to connect with many people before they find someone, but others don't. It just depends. As for my past, that's none of your business." She smiled at the last part, not upset with him, just enjoying making him squirm.

"Sorry. You're right; that isn't my business."

Marietta was making her way to them carrying a tray on her shoulder with steaming plates.

"Okay, dearies, here you go. I picked out different dishes so you can mix and match, if you will. I hope you like them."

First, she placed a dish in front of Ise. "There, dear, this is pasta stuffed with cheese and sausage." It smelled and looked terrific.

"And for you, young master, here is pasta with a cream sauce with shrimp. It's one of my favorites. Now, is there anything else I can get you two?"

They told her they were fine and that the meal looked wonderful.

Legon watched as Iselin bowed her head, feeling her emotions as she prayed. He waited for her to finish. She looked up at him and smirked. "You are confused," she said.

"I just don't understand. Religion isn't a big part of life in the Cona Empire. I know that our people have beliefs, but I don't think I understand them," he confessed, then added, "Sorry."

She chuckled. "Why are you sorry? Would you like me to tell you more?" she asked. Legon nodded his head. "Well, you have heard of the two great dragons, the white and the black, and that they used magic so strong that they split Elves into three races: Elves, Iumenta, and Humans.

"Here is what we believe: we believe that the dragons were brothers and that their father was a gold dragon that created this world. The brothers were to take care of it." Legon said he understood, and she went on. "The black dragon wanted to rule over us, but the white wanted us to have freedom to learn. The early Elves took sides as the disagreement between the brothers grew stronger. At one point, the dragons fought using magic so strong it changed the land. There were three groups inside of Elvin society at the time; those that followed the black dragon, who turned into Iumenta, and those who followed the white. We became the Elves you see now. Lastly, those who were undecided were Humanity, and they did not change."

Legon was deep in thought, but he was keeping up. "But why doesn't anyone remember this then?"

Iselin smiled. "We weren't immortal at first. It took generations. We have some ancient texts that we read, and we have faith."

"But the Iumenta don't."

"That is correct. We do everything we do in the name of the white dragon. We try not to be overt about it; however, it will be something you will need to understand if you are to lead in our society." She grinned. "Do you think I'm crazy now?"

Legon took a few moments to answer. "I have more questions for you, but crazy? No. I've been haunted by dreams with the black dragon, and when I turned into an Elf, I saw a blue eye that I always assumed was the white. I don't know how I know this, but... sorry, I don't know what I'm saying." He felt uncomfortable, and he knew Ise could sense that and dropped the topic.

"So, I hear you are nervous about addressing the rest of the house?" Iselin said. She was referring to a speech that Legon was to make once in Seeon, the capital city. He would be making many of these speeches, and he was not looking forward to it in the least bit.

"You know, I think I'd rather fight a dragon." Iselin laughed, and he went on. "I have always been a doer. I get up, work, go home, see friends, and get in fights. Everything I do and say is direct, but from what I have read about statecraft, none of that is effective. I hate people paying attention to me." He remembered something from when he was a kid and laughed. "When I was young, my father made me go into the center market and stand on a box and talk about our butcher business. I threw up," he said.

Iselin chuckled. "Aw, that's no good. It seems to me that leaders are either comfortable with combat and the direct side of leading or speaking. Most of the other heads of houses don't leave the Pawdin Empire, even in times of war. They lead by speaking, but you will lead in the field, I think."

He agreed. "I will be there when Bailaya falls, you can bet, but I will need to be at least a decent speaker as well."

Iselin and Legon spoke for the rest of dinner about public speaking and using the Jezeer to master Legon's voice. Legon loved it—not the conversation, but feeling in her mind and the other way around; never once was anyone confused.

SASHA WAS LOOKING OUT OVER THE CITY FROM THE training house. Her tour of Manton was enjoyable, though the city didn't have much in the way of attractions. Sydin took her to the training house so she could see Sara and Keither.

Sara came bouncing out of the front entrance, towing Keither. They were followed by an olive-skinned girl who looked slightly apprehensive. Sara beamed at them and threw her arms around Sasha. As Sara's companion got closer, Sasha's personal guard twitched slightly, and the girl looked at them warily.

"Did you get moved in?" Sasha asked Sara.

"We did; thanks for the place. This is my friend Sam..." Sara paused, looking for Sam at her side, then she turned. "Sam, come on! Don't be rude; say hello." Sam looked at Sara in shock. When she spoke, she gave Sasha a slight bow.

"Good evening, my Lady; it is an honor to meet you."

"It's good to meet you too, Sam. Are you keeping Sara under control?"

Sasha's guard chuckled and said, "Not likely."

"What is that supposed to mean?" Sara asked the Elf sternly.

Sydin answered. "He's only saying the obvious. Don't act offended; I don't think you know what that emotion even is."

"Maybe you're right," Sara said, brow furrowed. Then she looked at the guard again. "But you're on my list, buddy."

The Elf, whose name was Sinton, held up his hands. "I would never want to incur the wrath of one such as you." He smiled.

"You better not, Sinton. I know your wife..." she said playfully.

"You'd better watch it, Sinton. I think she means business," Sydin said.

"Oh, I'm all aquiver, Sir."

Sasha turned her attention to Keither. "So, Keither, do you like your new place?"

"It's nice, but a little high up, if you ask me."

She looked at Sara, who rolled her eyes. Sam appeared to be fighting the same urge. "It's on the third story—hardly a mountaintop. Anyway, tell us about your flight. Was it fun, or is Sydin like an old lame horse?"

Sam went rigid. It was obvious she would never in her wildest dreams speak to an Elf like this. Sydin was used to it by now. "Old horse! My age should inspire respect, not... whatever this is."

Sasha placed her hand on Sydin's elbow. "He didn't drop me, and it was fun. You should try it sometime."

Sara showed them around the training grounds and told them about her first day of training.

"Sash, you would do so well here. Just from the little I assisted you, I've been way ahead of everyone. Plus, the Elf who teaches us is gorgeous, and he's nice."

"Well, I'm glad you like it here and that the scenery is good." Sasha was happy to see her friend settling in.

"And Keither, how are you?" Sasha asked.

He smiled a bit. "Better, now that Pada and I are going over reading people. I'm not sure I'll ever figure out any of the physical stuff, but my formal training doesn't start until next week. Are you looking forward to going to Seeon? Pada tells me it's a beautiful city."

"Yes, I am, and the Propero looks like an incredible ship. I've never been on the ocean, so it will be a fun adventure." And she thought it would be; the ship was lovely, and with magic, she wouldn't get motion sickness in even the most horrific of storms. They continued talking until long after the sunset, when Sydin said it was late and reminded them that they were leaving early in the morning.

"Are you going to see us off tomorrow?" Sasha asked Sara.

"Yes; I want to say goodbye to you two, so we'll be there bright and early," Sara said, smiling widely.

Keither added, "How is Legon's date going?"

"I don't know; let me check..."

She paused and tried to connect with Legon. He was on the other side of town, and she wasn't sure if she could contact him that far away yet. She strained and felt a glimmer of his consciousness. It was faint, and he wasn't paying attention to the contact.

She pursed her lips. "I think it's going well. He's too far away for me to contact, but I think he's happy."

"Well, good for them," Sara said, beaming.

———

LEGON FELT A SLIGHT BUZZ AND STOPPED WALKING. ISE'S hand pulled on his, and she stopped.

"What is it?" Then pausing, she looked for herself. "Ah, they're checking in. Do you think they know we're having a good time?"

"I don't know; I think so. The contact with Sasha is fuzzy. Can you contact anyone from that far away?"

"Yes; it just takes time and practice."

Her face went blank. "Sydin says they were just curious. I told them we were at each other's throats."

Legon laughed. "Did he buy it?"

"No; not like it's going to matter. Sasha will break into your mind within five minutes tonight. I wouldn't even try to fight her."

"Oh, I won't."

The connection between them was getting stronger now, and it was nice to see that she was in no rush to get back to the ship.

"You said that with time and practice you can contact people from far away?"

She picked up on his thoughts. "You will be too far away for any real communication with our minds, but the ship has long-range communication capability, so I expect to hear from you."

He felt like an idiot getting all warm and fuzzy inside. It made him feel better knowing that Ise felt the same way. They didn't talk much the rest of the way back to the ship.

Guards were posted by the ship, so Legon knew Sasha and Sydin were back. Iselin paused at the gangway.

"Well, thank you for a wonderful evening. I look forward to doing it again in the future." This was formal for her.

The image of the guard flicked in his head, and he understood.

"You're not staying here?"

"No; I'm not going with you, so there's really no reason for me to stay on the ship, but I will be by in the morning to say goodbye."

This felt odd. It was supposed to be the other way around... the guy walking the girl to her door. There was a moment of awkwardness as he leaned in to give her a hug. He wanted to kiss her, but not with everyone watching. Their connection told him she was thinking the same thing. As he pulled away, he thought, *aw screw it*, and turned his head, planting a kiss on her lips. There was surprise, then amusement. She kissed back, and they parted after a moment. He was vaguely aware of his men turning away from them. Ise just smiled at him, winked, turned, and walked away. He stumbled up the gangway, receiving a few thumbs up from his guard.

CHAPTER 6
THE SPICE OF LIFE

"Sometimes we find that we have always been what we wanted, but just hadn't seen it."
— Diary of the Perfectos Compatioa

Barnin rested his hand on the hilt of his sword. Poison, his horse, was under a tree, and with the dark of night, they couldn't be seen at all. This was ideal, as the caravan he was planning to attack was approaching. The caravan appeared to be made up of two horse-drawn carts, so it was hardly a threat. Barnin didn't see any security to speak of; after all, what idiot would attack supply trains this far into the Empire? Still, that didn't mean that he and his men could be reckless, so he told Heath to check the area. Heath's eyes went out of focus, and Barnin noticed his lips moving as if he were muttering. Barnin would never say it, but that seriously creeped him out. He wasn't a huge fan of magic, though that was mostly because he couldn't use it. But Heath was a decent guy. *Get your head in the game,* he thought to himself. He ran his finger over the smooth brown leather of the saddle, waiting impatiently for Heath.

"There are four; two on each cart. None of them can use magic, and there don't seem to be any wards protecting them either. Do you want me to take them out?" Heath asked.

Barnin knew Heath could kill the men on the carts without anyone even having to draw a blade, but Heath's magic could wear out, and this could be a trap. *Better play it by the book,* he thought.

"No thanks, we might need you if this is a trap. I don't think it is, but you never quite know with the swine."

The carts were close now. Just a bit longer, and they would be surrounded by Barnin's unit ... not that you needed to surround four men. Barnin signaled for the six archers, or snipers as they liked to call themselves, to get ready. Then he thought better of it and signaled to the lead archer, sniper, *whatever,* to not take a kill shot. They needed information. The man nodded and readied to fire. With a flick of his wrist, Barnin gave the order, and six arrows flew through the air. All of the men went down, only one with a scream. His men rushed out of the brush and quickly secured the carts. It was far too easy, and Barnin figured there had to be more carts coming.

As ordered, one man was alive, albeit not for long. Two arrows pierced him, one in the shoulder and the other in the right side of his chest. He was gasping for air, not even bothering to scream. Barnin got off Poison and walked up to the man, his eyes rolling in pain and fear.

Barnin grabbed his tunic. "What are you hauling, and are there more in your party?"

The man sputtered, but to his amazement replied, "We... we have spices. That's all. There aren't any more with us, but back up the road, there are a few others from another party," he coughed. "Please, I don't know what you want; this is a government shipment. We mean you no harm."

"Check it out; I want to know if he's lying," Barnin barked to his men.

There was a rustle of fabric as his men checked the carts. He heard Ankle's heavy footsteps approach.

"Sir, we have won the war. Without salt and pepper, they will kneel at our feet," he said in mock triumph.

Barnin let go of the man and turned. "It's really only spices?"

"Yeah, but don't let that fool you, Sir; this is a win. Have you ever had bland meat?" Ankle faked a gag.

"Oh, shut it. Orders are orders. Burn it unless we need anything."

He turned back to the man, who started to speak again, "Wh... what war?"

"You work for the Empire, right?"

"Yes, but we aren't at war with anyone other than the resistance, and that's far to the south."

"About a day's ride from here," Barnin explained.

The man's face hardened, all confusion gone. "Rebel idiots. You won't get far. I hope this was worth it for you."

"Oh, it was; now we know where the rest of your group is. Thanks so much," Barnin said, patting the man on the shoulder without an arrow in it.

The man's eyes widened, realizing his mistake. He didn't have to worry long. Barnin gave Heath a nod, and the man's body went limp.

Ankle was back at his side. "What now, Sir? If there are guards, they will see the fire. Should we light the carts and wait for the other train's guards—if they have any? We could ambush them and then hit the train once it's unguarded."

"Yeah, that's what I'm thinking. From what we've just seen, we definitely aren't expected, so the guard probably won't even be from the army. Let's set up just up the road."

They reset and waited as before, letting the burning carts do their job. It smelled like a restaurant was on fire with all the spices burning. It was a solid plan. Soon they heard horses racing to the flames. Barnin guessed it to be about six.

Barnin glanced at Heath. "I'm on it already. There are no Venefica here; I'm absolutely positive," Heath said.

"Didn't think there would be," Barnin said, almost bored. "Stay out of sight and go to the convoy. Disable the rear cart; I don't want them running away. If it looks like it's guarded, head back here."

Heath turned his horse and disappeared into the dark. The men looked uneasy but stayed focused. They could see the horses now—it was time. As the horsemen passed, they didn't even take the time to look around; they were obviously hired help. Barnin's men didn't need an order when it was time to attack; they operated as a single unit. They closed in on all sides, hemming the horsemen in and cutting off their retreat. The horsemen realized too late what was about to happen. They spun, trying to go back the way they came. Barnin and his men flowed out from the dense forest, quickly surrounding the horses. The horsemen were shouting at one another, giving conflicting commands and losing all semblance of order. Barnin gave no command. The air rang with blades being drawn. He felt his own sword sliding out of its sheath on its own accord. A woolly man in a dark tunic and pants pulled his reins, causing his mount to rear. Poison slammed into the opposing animal, sending the rider sprawling. As the man lifted himself from the ground, Barnin swung, removing his head in a shower of scarlet. Looking up, Barnin saw the rest of the horsemen go down. As before, it was too easy, and it would be for a while. He needed to stay on guard. Sooner or later, there would be Venefica and real soldiers.

"Cut the saddles from the horses and scatter them," he commanded. "Two groups—one with Ankle up the left side of the trail, the other with me. Move quietly and in the shadows; wait until you get the order to attack."

They moved up alongside the road, keeping silent. He could hear yelling and arguing in the distance—Heath had done his job.

Soon he could hear the words being exchanged. A worried voice rang out, "Robbers! It's a band of robbers; see the fire!" Then another shouted, "Stop this stupidity! The guard will take them! Look at what you've done! Craig broke his wagon! Calm down, calm down!"

Barnin could see the convoy now, which looked like ten wagons and possibly thirty men. He whistled sharply and spurred Poison out of the trees and into the convoy. His men yelled as they slashed their way through the wagons. All of the men in the party were on foot. Barnin downed two before the others even started to collect themselves. An arrow hissed by his head, and he turned to see the remnants of a yellow flick, one of Heath's wards deflecting the projectile. Heath rode by, holding up one finger, showing Barnin how many times tonight he'd saved his life. Barnin snorted and moved along, not finding much in the way of resistance. Ankle sounded the all-clear and ordered the men to search the wagons.

Josher rode up to him, not looking nearly as smug as he did back home. "Sir, I found these."

Josher handed Barnin a stack of paper that, at a glance, showed shipping routes. "Where did you find this?"

"The second-to-last wagon. The man I killed was trying to burn them."

"Good work."

"What are they, Sir?" Josher asked.

Barnin called for Ankle to come over. When Josher looked like he was going to leave, Barnin held out his hand to stop him. "Wait a moment."

"What is it?" Ankle asked when he arrived. Barnin didn't fail to notice the gore splattered all over him. The kid wasn't afraid of anything; that was for sure.

"Look at this." He held out the documents. "I think this is shipping information, convoy routes and such. Josher here saved them. If they are what I think they are, then this will make our job a lot simpler."

"May I, Sir?" Ankle asked, holding out a hand.

Barnin handed over the paperwork. "Good work, Josher." Then to Ankle, he went on, "I want to get on this. If they are routes and manifests, then we will only have a few days to take advantage of the information."

Barnin turned to the sound of one of his men approaching. It was one of the new guys. He didn't have a clue what his name was, but he was a transfer from another group.

"What is it?"

The man stopped, winded. "Sir, sorry to interrupt, but I think we've found something."

Found something? They weren't supposed to find anything. They hadn't been given any information that something of interest was on the move. "What is it?"

"Black armor and cloth, Sir. It's the same kind some of the army was wearing during the battle; a whole wagonload of it."

"I guess I don't see what's so big about that." He didn't, either. He'd heard a few stories about a group of soldiers in black armor during the fight at the Precipice, but he hadn't seen any of them. He figured it was just tall tales, people trying to justify getting hurt.

"Sir, I fought some of them myself. They're just men, but..." he paused, shaking his head, "Sir, I've never fought men like that before. I've seen men that have been trained to that level, of course, but never a whole unit of them."

Barnin thought for a moment. He'd trained with this man. He wasn't a terrible fighter, and he'd been in the services for a while.

"Do you want me to check it out?" Heath asked.

"No, call it in to the Precipice. We're out here trying something new, so it's fair to assume the enemy is doing likewise."

"What do you want me to say?"

"Take a look at the wagon in question. Send back everything you see. Tell them we think it could be some new elite unit."

Heath ran off, and Ankle drew in. "Elite unit?"

Barnin lowered his voice. "Think about it, Ankle. Are we so different? We have been using guerilla tactics for some time now, and we have units that are the best of the best, right?"

"Yeah, but they don't..."

"Don't have special equipment and armor, yeah; I get that, but why not? You've heard the stories the men are telling ... these could be their best men sowing mayhem and shaking our confidence."

Ankle didn't look convinced but didn't push the point either. Heath sent in his report, and they moved up the road toward the next target.

———

Telunone scowled at the report on his desk. Enrich was across from him, reading his copy of the same report.

Enrich spoke first. "So, what do you think this is? Just the men getting jumpy out in the field?"

Telunone huffed and rubbed his face with his hand. "I honestly don't know. It makes sense that the Empire has elite units. They've been claiming the Human royal guard has been that for years. Maybe they just put it into practice."

"Yes, but the Human guard is just show. It's a mind game."

"Exactly, and that might be what this is too. But if it's not, why have the men stick out in your ranks?"

Enrich leaned back, making the chair creak. "Well, my friend, you're the one who has been fighting these pricks for hundreds of years; what do you think?"

Telunone smiled; he liked Enrich. He was a good leader and knew how to use humor to break a mood. "I wish I knew. The problem is Parkas has more than enough resources to do something like this, and he is more than capable of doing something new. It was he who planned much of Hoelaria's takeover. I think for the time being we need to watch and wait. Plus, House Evindass trusts Barnin and his command, so I do as well."

Enrich straightened. "I would agree, but still; if it's possible, I would like to broaden our patrols if the Empire is planning on sending in special... well, what are we going to call these types of units?"

"I liked where you were going with it—'special forces,'" Telunone offered.

Enrich smiled. "Well, most people like my ideas, but yes, these 'special forces'—we need to watch for them. They could be planning raiding parties of their own."

"I agree, and there might be something to this idea. I will meet with the great houses and see about some special forces of our own."

"Don't you already have elite units?"

"We do, but not formalized. It's something to look into. Plus, I think Legon and Sasha were thinking down these lines already. I'll talk to Iselin when she's back."

Enrich's eyes widened just a bit at the sound of Iselin's name. She seemed to have that effect on Human males. Telunone smiled. "Would you like to deliver our findings?"

Enrich grumbled and got up, giving him a quick farewell. Telunone looked over the report again, waiting for Iselin to return.

CHAPTER 7
SPRAY AND MIST

"Power is force and force is power, but what came first? And what holds each in check? Does time? The real question is how did we give power and force so much control?"
— Excerpts from The Diary of the Adopted Sister

Arkin reached up and knocked on Iselin's door. After a moment, she answered in just a robe, obviously not ready for the day.

"A little early, don't you think?" she said, with just the slightest hint of annoyance.

He smiled. "How do you know Legon and Sasha aren't in trouble?"

Her eyes went out of focus for the briefest of moments. "He's asleep, and I'm sure Sydin is more than up to the challenge of keeping them safe." She glanced behind her at a disk on the wall that told time and growled, "Five in the morning. What are you doing up?"

"You know he's asleep? And are you going to let me in?"

She scowled at him, but Ise was never on top of her game in the morning, so she let him pass. Arkin sat down on one of the cream sofas as Iselin brought him a glass of water and sat down opposite him.

"So, are you going to answer my question?" he prodded.

She raised an eyebrow.

"About how you know?" he explained.

"Oh yes, about that. Well, lots of reasons—the least of which is it's FIVE AM!" She took a sip from her glass. "But he's not all that far away, is he? I'd sense something major. I think you know how these things work."

Arkin couldn't help but smirk. "So it went well last night?"

She laughed. "Really, you came here to ask about my date? You're like a teenage girl, Arkin. Don't worry; I won't tell them. They all think you're some brave warrior." She winked.

"Well, no, I'm also here to say goodbye. I'm leaving this morning, and I thought that asking you about last night was polite." He knew she wouldn't fall for it.

Of course, she saw through him. "Yes. We connected quite well, I must admit." She shifted in her seat. "But where are you going?"

Most Elves were skilled in concealing their emotions, mostly because everything they did was so fast. But he couldn't help but see her slight smile when she mentioned her connection with Legon. She was so much the same and yet so different than he remembered her. She had grown up; there was no denying that. Long gone was the stick-thin tomboy he had known. She was a woman now, and an extremely talented and beautiful Elvin one at that.

"North, but I'm not sure where yet. I have a lot of contacts to build up again, you know."

She nodded, and silence grew. When she spoke again, there wasn't the usual carefree tone in her voice. "You did well. You know that, don't you?"

"They are here, and that's what counts. That was the mission. Glad it didn't go the other way."

She leaned in. "Stop."

"What?"

She gave him a stern look. "I know you, Arkin. It's not your fault."

He got up suddenly, not wanting to let this subject start. "I really must be off, Ise. It was good seeing you. I wish you and Legon the best."

He turned and walked out the door, unable to look at the eyes he felt boring into him.

———

LEGON TRIED TO SILENTLY PULL ON HIS BOOTS, NOT wanting to wake anyone nearby. As he stepped onto the deck, he was greeted by Tuneal, who handed him a hot cup of Socolata.

"How did you know?" Legon smiled, taking the cup. Tuneal just grinned.

At that moment, he felt the slightest touch of another mind. He focused on it. The connection was weak but felt familiar. He tried to widen the connection.

"Ise?"

"Good morning. How are you?" Her thoughts were concerned, but not about him.

His heart picked up a bit, and Tuneal chuckled. "Tell Ise hi for me." He looked inquisitively at him.

"I was once your age, too. A date with a very pretty girl tends to leave an impression. Of course, the smile on your face and your heart pounding was a bit of a tipoff, too."

Laughing from Ise brought him back. "Sorry, how are you?"

He, of course, didn't need to ask. He could feel how she was as she could feel him. "Sorry."

Her tone was amused. "Don't be; you're fine. It's hard not to ask questions, if you know what I mean."

"Where are you?"

"I'm back at the dome. I thought about staying in Manton, but it's not a long flight. Did Sash have fun with Sydin?"

Legon laughed. "Do you think she was going to talk about that last night?"

"I suppose not; how late was she interrogating you?"

"Late."

There was a moment's hesitation. "Normally I wouldn't recommend this, but as you two are so close, you could always share your memories with her."

He thought about that but then decided otherwise. "You know, I think that would lead to more interrogation."

Tuneal walked up to him. "Um, Prosa, sorry to bother, but one of the Human admiralty is here to speak with us."

Sasha walked out onto the deck of the Propero, enjoying the sea air filling her lungs. The ship didn't move in the still water. The morning air was thick with mist, and the entire city of Manton was cloaked in a dense fog. She made her way across the deck to see Legon speaking with two men, one a silver-haired Elf and Captain of the Propero, Tuneal. To Tuneal's left was a man she didn't recognize but who was obviously Human. The group turned to her as she approached.

"Morning, Sash. Sleep well?" Legon asked.

"Good, the Propero is amazingly comfortable."

Tuneal beamed at the compliment, but the Human man spoke. "Yes, but I dare say you wouldn't think that of our ships. You Elves certainly know what you're doing."

She took a moment to look more closely at the Human man. He was wearing a uniform that suggested he was in the Human navy, though by his age, she suspected the only thing he sailed these days was a desk.

The man went on. "I just came out here to bid you farewell and to let you know there have been some raiders sacking cargo ships reported lately. We haven't a clue if they are Empire or just pirates. So far, they've stayed clear of Elvin ships and warships, but it's foggy today. Maybe we'll catch them off guard." The man sounded disappointed, as if he wanted to be one of the captains hunting the raiders.

"You sound like you want to join the hunt," Sasha pointed out.

The man looked at her and smiled widely. "Well, truth be told, I do miss it out there. Used to command a whole armada, but the sea is hard on the old, and the wife, well..."

Sasha laughed. "Wanted you home, I take it?"

He smiled impishly. "Yes. Your lot can be persuasive. Well, best of luck to you, ma'am." He took his hat off and nodded to her as he left the ship.

Tuneal walked him off the ship and came back. "Well, we are about to set off. Perhaps a tour of the ship is in order." He pulled two little rope bracelets out of his pocket, handing one to each of them. "These are locators. The crystal takes energy from your body to power two spells. One is a sea sickness spell so you don't feel sick. The other is activated if you fall overboard. It will alert the ship and shine bright so we can find you. Both spells take little power. You shouldn't notice the drain in the least bit."

The bridge of the ship was on the same level as the deck, with the helm directly above it, though an additional wheel was inside the bridge for when the ship was in battle. Presently, the large windows running along the back and sides were open, letting the gray of the morning in. Soft, honeyed light came from sconces along the walls. Tuneal walked to a podium toward the back. Sasha and Legon followed close behind, wondering what was Human and what was Elf. Much of this question was answered upon seeing the top of the podium, or rather control panel. Tuneal ran his hand across the bejeweled surface, causing lights of every shade and color to pop into life.

"Like a dragon dome, the Propero uses a large center crystal to run things, allowing us to target, navigate, and even see other ships and dragons. Mind you, the crystal is nowhere near that of a dome's. It also is what provides the ship's growing instruction and long-range communication."

Legon's eyebrows rose. "How far away can we communicate?" He was obviously curious.

"Well, to Manton by voice and even image, and to immediate ships, but with written communication and some voice messages all the way to the capital." There was a note of pride in Tuneal's voice.

Admittedly, Sasha was as flabbergasted as her brother was. She could feel waves of amazement rolling off his consciousness. They walked about the ship, taking in its marvels, and as in the dragon dome, she couldn't help but be a little intimidated. The end of their tour found them on the bow, poking their heads over to look at the platinum that ran deep under the keel.

"What do you think, Un Prosa?" Tuneal asked.

"To be honest, I am a little overwhelmed, but amazed. How new is she?" Legon asked.

Tuneal laughed. "Un Prosa, this ship has serviced Evindass since the War of Generations."

"But that's impossible. That would make it over two thousand years old!" Sasha exclaimed.

Tuneal smiled in a way that she was used to by now, the smile that was patient with their newness to the world of immortals.

"Now it is time for us to depart. If you like, you may join me on the bridge."

"Yes, that sounds interesting. Sash?" Legon said.

"I'll stay here, thank you. I've never been to the ocean, and I can't wait to see it."

Legon left her with a friendly squeeze of the arm. She knew he worried about her episodes, but for once she did not join him. The Propero made her feel excited. She was going to a new home. She was going to see the sea. The ship's ties could not be loosened fast enough for her.

The harbor faded into misty oblivion as the ship left shore. There was a slight sound of the sails catching the wind, and spray crept up the bow, dappling her face with saltwater. Magic told her that she was far away from the shore, and the only sound was that of the Propero gliding along. Her muscles relaxed as all thoughts of danger faded with the distant shore. She felt her eyes close as her hair drifted around her face.

A nudge in her mind brought her off the edge of bliss. The feeling was agitated. "Sasha, there are three ships on the horizon out of sight. Get yourself to the bridge," Legon's voice rang.

She moved quickly, spotting Legon and a few other Elves on the top next to the wheel. "What is it?" she asked.

"We think it's the raiders. They're adrift. Most ships won't move with this fog and so close to shore," Tuneal said.

There was the stress again. "Will they see us?" she asked.

Tuneal answered, "Most assuredly." He didn't sound scared or even concerned.

"Can they catch us?"

Tuneal raised an eyebrow at her and smiled tauntingly. "Dear Un Prose, are you saying my ship, your ship for that matter, cannot handle three Human barges?"

She was confused. "I thought you said they were raiders."

Another Elf spoke, the first redheaded Elf she'd seen. His brown eyes blazed. "Compared to thy ship, mine lady, they be but logs adrift!" And with that odd pronouncement, the Elf leapt into the air and onto the deck, crying commands.

She wasn't sure what to say or if she should laugh or not. Tuneal chuckled. "Neenor has a taste for theatrics. Plus, he's been at sea an extraordinarily long time."

"I like him," Legon said. "Makes me feel like it's not a bad thing that we are headed toward three ships that would most likely want to kill us."

Tuneal grunted. "Don't fuss over them. If they saw us, they'd be sailing the opposite way. Go stand with the archers at the front of the ship, Legon; you will see."

Deep below deck, the Propero's main crystal fired commands to the ship, raising wards and sending messages to the fleet and targeting the enemy vessels. Slipping spells ran along her hull, reducing friction from the water to almost nothing, and she crept forward faster than before.

Sasha felt the air on deck change as fire suppression wards activated, and with a *whoosh*, the Elves on board raised the sails. From her peripheral vision, she caught the sight of long oars extending into the water. She still couldn't see the raiders with her own eyes, and she could only see their outline with Legon's more powerful ones.

Water turned as the oars moved faster and faster. She felt the ship speeding forward and the wind blowing her hair. The oars were no more than a blur now, and she could see the outline of three ships in the distance through the mist. She steeled herself into the ship's main crystal as it activated spells to aid the ballistae. Their course was straight at the center raider. What was Tuneal playing at? Was he going to play chicken with the ships? Something in her mind clicked—images of the beautiful platinum bow that Sydin told her was a strong alloy, and its finely tapered edge that so resembled a blade.

The raiders were close now. There were signs of the men running about, trying to move before the Elvin ship attacked. Bolts from the ballistae at the bow of the Propero launched into the sky, bursting into flames after twenty feet and hurtling across the void. As they hit the ships on either side of the center, bellows of fire ten feet around engulfed the landing spots, covering the two ships in flames and death. Sasha closed the connection with her brother as his ears picked up the screams of agony that hers could not yet hear. Still, the center ship was unscathed. She didn't need to feel the main crystal activate the cutting spell on the forward edge of the blade to know what the gleaming silver front was used for.

When they were mere yards from the center ship, the Propero sounded a collision alarm. The oars snapped back in the ship, and she grabbed hold of something without thinking.

Then they hit. She wasn't thrown from her feet. The massive ship barely shuddered as it hit the other right in its center. The other ship didn't seem to put up a fight—it disintegrated into a jumble of wood and bodies as they passed through. As the Elvin archers came level with the exposed decks, they fired at the scrambling crew. Then it was over. The stern slipped through the wreckage, the oars came back out, and the ship was propelled forward.

LEGON STOOD NEAR THE FRONT OF THE SHIP WITH HIS BOW at the ready. The water was hissing against the blade, and he saw the ballistae being prepared. The view of the opposing ships was easy for his Elvin eyes to see; they were growing larger. Scraggly men ran along their decks, readying themselves for a fight. The ballistae fired, sending wooden bolts toward the enemy vessels. As they left the ship, they burst into flames, landing on the decks of the ships. Sasha's mind pulled away as men burned. The center ship was growing closer, and he couldn't be bothered with the already-defeated two. He drew the bow back. Then, CRUNCH! Wood and debris flew, sending men and weapons every-where. As they came level with the enemy ship, Legon fired into the panic-stricken deck, each of the Elves' arrows finding their marks. He reloaded and fired before a Human eye could catch the movement, dropping two more, and then they were passing, and the oars were back out.

Legon stood transfixed at the two halves of the center ship as they slipped under the waves. On either side, the two others were doing likewise. Great clouds of steam filled the air from where the burning wrecks touched the water. He walked to the bow and looked over the edge. No surprise—the only thing marring the bow blade was a smudge of red paint from the other ship's waterline. The Propero slowed, and soon he heard the orders to lower the sails. All was back to normal. Now he understood the power of the Pawdin Navy, understood why Hoelaria refused an invasion. A thudding in the distance told him Sydin was on his way. He walked to the stern of the ship and saw Sasha looking back at the ruins. She was trembling slightly, but quieted at a touch from his mind.

The hulking black form of Sydin dropped from the fog. His hind legs touched on a bar at the back of the ship, and he transformed back into his Elvin form.

Agitation was plain on his face. "Are you two all right?" he asked, speaking to Sasha.

"Yes," she answered, shaken.

He shook his head. "Last time I stay in town to tie up loose ends!" He nodded to Tuneal.

"Is that how our Navy fights?" Sasha asked.

Sydin glanced at Tuneal for him to explain. "Yes, in essence. There is a bit more when we fight ships that are more up to par. What you saw today was nothing. These raiders are barely more than armed cargo ships. If they didn't kill so many people, we wouldn't have used such force."

A thought occurred to Legon. "The Iumenta can't make things grow. What are their ships like?"

Sydin picked up the thread. "Not like ours. They are powerful, yes, but still not on the same level. Their ships have a ceramic shell on the outer hull. It's extremely hard to penetrate and, being stone, fireproof."

Neenor was up with them now and gave a slight bow to Sydin. "But once that shell is cracked, the ship is simple to take down. Their bows are thick and strong like our metal ones, but they aren't as fast, and once their outer defenses are taken care of, they are done."

"That's good to know, so why use wooden ships for the Human fleet? They can't want Humans that outmatched, can they?"

Sydin shook his head. "It's not that. The ships are expensive, even for the Iumenta. It takes a long time to make them. The Human ships are meant to be fast and light to distract ours during a battle, giving the heavy ceramics time and space to bear down on us. Even then, it's a fight they'd rather not get in."

They didn't pursue the subject anymore, and Neenor went below to send word to Manton.

———

HUNDREDS OF MILES AWAY, EMMA FELT HER FOOT SLIP ON something. She would never know what, but she slipped. This morning she was in an unfamiliar part of the woods hunting for mushrooms. Laura sent her on Sasha's old chore, which up to just recently was kind of fun. Now that she was careening down a hill, she wasn't enjoying herself. There was a ripping sound, which meant her new apron wasn't so new anymore, and then SMACK! She came to a rather abrupt stop in what at first glance was some sort of pond. She lifted herself up and slopped mud and who knows what else off.

She looked down at her ruined clothes and winced at what was most likely a bruise on her side. Something in her hair moved, and she screamed, grabbing the spot and pulling out a tuft of muddy hair and what appeared to be some type of beetle. She threw it and slumped back down in the muck. She was so angry she felt like crying, and that's just what she thought she would do when an elk bounded into her little slice of heaven. It was a cow, and she looked frightened. For a fleeting second, Emma wondered if getting trampled by an elk was on today's agenda as well, but a thud in the distance made her pause.

She looked at the elk. "What was that?" The elk didn't respond but jumped at another distinctly louder thud.

Emma stood, all thoughts of yuck gone. What was that sound? There was a whooshing sound as a giant brown figure fell from the sky onto the elk, who tried too late to run. Emma felt her throat tear on the inside with her scream. The Iumenta dragon turned its head to her, and she screamed louder, seeing part of the elk hanging from its mouth. As the two locked eyes, she turned and ran as fast as she could. She didn't know where she was going, and it didn't matter. She crashed through underbrush, feeling her skirt tearing around her. From behind, there was a crack, a roar, and a THUD as the monster took flight. Leaves were catching in her hair and branches whipping her face. She was panicked and didn't know what she was doing; just that she had to run. The sun was obscured as the dragon closed overhead.

Please let the trees protect me, please! she begged silently as the dragon almost seemed to chuckle overhead, and she was surrounded in a brown glow. Her body rocketed up and through the canopy; her face burned as a branch slashed a gash across her cheek. She tumbled through space high above the trees, cartwheeling toward a clearing. Before she hit, there was another flash of light, and she slowed, then hit the ground, knocking the wind out of her.

She rolled on her back and looked at the figure bearing down on her. The brown scales leached light from the surrounding sky, and the dragon's black teeth glistened in a sick impression of a smile. As she attempted to stand, the dragon landed in front of her. Two of its claws barely missed her head as they passed on either side, pushing her to the ground and holding her with unimaginable force. Did she scream? Did she beg? What was she to do? She chose option one, screaming and crying to try to throw the beast off. It chuckled again as it stabbed its mind into hers.

The voice was surprisingly female. "Stop your sobbing and screaming, ape!"

She went quite silent, though the free parts of her body vibrated with fear. The dragon twisted its neck, lowering a massive yellow and brown eye level with her face.

The voice came again, cold, cruel, and taunting. "What are you doing, girl?"

She didn't answer. She couldn't speak.

"I asked you a question, ape. You'll answer if you want me to kill you painlessly." She felt the joy in its mind, and she knew she was going to die.

"P...p...please don't hurt me. I didn't mean to disturb you. Please don't."

"WHAT WERE YOU DOING?"

"G... g... g...getting mushrooms."

"Why?" the dragon asked, this time less sharply.

"I'm the healer's apprentice. She told me that we..."

She was cut off. "What town?"

"Salmont."

The dragon let up some pressure, and she could feel its hesitance to kill a healer. Aware of her thoughts, the dragon looked at her. "Don't think yourself too special, but healers in the area are hard to come by. I dare say you will be missed."

The thoughts weren't of concern for the welfare of Salmont, but more of the workforce and possible need for healers soon.

"Wh...wh...why do we need healers soon?"

"It is not your place to question me. Hmmm, Salmont." The dragon's thoughts grew abruptly angry. "Do you know an Elf?"

"A what?"

"Elf, idiot girl! An Elf—pointy ears, a sickening love of plants—an Elf, fool!"

"No elves live in Salmont."

The dragon roared at her as the probe in her mind dug in painfully. Her fear pushed the probe back. The sound made her ears hurt, and she screamed again. "Please, I don't know. I'm sorry. Please, I'm so sorry."

"What are you sorry about, you worthless little twit?"

Between sobs, she tried to say that she was sorry she didn't know an Elf.

"Why would you want to know an Elf, idiot girl?"

"So I could tell you, and you wouldn't hurt me."

Her head throbbed at the laughing in her head and from the dragon's mouth. "That would merely condemn you to death. Pathetic beast, go on your way."

The dragon's wings unfurled, and it took off, leaving her on the ground shaking. Emma rolled and vomited. She couldn't get up. She was terrified, so instead, she curled in a ball and waited.

CHAPTER 8
THE SHIFTING VEIL

"I was once asked what it was like when I realized that I was not alone; as then, like now, all I can say is thank you."
— *Confessions of Love, The First Wife*

Barnin slumped in his saddle as he crested the hill and the white towers of Manton came into view. He was tired, sore, and had a funny itch from some plant he had slept on. All in all, it was good to be home. The mid-afternoon sun glistened off the harbor, casting the hillside city in shifty shadows. It reminded him of some epic tale from when he was young.

"Ah, Barnin the Great," he said aloud. One of the new guys gave him a look. "What, you don't think I'm great?"

The man chuckled. "You're amazing, Sir."

"That's what I thought."

Of course, the city was packed, the streets clogged with midday traffic. He longed for the small-town days in Salmont as he made his way to his apartment.

As he dismounted, a small boy came running up to him. "Bed your horse, Sir?"

"Do what to my horse?" he asked a little shortly. He didn't know who this kid was, but surely he wasn't stupid enough to steal a horse from a soldier.

A nasally voice from behind him answered, causing him to spin on the spot. "He wants to know if he can take your horse to its stall, feed it and all that."

"Keither!" He hugged the boy—well, tried to hug him. He was a lot to hug. "What are you doing here?"

"I live with Elves, remember? Anyway, give the kid a break."

A year ago, Keither wouldn't have so much as looked Barnin in the eye, let alone told him to give someone a break. He tossed the kid a coin and said a silent prayer that Keither was right and that he would still have a horse tomorrow.

"Help me with my pack?" Barnin asked Keither.

Keither picked up one of the many packs Barnin had at his feet. They walked into the dimly lit entrance to his building and up to the top floor. The place was quiet and catered mostly to soldiers, meaning it was nearly empty all the time. They walked into the one-room apartment, and Barnin gave the soft bed a fleeting look.

"Just set that on the bed." He stripped off some gear. "We can grab something to eat if you want, but do you mind if I clean up real quick?"

"Of course not. I'll contact Sara and see if she's available for lunch. She may not be, though; they keep her busy." Keither's eyes went slightly out of focus.

Barnin left the room with a towel in hand. He hated magic. It made his skin prickle, and while Keither wasn't doing magic, the mind-talk stuff was just the same in his book.

If there was one thing you could count on in Manton, it was a hot bath. With the place all but empty, he had the center bathroom to himself. It felt fantastic to clean off all the grime from the road, and shaving with hot water wasn't bad either. When he returned to his room, Keither was sitting on the bed reading a book.

"What ya reading?" he asked, not actually caring.

"It's a history of House Evindass."

"They have those?"

"Yes," Keither said slowly. "It's called a library."

Barnin snorted. "I can still beat you up, you know that?"

Keither rolled his eyes. "I haven't heard that in a while."

"Just so you know. Is Sara meeting us?"

Keither rose from the bed. "She is, but she doesn't have much time." He gave Barnin a look. "Why are you scratching yourself so much?"

The itching was getting pretty serious now, but he wasn't about to admit that he slept in poison oak or something. "Shut up. Where are we going?"

They made their way to a little bakery, where they saw Sara sitting outside at a small table. She was in the standard pale green of healers, so Barnin figured she came from the training house. She hugged him when he got to her.

"Hello Barnin, how are you doing?" She looked him in the eyes the way all healers did.

"I'm good. Tired, but good. You don't need to fix me."

She smirked. "That's up for debate, but let's get food. I skipped breakfast."

As they ate, they made small talk, and Barnin noticed, not for the first time, that Keither was paying a decent amount of attention to Sara. Barnin smiled into his glass, but at the same time, he was proud of the boy. It was about time he figured out the opposite sex existed.

"So, how much have you learned?" he asked Sara.

She exhaled. "It's the most amazing thing. I never thought I would enjoy healing, but I love it; it's so incredible. You would not believe what we can... what is wrong with you? Why are you scratching yourself so much?" She looked at Keither for confirmation, and he shrugged.

"I'm a man; we itch a lot," Barnin said dismissively.

Her eyes narrowed. "I'm aware. You didn't get into poison oak or anything like..."

He cut her off, maybe a little too abruptly. "No, what kind of idiot would sleep in poison oak?" He shifted in his seat, fighting the urge to itch.

The smile on her face said, *He's messed up.*

"Barnin, I didn't say anything about sleeping in it. Please, oh please, don't tell me that."

"It was dark, and the ground was hard, okay? We don't stay at inns or anything," he said defensively.

She was laughing now. "You idiot! You slept in poison oak? Did your parents drop you as a baby or something?" She got up and walked to him. "Here, let me take a look."

"I'm fine, I..." She was giving him that look that all healers do, the one that said *shut it and do what I say*.

"Geez, do they teach you that look on the first day or something?"

She didn't answer but placed her hand on his chest with her eyes closed, muttering something. A slight silver glow wrapped around him, and the itch stopped.

"There you go; all fixed. I have things to do. See you, Keither. Barnin, please try to not sleep on the soft leaves from now on." She walked off.

———

KEITHER WATCHED HER LEAVE. AS SOON AS SARA WAS OUT of earshot, Barnin rounded on him. "So why aren't you with her?"

He was confused. "She has studying to do..."

"No, I mean *with* her," Barnin said, emphasizing the 'with.'

This was not a conversation Keither wanted to have with Barnin. "I don't know; I think that when it's time, we will, you know, it will just happen."

Barnin nodded. "You're scared, aren't you?" He continued, not waiting for a response, "Look, she's a good-looking girl, and truth be told, she has a good personality. You need to get a move on before others do."

"I know, I know." And he did. He was aware that sooner or later, Sara would get over her distaste for most men and pick someone.

Barnin held up his hands and, to his surprise, sounded sincere. "Look, Sara has been through more than anyone should. She deserves a good guy. You're a good guy, Keither. Hold up, let me finish; I don't need to tell you what it's like out there. Life is short. Don't wait for it to throw you a bone."

He didn't know what to say. He wanted to change the subject, but Barnin saved him the trouble with a shudder.

"What is it?" he asked.

Barnin scowled. "What? Oh, nothing." He paused. "No, not nothing—doesn't the whole mental network junk freak you out?"

This was an odd change of topic. "At first, but not anymore. It's great if Sara and I need to talk, or if Legon is close by; we can. How do you think Sara knew where we were today?"

Barnin didn't like that. "So how can you not land her then? I mean, if she can find you and all, aren't you two sharing dreams yet?"

Keither laughed and waved his hand in dismissal. "She doesn't know where I am; I told her where. And no, we don't share dreams—you can't. And we don't always talk with the link. Plus, even when you do, you can filter what the other sees."

Barnin appeared to like the filtering part. "What do you mean you can't dream together? Is that against the rules?"

"There are no rules, but the subconscious works differently. I could, say, access her mind enough to give her strength if her conscious mind was used to my contact. Or, I could maybe see if she was sick or injured. But actually see a dream? No. The subconscious is too convoluted for that. Even Elves who have been married for thousands of years don't know what goes on in the other's dreams."

Barnin nodded his head in a jerk. "Well, all right then."

After lunch, things were a bit awkward, and Keither got the impression that Barnin was focusing on his mental protection, most likely suspecting him of reading his mind. He could have told him that once your mind was guarded, you didn't need to put more effort into it, that it worked on its own, but it was kind of fun to see his eyes squint from time to time. He was starting to look constipated, and people were beginning to stare when they finally left.

PHAEDRA CRASHED THROUGH THE UNDERBRUSH. ARKIN WAS barely able to keep his hold of the reins. He wanted to slow down, but the snapping from behind told him the three Iumenta were still following. Luckily, Iumenta, like Elves, didn't ride horses much—if ever—and Phaedra's long legs helped her outpace the filth. It was a given that the Iumenta could jump from tree to tree like the Elves, but unlike the Elves, their homeland was rumored to be open space, so they might not be willing to jump in the trees. Still, they weren't magic users, and that was good news. It was dusk, casting the forest into near darkness. He couldn't see anything. A branch ripped his shirt, cutting his chest. He swore.

A crack from above told him that one of them was in the trees and gaining. He chanced a spell slicing a passing tree. There was a THUD and groan from his other side. One down, but how to lose the other two? A thought came to him. He reached out with his mind, finding anything in the air. There was a small herd of deer— they would do. He raced toward them, freezing them to the spot with his mind.

The Iumenta were still coming, but further back now. He only had one chance to make this work. He burst into the clearing with the deer and scattered them with a thought. They bolted into the forest, loudly bowling their way through bush and brambles. His mind shot out again, panicking the animals and causing them to thrash and run aimlessly. Phaedra darted back into the woods, carrying him away from the mayhem. Through one of the minds, he saw the Iumenta enter the clearing. Even with their more sensitive ears, they wouldn't be able to hear him with all the panicking animals.

Not having long, he stopped and dismounted, urging Phaedra to the ground and covering them with brush. He could sense the deer's minds disappearing as the Iumenta killed them off. As the last deer's neck was snapped, he placed the spell. If he stayed still and the swine didn't get close, they wouldn't find him.

The horse didn't move, the spell being for her as well. He couldn't afford to reach out with his mind on the chance he would touch the Iumenta. He heard them closing in, one still in the trees.

They were speaking Glosso, the language of the Elves, and Iumenta, so he didn't catch everything they said, but he knew enough to see that his ploy hadn't completely worked.

"Try to scare the horse; make noise," a voice hissed in the tree above him.

Snapping and the sound of metal on metal filled the forest, but Phaedra couldn't hear. They paced around, sniffing and looking. Arkin could tell they were young and didn't have experience in the woods. If they had been older, they would have been able to track him to his spot in a moment. After a while, they left the area, but he didn't dare move until morning.

EDIS PACED UP AND DOWN THE SMALL FAMILY ROOM. "DID she say what part of the woods she was going into?" he asked, flustered.

Laura was wringing her hands. "I don't know where she is. She's never taken more than a few hours, and it's so late now."

In response, Edis turned to look out the window into the pitch-black night. Clouds were obscuring the moon, and he knew there was no seeing in the forest, but that was hardly the issue.

"Are you sure Elaine was correct?"

Laura stiffened, but not from him. "She said it went right overhead, taking light from the sky. What else could it be? I've seen them before when I was at school, remember?"

He did remember, and at the time, he thought they were interesting, but as his youth faded, so did his interest in dragons.

"I'm going to go look for her. Maybe she saw it and fell or something." The something was what neither wanted to think about. Elaine said that its mouth had red on it, but that didn't mean it was Emma. It could easily be animal blood.

Further concern became useless as Emma slid into the house through the back door. Edis whirled and felt the blood leave his face.

"So sorry... I didn't want to wake..." Emma didn't finish. Laura and Edis crossed the room in one movement and both wrapped their arms around the trembling girl, who started to cry.

As they stepped back, Laura spoke first. "Was it the dragon?"

Emma's head bounded up and down, and her face paled.

Edis pulled the girl in close, like he used to do for his other daughter. "It's all right, love. You're safe now. Are you hurt?"

There was a cut on her face; she was covered in dirt, and her clothes were torn up.

"I'm all right," she said, not sounding it at all.

"What happened, dear? Did you fall?" Laura asked.

She shook her head no. "I fell down a hill and landed in the mud, and then the dragon flew down. It ate an elk that was nearby, and when I screamed, it saw me, and I ran. But then I wasn't running. I was glowing and flying, and then I hit the ground, and she was on me."

Edis stopped her. "*She* was on you?"

"Yes, the dragon was a she, and she wanted information. She wanted to know if I'd seen an Elf. She didn't give her name. She laughed at me and pinned me down with her paw and then flew off." Emma sunk into a chair.

Edis felt ice water filling his insides. Laura looked like she felt the same. She gave him a worried look, and then it clicked in her mind.

"So, it just wanted to talk to her?" Brack said the following day.

They were standing in the back of the butcher's shop.

"Yeah, right scary if you ask me. What is a dragon doing near Salmont?"

"Well, hunting. Maybe it just wanted to eat."

Edis gave Brack a look. "What? And figured it would ask some questions while it was at it?"

Brack shook his head and shivered. "Well, that's simpler to think of than the alternative, which is that it was here for a reason. An Elf? Honestly." He took a drink from a glass on the back counter. "You don't think it was looking for your boy, do ya?"

That's exactly what Edis did think, but he wasn't about to say it. "Does Legon seem like an Elf to you?"

Brack grimaced. "No, but they came looking for him, didn't they? And considering the place we found him in, maybe they think... I sound crazy. It's just all this talk lately."

"What talk?"

Brack looked confused. "Oh, that's right, you haven't been to the tavern in some time." He looked around furtively before going on. "They say there's some new Elf Lord that's got the Queen's iron knickers in a dither, but the rumor is that he lived in the Empire for years. Hogwash if you ask me, but maybe if Emma is proof, there is something to it."

Edis didn't want to talk about this anymore and changed the subject to something less terrifying than a war with the Elves. After a bit longer, Brack left, saying he wouldn't tell anyone about Emma.

THE HANDLE TO THE WOODEN TRAINING SWORD VIBRATED painfully in Keither's hand as he blocked a blow from Barnin. His combat training hadn't actually started yet, but Barnin insisted on working with him before he went back to raid caravans. Barnin thrust at him, and he parried, barely, and tried to slash back. This was not a smart idea. Somewhere between blocking and swinging, Keither lost his grip on the stave. Dropping his weapon wasn't new. The problem was Barnin's stave that was on its way to Keither's head. There was that split second in which time slowed down. Barnin's eyes flashed, realizing too late that there was nothing to stop his stave. Well, there was something to stop it, just not something Keither wanted to use.

There was a dull THWACK. Keither didn't feel it yet, but he would. His head wrenched back, and he toppled over. Now he felt it, and his hand flew to his face where blood was pouring down his chin and shirt. Pain throbbed from the center of his face to seemingly every part of his body. This wasn't his first time getting hit in the head. Last time it was the royal guard, but the wood hurt way more, and his eyes popped with stars.

His ringing ears picked up a voice. "Are you all right?" The voice was Barnin's. He didn't sound panicked.

His eyes focused, and as he stood, the concern on Barnin's face left with a smirk. "Well, now you won't drop your sword. Come on, let's keep going."

Let's keep going? He was appalled. He was hurt; they weren't going to keep going. To his horror, he heard the last voice he wanted to hear.

Of course, Sara was home with her friend Sam. Both girls ran up to him, and Barnin snorted.

"Are you all right? Here, let me look at you," Sara said, pulling his hands away from his face.

She muttered something. "It's broken." She glared at Barnin. "What did you do?"

Barnin fired up. "I was teaching him, and he dropped his stave. Don't look at me like that! My nose has been broken a dozen times. He'll be fine. We just need to move it back in place."

"Move it back in place? Well, obviously that's what you've done on yours," Sara shot back scathingly.

Barnin scowled. "What's that supposed to mean? Come here, Keither; it will just sting a bit."

Keither backed up. "Get away from me!"

Barnin scowled. "Don't be a child; come here." He moved to grab Keither. "Stop it now, come on, I can see your vagina. Here, let me fix it."

At last, Barnin had gone too far. Sam, Sara's friend, puffed up, and the normally charming girl looked terrifying. "You can see his what? You sexist pig!"

Now Barnin was on the defensive for probably the first time in his life.

Sara walked up to Keither, and silver light flashed. "Sorry about that; I had to do it quickly before Barnin and Sam start killing each other. Are you all right?"

"Yes, thank you," he said, but it wasn't his voice that answered. It wasn't nasal like before.

Sara looked at him with surprise. "You must have had a problem with your voice before; you sound a lot like..."

"Kovos," is all he said.

Memories of his brother and his death came to him, and looking down at Sara, all of his promises to himself came back. "Barnin, stop flirting with Sam; she's out of your league. Let's go again."

Barnin turned wide-eyed to him. "You sound like..."

"I know; Sara fixed me. Now again."

He picked up his stave, and as he rose, he saw Sara's lips twitch in a smile. Sam took the opportunity to punch Barnin in the arm and returned to her friend.

LEGON FLOPPED DOWN IN HIS BUNK, EXHAUSTED FROM A day of learning the ins and outs of working a ship, but at the same time, he was too keyed up to really go to bed. He glanced into Sasha's head to see what she was doing—no surprise, she was reading a book of Elvin poetry. Legon didn't have anything against poetry, but the book Sasha had was about lost lovers and all that. He sent her an impression of dry heaving, and she blocked him out. At some point, he fell asleep.

He felt a sharp pain in his arm and woke with a start. "Ouch, what did you pinch me for?"

Sasha was kneeling next to him. They were in a misty field. He could hear waves crashing in the distance.

She spoke. "You'll be fine; you wouldn't wake up. What is this place?"

He got up, and she steadied him. "For a dream, Legon, you sure are needy. You're normally stronger in my dreams."

He arched an eyebrow. "In your dreams? You're in my dream."

She rolled her eyes. "What is this place?"

"It's the field where I see the dragons. Well, the white one is here, but I've never seen him." He pointed behind them. "Don't go that way; trust me."

She nodded, looking nervous. The waves were new. He'd never heard them before. In fact, it had been a while since one of these dreams, and he hoped they weren't about to start up again.

Sasha's hand gripped his arm firmly, and she whispered. "Do you hear that?"

He almost forgot to listen for it. "Yeah, that sound through the mist is the white dragon. I don't think you'll see him. Maybe some blue, but that's it. I'm not even convinced it's the white dragon. It could be a blue one."

The sound of heavy breathing was drawing closer. The mist seemed to be thinning before their eyes. He gasped, and Sasha yelped as a giant white dragon's foot parted the mist to rest before them.

The scales were white and glowed, casting shards of light from them so that little rainbows of light danced across the ground. The dragon extended one golden claw and poked the ground with it, then pulled back into the mist. Where the claw touched, a plant started to shoot from the ground. Soon it grew into what looked like a rose bush. Buds appeared, and lavender roses bloomed, filling the air with their rich scent.

"Sash, are those lavender roses?"

She leaned closer, as if speaking above a whisper was inappropriate. "Yes, they are extremely rare. Only the Elves really grow them, but they make roses in every color and shade. Is that a caterpillar?"

Sure enough, there was not just one but several caterpillars crawling up the stalks of the plant. As they moved, they began to change, forming into white butterflies. One took flight and fluttered past them, its wings glowing white and veins of deepest purple running through them with wisps of gold along the tips. They were beautiful, but the bush was starting to wither away and die as the butterflies left it. Soon they were all gone, and the bush was dead.

Legon spoke. "I don't understand. What are you telling me?"

There was no reply, but he saw a flash of blue and awoke in a cold sweat, just like any other time.

He lay there for a time when he heard his cabin door open. "Hey Sash, can't sleep?"

He looked at her; her face was covered in a sheen of sweat. "What's the matter?"

She sat at the bottom of the bed. "You know those dreams you had about the dragons?"

"Yeah, I just woke from one. You were in it."

She stiffened. "Was there a lavender rose bush and butterflies?"

"Yes." A chill ran along his spine. "How did you..."

"I was there. You talked to him."

He was starting to feel extremely uneasy. "He didn't answer. How do you know that we can link in dreams?"

She nodded. "Who said we were dreaming?"

CHAPTER 9
COREUM

"All seek the most common denominator in life. In that is great strength and weakness."
— Articles of the Mahann

S ydin scowled. "This doesn't make sense. You can't mentally link when you are unconscious, or even half asleep for that matter." He paused to think. "This is something to look into. Maybe there is something different about you, Legon, coming from both Human and Elvin descent, though I find it unlikely."

Sasha knew there wasn't any point in pursuing the subject anymore. Sydin was just as stumped by the dream as they were, and it hadn't happened again.

The air was thick and heavy. They were almost to the rendezvous with the fleet that would escort them to Seeon. Once again, she was thankful for magic. The cooling spell she was using made the hot, moist air feel good on her skin, and it kept her from sweating.

"Sydin," she started. "Can you tell us more about the ship? How does it respond in a fight? I'm interested."

His face relaxed, no longer having to figure out dreams. "Sure thing. Where to start, where to start... Oh yes, well, as you have been told, there is a central crystal, but the ship has other features as well. You know some of them, but others you likely don't."

They were taking another tour of the ship and learned how it was able to stabilize itself so it didn't capsize, regardless of the weather. They also learned about its ability to feed from the ocean like a water plant to provide them with food and clean water. Elvin ships could stay at sea indefinitely because of this feature. The ocean is full of nutrients, so all the ship had to do was collect them, which it did with roots drifting from the belly. She was interested to find out about the bow, which was an alloy, including high amounts of platinum that kept it from corroding.

Sydin told them that during the War of Generations, Elvin and Iumenta ships would ram each other and send spells and bolts from ballistae. The ships could even fire upon dragons with some level of success, though not as much as a dragon firing on another dragon.

"You will love the carriers; they are truly something," Sydin said.

"Carriers?" Legon interrupted.

"Yes, there are large ships that carry dragons; they are called Dragon Carriers. Simple, I know, but the ships are massive, holding up to ten dragons. In a fight, you won't see the carriers get into many battles. They tend to hang back, being difficult to maneuver."

Sasha tried to picture the carrier in her head but couldn't quite figure it out. "Sydin, were you ever on one?"

"A carrier? Yes, many times. Most dragons have been, though Ise doesn't like them as much as most."

Legon fidgeted when Sydin mentioned Ise. Sasha tried not to show her amusement. He liked her, and Ise liked him, and because Sasha was the one who pushed the relationship so much, she figured if they ended up together, she would get credit.

"Is it hard being away from your wife?" Sasha asked, sensing the question in Legon's head.

Sydin considered the question for a moment, and after glancing at Legon, smirked a bit. "Yes and no. We've been together for a long time, so even with a great distance, if anything major happened, I would sense it. But yes, I do miss her. However, most couples don't go long without being around each other in our society."

ARKIN WAS CLOSE TO THE CITY OF COREUM. THE TOPS OF buildings grew from the plains as he crested the horizon. Coreum was one of the largest of the southern cities, located next to one of the sizable bodies of water, Coreum Lake. Arkin enjoyed the city with its all-wooden construction and bustling streets. Despite its size, it still had a small-town feel about it. Everyone seemed to know each other, or they had a friend or a family member who knew someone. It was for this reason Coreum was the perfect place to recruit talent, and it was still one of the only major cities that was outspoken about its distaste for the Queen. *But when you are the hub for most of the agriculture in a country, you can do just about whatever you want,* Arkin thought.

He passed through the main entrance without any issues. The streets were clogged with end-of-day travelers. To his left, he could hear an open market where people were buying whatever they needed for dinner, and wholesalers were wrapping up deals and leaving for the day. Arkin made his way to the White Dragon, an inn he knew well. Above the door was an elaborate carving of a white dragon standing on something black and scaly. He shook his head as he walked in the door. *How much more blatant could they be?* The White Dragon was an ideal place to stay if you were an Elvin spy, for the simple reason that no one in their right mind trying to blend in would stay in a place that screamed "I hate the Empire." It was for this reason the government didn't think much of you if you stayed there. *There really is something to be said for hiding in plain sight.* He walked through the packed dining area, not recognizing anyone, and stopped at the counter.

A man with a long white beard walked up to the bar. "What can I get ya?" His voice was rough.

Arkin stared for a moment. "Richard?"

"Nope, I'm not fer sale, but my wench of a wife is if you want." He turned his head. "Wench! Come here and show this chap a good time!"

A woman at the other end of the bar, who Arkin knew to be

Richard's wife Ivy, made a rude hand gesture and went back to what she was doing.

Richard pointed at her and leaned in. "See what I have to deal with since you left, Arkin?"

Arkin smiled. "You remember me, huh?"

"Yes, I do. You still owe me money, and don't think I haven't been adding up interest."

Richard rummaged in a pocket and pulled out a worn and abused piece of parchment that at first glance looked like a shopping list, but was actually a list of names and amounts owed. Arkin rolled his eyes. "It's been what, fifteen years? You have kept that for fifteen years?"

"No, of course not. Some people pay. I've just transferred names. Do you want to pay your balance, or do you want Ivy?"

Arkin glanced at Ivy, who obviously remembered him. She smiled and pointed at the door, indicating for him to leave. "How about a room and I'll pay off the debt; how much is it?"

"You sure you don't want her? Well, fine. We'll just tack on an extra five pieces, and that should cover it."

Arkin was dumbfounded. "And that's with interest?"

"Yes. And don't think I'm going down any."

"Richard, that's what—two beers?"

Richard looked up, doing the math. "Yep, about right." He turned to his wife. "WENCH! This pecker needs a room."

He looked back at Arkin. "I'll come see you tonight. I'm sure you're not here for any good, but I want you to pay up front. I'm not a bank."

Arkin made his way to his room and settled in. He woke to the sound of a knock at the door. It opened, and Richard and stone-faced Ivy entered the room. They sat at a desk across from the bed.

Ivy spoke first. "Where have you been the last fifteen years, huh?"

He smiled. "Busy. I see you two still hate each other."

Richard smiled. "It's the best front we've found, huh wench?"

Ivy didn't respond. "We deserve answers, Arkin. I swear I will chuck you out..."

He held up his hands. "I was in deep. I'm sorry if I worried you; it was never my intent to hurt anyone."

She snorted. "So how deep were you that you couldn't send word to your aunt?"

This wasn't a topic he could bring up easily. "Have you heard anything new lately?"

Richard piped up. "We heard Evindass has a new head, and that he's behind some serious raiding action, but I suppose you already knew that, didn't ya, if you're here?"

Arkin smiled. "Well, now you know what I've been doing, don't you? I can't talk about that now; I have work to do. Are you still in the game?"

"Which one?" Ivy asked.

"Tell me the run of the land. I've been out too long."

Richard sighed. "It's been hard getting things across the border, as you know, but once they are here, it's simple."

Arkin interrupted. "How is Coreum still the center for trade?"

"Well, at one point in time, Coreum was the center of the Human lands, wasn't it? Even after the war, trade went relatively unhindered with the free lands. Hoelaria was too busy consolidating power to worry about where food moved from and to. By the time she got around to addressing the problem, it was too late. Coreum was reestablished. It took her another thirty years to truly hinder smuggling, and by then the farm communities were wise to her and came here to trade. You know this; why do you ask?"

"I want to make sure I'm in a hub, and a safe one."

Ivy spoke up. "You are, but not if you want to get something across the border—that won't happen. Too much military. Even the trade in smuggling refugees has all but come to a standstill. It's making for a lot of idle hands, if you know what I mean."

He did. If there wasn't the business that there was before, crime would rise and other problems would arise, but that also meant that there were a lot of skilled smugglers and mercenaries waiting to be recruited.

He explained his plans to his aunt and uncle. They took it better than he thought they would and even knew a few people to talk to.

"Is there going to be anything else we need?" Richard asked after a few hours of talking.

"We will need a route into Manton so we can get money from Evindass until we can support ourselves with front companies. We also need to set up a better network to communicate with our minds. The relay system just won't do for something like this."

Ivy agreed to figure out the network issues, and Richard would make sure they could move funds from Manton securely. Arkin was relatively happy with how it went and was looking forward to a few days of recruiting before heading to Salez to talk to House Grey. Ivy would make a great communications leader. Richard and Ivy were perfectly placed as well. If things got too hot, they could leave. No one suspected them after all these years; Richard was just a barkeep who dabbled in setting smugglers up. Ivy was just the unpleasant person Richard had been forced to marry, or so people thought. Both came off rude and a bit dim, but neither was, and Arkin knew his aunt to be a certified genius, having taught him almost everything he knew.

LEGON STOOD ON THE BOW OF THE PROPERO. HE WAS waiting to see the main envoy come into view. Shortly after their encounter with the raiders, Sydin told Legon and Sasha that it was customary for the head of house to sail in the house ship, but due to Manton's proximity to the Empire, this was a bad idea. The house ship would be accompanied by many warships, and that was the problem. Unguarded, it was a tempting target, but with its escorts, it was too aggressive, so now Legon waited, anticipating House Evindass's ship, the Lux.

Sasha came up next to him, expectant, looking forward to seeing the Lux as well. Her hair swirled around in the sea breeze, and she smoothed out the turquoise fabric of her dress. In the distance, his ears heard the telltale thud of a dragon's wings, and he knew that dragons were flying over the Lux's armada. He wasn't surprised to see flecks of red and brown surrounding the Propero as two huge figures dropped from the sky, glittering in the bright sun. The two dragons began to fly circles around the Propero, keeping pace with it and guarding it from the sky. They had made it to the armada.

As they came alongside the armada, a sleuth and a frigate broke from formation to skirt around the Propero, bringing it into the safety of the armada. Legon couldn't help but be awestruck by the fleet before him. Toward the back was a ship with two hulls, and atop each were five massive masts. It was long and odd-looking.

"It's a carrier," Sydin said, coming up next to them.

Sasha gawked. "How many dragons are on one again?" she asked.

"They hold ten."

She pointed to the ship in the center. "What is that?" she said, amazed.

"That, my dear, is the P. E. S. Lux."

The Lux rose from the water, graceful and brilliant. The white hull sparkled in places, and Legon took in the four-masted ship in all its glory. The Lux towered over them as they came alongside. From the gold-gilded rail, a plank extended until it rested on the deck of the Propero.

Sydin spoke again. "Sasha, I will help you up the plank. I'm sorry to say it wasn't designed with Humans in mind."

That it wasn't. It was steep, and on the undulating sea, it would be hard for non-Elves to traverse. Legon watched as Sasha attempted to walk the ramp with little success. Finally, Sydin put his hands around her hips, steering her up. Legon crested the railing and stepped onto the deck of his ship. They were greeted by many Elves, all in robes of the deepest purple. Sasha stood next to Legon, and in unison, all of the Elves aboard the ship knelt. He turned to Sydin to find him also kneeling. As his gaze swept the decks of the fleet, all the Elves on each ship knelt, facing the Lux.

Legon was supposed to say something, but he didn't want to. This was one of those times when everyone was looking at him, and he'd rather swim to Seeon. He cleared his throat. "Thank you; it is an honor to be with you," was all he could think to say.

They rose, and a man with brown hair approached him. "Un Prosa, it is we who are honored. It has been too long since the Lux was put to its proper use. Welcome aboard."

A woman with bronze hair walked to Sasha. "Un Prose, I am Elna. I will be your handmaid while on board."

Sasha responded warmly. "You don't have to do that; I can manage."

Sydin spoke softly to her. "Sasha, this is Elna's job. While it may seem odd to you, refusing her service would be a great insult."

Sasha corrected herself. "Oh, I'm sorry, Elna. Thank you. I'm looking forward to getting to know you."

Elna smiled warmly, not bothered in the least. Sasha spoke again. "Maybe you would be willing to help me understand how my brother's society works so I don't offend anyone?"

Elna's response was kind but firm. "Your society too, Un Prose. Never forget who you are. And of course, I would love to teach you." She turned to Legon. "Allow me to introduce my husband, Pras."

A man with brown eyes and long, flowing brown hair came up next to Elna and bowed. "Un Prosa, I will be your butler while on board. Anything you need at all, please let me know."

With that, a procession of people introduced themselves, and in time, the crowd on the deck dispersed to various parts of the ship.

———

Sasha took in the ship as they made their way into a door at the stern. Elna glided beside her down a set of stairs onto a landing. "This way to your quarters, Un Prose," Elna said.

Sasha wasn't all that comfortable with the whole 'Prose' thing, but she didn't want to offend Elna. "Elna?" she asked.

"Yes."

"Do you mind calling me Sasha?"

Elna smiled. "You asked me to teach you about our culture."

"Ummm, yes," Sasha replied.

"Un Prose is what you are called, and in public, you are obliged to be Prose. However, in private, it's acceptable to speak with more familiarity. So if you prefer, I will call you Sasha."

"Thanks, and thank you for putting up with me."

Elna spoke. "I'm not putting up with anything. It will take you a long time to get used to your new life." Her voice was warm and kind.

Sasha relaxed, and Elna opened a large double door. They stepped into Sasha's quarters. The apartment was elegant, with a raised ceiling that went beyond the main deck. A doorway led to her bedroom. At the end was a window as tall as the room that curved out away from the ship's stern. She walked to the window and looked down into the turning sea below. To her left was an enormous bed. With the sight, something struck her.

"What is it, Sasha?" Elna asked.

"I can't feel the ship moving," she said.

Elna paused for a moment. "That's right; you've never been on the sea. The Propero, while powerful, is made for war, and all of her spells are directed accordingly. The Lux is designed for luxury, and so are her spells. This ship has powerful wards, of course, wards far stronger than the Propero's, but the Lux has much more energy. You don't feel the movement of the ship because the Lux is keeping you from feeling the movement of the sea. If you like, reach out with your mind, and you will feel movement again."

Sasha gaped. "The ship is keeping me from feeling the sea?" The spell seemed straightforward enough, but that the Elves put so much effort into the comfort of the ship amazed her. The air was brisk and pleasant as well. Obviously, the climate inside was controlled, and she caught the scent of wildflowers, the same wildflowers that grew in Salmont. She felt sad for just a moment. "The air reminds me of home," she said.

Elna answered. "Yes, we thought you might like it. You are sad... would you like a different scent?" Elna said, reading Sasha's emotions.

"No, no, this is good. It just made me miss my family, that's all, but this is good. Please show me around."

LEGON SANK INTO THE MOST COMFORTABLE BED HE HAD ever laid on. Instantly, he wanted to take a nap. "Pras, do you mind if I sleep for a while?" Pras laughed. "If you like; would you like me to bring you lunch, or would you like to tour the ship and eat in the mess hall?"

Legon thought for a moment. "I think I'll take a tour of the ship first." He wanted to know more about this man. He'd been around Elves for a while, but only those in the military. "Tell me about yourself." He followed Pras to the door and out into the hall. Sasha and Elna were entering the hall at the same time.

Elna answered for Pras. "We live on the Lux. This has been our home for a long time now." Pras took over. "We have lived on this ship since it was remodeled in 203 A.G." Elna spoke next. "The Lux rarely leaves the capital, so we can see our children, but we love it here and will stay on unless you decide otherwise." Then, as before, Pras took over. "We will always serve you and be with you, but in the capital, there will be people assigned directly to you in the house." Then Elna spoke. "They like us to live in the house and would be here today if they weren't preparing for your homecoming."

He was getting used to this. Some couples did everything they could to be of one mind when together and would quite often finish the other's sentences. This was normal for them. He wondered if Iselin and he would be like that. He doubted it. They both enjoyed their individuality, and if they did stay together, they would be just as close as Elna and Pras, but they would still keep their own identities.

The group made their way down a long corridor to the bow of the ship. They entered a large dining room. Legon strolled to a window, whose length ran along the whole forward edge of the bow, giving one the impression of flying. Indeed, few things about the Lux were built for practicality. He turned to the soft sound of platters being set on the table. Sasha was looking up at the ceiling and the vast chandelier attached to it. Right above the table hung a ruby crystal that was nearly the size of the table. It looked like a collection of rose petals all connected together.

Other members of the crew joined them for lunch, and Sasha and Legon spent most of the afternoon learning about the Lux. Finally, after dinner, most of the crew retired, and Sasha and Legon sat soaking in a tub filled with hot water that could hold eight or nine, located on the top deck of the bow. He stared up at the open sky, seeing more stars than he thought possible.

Legon spoke. "What do you think of this?"

Sasha took her time answering. "I'm not sure. It seems like a dream to me, ya know? On the one hand, I feel guilty because we are now living better than anyone in either of the Human lands."

"But?"

She took another moment. "But this seems right to me for the Elves. I mean, they are immortal and can grow things with their minds. They don't have the same worries as most people do. They have more time and skill, so why not live a comfortable life? I think it's also unfair to compare the Lux to normal ships because we are heads of a great house. The rest of society can't live like this."

He knew what she was getting at. All Elves lived in almost the same level of comfort, but where he and Sasha had houses and ships, most people wouldn't. Would they? He reached out with his mind and asked Sydin.

Sasha looked at him, waiting. "Sydin said he would join us." She relaxed.

When he joined them, Sydin explained that while as heads of a house they did have more than most, many Elves had several houses. He also explained that they were much larger than Human dwellings in many cases. In the cities, Elves had apartments, but that property stayed in families, and as a result, people would spend seventy or eighty years in one spot and then move elsewhere in the family estate.

Before he went to bed, Legon tried to see if he could contact Ise. He went to the ship's main communications center and accessed what he needed. He wasn't expecting to see her face fill the crystal. "Hey, how are you? I can see you."

She smiled. "That's good; you aren't blind. I'm fine, why? Are you surprised to see me?"

He chuckled. "I wasn't able to before; is it because this ship is so powerful?"

"Yes, and you are close to the coast. How was your day?"

They spoke for a long time until after a few yawns, she told him to go to bed. He returned to his cabin and slipped under the silk sheets, feeling himself sink into the bed and fall asleep almost instantly.

"Legon... LEGON! Wake up, you lump!" Sasha's voice said, irritated and nervous.

"Wh...what? Sash, let me sleep, will y..." he trailed off as he sat up in the misty field that was filled with lavender roses.

CHAPTER 10

SIGNS OF THE TIMES

*"When did the world change, you ask? I cannot tell you, because like then,
from the dawn of time nothing has remained constant."*
— *The River of Change*

E dis scrubbed the spotless counter. He was pretty sure that if he kept rubbing, the surface would start to wear away, or his hand would cramp... again. He huffed and tossed the rag across the room. The door tinkled, and he turned to the customer, but it was no customer.

"Sorry, it's just me." Emma smiled.

The kid was looking better and even daring to go into the woods again. Why, Edis didn't know, but she went anyway.

"It's always good to see you, dear. How are you today?" he said to her.

She nodded. "Fine. I take it you have nothing to do?"

He didn't have anything to do; no one was selling livestock right now, and of course, after the dragon, no one was going into the woods to hunt, meaning Edis had nothing to do and no money coming in.

"Nope, no one has livestock to sell. It all dried up because of that ruddy dragon, and people are too..."

"Dumb and scared to come out from under their rocks? Yes, I know," she said, smiling again.

"Hmmm, I told you that, huh?"

She winced. "Not today."

She plopped herself on the counter. "I thought I would come and keep you company."

Now it was his turn to smile. "That would be welcome. Doesn't Laura have things for you to do?"

"No, as no one is leaving their houses, they aren't getting sick or hurt." Her cheeks flushed. "But she says we will have a lot of babies to deliver in about nine months."

He chuckled. "Yes, boredom has that effect." He noticed a flyer in her hand. "What is that?"

"A notice about road curfews. Apparently, it's unsafe to travel at night now, so we need to stay within town limits and off the roads." She rolled her eyes.

Edis didn't comment, but this bothered him. He too had seen flyers like this. There was even talk that the Queen was considering drafting people for the army, something that hadn't been done in living memory. He wasn't worried about getting drafted; he was old, but once Emma was done with her apprenticeship...

She interrupted his thoughts. "What do you think is going on?"

He shook his head. "It's hard to say. I don't think the Queen will act against the free lands, but it sounds like they are moving against her."

The question made him look at her closely. Her eyes were slightly puffy. "I'm sure they are safe." He answered the unspoken question.

She looked down and fidgeted more with the paper. "Do you really think so?"

EMMA MADE HER WAY OUT OF THE SHOP SOMETIME LATER and decided to go and get some produce for dinner. It was odd. Edis thought that people were scared of Iumenta dragons in the area, but in

reality, most of the people didn't think a thing of it. They were frightened by the possibility of robbers, and even, to her surprise, a few questioned her about the incident, asking why she was in the woods and
what would make a dragon suspect her. But these were mostly those
who traveled frequently. The core of the town was just scared and angry
because of the threats to their lands and safety. Still, there were other
signs that not all was well in the Cona Empire, and there were signs that
not many seemed to notice. It came mostly in the way of news. Something didn't seem right about it. There were articles posted to message
boards proclaiming victory in the south, but they were recruiting more,
and it was now deemed unsafe to travel at night, so how could the south
be conquered? Also, when had the Empire gone to war with the rebel
south to begin with? When she asked, no one knew when the war had
started. Most people just seemed to think that it had always been
going on.

As she rounded a corner, the sun momentarily blinded her. She held
her hand up, measuring it in the sky. "Dang it," she said under her
breath.

It was getting late in the day, and people would be heading home
soon. She could already see it in the streets. She picked up her pace,
wanting to catch the market before all the farmers hurried to the safety
of their houses.

This line of thought turned out to be correct. It wasn't easy for her
to find what she wanted, and the farmer gave it to her for next to nothing, just wanting to be done for the day. She headed home unhappily. If
she had gotten a deal due to some tricky haggling, she would be proud
and happy, but that wasn't the case. There was no need to haggle so late
in the day. Fear of robbers on the roads made the deal for her. She paid
the merchant more than he asked for, and that was something.

The streets were quiet now. Only the sound of the dirt and gravel
under her feet made a sound. The townsfolk didn't hide at night.
Salmont proper was more than safe, but with the market and shops
closed, there was a lull as people went home and spent time with family.
Later she might go to the tavern. It would be packed in a few hours.

The next morning, Emma decided to go for a walk in the woods.
She needed to conquer her fear of them, and getting out of town would

be good for her. Edis offered to close the shop for the day and go with her, but she declined. There were other things that she needed to work through.

With a bit of effort, she was able to procure an old pair of Legon's pants from when he was much younger and smaller. They fit relatively well and seemed to be in reasonable shape, despite their age. Laura raised an eyebrow when she saw her.

"You get confused, dear?" she asked with a smile.

Emma smiled. "No, I just don't want to ruin another dress. I want to go up the north face of the valley, and it's not easy hiking."

There was no need to explain why she was going up the north face, as the east was too steep for any but the most experienced climbers, and the last time she was on the west, well, she wasn't thinking about the west right now.

Not wanting to get any more looks than normal, she wrapped around Salmont, making it to the base of the hills around mid-morning. Once she was at the tree line, her insides filled with ice. What if that dragon was out again today? She pushed the thought from her mind. The forest was too dense here; it wouldn't be good hunting, and besides, a dragon hadn't been seen for a while now. It was probably safe. She adjusted the small daypack on her back and started into the thick woods.

Sound stopped once inside, and the light dimmed green through the canopy high above. The feeling of foreboding only grew as she went deeper. She could see maybe ten feet in front of her, and without sound or a marked trail, there was the risk of getting lost. That fear soon outweighed that of the possibility of dragons. Once she calmed herself, it wasn't difficult to find her bearing. She knew enough to not get permanently lost, at any rate.

As she moved, her shirt clung to her sweaty skin. It was uncomfortable and something she wasn't entirely used to. Her mind wandered about the many possibilities at hand, the first and foremost her education. Well, that was the first that she could control. The true first was Kovos, but she wasn't going to think about him now. Her options were clear. She would be able to stay in Salmont until her apprenticeship was over, and from there she would go to Salez and finish the higher levels of training. Laura could, of course, teach her everything, but she needed certification from the Empire. Right now she could claim being a level one or a nurse. That could keep her in Salmont maybe, and she could find work in most of the towns in the territory. If she went to school, she could become a level two or three healer and could live almost any place she wanted. Also, if she was asked to go to the battlefront, she would be well away from any fighting. Already the nurse's band on her arm made her all but immune to any violence. Not even a band of robbers would hurt her. They could take her and force her to fix their wounded, but nothing more. Healers, like smiths, were too important and rare.

She stuck her foot through tall grass, and it landed on soft level ground. As she made her way between the current of grass, she found herself in a small clearing, except it couldn't be called a clearing. Her eyes and mind tried to make out the shape in front of her. It was a tree, but it wasn't. The base of the trunk bulged with holes that looked like...

"Are those windows?" she said out loud.

Hesitantly, she moved to the tree, or structure, or whatever it was. Instinctively, her eyes flashed around and stopped on a white stone lying on the ground. She went to it and knelt. It was square. She leaned closer and saw an engraving: *Umquam Omitto*. What did that mean? Then it hit her, and she moved quickly to the side, realizing that she was standing on a grave.

She whirled to the tree that she now knew. The story of Legon's past —the one she only knew bits about—came to her in a rush. The memory flooded her. Lying in Kovos' arms as she tried to fall asleep, he was prattling about Legon and how he was found. She thought Kovos was playing with her, or that maybe she was asleep, and then the next day he was gone. She never gave his ramblings that night any thought, but now she remembered. Her feet moved on their own accord to the little dwelling. Part of her screamed to run away, told her not to go in, but another part, a more rational part, told her there was no danger here, not anymore. The bark was rough under her slender fingers. Her hand moved up the oval doorway, and she walked into the little room.

Chills ran the length of her spine as she entered the one-room dwelling. Even after years of abandonment, chairs, tables, and other belongings covered the floor. The floor was one piece of wood with large splotchy stains she assumed were from blood. The sweet scent of sap was almost inviting, a direct contrast with the scene before her. There should have been a thick layer of dust coating the interior, but the finger she ran across the curving mantelpiece showed less than what you could find in Laura and Edis's house. Was this place still inhabited? She knelt over the empty fireplace, or at least that's what she thought it was. There was no stone, just seamless wood. Her hand found a small ridge under the hearth, and she lifted without too much force. She looked at an empty space, just the size for a small child. She picked up a small yellow blanket. The fabric was stiff with age, but she could tell at one point it had been soft. The compartment closed as silently and easily as it had opened. One hand still holding the blanket, she lifted herself from the ground, holding the wall for support. A bump in the wood gave, and she leaped back as flames burst into existence in the fireplace. This was bad; it was just wood. Panicking, she did the first thing that came to mind and pushed the bump again. The fire stopped. There was a small *plop* as her mouth fell open. The wood looked just the same as it did before, but there had to be a fire; she could still feel heat from the fireplace. Carefully, and still holding onto the blanket, she made her way out of the house and hurried as fast as she could toward town.

"Hello, dear, what is that you have?" Laura asked as Emma entered the house. Then, taking a closer look, asked, "What happened? Is everything alright?"

Emma looked down at the little blanket and dropped it. She didn't even know she was still holding it.

"What's wrong?" Laura was looking a bit frantic now.

"I found the house," was all she managed.

Laura looked confused. "What house?"

"The house, the one they found him in. The one that's a tree, not a house."

"What house that's a tree?"

"The one they found Legon in; there's still someone living in it. There has to be; it makes fire, and there's no dust." She was starting to ramble. The logical side of her brain told her to calm down and not be upset. No one lived in the house anymore. Also, she knew what Kovos said. Edis told Legon about it. She just thought maybe Edis had been under a lot of stress when he saw it and remembered wrong. Emma thought perhaps it had been a treehouse of sorts, but it wasn't. It was a tree, and it was alive.

"I'm not sure how much more I can take... dragons, trees that are houses, my family dying, Kovos gone, the problems in the south, wh..."

"Stop," Laura said, placing her hands on Emma's shoulders. "Breathe. It's all right."

But it wasn't all right; it had never been all right. She was supposed to be in some little mountain town away from everything! Nothing was all right, and nothing was what it seemed.

***

SARA TOSSED A RAG ASIDE AND WALKED OUT OF THE ROOM. What was the lesson here? The patient was going to die. Why were they still trying so hard with him? She wasn't in a pleasant mood, and her shoes clicking on the granite floor weren't helping matters. Her right foot clicked "you can't save anyone," and her left "you're going to fail," on and on.

"You ok?" It was Sam.

"Maybe this isn't what I should be doing." It wasn't a question, just stating the obvious.

"You don't want to go into combat or anything, do you?"

She shook her head. "No, no, of course not, but why do I have to use magic? Why can't I do something else?"

Sam pursed her lips. "Ok, well what do you want to do? Don't look at me like that. This isn't the Empire; you can do whatever you like."

"Yeah, but we don't have that many Venefica..." Sara trailed off. Also, there was the fact that Legon and Sasha were heads of a great house, and quitting or failing out of school wouldn't look good. Not to mention that it would be extremely ungrateful of her.

"Are you worried about disappointing them?"

She frowned. "That obvious?"

"Come on. Anytime someone mentions House Evindass, you perk up like you were in the inner court or something." She paused. "You know they wouldn't mind if you quit; I bet you could even move to the capital." Her eyes went wide. "Can you imagine what it must be like?"

"I'm sure it's like the dome."

Sam went on. "Maybe. I bet it's amazing. I hear that all the Elvin cities are. I've never been in the dome before; what's it like?"

This was another reminder of the privileges Sara enjoyed. "It's nice. I guess I can take you in sometime."

They had been walking side by side when Sam stopped. Sara took a couple of steps back. "What?"

"You can't just go in. Only high-ranking people go in there."

She smiled. "This weekend. Come on."

It was mid-morning when the dragon dome loomed before them. Keither rode Pixy next to Sara. "It's going to be good to see Ise again," he said.

"And Cat," Sara prompted.

"That's right," he laughed.

"Isn't this a little far for a joke, you two?" Sam said. She didn't believe that they could get in the dome at all, but came anyway for something to do.

Once dismounted, they started their way up the side, Sam looking more and more apprehensive. Keither seemed to have more confidence in his step.

"You starting to get the Jezeer?"

It looked like she pulled him away from some train of thought. "Starting to—yeah—and Barnin, when he's around, helps out a lot."

When they were almost at the top of the dome, a slender figure in pink could be seen. Sara and Keither waved.

"What are you doing? We are going to get sent away. Oh no, here she comes," Sam said, terrified.

"Sam, have you ever seen an Elf hurt someone?" Keither said, confused.

"That's hardly the point, is it?"

She knew Ise could hear the conversation and didn't raise her voice. "Are you going to eat us?"

Sam looked mortified, but Ise's voice didn't sound angry in the least bit. "Too greasy," she said, making a face.

When they were a few feet away, Iselin walked forward and gave Sara and Keither a hug, then turned to Sam. "You must be Sam?"

"Yes ma'am. H...how did you know?"

"I talk to these two. Come in; have you had lunch?"

Sam tugged Sara's sleeve. "What is it?"

"Did you see her eyes?" Sam whispered.

"Yes, she's Ascended, we know. Don't be awkward."

Sara was surprised at how good it felt to be in the dome again, with its woodsy smell and pulsing energy. It was alive, and in a way, when she was here, she was alive in another way too. Maybe she would go to the capital...

Sam ohhh'd and ahhh'd at all the right places and was quickly getting over her fear of being in the dome, but still seemed a little uncomfortable.

"It's alien, I know, but by morning you'll love it," Sara gushed.

"We're staying here?"

Iselin spoke. "Yes, I have arranged guest quarters for you. You're in your old place, Sara."

KEITHER STOOD IN FRONT OF THE WALL-HEIGHT MIRROR examining himself. He was in Mantic's apartment, a far nicer accommodation than he'd enjoyed the last time he was here. He pinned an Evindass pin to his vest, making sure it was level and gleaming. His fingers slid over the emblem wrought with silver, amethyst, emerald, and sapphire. The emblem was so simple, yet it burst with meaning. The Human houses never truly got the meaning of a crest. They opted for elaborate symbols that were empty. The green of the emerald was for life, emphasized by the tree showing life growing. The blue sapphire spoke of spirituality, once again emphasized by a shape, this time of a triangle. Last, the majesty and royalty of the amethyst in a dot represented the circle of eternity.

Cat wound her way between his legs, and he reached down to scratch behind her ears. It was time to go to the dining hall. On his way out, Mantic stopped him.

"Here, I think you might enjoy this." He handed him an old but well-kept black leather volume.

"What is it?" he said, and he ran his fingers over the embossed cover.

"'Who is it by' is the better question."

Keither raised an eyebrow but opened the book to read the author. "Hoelaria!"

Mantic smiled. "Yes, it is one of hers. It's good to know your enemy, Keither, and don't forget at one time the Elves and Iumenta weren't at each other's throats. We fought, but we respected each other's intellect."

"But Hoelaria?" He was incredulous that someone so high in the Elvin command would have this.

"She's thousands of years old, Keither, and moreover a master of the Mahann. Read it; there is poison and wisdom contained therein. Now, off to see Iselin. I don't want on her bad side. She will explain more to you if you like."

He entered a private dining room. The girls were just getting seated. Sam looked awed by all the Elves, and it took him a bit of effort to remember that they kept themselves apart from Humanity for this reason. Humans were easily overwhelmed by the immortals. It dulled the mind after generations.

Sara was in a lavender dress, the pin of Evindass above her left breast like his own. She was showing support for House Evindass in every way she could. She must still feel guilty, he thought. Sam fingered the red velvet of her dress. She wore no emblem.

Iselin walked in, and Cat darted to her. "Sorry I'm late; may I look at that book, Keither?" She held out her hand.

He handed her the book and sat next to her at the table. An Elf walked in with a tray of food and set it in the center of the table.

"*De Situs ne Cogitatio*—one of Hoelaria's. It's a fascinating read." She put the book down next to him.

Sam spoke. "Hoelaria? The Queen?"

"Regent," Ise corrected. "Yes, and yes I've read it and many other Iumenta books, as have they read many Elvin."

Keither had been thumbing through it on his way down. "Ise, may I get your thoughts on a section I read on the way down?"

She gestured for him to read the section.

Humanity is ruled by time, whereas we are not. The mortal mind cannot fix its gaze on the horizon long enough to travel to any desirable destination in society and ideology. Thus cause issues, an infection that will end the races. Ergo, they must be subjugated in mind, body, and spirit in order to avoid the Multo Fino or The Great End in their language.

"Yes, the great end would be the end of society, though I find it unlikely. There is some dispute about this. That's the crux really, of the Iumenta and Elvin disagreement about Humanity. You see, the Iumenta believe with your race's ability to breed, and the fact that you are sentient beings, you will cause the end of us all."

"How can we do that?" Sam asked, a little offended.

Keither answered her. "We shift too much. We are a pendulum going from extreme to extreme. This is evident in our history. Even after taking the old wastelands of the War of Generations, we fought amongst ourselves. It was the Elves that brought us together, helped us like a parent would a child kept from extremes."

She didn't look convinced, but he went on. "That is why the Elves don't push us too hard. They don't want to subjugate us, whereas the Iumenta believe that is the only way."

He helped himself to some food while Ise continued the thought. "We have interceded many times. It's not that you are different from us, but that you don't have former generations to see the mistakes of the past. You have lived with Elves in the training house; you must see this."

Sam nodded. "I think I understand."

Sara took a drink. "Is this what the war is about?"

Ise shook her head and held her hand out for the book. He handed it to her.

No two ideologies can exist in one space at one time. One will perish and one survive; this is an inevitability, and for this cause we must destroy the opposition or they us.

"That is what the war is about." Iselin forestalled questions. "It's not that we aren't open-minded; we are with many things. However, two ways of ideology cannot coexist unless both parties are near destruction. Yes, they may be cordial, but always fighting one another, be it in word, action, or thought."

"So 'you're wrong and we're right' is the center of this whole thing?" Sam asked.

Ise took her time. "Yes and no. We are blood enemies and would kill one another anyway. Indeed, even our bodies appear to hate one another, whereas a Human can breed with an Elf or Iumenta, though there are no known cases of the latter. An Elf and Iumenta cannot have a child together since our species are too different. Yes, the ideologies are why we fight, so different are they. We would let them live if they would let us live; however, their way of thinking is to kill all opposition. They struck first many of the times, and to this day no one really knows the true start of the War of Generations. Now, let's eat and have a good evening." And with that, the topic was closed for discussion.

Legon sat in Sydin's tight cabin with Sasha as Sydin explained the new world they were going to.

"We are about a day out. Over the next few months, you will learn a lot. As you can guess, there are responsibilities to being the head of a house. I'm not here to teach you most of those. Unless you decide to move or replace me, I am in charge of your military.

"This is common in all houses. Now, Arkin told me that you two have developed some slight hand signals for communication."

Both Sasha and Legon's heads shot up, but Sasha spoke first. "How did you know that?"

Sydin smiled mischievously. "Well, Arkin was a spy, after all, but also because coding is so important in statecraft that he fostered that by planting the suggestion of signals when you were toddlers."

They really never got anything by the carpenter, did they?

Sydin went on. "There is a sublanguage, common words that mean different things. Each house has several of these languages. You will need to know the sublanguages for your security."

"Are we not safe in our own city?" Legon asked.

Sydin shook his head. "Extremely safe, but caution is important."

At first, the idea of code and sublanguages that only a single house knew seemed like a waste of time to him. With the mind's ability to talk, you were perfectly safe; there was no breaching the connection. But as time went on, he realized that the mind talk was only effective over a short distance. There were ways of communicating over vast spaces, as he did every night with Iselin, but that signal could be intercepted; it was not secure. They learned that even Arkin had given every report in code in case one of the relays could not be trusted. Paper documents also contained codes. The words were seemingly meaningless in the code —simple everyday conversation. Legon began to realize that you could be having two conversations at one time, incorporating tone and signal language. They learned that in many ways, statecraft was learning this way of communicating, using hints, symbols, and inflection to communicate many things. Legon's communication to the Iumenta command began to take on new meaning. Before, he didn't understand why they were wary of a house leader who was so blunt and arrogant. He understood now. They were looking for the meanings, trying to figure out what Legon's true motives were. It was the utter simplicity of the message that confused them.

Sydin also helped work with Legon on the speech he was to give during his homecoming celebration, a speech he had no desire to give. To his immense relief, Sydin and Legon's other house advisors had written the address for him, not from any lack of faith in Legon, but rather in the knowledge that Legon did not have a firm grasp on the Elvin language, nor had he ever written a speech in his life.

"Will someone always write my addresses?" Legon asked.

"Sometimes yes; you will have a speechwriter on staff. Their job is to take care of doing a lot of the legwork; it can take hours to write a speech. You will on occasion want to write something on your own, but for most occasions, you will give instruction to your writer, and they will write the speech and then give it to you to approve," Sydin explained.

"Instructions?" Legon asked. "And what about Sasha?"

"Instructions in the sense that you will tell them what the speech is to be about and the feel you want—if you want any facts or numbers.

They will do the research needed and put those points in the speech. As for Sasha, yes; she too will have to address the house from time to time, but not as often as you, Legon."

"That's good to know. I feel a little better, but everyone seems to really like Sasha. Don't you think that maybe she should be the house's mouthpiece?" Legon offered.

Sasha wasn't having it. "Legon, you are the head of house, and you're so brave. It should be you, and besides, it's so enjoyable watching you choke," she said sweetly.

It was late in the night before Sydin let up, and Legon's head throbbed with the stress of learning too much. Most of the nation lived in relative relaxation, but the higher-ups did not enjoy that luxury. He would still be putting in a full day's work and then some.

"I think my head is going to pop," Sasha said outside her door. "Why do you think he waited until now to tell us more about how life will be when we get home?"

"I don't know. I think they have been letting us settle. By the sound of it, we will have a lot to learn in the coming months and years."

She nodded. "Tell Ise hi for me."

He said he would and went to the communications room of the ship. There, built into a podium against the wall, was a pentagon-shaped crystal that shone with the image of a beautiful blond woman.

She smiled at him. "How was your trip?"

He couldn't help but grin. "Good, we've been learning code."

"Don't say any meanings over this, but that's good." She smiled. "Sorry."

"You're fine; the reminder is good. How were Keither and Sara?"

"Fair. Keither is doing well. Sara struggles. The training she received on the road put her months ahead of any other Venefica healer. She seems to think that the few weeks she's been in school should have given her the abilities that Sasha has. Keither is finally showing progress with the Jezeer. Once something clicks with him, he learns incredibly fast."

"He does learn quickly. Sara is impatient, but not in a bad way. I'm glad she has a friend."

"I like them. I want to stay and talk, but I need to pack up to leave for Seeon."

"How long will it take you?"

She thought for a moment. "Not long; the route you took was longer. Truth be told, I think the city wanted more time to prepare, but even then I will be jumping. I will see you when you get there. There is going to be a big celebration." Dragons were powerful enough that they could move instantly from one point in space to another. However, it took massive amounts of energy, and unless they were moving, line of sight was all but impossible. Crystals were used to guide dragons from one point like the Precipice to another like Seeon.

He liked the sound of that. "Will they last long?"

She rolled her eyes. "The whole house will be putting itself out for this. It will take days. Trust me; your face will be sore from the smiling. Now, I must go. I'll see you soon."

Two emotions raged inside him. The first was disappointment that they couldn't talk longer. He didn't know why, but he was already extremely attached to her. The second was excitement because seeing her face to face would be far better than this crystal.

"See you soon. Oh, Sasha says hi."

She smiled. "Give her a hug for me." She kissed her fingers and touched the crystal before she left.

CHAPTER 11

HOMECOMING

"Environment is what has the greatest impact on emotion. The problem is most people think of the environment as the place they are in, as opposed to a state of mind."
— Teachings of the Restored Queen

Iselin finished her last walkthrough of her apartment, making sure that nothing was left behind. She had brought few personal effects when she was deployed, and most of those were being shipped home. She walked out of the apartment for what she hoped was the last time. Her stay at the Precipice dome hadn't been an unpleasant one, but she was looking forward to being home and seeing family and friends.

She made her way, Cat trotting behind her, to the center chamber of the dome. She'd said her goodbyes and didn't pause when she reached the hangars and looked up and out of the opening to the mostly clear sky.

At first, ascending was not uncomfortable, but an odd feeling. Now it wasn't. She concentrated on the power within her and willed her body to change. To those watching, it seemed to be an almost instantaneous thing, but while you were doing it, time all but stood still. The air shimmered as her clothes faded into oblivion. It was this that first made ascending awkward. She felt naked, but she knew that her body was blurred and couldn't be seen in the split second of transformation. Heat coursed down her arms, and they shot out to the ground, rippling with scales and muscle. The ground moved away as her neck stretched and heat ripped down her spine. The burn of it should have hurt, but it didn't; it felt fantastic, like power or energy being liberated from her body, and it was. She stretched, and her wings burst from her back and she flicked her tail through the air.

Now that it was done, she looked down at the floor below her to Cat, who was just a little fiery furball now. With a flick of her mind, the familiar turned into a ball of energy and flew to rest behind her right horn. The world was so different as a dragon. Normal people couldn't see energy, couldn't truly see magic, but dragons could. She watched the Elves moving around the hangar floor, all of them glowing with power. All Elves had some level of magic, even if it was limited to plant manipulation, so all Elves radiated energy. It was a calico collage she looked down on now. From the other dragons, she saw bands of energy moving around as they did various tasks. In this state, she could sense the currents in people's bodies as their brains sent signals to muscles. This was difficult for all new dragons, probably much the same way it would have been for Legon when he changed into an Elf. The thought of Legon pushed her thoughts of the world around her away, and she readied herself for takeoff.

Iselin coiled up and launched herself into the air, feeling her wings unfurl and drive down, thrusting her up. She loved the feel of the wind against her body and the sensation of it in her wings. She spiraled higher and angled to the south. As she made her way to the crystal that controlled the outgoing jumps for this area, she accessed it and the network it connected to. Jumping was the magic that would allow her to travel from one point in space to another instantaneously, but guiding herself over long distances was impossible. That's why there were jump crystals. They connected different points, allowing Ascendeds to jump anywhere in the Empire. She tapped into the crystal, selecting Seeon as a waypoint and then refined her selection to the central jump spot. The connection came back, telling her the air was clear and to begin her jump. Iselin started the spell that would carry her body the distance, letting her mind connect fully with the crystal, letting it guide her. She began her countdown and checklist: THREE: all her wards in her immediate area were disconnected, TWO: she snapped her wings against her body and her mind saw its destination to the exclusion of all else, ONE: she engaged the magic, seeing a bright dot of pink in front of her and felt the giant ball of magic behind her, JUMP. The ball behind her rushed over her body, and for a moment, she didn't exist. Then she was in a tunnel of pink. Her wings snapped tight to her side, sliding down the magical corridor. The tunnel opened, and just as fast as it had begun, it was over. Her wings caught the air, and she soared high above Seeon's central district.

LEGON LOOKED AT HIMSELF IN THE MIRROR. HE WAS becoming accustomed to Elvin dress, but he still didn't quite recognize himself. He adjusted his shirt and looked at Pras. "Do I look all right?"

"Wonderful, Un Prosa," was his reply.

Today was the day that the Lux would be arriving in Seeon. Seeon was a harbor city located at the end of a long bay that extended some distance into the Pawdin Empire. Legon fidgeted with the white robe he was wearing. The clothes were odd to him. His robe had no sleeves and didn't tie together. Until now, the only robes he had really ever seen were his mother's and Sasha's dressing robes, and these robes were nothing like them.

"Is there something wrong, Un Prosa?" Pras asked, showing no sign of emotion.

Was there something wrong? Yes, there was. Legon was to lead one of the Great Elvin Houses, and he didn't even know the language. "I'm a little nervous, you could say."

Pras smiled but didn't say anything. Legon liked Pras well enough. He was friendly, but unlike Sydin, Pras wasn't all that helpful and almost never showed emotion. Legon stopped playing with his clothes and walked to the door and into the hall. After a moment, Sasha came out, looking as uncomfortable as he did. Her white dress flowed more than normal Elvin wear. White was the color that heads of house wore for momentous events like today. In fact, the white robes that he wore now would be a standard article of clothing for him. Sasha was wearing something similar, though hers only seemed to accent the dress.

They made their way to the deck of the Lux, which was pulling into a slip in the harbor. Like Manton, Seeon rose from the water in a graceful hill. Legon cast his gaze over the city, and his breath caught.

He knew that the city would be grown from trees, but the diversity of it staggered him, and the color. He was prepared for Seeon to look like a forest, but it didn't; the buildings were organic-looking in the extreme, but many were large and towered several hundred feet in the air. But the thing that caught his eye the most was the flowers. All of the buildings had flowers growing on them. Every color in the rainbow was represented, but the dominant theme was the house colors. In front of him, on the side of the hill, was the crest of House Evindass grown in flowers. The crest spanned dozens, if not over a hundred buildings. Bands of white and purple ran across all sides of the harbor, which the entire city had coordinated for his and Sasha's homecoming. His eyes focused on the flowers, and with a slight chill, he realized that many were lavender roses.

Sasha spoke in his head. "Do you think this is what our dreams mean, or is it just a coincidence?"

"I don't know. There is virtually every other type of flower here, and they are all in house colors."

His uneasiness over the flowers soon evaporated as he continued to view the city and the thousands of flags and banners that wafted in the air. Their guard took their places around Legon and Sasha, and they made their way off the ship.

As Legon stepped on the pier, there was an explosion of sound as the city cheered and chanted. His current guard moved out of the way to let the house guard take their places. They moved protectively around him and Sasha.

SASHA COULDN'T HELP BUT BE AMAZED AT THE SIGHTS before her. Never in all her life had she imagined something like Seeon. The Lux was unreal to her, but it was nothing compared to the city and all its trees and flowers. Everything around her seemed to pulse with life. She knew that up to this point, their guard was temporary soldiers consisting of an assortment of the best fighting units from the Dome, all loyal to Evindass. Now she was under the protection of the house guard. The entirety of her personal guard had fought in the War of Generations, and none was under a class five magic user. She was even assigned one Ascended class seven. They wore heavy-looking overcoats of the deepest purple with fenrra sprouting at their backs and fenna at their sides. They were rather severe-looking, and if she was being honest with herself, they were altogether terrifying, even the women.

They made their way up a long, cobbled road. The city grew around her, and she marveled as Elves hung out of windows high above to see the new heads of house. Every now and then, one of the dragons that flew with the Lux would pass overhead. She didn't understand all of the security. They were in the capital; there were none here that would hurt them, she thought. In truth, she was having a bit of a hard time taking everything in. With the house guard so close to her, they were all taller than she was, and she couldn't see over them. She thought about hopping a bit to see over them but decided better of it. She connected with Legon to look at the world through his eyes, but he was just as crowded in as she was.

She noticed the presence of another's mind in his. "ISE!" she shouted over the connection. "How are you? Did your jump go well? Why didn't you come to meet us at the dock?"

She felt Iselin's emotions across the link, telling her to hold up. "Whoa there, Sash, one at a time." Ise's thoughts were happy. "In order; first, I am good. Just getting some things at the house taken care of before dinner tonight. Second, my jump went fine. Pretty standard, really. And lastly, your homecoming is more for the people than you and I. Didn't want to get in the way of the house guard."

Legon spoke. "How would you get in their way? They don't talk much, do they?"

Sasha sensed Iselin's uneasiness. "They are a little severe, yes; but don't be too hard on them. They let your father go off on his own, and we saw how well that worked out. The guard considered it a failure on their part. They feel it was their responsibility to follow your father, even if he didn't want them to."

Sasha understood now. Evindass had lost two heads of house in the last thirty years. The first were Legon's grandfather and grandmother. Their deaths were not due to any sinister deed. Legon's grandmother became ill, and when she passed away, so had her husband. Unlike the Human world, inheritances were passed down to the youngest child, unless specified, so Legon's father became the next head of house. But it wasn't more than a few years before he too died. All of this made Evindass unstable, an unknown in the Pawdin Empire. Sasha and Legon would have to work hard to ensure society that the house was strong and ready for the future.

Sasha wasn't paying strict attention anymore. She couldn't see anything anyway. She thought they came to an open area because she couldn't see buildings overhead anymore. She looked forward and up the hill in front of her. She gasped. It wasn't a hill but rather a building, five or six stories tall and extremely long. Its sides were draped in ivy and flowers. They approached a double door, the top of which she could only see over the heads of her guard. The door opened outward, and she knew that she was home.

Legon walked into a room high in the palace that was now his home. He was dazed thus far with the day. In the room waiting for him were two Elves who walked up to him and Sasha. One had long sandy hair and green eyes the same shade as Legon's, and to Legon's amazement, purple flecks that were the same shade and color of Legon's magic.

He introduced himself. "Hello Legon, I am Tenick, and this is my wife," he said, gesturing to the bronze-haired woman next to him. Legon noticed right away that Tenick did not call Legon 'Un Prosa,' which meant that he was family.

"Hello Tenick, it's nice to meet you. This is my sister, Sasha," he said, pointing to Sasha.

Tenick smiled. "And my niece now as well. I am your uncle, the next youngest to your father," Tenick explained. Tenick looked Legon over. "You have his eyes and her hair."

"You are Ascended?" Legon asked.

"Yes, a class seven like your father. Magic runs strong in our family, though our magic's color being the same is a coincidence, I think."

"Oh, I was wondering that... are you sure you don't want to run the house?" Legon said without thinking.

Tenick laughed. "That was unexpected, but then you are your mother's son. No, Legon, I have absolutely no desire to run the house. It has been a fear of mine for many years now."

Legon could read on his face that he was telling the truth. It was a relief to Tenick to not have to take care of the house. "I am sorry, Tenick, I know nothing of our family. I would like to get to know them, but only if that's what they want..." he trailed off. He wouldn't have thought it, but Legon was nervous that his Elvin family wouldn't want anything to do with him. He'd never met them, and he was from a Human mother.

Tenick's face darkened for a moment. "Legon, never think that we do not want you or Sasha in our lives. We loved your father, my brother, and your mother deeply. I can tell you that every member of the family has prayed to the white dragon every night in earnest for your safe return, and yours too, Sasha. Indeed, we were worried that it would be you who did not want to meet us."

Tenick looked at Sasha. "Had we known what life you lived, we would have stopped at nothing to bring you home to us. You are just as much a part of this family as Legon."

Legon looked at Sasha, feeling her emotions, seeing her eyes well up. "Really? You don't even know me, and you wanted me here?"

Tenick's wife stepped forward, taking Sasha's hand. "You are family. We didn't need to know you to love you," she said.

Legon looked back to Tenick, who looked like he wanted to say more, but instead, his eyes went out of focus. "I am sorry, we will talk more. I was hoping for more time with you today, but you need to address the rest of the house," he said.

"I guess we should get this over with," Legon said.

The door to the room opened, and Legon's advisors, along with Sydin and Iselin, entered. Elves drew back curtains along the wall, opening the room up to a small terrace. Legon stepped outside with Tenick next to him as a mob of Elves below cheered.

Tenick walked up to the rail of the terrace, and a little crystal the size and shape of a marble hovered right in front of his mouth. Legon looked out at the crowd, seeing larger crystals levitate. The clear marble in front of Tenick's mouth glowed blue, as did the crystals in the crowd.

As Tenick looked around, the crystal stayed perfectly with his lips, and as he spoke, his voice was carried to the crystals in the audience and amplified. "Hello, loyal followers of House Evindass. Today it is my great honor and privilege to introduce my nephew, Legon." There were deafening cheers. "We are happy to have him and Sasha home where they belong. Legon will be addressing us shortly." Tenick spoke for a while about the history of the house and where it was going, then the crystal by his mouth went clear again and moved to hover in front of Legon as he walked up to the rail.

His mouth and throat were beyond dry. He felt spells meant to keep him from throwing up draining power from him. But he also felt the minds of his entire advisory staff, Sasha, and Iselin, along with those of Tenick and his aunt. All sent him calming thoughts.

The crystal glowed blue. Legon spoke in the language of the Elves to his people for the first time, but no sound came out when he opened his mouth. He swallowed back thick saliva and tried again. "Good after-noon," he said, and Elves applauded. "Thank you, th... that is very kind." Did he just stutter? "...it is an honor to be amongst you..." he couldn't remember what came next. Sasha spoke the words in his mind. "I look forward to leading this house... I have... come from... a land far different than our own... one where freedom does... does not exist." He swallowed again. The audience made no sound. "This house has seen... man... many trials over the last few—years." He recited a script for fear from the Jezeer in his mind. "But we will over...come, these t... trials." The fear scripts were doing nothing for him. "Thank you again for allowing me to be your leader and y... your servant. It is an honor." And the crystal stopped glowing.

The gathered Elves cheered, just as they had before. Legon stepped back into the palace, feeling his heart slow down. Tenick was back at his side, and Legon looked to him. "Do you think I messed everything up?"

Tenick smiled. "You heard them cheer, didn't you?"

"Yes, but Elves are polite..."

Tenick chuckled. "Yes, we are. Everyone in the Empire knows where you have been and knows that you have no grasp of our language or culture. They also know that you have never had to speak to a nation before. That you didn't pass out was enough for them."

Legon wasn't sure he felt better. "Well, at least it was just some of the people of Seeon, I guess."

Everyone except Sasha looked guiltily down at the floor. "What, all of Seeon?" Legon asked.

Sydin looked up. "We knew you were terrified to talk to the few hundred Elves outside, so to keep you from worrying, we didn't tell you that your address was broadcasted to the entire Pawdin Empire..."

Legon felt blood drain from his face as emotions ran in his head. Finally, he laughed and laughed hard. Everyone looked at him like he'd gone mad. "Well, in most situations, you can laugh or cry. I pick laugh, and at any rate, I guess the bar has been set pretty low for me. I shouldn't have too hard of a time improving."

ARKIN PASSED UNCHECKED THROUGH THE GATES OF SALEZ. He hadn't run into any problems on his trip north. People were fleeing the southern lands in droves, and he was able to blend in with the crowds. He knew this was due to the increase in activity along the border. People from all over were scared. Some were fearful of the resistance, and others feared their own country, but for either reason, people moved north, away from the friction. Rumors about raiding parties deep within the Cona Lands were already spreading. Arkin knew these were units like Barnin's, and he hoped the kid would be able to keep his head on his shoulders. No one noticed it yet, but the Elves had stepped up their presence along the border too. He wondered how long it would take the Iumenta to start diverting dragons to the south. *Does it matter?* he asked himself. No, it didn't matter. He had more than enough to do, and it was time to get busy.

The sun was down, and he was having a hard time finding his way to the meeting spot, but he managed. He made his way up to a large house with a slightly gray exterior. He chuckled. Monson wasn't without a sense of humor, so Arkin shouldn't be surprised to find that the Gray family lived in a gray house. He walked up to the door and knocked. The rough wooden door creaked open, spilling light into the narrow street. A balding man with a friendly smile looked him over.

"Good evening, Mr. Arkin. Please, come inside," the man said with a voice just as smooth and friendly as his smile. Mr. Arkin? What was that about?

Monson was sitting at a table with two other boys. One was short and stocky with sandy hair, and the other a tall redhead. "Arkin, good to see you again. These are my friends Casey and Authur," he said, gesturing to the two boys. He wondered if these two were going to be part of the new group or not. His question was answered as Casey stood up, followed by Author.

"Thanks for dinner, Grey. Author and I are going to go catch up on our beauty sleep. Come on, Author," Casey said, and Author muttered under his breath, "Don't call me Author."

Arkin waited for the two to be led out by the butler, who he found out was named Brian. "I thought you said the redhead was named Author? And do you think it's a good idea to meet at your house?" Arkin asked.

Monson shook his head and smiled. "It is, and don't ask." He was serious again. "I'm not coming with you tonight. That's why I was willing to meet you at my house; no one will think anything of it. You're going to be meeting a man of mine named Tom."

Monson was in the loop with what was going on, one of the benefits of mental networks. "Who is this Tom guy? Do you trust him?" Arkin asked.

"I trust him. He doesn't know too much, but he's good at finding help. He should be a dependable resource for you."

Arkin thought about it for a moment. Nothing about this assignment was going to be easy. He couldn't even trust his own men. No one could know too much; it wasn't safe. Monson gave him directions to where he was to go.

Arkin made his way to one of the business districts of Salez. He entered a costume shop and looked around. The walls were packed tight with garments. Arkin didn't pay them any attention, but he had to give it to Monson. This would be the perfect front. When he entered the back room, it appeared to be empty. Arkin's mind flicked out and touched the magic within him. He uttered a silent spell, and four balls of green light appeared in front of him. The spell was meant to identify those who were close to him. The balls would hover over someone, but these didn't.

Arkin spoke aloud. "Very good, but I still can see that there are four of you in here."

There was a shuffle of sound, and out of the corners from the loose boards on the wall, four people came out. A tall man beginning to bald walked up to him, running his hand over his chin, smoothing his black beard. "So, you're Arkin, huh? Don't suppose you know a way to completely suppress that spell, do ya?"

"Yes, I do. So who are you? And who is your crew here?"

A short girl with long brown hair and green eyes bounded forward. "I'm Stacy, and we aren't his crew," she said, tilting her head at the tall guy, who rolled his eyes.

Arkin eyed the girl. She looked keyed up. She had a grin that showed all of her teeth, and she was bouncing on the balls of her feet. "Stacy, huh?"

Stacy frowned and stopped bouncing. "Rachel then? Do you like that more? How about Samantha? Or Jenni, maybe Ginger, or Clare..."

Arkin held up his hands. "Stacy is fine. I take it that's not your real name, and frankly, I don't care. Who are the rest of you? What do you do?"

The tall man spoke up. "I'm Brian; I take care of the arrangements," he said, waving his hand around the room. Arkin made a mental note. Stacy took her turn. "I'm public relations, and I use magic class one." She smiled widely. *Right, so she's a con artist,* Arkin thought. A gangly kid with mousy hair stepped up. "Seth, retrieval expert," which meant he was a thief. Lastly, a normal-looking middle-aged man stepped forward. "I'm Tom, and I take care of supplies." This was Monson's man and the one who found the others in the group.

Arkin spoke. "I'm Arkin, and I'm in charge."

LEGON'S MIND WAS POSITIVELY BUZZING. THEY HAD BEEN going the whole day. There were feasts, festivals, and meetings. He was introduced to what seemed like everyone from advisors to some of the servant's children, who he was pretty sure weren't supposed to be in that part of the house. He walked into his apartment. The house was a palace and as such was gigantic. It was constantly housing an assortment of guests and diplomats, as well as family. He didn't meet too many family members today. Sydin told him that he was going to spend tomorrow getting to know his relatives.

As he walked into the vaulted room, he took off his shoes, not even noticing how large the place was. He walked to a set of glass double doors and out onto a patio that overlooked the harbor. He leaned against the thick rail and breathed out a sigh. He heard the door click and the sound of someone walking softly. He turned, smiling, knowing who it would be.

When he first saw Iselin, he was elated, but they hadn't gotten a chance to talk. But now the events of the day were done, and no one was here to bother them. She was still dressed up from the day in lavender, with her hair done like when they had gone out. If he was being honest, purple wasn't her color, but it was house colors after all. He leaned back on the rail, and she walked right up to him. His mind had been connected to her all day long, even if they didn't have any time together. She walked up and wrapped her arms around his neck, and his wound their way around her waist. He leaned his head forward and kissed her.

"Hey, how was your day? And have I told you that I love the mental networking thing yet today?" Legon asked. And he did love it. He hadn't seen Ise in person in a while, though they'd talked a lot. Before the network, he would never have kissed her. With the network, he knew she wanted it just as much as he did.

Iselin smiled, seeing into his mind. "Yeah, it is handy, isn't it? My day was fine. You know, now that we're close, you don't have to ask those questions."

Now it was his turn to smile at her thoughts. "Really, well what do you have in mind?" he said, giving her a squeeze. She responded by kissing him again.

Her lips were perfect, and in Legon's opinion, the softest, most wonderful things in the world. He instantly forgot all about his day. He ran his hands up and down her back. "You are an excellent distraction, you know that?"

"I try," she said as she winked.

Iselin rested her head in the crook of Legon's neck. His thoughts drifted to wondering what came next. She responded out loud. "It's awkward explaining courtship to you, you know that?" He didn't respond, and she scowled. "Well, from here we do whatever we want. Obviously, with the mental network, people grow close quickly. Most Elves only court for a couple of months before getting engaged. We are at the point where we decide if we think this relationship has a future or not. There are no flings in our society."

He thought for a moment before speaking. "I want to go for it, ya know, you and I. I know I haven't been around many of the other Elvin women, but I've dated plenty of Humans."

"And you know what I want, don't you?" she asked.

Legon reached in her mind just to make sure and kissed her again.

CHAPTER 12

PAWN E2 TO E4

"Once I saw a boy playing a game of catch with a dog and wondered if it wasn't really a boy playing catch, or with a dog, or if it was a dog playing chase with a boy."
— *Tales of the Traveler*

Arkin loved chess. It was his favorite game, and Stacy was a worthy adversary. The little con artist was accomplished at reading people and figuring out their every move. Her face scrunched as she moved a knight. He felt a glimpse of hope.

"Check," Arkin said with a grin.

Stacy scowled again and knocked over one of his pieces. "Mate!" she exclaimed.

Arkin growled. "Stacy, that's cheating. You can't do that. Now every time I'm about to beat you, you cheat. Take your defeat like a man already."

"But I'm not a man, thank you very much. Maybe you haven't noticed," she said, firing up.

Arkin rolled his eyes. He didn't buy it. "I know you're not a man; I meant it figuratively. And you're not picking a fight to get out of losing." He righted his Queen and waited for her to make her move.

Six moves later, she actually did have him in checkmate. The whole charade was just that—a charade. "You still cheated," he accused.

"There is no rule against using your opponent as a pawn. Chess is a game of strategy, anyway." She stuck out her tongue and flitted out of the back room, her long hair waving behind her.

Arkin frowned but accepted his defeat. He turned his attention to more serious matters. For the last month, all he had done was build up contacts and set up front companies. So far, he'd done well, but he needed more. There were still a few cities where he didn't have people planted. The costume shop had played its role well. Brian was right to use the place. Jesters and other entertainers from around the city would come looking for various items, and when they did come in, Stacy or Brian would get information. Entertainment was a terrific way to get into places. Lords and ladies would often hire entertainers for parties or other events. Stacy had done well with this, getting herself brought on as an extra for a few shows in town. As a result, she was able to find key people and give Seth more than enough information to get into any structure in Salez.

Arkin pulled out a crystal from a box in his pocket and placed it on a large sheet of parchment, pouring some ink from a bottle onto the paper. "Operamo," he said in a soft voice. The ink flowed across the page into lines and dots that then settled into words, revealing the document. He was given the idea for this by Iselin. She was an avid reader but known for keeping books for too long, and she liked to mark them up with notes. Subsequently, she didn't borrow books from anyone, but she developed a fascinating little spell that would copy any sheet of paper with ink on it. Arkin had made a few alterations to the spell and then placed it with one other spell in a few crystals. Seth would place the crystal on a sheet of paper and say a command. There was power in the crystal, so Seth didn't need to be a magic user. The spell copied the sheet's contents into the crystal so that later Arkin could make a copy. The crystal on the page now could hold the contents of about fifty sheets of paper.

Arkin blew on the wet page, letting the ink dry. Seth had managed to get his hands on landholding records, and Arkin studied them eagerly. He was starting to figure out all the workings of the city and those who controlled it. Seth didn't know why he was ordered to obtain certain documents, but he did as he was told. Arkin liked Seth. He was a good kid, even though he was a thief. The records that Arkin held now would be noted for later use when it was time to assassinate people in the Cona government.

Over the course of the next few weeks, Arkin was able to compile a clear picture of everything he needed to. He found the corrupt and those who could be blackmailed, and some who just needed to be taken care of. Ivy and Richard had done their part as well, helping with other front companies and staffing. Arkin had to admit that if they wanted to go straight, they could do quite well.

Tom walked in, sweeping his hand through his brown hair. He sat down and spoke. "I've been at it all day, but I think I found a potential one for you."

Arkin's eyebrow rose. "Tell me about it."

Tom looked across the room at a bottle of cider and raised a hand. The bottle glowed red and flew across the room into Tom's hand. Tom was a class two, just like Arkin, and while he wasn't as knowledgeable as Arkin, Tom liked to use magic. He was of the mindset that magic was to make the world a more accessible and easy place to live. As soon as he was out of the public view, he used magic for just about everything.

He took a long drink and started. "Okay, so they are looking for this killer. His method is to break into a house, tie up his victims, and bleed them out."

Arkin nodded, and Tom went on. "There are a few others in the area, but this guy is the only serial the authorities know of. He doesn't stick around long, and he's clean."

Arkin responded, "That's good. How does he tie them up? We don't want anything too complicated. Who are his victims? Do the authorities have any leads?" He stopped when Tom waved a hand.

"Hold up, boss, I'm getting to that. His victims look random, but we know they aren't; they never are with a serial. Here's the great part, though—the authorities don't have a clue who this guy is or what type of person he likes to go for. They are just starting to suspect that he is a serial killer. They don't even know if it's a man or not. They don't know anything. I'm sure the Iumenta could figure it out, or if a few Venefica were tasked with finding him, but the local law enforcement doesn't have those kinds of resources. Right now, they are standing around twiddling their thumbs." Tom smiled.

"Who is he?" Arkin asked.

Tom scowled. "How did you know I figured out who it was? You just took my big reveal."

Arkin shrugged, not answering the question. "Sorry, that was wrong of me." He finished with a smile.

Tom laughed. "Whatever. His name is Henry Punpkin. Odd name, I know. Anyway, I think he is targeting people who have wronged or upset him in some way. It's hard to tell. He lives just north of the river."

"Have you taken him out yet?" Arkin asked.

Tom blanched. "No." Arkin wasn't surprised. Out of the little band that he had, none were killers. They all fought the Iumenta, but none killed. That was fine. Arkin did kill, so it didn't matter.

The team took a few days to compile lists and information about local murders and rapists, the trash that had escaped justice. Legon was clear about this; they only killed those who had it coming to them and those who were a continued threat to the innocent. Arkin then selected a few officials who needed to be removed. Stacy helped him plot everything out. They bribed some people and finessed a few others. By the time they were done, they had a small list of assets who just needed to move up in society. Now it was time to make that possible.

The night they made their move, the moon was covered by clouds, casting the city in darkness. No one below could see Arkin, clad in black, as he scaled up the side of the building; he moved easily. His concealment spells blurred his outline to any who could see him. Without a sound, he made it to the window. All was not quiet inside. Arkin peered in to what he presumed was the living room, seeing Henry pacing back and forth, talking to himself. Seth had been watching the apartment ever since they decided Henry was the one they wanted to copy. Seth said that Henry was looking more and more agitated. Tom's research showed that Henry killed about once a month. It had been three weeks since his last known kill, and Arkin assumed he was getting ready to do it again. Arkin watched, and after an hour, Henry calmed and slipped off to bed. Arkin spoke a spell, and the window latch came undone.

He slid through the window and moved to the shadows. On a counter, Arkin saw a drawing of a young girl, the lines hard and harsh— almost hateful. Next to it were scrolls of text. Angry words jumped off the page. Presumably, Henry was documenting his feelings about the girl in the drawing.

> *How dare she kick me out of the Inn! There should be no closing time for regulars. She just wanted to be with that slob of a man. I'll show her... I'll show her what happens if she doesn't show me respect...*

Arkin read more of the text. It became more and more violent and descriptive. *Of all the reasons to kill someone,* he thought with disgust. Judging by the contents of the scrolls, Arkin figured Henry was about to change his method. His last few kills had shown more signs of suffering, Tom said, and judging by the plans on the paper, Arkin assumed he was going to keep escalating the violence. In truth, it was a little unbelievable Henry hadn't been caught by now. Arkin pushed it from his mind. He didn't know who the girl in the drawing was, and frankly, he didn't care. He didn't want an innocent person to die, but he couldn't obsess about every potential victim out there. *Besides, she's not going to be a victim,* he thought. Creeping into the bedroom, Arkin saw the sleeping form of Henry. Bile bit at the back of his tongue. This was not the part he was looking forward to. It was one thing to kill someone who deserved it; Arkin had done that plenty. No, it was that Henry was Arkin's practice. He would kill Henry the same way Henry killed all his victims. He would kill him and see if the authorities credited the murder to the serial killer they suspected. He sensed Seth enter the apartment to remove any evidence that proved Henry was the killer. Arkin breathed deeply and went to work.

After taking out Henry, his job moved quickly, and in the end, the local law enforcement believed that Henry's death was another serial murder. Stacy used one of her contacts at an organization that posted to bulletin boards to dub the murderer 'The Salez Slasher.' The news caught on quickly, and before long, the truth skewed, and the citizens of Salez lived in fear, fear that was supported as Arkin took out some of the local trash, refining his killing style. Brian arranged for fliers to be made around the killings, some giving descriptions of the Slasher, others pointing fingers at city leadership for not stopping the killings, and more. The descriptions were vague to the extreme, and as a result, people flooded law enforcement, accusing their neighbors and strangers, all claiming to have solved the case. The local authorities were utterly overwhelmed with the angry mobs, which made it impossible for them to do their job.

Arkin finished reading a statistical report published by Lord Sodomis's office. He looked to Stacy. "Crime rates are rising fast, maybe even too fast. We don't want too much attention yet."

Stacy shrugged. "You wanted to kick the hornets' nest. How are the other cities doing?" she asked casually.

Stacy, like the others, knew their group was only a single cell of a larger organization, but she didn't know much other than that. Arkin was controlling everything via a vast mental network. Other cities were coming along, but not at the rate Salez had. He would have never guessed that the Salez Slasher would have been able to make such a splash. He thought that perhaps there was always underlying fear in the area, but he couldn't see why. Now that law enforcement was crippled, the rest of the criminal underworld was taking full advantage, making things spin out of control. This was all part of the plan, but it wasn't supposed to happen so fast.

Stacy interrupted his thoughts. "What I don't get is why the Iumenta haven't started using their Ascended more."

"You know, you're the only Human I know who calls them that."

"Calls them what?" she asked, confused.

"Ascended. Most people call them dragons. It's just odd to hear another Human call them Ascended. The reason why, I suspect, is that they haven't had much of a reason to send Dragons yet, but now that local law enforcement is overwhelmed and people are panicked, they may be forced to. Let's hope all they do is use the Dragons to soothe the people, instead of the alternative." The alternative was that the Iumenta would simply take over the investigation themselves. Arkin covered his tracks well, but he didn't want that kind of heat yet. He heard Seth in the front room announce that the shop would soon be closed, and people needed to buy what they wanted or find somewhere else to loiter.

Stacy rolled her eyes. "He's great at stealth, but customer service..." She shook her head.

A moment later, they heard the door close, and Seth came in the back room. "You know, I like people a lot more when I'm stealing their money; not earning it, ya know what I mean?"

"Guess this means you aren't going straight?" Stacy poked. Seth laughed. "Not a chance, honey, not a chance."

Arkin rose. It would be dark soon, and tonight the Salez Slasher was going to make his first assassination.

Arkin and Stacy stood on a sloped roof on the east side of town. She adjusted the black cloth around her face, and they spoke in their minds. "It looks like this place has a few guards. I suppose with all the attention and burglary going up lately, we should have seen that coming," she said.

They crept up the roof to where the building rose to another level. Just out of reach was the ledge of the window they would be entering. Arkin reached around his back and produced an iron rod. Stacy had a similar one. She held hers about six inches from the wall, and it glowed gold from magic for a moment. Arkin grasped the rod and pushed off the wall with his foot, lifting himself. He held his rod higher than Stacy's, and it glowed green for a moment. "Come on," he thought to Stacy.

They used the two rods like rungs of a ladder and made it to the window. It was open. As they slipped in the open window, both pulled on their magic, causing the rods to fly back to their masters. Once in the house, they split, going on different missions. Stacy was to plant misinformation, and he was going to the master bedroom to take out a local politician. The house was silent tonight, and he had to work hard not to make any sound on the old wooden floors. He was hesitant to use more magic, but he risked a few spells to keep the floor from creaking.

Arkin peered into the room. His eyes swept to a large bed with the form of a sleeping man under the sheet—his target. Arkin made his way over to the bed. He raised his hand to place a spell on the man to keep him from screaming when he heard a loud thud and a yell from the other room.

"HEY YOU, STOP THERE!" a booming voice yelled, and then in his mind, he heard Stacy's, "I'VE BEEN FOUND!" The sleeping man sat bolt upright, took one look at Arkin, and screamed, "GUARDS!" Without a thought, Arkin shot a blot of green into the man's face, silencing him, and then he grabbed the first sharp object he could find and stabbed him in the chest. The man gurgled but was unable to cry out again. He pawed at Arkin as blood gushed from his chest. The door burst open, and a guard entered the room, followed by Stacy, who was followed by another guard. Arkin swore.

The first man didn't seem to notice Stacy and came at Arkin with a war hammer raised high. Arkin sidestepped the blow and let the guard pass him, taking out a cabinet with his swing. Arkin wrapped his arm around the hulking man's neck and wrenched him back, trying to cut off his air supply so he'd pass out. Stacy screamed. Arkin turned his head to see her dodging wild swings from the sword of the other guard, who was equally large, but like his opponent, unskilled. The two guards spun, facing each other for a moment, and Stacy barked a spell. The swordsman's eyes bulged as his blade flashed gold and shot forward, driving deep into the belly of the other guard. Arkin let go, slipping off his opponent's back right before the sword could make its way through its target, out the other side of the man, and into him. Arkin fell back and watched the guard he had been fighting raise his weapon and bring it down on the other guard's head. Both fell to the floor, one dead from a head wound, the other from bleeding out.

Arkin worked on instinct alone, wrenching a dagger from the belt of the bleeding man in front of him and driving it into the dead politician. Stacy, while a little ruffled, looked to be unharmed. "What are you..." she started, "... making it look like one of these guys did it and the other caught him? Come on, we need to leave before others show up." She didn't argue, and they darted from the room.

Arkin grabbed Stacy and pulled her into a room, moments before two more guards pounded their way up the hall. "This way," he hissed.

He pushed her to a window and opened it. She looked out, seeing a thirty-foot drop. Arkin didn't wait. With another bolt of green, Stacy was rendered mute. The look on her face was that of horror and confusion, and then he tossed her out the window. She looked up, a silent scream on her face, but right before she hit the ground, he spoke a spell, and she came to almost a complete stop before landing on the ground. He jumped, feeling the crisp night air rush by, and then he too slowed and hit the ground. It wasn't a soft landing, but neither was hurt.

Stacy had countered his silencing spell, and as they ran, she growled at him. "Could have told me. I thought you were chucking me as evidence or something." He didn't respond. He was still thinking about the look on her face. She reached into his head when he didn't answer and saw what he was thinking. "It's not funny, you jerk," she said, punching his arm. They didn't speak again all the way back to the shop, but he thought he heard her chuckle.

CHAPTER 13
CONVERGING PATHS

*"I wonder, do we truly understand just how we affect others? Somehow, I
don't think we can."*
— Conversations in the Garden

Legon and Sasha looked at a large map laid out on the conference
room table. Sydin's finger ran along the border of the Pawdin
and Cona Empires as well as the Cona Republic lands. "So far,
things have been working well. We see a dramatic increase in activity
here, here, and here," he said, pointing to various spots on the map.

While Arkin had been busy in Salez and with his new organization,
others had also been hard at work. The border was now teeming with
military and was all but impossible to cross. This was bad because
refugees could no longer make it to safety, but good because all was
going according to plan. Barnin had been part of the initial attack, going
deep into Cona lands and wreaking havoc. Those activities had been
scaled back considerably. Parkas was now guarding caravans with everything he could spare. Even now, Ascendeds flew the skies, making sure
supply routes remained safe.

Sydin went on. "From what we can tell, there aren't any Ascendeds being pulled from Cona lands yet to help secure the border, but that isn't to say that there hasn't been an increase in patrols."

"Where are they coming from?" Sasha asked.

Iselin responded, her voice like honey to Legon. "They are coming from Impa airspace. They know we can't attack those lands. I suspect they are pulling reserves and sending them south."

House Floren had come up with the idea of having Pawdin dragons fly in squads of five. As each house sent more and more Ascended to the border, the Pawdin Empire's air presence had done its job. Before, Ascendeds flew on their own or in pairs, as did the Iumenta, but in squads, they could be more offensive. The Elvin dragons would find solo Iumenta, and five on one meant that the Elves didn't take casualties, even when there was another Iumenta dragon. No matter how strong, the results were the same. As a result, in the last week alone, the Iumenta had lost ten dragons, the highest amount of Ascended casualties either side had suffered in two thousand years.

"Do you think they know what we are doing?" Iselin asked the room.

"They know," Legon said. "The question is, what can they do about it?" He pointed along the Pawdin border to a line of dots, each representing a dragon dome. "They can't invade at this point; we are too strong, and they know it. They won't risk their society again. But I bet they are banking on us feeling the same. If I were them, I would make a go for the Cona Republic. It's a small victory, but it's something."

Sydin nodded. "I agree; they won't attack the Mahj Proper," he said, pointing to the line of dots. Higher on the map, there was a similar line of dots around the Impa Empire, also representing the dragon domes that protected their lands. On the Pawdin side, when looking at only the dots of the various Mahj defensive lines, the country looked like the inside of a tree with rings of defense. Those defenses would take the Iumenta centuries to breach if they were to use Human forces, and that was why they wouldn't invade yet. Sydin went on, "We have done all we can. All we can do from here is keep pressure on them. I don't think it would be advisable to keep Human forces going into Cona lands. We don't want high casualties. Our goal is to waste Cona resources, not our people's lives."

"I agree," Sasha said, speaking for her and Legon.

"We need to find a way to make sure that the Cona Republic can survive this in case they are invaded," Sasha pointed out.

"Yes, we need to set up evacuation routes for the cities. Sooner or later, the Precipice will be attacked, and the dome can't repel a force that large. The dome was built more as a relations piece for the old Cona Empire," Sydin said. They spent the next few hours arranging evacuation routes and preparing communication for the other houses. Once approved, the plans would be sent to the Cona Republic to approve or deny.

SASHA MADE HER WAY OUT OF THE CONFERENCE ROOM AND was approached by an Elf with shaggy black hair.

He spoke in a liquid-smooth voice. "Good afternoon, Un Prose, I am Edling." His gray eyes fell to hers, and it took her a moment to speak.

"Hello, Edling. Umm, did we have an appointment?" she asked, embarrassed.

Edling smiled warmly. "No, my father was to teach you about crystals, but he thought it would be good for both of us if I taught you what I know before he takes over. Your assistant said you were free today," he paused and added as an afterthought, "Sorry."

Sasha liked him, and she was struck by the color of his eyes. They intrigued her. "That's fine. Let's go to my apartment so I can get a book for notes. Does that work?"

He motioned for her to lead the way. As she moved, Edling stepped in alongside her but seemed a little uncomfortable by the looks her guard was giving him. Sasha's mind flicked out to the closest of her guard. "Is there something wrong?" The guard's response was slow, and she felt a protective edge. That was different from normal. It surprised her. "You wouldn't notice, being Human, but he..." the guard struggled for words. "He showed a little too much warmth for someone just here to teach you, Un Prose."

She was confused and asked another question. "Too much warmth?" she prodded.

The guard huffed and thought in a rush, "His heart rate picked up; so did his breathing, and his pupils dilated."

"You mean he was checking me out?" she said to him. "Really?"

The lack of response was all she needed for confirmation. She found it hard to believe that an Elf would be interested in her that way. They were immortal and rarely went for mortals. But her guard was highly trained at reading body language, and she knew they wouldn't be mistaken. She gave Edling a sideways glance. Like all Elves, he was easy on the eyes, and he seemed friendly. He looked over at her, smiled quickly, and looked away. In her mind, the guard showed her what he saw, and she was amazed to see that Edling's cheeks had flushed. Sasha's guard wasn't happy about the pleasure she felt from this but didn't pursue the subject. After a moment of thought, she expanded her mind to her whole guard. "I forbid you from intimidating this Edling, or killing him, or telling Sydin or my brother."

There was silence, and then a response from one of the women. "Fine, but if he breaks your heart, I'm disobeying you." Sasha rolled her eyes.

Once they were to her apartment, she opened the door and signaled for Edling to enter. He looked uncomfortable. "You want me to come in?" he asked.

"Is there somewhere that's better? I have a huge terrace. It's shaded and nice this time of the day; can we talk there?"

He shrugged and gave her guard another glance. She entered her apartment, followed by Edling, and made her way to a bookshelf packed full of her notebooks and books from the national library about crystals. She pulled one off the shelf and motioned for Edling to follow her out onto the terrace. As they walked, she reached out with her mind and ordered some drinks. The terrace was shaded, as she had promised, and Sasha made her way to a small table and two chairs next to the railing. She relaxed into the soft fabric of the chair. Before Edling could speak, an Elf with long bronze hair came up to them with a bottle of Poti and two glasses.

"Thank you so much," she said to the Elf. She started to move to pour the drink when she stopped, forgetting that that would be rude to the Elf serving them. Sasha was getting more accustomed to being served, but it still made her uncomfortable.

As soon as the Elf was gone, Edling spoke. "You don't like being served, do you?"

"That obvious?" she asked, concerned.

"Yes, but it's also obvious that you don't want to offend anyone. You'll get used to it, I'm sure," he said warmly, and then went on. "So, why don't you tell me what you know about crystals?"

With that, Sasha launched into what she knew. Before she became a Venefica, she had always wanted to be a healer, and she still loved that. But she found that she loved everything to do with crystals more. Legon learned about them, and he respected their necessity, but he didn't have a lot of interest in the subject other than that. Sasha, on the other hand, spent a great deal of her free time reading about them. She spent hours in the palace library perusing the sections dedicated to them.

It didn't take more than an hour before Edling raised his hands, stopping her. "Un Prose..." he started.

"Sasha," she corrected, a little breathless.

He smiled. "Sasha, breathe. This isn't a test."

She breathed a sigh of relief. "I know that I should know more. I'm an Elemental and all, and I've tried to learn as much as I could..." He stopped her again.

Edling took a moment to answer. "Look, I'm going to be honest with you." He gave her a look that was half admiring and half exasperated. "I think you could go on for some time about this subject, and from what I can tell, you know more than I do about it."

She was brought up short at this. "Um... so I'm not behind?"

He laughed. "No, but I think I may be."

EMMA HEAVED, AND WITH AS MUCH STRENGTH AS SHE COULD muster, she finally pulled the boot free from its owner's foot. Then she looked at the other boot with distaste, gripping and pulling. The man groaned, and Emma stopped pulling. "Are you all right?" she asked. He didn't respond, and she moved to the other side of the bed, trying to stay conscious of the slanted roof; she'd hit her head twice this week. *How did Legon stay in here? He's taller than I am,* she thought. She leaned over the man's face, worrying about the beads of sweat rolling down it. "Sir, is your foot hurt?" she asked. Nothing.

"Laura!" she yelled out the door.

Laura's voice rose from downstairs. "Coming! I have something I think will work on the fever."

A moment later, Emma heard her coming up the hall, and Laura came into the room. "Did he wake up?" she asked.

"No, but he groaned when I pulled his right boot. I think he may be injured," Emma supplied. They had no idea what was wrong with the man. Emma wasn't even sure what his name was. He'd come to town a week ago, gotten a job at the tanner, and then today he passed out. They had no other information about him.

"I bet he's not sick in the way we are thinking. I would bet when we get that boot off, we are going to find a cut that's infected to high heaven," Laura said, pointing accusatorially at the boot. Then she turned and called down the stairs, "Edis!"

"What?" he yelled back.

Laura sighed. "Come here."

"Why?"

She lost her composure. "Because I asked you to, that's why! Because I have a sick man in your son's room, that's why, and because you love being in my warm, loving presence, that's why. Pick a reason and get up here!"

"FINE! Since the world is at an end, I'll come up!" Emma tried not to smile when she heard him say in a lower voice, "Crazy woman. I'm not a nurse, for crying out loud." His mutterings continued until he made it to the room, and he smiled at his wife. "Yes, love? What can I help you with?" he said in what was obviously an attempt at a pleasant tone.

Laura gave him a look. "I'm not crazy. Hold this guy down. He's out of it but might wake up, and we have to get this boot off him."

"Oh, we are torturing someone! Sounds fun. Why didn't ya say so?" He made his way to the man on the bed and held him down. Emma and

Laura went to work on the boot, and sure enough, the man woke up with the pain. He screamed and shouted accusations at them, having no clue where he was. Emma was worried about getting kicked or hurt, but after a few minutes, Laura barked, "Edis!" Edis nodded and looked at the thrashing man. "Night-night time!" He reached back and punched him, knocking him out.

"Thank you," Laura breathed, dropping the boot on the floor. Emma winced at the ravaged and infected foot. Once the smell hit her, she tried to hold her breath.

———

EDIS ONLY NEEDED A WHIFF TO KNOW THAT LAURA HAD HER work cut out for her, and that later tonight he would probably be helping with an amputation. But for now, his work was done. He didn't need to be dismissed and made his way out of the house and to the shop. He felt for whomever that was up there; he honestly did. But how often did your wife ask you to knock out a total stranger? Not often. And if he played his cards right, he could tell her his fist hurt, and he might get a little TLC himself. He whistled and went to work in the shop. A few hours later, the bell on the door dinged, and Laura walked in.

"How's he doing?" Edis asked, concerned this time.

"He'll be fine. I don't think he's going to lose that foot, but I'll watch it for a bit. He's up and talking." She looked at him. "How's your fist?"

Edis looked at his hand, which in truth was fine, but he shook it a bit. "Meh, it's fine... a little tender... I'm sure it will be good by morning." He tried to look like he was acting tough, like it hurt more than he said. She scowled playfully, walking up to him and taking his hand, rubbing it. "Faker," she accused. He wrapped his arms around her and kissed her, moving down her neck. She giggled. "So what if I am?" he asked.

She made a half-hearted attempt to push him away. "Edis, what if someone comes in?"

He smiled. "You're just taking care of what ails me, right, love?" he said between kisses. He stopped and held her, enjoying just being with his wife. Then he got serious again. "How'd he get hurt?"

Her blue eyes looked up into his. "On the road. He was trying to get away from the south, and then once he got to Salez, he said it was worse. Their crime is out of control. I guess he thought a small town was the way to go." She laid her head against his chest. "... said his company had some trouble on the road. There are not many patrols up in the north and central areas anymore, he said. Edis, I'm worried."

He squeezed her and rested his head on top of hers. "I am too, love, I am too." He stood for a moment and then said what was on his mind. "How do you think the children are doing?" Laura tensed. "I honestly don't know, but Kovos and Legon are strong..." she trailed off, neither hoping that Kovos or Legon would need that strength.

LEGON WALKED WITH ISELIN THROUGH THE HOUSE GARDENS, neither making a sound as they glided along the cobbled path, looking over the edge of the roof into the harbor. She laced her fingers in his, and they relaxed in each other's emotions. Legon knew that what they had wasn't uncommon. He knew that once two compatible people linked, they grew together quickly. Even now, it would be painful to lose her, and he knew she felt the same. There was no doubt in either's mind that they would be together forever.

"You're thinking about Arkin's mission more than normal, and your parents," Iselin pointed out. Though she had never met his parents, because of the connection she shared with him, Iselin worried and cared for Laura and Edis nearly as much as he did.

"We need to get people out of the Cona lands," he said.

"How? Small groups can cross the border, but I would think that would be ill-advised, and who could we send?"

Legon thought for a moment. "It would have to be Arkin, but not until he can spare the time. Salez has been a good case study. Once other cities progress, the Cona lands will destabilize quickly. The way I see it, the sea is the only way right now that's still an open option."

"But it won't be for much longer. Reports show that the Cona Empire is building more ships than ever before," Iselin said.

"Parkas isn't an idiot. He has to know that sooner or later we will start to hit shipping routes, and it's not as if they are going to send the Impa Navy to deal with it," Legon thought out loud. From what they could tell, the Queen was having issues pulling from the Impa areas. In reality, she wasn't Queen of either land. While recognized by the Cona Empire as a Queen to the Iumenta government, she simply had more power than anyone else. Because of her control of the Cona lands, she had taken control of the Impa Empire, but her power was not absolute. Legon's advisors found it unlikely that the other Impa leaders would be willing to divert too many resources away from the homeland. This meant that Hoelaria was going to be forced to use more and more Human resources.

"We will give Arkin a bit more time, and then I am going to send him and Barnin to collect my parents and Keither's. We will see if Kovos' girlfriend Emma wants to come too." As far as he was concerned, Emma was family now. Kovos would have married her if he hadn't gone with Legon and Sasha. Legon would do whatever he needed to make sure she was taken care of.

Iselin sent soothing thoughts Legon's way. "It's not your fault," she said simply.

"I know, but I still owe him for saving us and for everything he did for Sasha."

Sometimes when he said Sasha's name, he felt Ise pull away from him, and in that moment, he would feel anger, fear, and shame. But then she would guard her emotions and change the subject.

They were on a bridge over a small stream that ran off the edge of the roof and down the side of the palace.

Legon stopped her. "Hey, what is that?" he asked softly.

She knew what he wanted and couldn't avoid the question. He looked into her blue-green eyes, and the flecks of pink almost darkened. "I love Sasha like a sister, you know that." He nodded, and she went on. "I know you suspect that I am jealous, and it may look that way, but I'm not."

"Then what are you?" he asked.

She looked down. "We both know where this is going. We may not have said it yet, but I love you, and you love me. We will continue to connect, and someday when one of us dies, the other will follow close behind." He liked that thought. She went on, "But here is the thing... you are so connected with your sister, which is a good thing, but at the same time; what happens when she grows old..." Her voice tapered off, and her thoughts continued on.

He understood now. He could see why this would bother her. As she let down her defenses, he saw how this would affect Sasha as well. Her life was intertwined with Legon's permanently. More so, he saw that Iselin was angry because this would cause pain someday, and she was scared about what would happen, and ashamed for feeling negatively about it. When Sasha died, Legon ran the risk of losing his mind, and with that, so could Iselin.

He could tell she didn't want to talk anymore about it tonight. She didn't want to share what she already had, and he wouldn't force her further. He smiled. "You know, you're wrong about one thing."

She had turned away to face the harbor and now turned her head to him, her eyes red. He turned her to face him and wiped a tear that was about to escape from one eye. "You said that we hadn't come out and said that we loved each other, and, well, you kind of just did." He smiled.

"Yeah, I guess I did."

He kissed her softly. "I love you, too." And in that moment, nothing else mattered to him.

SASHA'S SHOES MADE A STACCATO CLACK ON THE HARD floor of the hallway. Edling had stayed for dinner, and they spent all afternoon and evening talking about crystals. He joked that he didn't know what he was doing, but he was very knowledgeable about most of the basics. She came to a stop at Legon's door and opened her mind. "Knock, knock." She entered his apartment and made her way to his study. He was sitting at his desk, reading reports of some kind.

He looked up, rubbing his eyes. "Hey, you're up late."

"You too," she pointed out.

He smiled and put the report down. "Ise and I had a good talk tonight, and I couldn't fall asleep."

"A good talk, huh?" she questioned.

Legon took a moment to think it over and then showed her part of the evening. Sasha said, "That explains why she's shown irritation before when I've talked to her about our link. Poor thing, she must have been terrified to show you this."

"I think she feels bad, but I'm glad it came up. It was something we needed to know."

Sasha sat down in a chair on the opposite side of the table. "So, what do we do? I don't want..."

"Don't start that. We just need to take things into account. No one is upset with anyone, just the situation." He changed the subject. "How was your lesson?"

She thought about protesting the change in topic but came up short. There wasn't anything else to talk about. The situation was what it was, and there was no changing that, and everyone knew and accepted that fact. She placed a few crystals on the table. "We were at it all day. These are a few basic crystals." Legon looked them over, and she pointed to each in turn. "This one Edling helped me with because it's plant-based, like all Elvin crystals. But these two I did on my own. He taught me one of the few known Iumenta techniques. You need to be a Venefica to make them, and having an elemental minor is helpful too."

Legon perked up. "I assume the technique is from the War of Generations. Is there much known about it?"

Her tone turned business-like. "Surprisingly, no, there isn't. Once we found a way to use plants, research on the Iumenta style was put on the back burner until the end of the war, and at that point, no one wanted to study anything from them. They're hard to do, and they can't hold much power. They are really primitive," she said, examining them. "I have an idea."

Legon smiled, reading her thoughts. "I like it. Try to combine the techniques. Do you know if anyone has tried to before?"

"At first, yes, combining the techniques was the only way, but as I said, when Elves could make better, stronger ones without as much work, they did. The Impa Empire was just too much of a threat at the time to do much else. But I think this could be good research. The Iumenta now have more advanced crystals than we do, and I don't think we could catch up to them just trying to mimic their work. But maybe by combining..."

"Good, why don't you make this your priority? Talk to Edling's father," Legon said. She was happy to see that this was as much an order as anything else. Not an order to her so much; she could do whatever she liked, but he knew that this was what she wanted and was giving her permission to use his authority.

Something in her thoughts had tipped him off. "So you like this Edling guy, huh?" he said with a smirk.

She was getting ready to fire up but came up short at his emotions. "You're happy? I thought you would be all 'overprotective brother' and threaten to have him killed. Not that I think anything will happen; he's leaving at the end of the week. He was just here visiting," she finished.

"Sash, look in my mind."

She did and saw how he and Iselin were. She saw that with the mental connection, they had grown closer than people who had been together for years. In just a few months, they had built something truly amazing, and each understood the other on a profound level. Further, she saw that with the network, there was no room for deceit. You couldn't hide anything, and it was hard to hurt someone you were with. Every time Legon or Ise would offend the other, they could see what each felt, and the issue was resolved before anyone could get their feelings hurt.

"Do you see how happy I am, Sash?" he asked.

And she did see. She saw that while Legon and Sasha would always be connected, it pained him to think that she wouldn't have a chance at this happiness. That there was a chance that Sasha could find someone was the greatest news he had heard all day. Then his thoughts became playful. "But if he does break your heart, I'm going to tell Ise to eat him." He smiled.

She laughed, and they talked late into the night about Iumenta crystals.

CHAPTER 14
EXODUS

"Sometimes it's not the how that matters, but the what."
— Excerpts from The Diary of the Adopted Sister

L egon should have felt nervous, but he didn't. He didn't because he already knew her answer. The thing he was having a hard time with was deciding how to do it.

Iselin looked at him, her eyebrow raised, fighting a smile. "You don't have to do this, you know. Elves aren't Humans," she pointed out for the millionth time.

"I know, I know, but it just seems so wrong to me. Look, I didn't ask your father's permission. I'm going to do this the right way."

Iselin rolled her eyes. "We don't do that... do not get on your knee..."

"Iselin, I love you more than anyth—"

She huffed, cutting him off. "Yes, the answer is yes. We're mentally connected; have you forgotten we have a date picked out? We just need to get the crests on our backs taken care of."

Legon ground his teeth. "Fine. That was some proposal! Why am I going to spend the rest of time with you again?" Iselin rolled her eyes again, and Legon felt her call Sydin. It had been three months since they had said they were in love, and now they were engaged. It was all so simple to him. As she said, Elves didn't even propose. Both parties came to the decision to get married, and that was it. He remembered when that happened for him and Ise. Two nights ago, while on a walk, they both just seemed to know. There was no pageantry about it, no ring, no nothing; they knew, and that was that.

Soon Sydin came strolling to them at the same little bridge where they stood not so long ago.

Sydin smiled warmly. "What can I do for you, Un Prosa?" he asked.

Legon squeezed Iselin's hand. "We're getting married. Can you fix our crests?"

Sydin beamed. "About time, you two! That's great news. Did you tell your sister?"

Iselin laughed. "How could she not know?"

"Turn around; this will only take a moment," Sydin said.

Legon turned and saw two flashes of black. There was a cold spot on his back, and then everything felt normal. He craned his neck around to see Iselin's crest on her back, a vivid pink that stood out. In the center, where there used to be a solid dot, now the dot was hollow. It would stay that way until they were married, and then his crest would be placed in the center of that dot, the same on his back. Their crests would repeat inside themselves, giving them the appearance of going on forever.

———

SASHA WATCHED FROM LEGON'S MIND AS HIS AND ISELIN'S crests were changed. Her eyes filled with tears, and she felt an immense weight lift off her. Her whole life, she had worried that Legon wouldn't find anyone. She worried that he would never try and instead put his efforts into keeping her safe. Now she didn't have to worry about that. She disconnected from the two of them, giving them privacy. Still, the whole process was alien to her. After coming to the agreement to get married, there wasn't much else. The whole affair was treated with the same level of energy as any mundane task. Sasha decided that their wedding would be a different matter. At her disposal were the vast resources of House Evindass. Images ran through her mind, and she was surprised when an almost crazed giggle escaped.

"It will be the wedding for all time, never to be outdone," she said, and then just for fun added, "Muahahahahaha."

ISELIN WOKE IN A FIELD. SHE LIFTED HERSELF, REACHING OUT with her mind but finding nothing. She stood, concerned, looking around. *What is this place? It looks familiar,* she thought. It looked like a dream Legon had shown her, but it couldn't be. She heard voices and moved toward them. As she walked into the mist, she realized she was in a field of lavender and red roses. She was on a small path, and the voices were just ahead. Two figures came into view.

"What is this?" she asked.

Legon and Sasha spun, looking startled. Legon spoke, "Iselin?"

Iselin walked up to him and tried to take his hand. He flinched away. "Don't touch me; it will end," he said.

"What will end? Is this a dream?" she asked, perplexed.

Sasha answered, "Yes, it looks like you're a part of them now, sorry Ise." Sasha took a breath. "You need to get up to speed before he gets here."

"Before who gets here?" she asked.

Legon spoke. "The White Dragon, we think. Ok, look at this field around you," he said, sweeping his hands out around him. "These have been here for about a month. If tonight is like other nights, we are going to see a tree grow..." he stopped, and she heard a THUD in the distance.

"Wh—"

"Shhhh... it's happening," Sasha said.

A little stung, Iselin stopped speaking and looked ahead into the mist. Just ahead of them was a small clearing. She jumped as a large, white-scaled paw parted the mist and drove one golden claw into the ground. She knew that paw, and the dragon that went with it—every Elvin Ascended did. Like the Iumenta, when an Elf ascended, they saw one of the original dragons. The Iumenta believed this to just be a figment of their imagination—some learned response—but the Elves knew it to be otherwise. All Iumenta saw the black dragon because they were his, and all Elves saw the white. A chill ran down her spine as she watched a tree grow from where his claw had touched. The white bark shot into the air, unfurling long branches that grew thick. Buds burst with silver leaves that had gold coloring the edges. As the tree grew, lavender and scarlet flowers dotted it, shedding some of their perfect petals to swirl and play in the breeze.

"Look," Sasha said, pointing to the base of the tree, where a green vine was making its way up the trunk, bright pink roses blooming up its length. It took Iselin a moment to realize that the lavender and red flowers were the exact same shades of color as Legon and Sasha's magic. She looked again, wary of the vivid pink roses, recognizing herself.

WHEN LEGON WOKE UP, HE FELT ISELIN'S FAST APPROACH. He got out of bed, putting on a silken robe, and walked, yawning, out onto his terrace. The orange rays of the sun were just touching the hilltops on the opposite side of the harbor. Ise's sparkling form floated on the cool morning air toward him. She swooped in, transforming just as her foot touched down. Legon's eyes popped a little, seeing her in a dressing robe.

He smiled. "I like being engaged," he said.

Iselin didn't beat around the bush. "What was that last night?" she demanded.

Legon breathed out a sigh. "A dream, we think."

"You think?" There was a note of hysteria in her tone.

He motioned for her to follow him to a bench. She did, sitting down next to him, still facing him and waiting for a response. "Let me see if Sasha is awake," he said, and then instantly regretted it.

Iselin's confusion turned to anger. "No, you tell me, Legon! What was that? You don't need Sasha for everything."

He held up his hands. "Love, stop. We don't know exactly what they are. I want you to get both theories before you make a judgment, that's all." He tried to soothe her with his mind, but she wasn't having it. "I don't know what they are. I had them before I was an Elf, but in those, the Black Dragon was there too." He felt her fear and rushed on. "But he hasn't been there since I became an Elf, or at least if he is, then he has kept quiet." Legon shivered, remembering the red eyes and hulking form of the Black Dragon. He decided to show Iselin what he had seen in his first dreams, and she shivered too.

She spoke, watching as he played what he remembered of his dreams for her. "That's awful. It's the other brother for sure."

"So you think we are seeing the two brothers, then?" he asked.

Iselin's voice came, calmer this time. "Yes, when one ascends, they see one of the dragons, sometimes just a bit, and some see all of them. In a few cases, they will speak to whoever is ascending, but we don't talk about it. For Elves, it is extremely sacred."

Legon wasn't going to ask what happened for Iselin, as he didn't want to violate what was obviously a very private memory. She put her hand on his leg. "Not too sacred to share with you." She smiled. "I won't show you, but I saw him, and he spoke to me. I won't tell you what he said, but it was the most defining moment of my life."

"He has that effect. He said something to me, I think, when I changed. I only saw his eye, and I can't remember what he said." Legon looked down, straining his memory.

At that moment, Sasha walked out onto the terrace in her dressing gown. "I figured you two would be up. Sorry if I was rude last night, Ise."

"Don't be. What are your thoughts?" Iselin responded.

Legon could tell from the circles under Sasha's eyes that she woke up early and hadn't made it back to sleep. She sat and spoke, "I think that tree is our life. I am just as much a part of Legon as he is of me, and now Iselin, you are part of us too. But it's not complete."

Iselin looked confused, not being as connected with Sasha as Legon, and he picked up the thread of Sasha's thoughts, explaining, "You see, we always see the tree. Sometimes it dies, but sometimes—like last night —it doesn't. Anyway, seeing pink at all was new. I'm sure you figured out that each color is one of us. The pink roses are just making their way up the tree because we just decided to be together forever, do you see what I mean?" he asked.

Iselin nodded, overwhelmed, and Sasha went on. "Legon, we need to get Mother and Father out of Salmont. I don't care if Arkin is ready."

Legon answered, "I agree. We should get Keither's family out too. Sara's parents left town long before we did. They will be impossible to find." He felt the urgency emanating from Sasha, and surprisingly Iselin as well. "You two can talk about the dream or whatever. I'm going to contact Arkin."

With that, he stood and left them to talk.

ARKIN TURNED AROUND, HEARING THE CLICK OF THE DOOR. Barnin and a red-haired man walked into the back room of the shop. Barnin didn't smile when he turned to see Arkin.

"Nice place, Arkin," he said sarcastically.

"It's not as good of a cover as the carpentry shop, but not bad."

"Right," Barnin said, looking around. "This is Heath; he's a class one."

"Good to meet you," Heath said, looking wary.

"It's safe; don't worry," Arkin said, reading the look on Heath's face. "We need to leave as soon as we can," he added.

Barnin got to business. "I just don't like being here. I'm sure you understand. We know we are getting people out of the Empire. You can fill us in on the road."

Arkin was ready to go and just about to leave when Stacy walked into the shop, her long curls bouncing. "Who are your friends?" she asked, smiling warmly at Barnin and Heath.

"From the Cona Republic," Arkin responded, earning a disapproving look from Barnin.

"I'm Stacy; good to meet you two," Stacy said, bouncing forward. The two men shook her hand and relaxed a bit. Stacy turned back to Arkin. "Do you need anything before you go?"

"No. Keep me posted on everything. I won't be back for a while. I'm leaving you in charge of Salez," he said, picking up his bag and walking to the door.

Barnin, Arkin, and Heath made their way out of town. Once clear of the city, Barnin and Heath relaxed.

"So who is she?" Barnin asked, jabbing Arkin's arm.

"She's part of this cell. Why are you looking at me like that?"

"Robbing the cradle, huh? Good for you, old man," Barnin teased, and Heath laughed. "Barnin said you had some talents. He didn't tell me that was one of them."

Arkin huffed. This was going to be a long trip.

BARNIN LOOKED DOWN AT HIS HOMETOWN. IT LOOKED THE same as it did when he left. He looked down at his old house, seeing smoke float from the chimney. *So someone bought it,* he thought. His parents left town around the same time he had. He wasn't sure where they moved to, but he figured they were taking care of themselves.

He turned to Arkin. "It's a good thing you brought that other horse. I don't think Emma will have one. It's hard to tell, but it looks like there are two at Kovos' place. How do you want to work this?" he asked.

"You get Brack and Margaret out tonight if you can; I'll wait here a few days. Tell them to post a sign about being out of town or something. We don't want the townsfolk to wonder why they went missing." He paused. "Heath, if they don't want to come, put them to sleep and then contact me, and we will get Laura, Edis, and Emma out tonight instead."

Barnin didn't care for this part of the plan. There was no reason to suspect that anyone was in danger, but Arkin didn't appear to be taking chances. Barnin was going to have to explain to Brack that his son was dead. Arkin would have done it, but Barnin wouldn't let him. People couldn't know that Arkin was back in town, and if Barnin was being honest with himself, he figured Brack would lose it and blame Arkin, making a scene.

"Are you going to be alright getting them out?" he asked.

Arkin looked at them. "Yes; we are going to head west, straight to the coast. If we take normal roads, that will add a month to our travel time. This way we can make it in three, maybe three and a half weeks. Do you remember the locations of the safe houses and food caches?"

Arkin had gone all out for this, arranging food drops, the whole nine. Barnin was amazed at how many contacts the man had. It made traveling fast and easy. They wouldn't have a hard time until they hit the border. "Yeah, I do. Don't worry, we can get across without any problems. It is only the large groups that have issues making it across the border," he said, forestalling any questions, then adding, "What are you going to do if you hit trouble?"

Arkin smirked. "Take care of it; why?"

Barnin fought a grin. "Are you sure? That's some nasty country you're going to be crossing, and there are two of us in case we run into any issues..." he trailed off, seeing if Arkin would take the bait.

Arkin scowled. "Barnin, I've been doing this a lot longer than you, and I'm a class two. I think I can handle it," he said, his tone clipped.

"That's what I mean; you're like sixty, aren't you? I mean..."

"Forty, and I can still take you..." Arkin said in a deadly whisper. Heath snickered.

Barnin slapped Arkin's shoulder. "Yeah, I still got it. Don't get killed," he said, standing and walking off before Arkin could retort.

A day later, Barnin and Heath waited outside of town as Brack and Margaret approached on horseback. They rode out to see them. "Did people buy it?" Barnin asked.

Brack was still shaken up about the news of his son but raised his chin. "We told people we were going to visit my parents. They won't be looking for us for a few weeks. How are Laura and Edis going to get out?" he asked.

"Another team is taking them and Emma out; don't worry about them. Come on, let's go."

There wasn't a lot of talking; Barnin didn't know what to say, didn't know how to console them. All he could do was promise that Keither was fine and waiting for them. It was morning, and they were about a day away from the end of the road, where it would split in three directions.

"Heath, are you in range?" Barnin asked.

"Yeah, but not for long; what do you want me to do?"

"Call it in. Tell him we're clear."

Brack and Margaret looked confused. Margaret spoke, "Call it in? What do you mean?"

Barnin looked to see Heath's eyes slide out of focus and then back in. He nodded to him, and Barnin spoke. "Heath can use magic. He's telling our guy in Salmont that we haven't had any problems and to go get Legon and Sasha's family."

Brack coughed a hard laugh. "What, he's not doing it himself?"

"Who—Legon? No, he can't," Barnin said.

Brack shook his head. "Ungrateful. He gets our son killed and then won't even stick his neck out to save his parents. What is he doing? Probably doing something with that demon girl."

Barnin's hands gripped the saddle, and he tried to calm himself. Heath spoke out, "Who is a demon?" he asked, his tone acidic.

"What, you don't know? Sasha. The little tramp is possessed. Should have taken her out a long time ago," Brack said, and Margaret nodded.

Barnin moved in a flash, drawing his blade and blocking Heath's just in time to save Brack. "Heath, no!" he shouted.

Heath was growling in Elvish, and Barnin saw his hand rise. "They don't know what they are saying. Don't do this."

Heath looked at Barnin and then past him, pointing to Brack and Margaret, who looked mortified. "Why should we save them? They insult those whose feet they aren't worthy to clean!"

"Now, you wait here just a moment..." Brack started but was cut off by Barnin.

"Brack, Heath, stop." The two men didn't speak. "Heath, they don't understand. Think of where they live." He turned to Brack. "Don't say that Sasha is a demon; she has a medical condition." He held up his hand, cutting Margaret off before she could speak. "Look, there is something I'm not telling you." He paused. "When Kovos died, Legon was trying to save him, trying to kill an Iumenta with magic." Brack's face blanched. "When he used that magic, he changed. Brack, Legon's an Elf, and not just any Elf. He is the head of a great Elvin house. Sasha is his adopted sister, and the Elves recognize her as a lady of a great house now."

Margaret spoke first, incredulous. "You mean they are royalty?"

Heath spoke, more subdued. "Yes, both are, and the Cona Republic sees them as such. Legon didn't come because it was too dangerous for him, and it's not like an Elf can just move around the country now, can they?"

Barnin explained everything to them, leaving nothing out. He explained dragons and magic to them, telling them how they had been influenced. By the end, both Brack and Margaret looked even more defeated than they had two days ago.

"So, we have been used? We have had our hearts and minds twisted to make for a better workforce?" Brack asked. Barnin nodded, and Brack spoke again, "And they killed our son and made that poor Sara girl into a whore?"

Margaret spoke. "And Sasha? What, they don't want those with problems influencing the breeding population, so they make us hate them?" she asked, choking.

"Yes. When you get to Manton, you will see. There are people like Sasha. There are those who are blind, deaf, crippled—you name it. For many of them in the Cona lands, once they are taken into the Queen's care, they are just slaughtered like lame horses. Sasha, however, was functioning, so she would have likely shared Sara's fate," Barnin said.

Margaret looked like she was going to be sick, but a fire lit in Brack's eyes. "What do the Elves and the resistance need to kill the Iumenta?"

Heath answered, "The Cona Republic needs able smiths."

"Then we need to get a move on, don't we?" Brack said, shaking with anger and determination.

———

ARKIN SLID HIS HAND ALONG THE WALL OF THE COTTAGE FOR what he hoped was the last time. This was her house, his first failure, his best friend. Over the years, this place was an addiction for him. He kept coming back, never changing anything, just walking around and sitting by her grave. This would be the last time, he told himself. There would be no reason to come to Salmont ever again.

Heath's voice came fuzzy in Arkin's head. "We are clear."

"Good luck," Arkin said, and Heath was gone.

Arkin walked out of the cottage, resisting the urge to look back at it. Carefully, he made his way around town until he was in the woods just beyond Edis' property. Here he would wait until nightfall.

EMMA WALKED IN THE BACK DOOR OF THE HOUSE WITH A sheet from the clothesline. She looked behind her to the woods, feeling like she was being watched.

"What is it, dear?" Laura asked kindly.

"Nothing. You know how sometimes you feel like you're being watched, but there isn't really anything there?"

Laura smiled. "That's just good old-fashioned paranoia, and perfectly normal..."

Edis came in the front door. "I'm beat. What's for dinner?"

"Good to see you, too," Laura said frostily.

Emma contented herself by listening to Laura and Edis' friendly bickering. She helped with dinner, and afterward, she was at the table reading when she heard a knock at the back door.

Edis got up, moving to the door. "Who would come in the back?" he said, opening the door. "Arkin?"

Emma turned in her seat to see the town's old carpenter walk in the back door of the house, take a look outside, and close the door. "Good, you're all here."

There was a rush of voices, everyone asking questions and Arkin trying in vain to stop them. "I will explain everything, but you have to let me talk," he said firmly.

He sat at the table, and Laura and Edis sat on either side of Emma, just like she was one of their children.

Arkin spoke, "There is a lot you need to know. It's best I start at the beginning."

Arkin explained Legon's parentage—about his mother being Human and his father being an Elf. Then he told of their trip and of the royal guard. Emma tensed with Edis and Laura when he said what was about to happen to Sasha. Emma reaffirmed her vow that she would someday make everything up to Sasha. Arkin went on talking about finding Sara and what had been made of her. He showed them magic, producing a small emerald flame in his hand. It was too much for her to take in. Never had she suspected that Arkin was more than a carpenter. All of a sudden, her encounter with a dragon didn't seem so unlikely.

Arkin stopped and collected himself. "We were in a co-op. There was a Dragon. We ran, but we were found." The silence in the room was palpable, and Emma felt fear take control of her as she listened on. "We were found, and it turned into a fight. Legon and I used magic, but there was an Iumenta..." Her heart seemed to stop working. Everyone knew that Iumenta were powerful. She knew how good both Kovos and Legon were at fighting, but she still knew that neither of them could hold a candle to an Iumenta.

"Arkin, what happened to my children?" Laura asked, terrified.

"Legon was trying to save us. He used a spell and put all his energy into it. When the Iumenta came in, Kovos moved to it, and Legon was trying to save him. The spell was too strong, and it reverberated back on him. I've never seen anything like it before..." Arkin looked Edis in the eyes. "The Human in him died, and he turned into a full-blooded Elf." Everyone was dumbfounded, but Arkin wasn't done. He turned a pain-filled gaze to Emma and spoke in a whisper, tears in his eyes. "When it happened, Legon's spells stopped working, and before he could get them up again to help Kovos..."

Emma's blood ran cold. "No, Arkin, no! Please—no, no no no no, please no..."

He looked down. "I am so sorry, Emma. I know it doesn't help, but we did everything we could." He stopped and added almost as an afterthought, "If it is any comfort, you were the last thing he thought about."

"NO!" she wailed, turning into Edis as he pulled her in. Laura's arms were around her too. She heard them ask if Sasha and Legon were okay, and Arkin said that Kovos' sacrifice saved them all, but it didn't sink in with her. It didn't matter. He was dead; her love was dead. There was no hope after all; there never had been. She had nothing but the two people holding her now, and she clung to them with everything.

"Legon and Sasha are the head of House Evindass, a great Elvin house. We need to get you out of here tonight," Arkin was explaining.

Emma heard this. "No, please don't leave me," she begged, looking into Laura and Edis' faces. "Please, I'll do anything, just don't leave me alone," she sobbed.

They squeezed her. "We won't, sweetie. Don't you worry; we aren't going anywhere without you. You're ours now," Edis said.

"Emma, Legon and Sasha both see it as their duty to take care of you. If you wish to live in the Human lands outside of the Cona Empire, a house will be provided for you. But they would like to offer you a home in Seeon, if you will take it," Arkin said.

"Seeon?" Emma asked, feeling relieved that she could stay with Laura and Edis.

"Yes, that's the Pawdin Empire's capital. House Evindass is in charge of it. You would be living in the palace with Legon, Sasha, Laura, and Edis, if you like."

She clung to a new idea. Kovos protected Sasha and died trying to protect her and Legon. She owed Laura and Edis everything, and she needed to make amends with Sasha. She clung to the new reason to live. "I would love to live with Sasha and Legon." She would serve them, would be the best sister there had ever been. She would assist them in any way they needed, would help them take out the filth that had killed her Kovos.

"Are you sure? You can think about it if you like," Arkin said.

"My husband gave up his life to give us a better future. I will give my life for the same." No one questioned her calling Kovos her husband, and while she felt a part of herself die with his loss, she felt resolution about what she would do. Arkin explained what Legon was called and what people thought him to be, that he was to cleanse the land. He explained Sasha's role as a compass for him as well. This too made her feel the rightness of her choice. She dabbed the tears from her eyes. She would cry later, would mourn later. Right now, she needed to focus on the matter at hand.

Arkin told them to take only what they would need, and he told Emma that he had a horse for her. She took some clothes and a diary.

She paused and went to a box that held a necklace Kovos had given her. It was the only thing she had to remember him. She took it to Arkin.

"Arkin, this is all I have left of him," she said, trying not to lose control.

He took the necklace and muttered, making it glow green, and handed it back to her. "There you go. It will be hard to break now. Once we get back to the Elves, they will make it nearly impossible to break. Also, I placed a spell on it that will make it so you will always know where it is."

"Thank you, Arkin." She took a moment. "And thank you for doing what you did. I know this wasn't easy for you."

Arkin placed a hand on her shoulder. "Emma, I will tell you anything you want to know once we make it to the ship, but for now just know that it was the greatest honor to have fought with your husband." She saw the loss in his eyes; saw that he too had paid a terrible price. Hadn't he lost a friend? He had lost Legon's birth mother. Emma had seen the house with her own eyes, seen the horror that Arkin walked into all those years ago. She couldn't look at him the same way again. She knew that he would be an inspiration to her. He had given his whole life to avenging the death of his friend. He'd spent years hiding, sacrificing. She could do that. She would do that.

Emma walked out of the house and got on her new horse. She knew they would be heading to the coast, and she also knew that she would never see this town again. As they rode, she turned, looking back at her place of birth. "Goodbye, Mother and Father," she said, and turned back around and rode into the dark woods.

CHAPTER 15
JOURNEY

"It can be hard to see, but once you do, you find that everything is the same, just different."
— *Diary of the Perfectos Compatioa*

E mma shifted in her saddle, trying not to hit a tree. They were almost out of the mountains, and she was looking forward to being on roads again. Arkin was different now from how she remembered him as a child. There were some similarities, but she now saw that his whole life had been an act. He moved ahead of the group, scanning the land with all his senses. The first night, Arkin had demonstrated to everyone the ability to speak with thought. She, like everyone else, couldn't reach out and contact anyone yet, but she was starting to become more comfortable with Arkin in her mind. At first, it felt like a terrifying violation to her, since her only experience using her mind in this way was when she was confronted by a dragon. But Arkin's mind wasn't cruel or alien to her. It felt like talking in a normal fashion.

Once one becomes aware of their mind being touched, the mind is able to sense and block another's. This didn't happen often, but she was surprised that it happened at all. Arkin told them about how the Iumenta controlled the hearts and minds of the people with fiery little thoughts. She didn't buy it for one second, but sometimes she heard a whisper. It was low and subtle, just a little notion. It only lasted for a moment and then it was gone. Sometimes it was just an emotion—fear or anger, sometimes happiness. Many times the emotions came with a thought. If Arkin hadn't said anything to her, she probably wouldn't have even noticed them, but now...

She felt that now and decided to ask. "Arkin?" she called.

He turned around and rode over to her. "What is it? What's wrong?" he asked, reading the look on her face.

"I hear stuff sometimes, like now. I think of the Queen and then feel happy, but sometimes I think of displeasing the Queen and feel scared. What is that?" she asked.

Arkin's brow furrowed. "Clear your head and do what I taught you to block thoughts."

She complied, and the feeling left her. "It's gone?"

Edis and Laura were alongside them now, and Arkin stopped everyone. "Let's take a break, and I can explain to you." They dismounted and retrieved their water skins. "You all can hear now because I have touched your mind. Emma, I'm a little surprised that after your encounter with the Iumenta dragon, you didn't start hearing and feeling things. You have always been subject to these thoughts, but they have been too soft for your conscious mind to pick up on. What you are hearing is an Iumenta dragon." He forestalled a panic. "Don't worry; it is far away. We have nothing to worry about. The blocks on your minds will always stop them if you want. It's a matter of what your mind is willing to accept in it. You will have to raise your defenses from time to time, but it's really not that much of an inconvenience. Once in Seeon, you won't need any defense at all, but every time you enter the Cona Empire, you will feel most unwelcome, so be prepared."

"How does this control us?" Laura asked.

"It doesn't. All it does is put ideas into your head and gives them a place to grow. Like that feeling you felt of Regent Hoelaria being upset and then feeling fear. After years of thoughts being planted into your subconscious, you will begin to believe that way on your own." He read the fear on all of their faces. "It takes people months, sometimes years, when they leave the Empire for these thoughts to dissipate. Don't worry; areas like Salmont are not as affected as large cities where the Iumenta are close." No one looked convinced, and Edis said, "So how do I know that my beliefs aren't what the Queen wants me to believe?" Arkin held up a hand. "The Regent," he corrected. "As I said, they are small, and now you can feel it. Before, you may have noticed yourself thinking something that seemed wrong and wondered how the thought got in your head. Remember that you choose what your mind accepts. Even if the thought wasn't put there by you, you have the choice of whether to keep it or not." With that, Arkin closed the topic, saying that the break was over.

Arkin took the lead again, and before too long, they were on some type of road dappled in midday sun. Emma's eyes swept the dense trees on either side of the narrow road, breathing in the scent of dust. She sneezed from it and figured horses or a cart must have been by recently, kicking up the dry dirt. In front of her, Arkin stopped, holding up his hand.

Edis was about to speak when Arkin's voice came across the mental network. "Don't say anything; we aren't alone."

ARKIN FELT THE OTHERS' APPREHENSION. THEY WEREN'T concerned about any danger, and why would they be? Most people traveled around the country in relative safety. It had only been in the last few months that traveling had become even remotely hazardous. Arkin's nostrils filled with dust, and his eyes raked the ground, seeing tracks that looked recent. This area was still out of the way. The road was not a high priority for guards, and moreover, the light traffic made it perfect for an ambush. His mind flicked out to a hawk. It circled high above them, looking where Arkin directed it. Just around the next turn, he saw them —seven men lounging around. An eighth entered the bird's field of view, heading away from where Arkin's party was stopped. The man seemed to be talking and pointing down the road toward their party. The men took places on each side of the road, setting up an ambush.

Arkin spoke over the network. "There is a band of robbers up the way. You lot stay here while I take care of it."

"How many?" Edis thought.

"Eight," was Arkin's reply.

Edis spoke out loud, but softly. "I'll go with you; you need help."

Arkin shook his head. "No, I don't. You stay here." Edis looked like he was going to go anyway, so Arkin connected with Edis' horse, giving it an overwhelming desire to stay put. He heard Edis grumble at the horse, but Arkin was on his way.

His plan was straightforward. He was going to just spring the trap the robbers had set. He rode, picking up speed, and rounded the corner. There was nothing waiting for him. His connection with the hawk showed him that the men were there hiding, presumably waiting for the rest of Arkin's party. He was unfazed. Really, it didn't matter to him. He took his time pulling out his bow and stringing it. Still, the hiding men did nothing. He saw that they had weapons drawn and were signaling to each other, telling the others to hold and pointing down the road. *Amateurs,* he thought.

After a moment of thought, he decided that avoiding violence would be the best plan. He didn't care for Legon's family to see a bunch of people hacked to death. "I know there are eight of you. I know you think you have a pretty good little trap set here, and I know that you are waiting for the rest of my group," he said loudly. Nothing happened. *Honestly,* he thought. He turned to look into the brush where one man crouched, barely out of easy sight. "You there, I can see you," Arkin said coldly. He continued on, "Look, I don't want to have to kill you; it's not good for anyone. So just come out so we can pass, and you can set up for the next group."

Finally, a response. "Or, we could just kill you and be done for the day," a jeering voice rang out. There was a small chuckle from the bushes around him, and Arkin knew where this was going. "Very well," he said.

In a flash, Arkin knocked an arrow and drew his bow, sending the projectile hurtling in the direction of the man he could see. There was a gasp and thud as the man fell dead. The trees exploded with the other men shouting and firing arrows at him. All but one missed him by a long shot. One of his wards glowed green around him as it deflected the only arrow with true aim. Arkin felled two more men with the bow. A longhaired man bowled toward him with a wild battle cry. Arkin moved his mount and dodged the blow with ease, drawing his own sword and taking off the man's head.

EDIS FINALLY GOT HIS HORSE TO MOVE. HE CHARGED around the corner as he heard yells and screams. *What is Arkin thinking?* As he rounded the corner, a fight came into view. Bodies were lying in pieces on the ground, muddying the dirt. He jerked on the reins and watched in detached horror. Arkin was off his horse, his broadsword lashing out like the strike of a snake. Each move brought death to one of his foes. The last two men Edis could see alive rushed Arkin—one with an axe and the other with nothing more than his bare hands. Arkin turned to the unarmed man and barked, "Flamma." Emerald fire erupted from his right palm in a ball of bright fire and death. It struck the man's chest, engulfing his upper body, and then the fire died, leaving only a charred ribcage in its wake. The rest of the dead man's body fell to earth, his incinerated chest merely smoking. Edis couldn't take his eyes off the sight. He didn't even watch Arkin kill the other man.

"Edis, are you injured?" Arkin's voice asked, concerned.

Edis moved his horse forward, trying to avoid bodies. "Edis!" he said, this time demanding. Edis looked up at Arkin. Crimson dotted his face. His white shirt was scarlet, as was the blade in his hand. But that wasn't what really transfixed Edis; it was that Arkin was totally unaffected by this. The look on his face was apathetic, like someone who had just taken out the trash.

Arkin came up to him, placing his hand on his forearm, giving it a shake. Edis shook his head. "I'm not hurt," he said, then after a moment, "I don't want my family to see..."

"Of course not. I will move them; you just take a moment."

BLOOD SPRAYED FROM LEGON'S ARM, AND A MOMENT LATER, his healing ward staunched the bleeding. He staggered back, his fenna feeling like lead in his hand. Mage, one of his guards, circled, giving Legon only a moment's rest before lashing out again with his fenna. There was a deafening clang of metal on metal as Legon barely blocked the blow, his knees starting to buckle. *How can his attacks be this strong? He's not even tired. Not even Sydin can hold up like this,* Legon thought, panicked. *Maybe if I attack him with some of the energy left in my blade, I can get in a few hits. I at least want to draw blood.*

Almost as if he were reading Legon's mind, Mage spoke, "I'm not Sydin." Then with a roar, he barked, "Flamma!" His fenna flashed gold as a long thick cord of fire and magic unfurled like a whip curling in the air, and as Mage swung his arm around, he sent the whip toward Legon, yelling, "INGENIUM!" Legon barely had time to try to block, and the spell hit his fenna with more force than he thought possible. His power drained in the blink of an eye. Gold surrounded him as Mage's ward activated, saving Legon from certain death. Still, the force of it sent him flying back, crashing into the wall.

Legon collapsed in a heap, breathing hard and having no magic left. He looked up to Mage, who had already sheathed his fenna and was brushing his long sandy hair out of his bright blue eyes. They looked cold. The vibrant blue was like ice as Mage walked forward and extended a hand.

"Do you need a hand, Un Prosa?" he asked, calm and collected.

Legon took the proffered hand, and Mage lifted him. "How did you do that?" Legon asked.

Mage smirked. "Un Prose, who was the last person you fought with a fenna?"

Legon thought, "An Iumenta at the Precipice, and Sydin before that when he trained me how to use it. Why?"

Mage nodded sagely. "You have never fought a master then." He held up a hand. "Please allow me to explain. You see, Sydin is an Ascended and is far more powerful than I, but when it comes to the fenna, he, like most of the Ascended, is not a master. You see, they never had to learn how to be masters of the fenna. Very few Venefica do. There are several levels to fighting with magic and several releases, if you will; the top of these is Binon."

Legon interrupted, "Was that the crazy whip thing?"

Mage smiled. "Yes, that is one of the forms of my Binon. Suffice it to say, Binon is the maximum release of magic in a concentrated form. You have experienced this in some way, I think."

Legon thought about if he had, and Mage kept speaking. "When you changed, didn't you use a spell with so much power you thought it might kill you?" Legon nodded, and Mage went on. "You felt like in that moment that you could die, that the entirety of yourself was in the spell?"

"Mage, I've never told anyone that. I know that you can't die from casting a spell, so it felt silly to say I had felt that way. How did you know?"

"That is Binon, but at that time you were only part Elf. Now if you can attain that release again, you will be much stronger. You were in a life-and-death situation, and that is why you were able to do what you did; however, it is much better to learn and master this skill so that you can use it at will, as opposed to waiting until you are at death's door. I will explain more to you, but only after you have had something to drink and eat. Come, Un Prosa, you look horrible."

They made their way to Legon's apartment, Mage not walking quite evenly with Legon. They entered the spacious main room, and he noticed that there was a sheathed fenna lying on a cabinet next to the door that led out onto the terrace. It took Legon a moment to figure out why it was there.

"Oh, they are done with it already. I thought it took a long time to make one?" Legon said, turning to Mage.

The latter walked to the fenna and picked it up. "Un Prose, they do take a long time, but you are the Head of House, after all."

Before leaving the dragon dome at the Precipice, Legon had met with a weapons master. She had taken a list of measurements of both his physical and magical attributes to send to Seeon. Fenna were powerful weapons, but Legon didn't learn much about them until he was in his new home. Mage had explained that fenna were made for each Venefica, designed around them to make them stronger and more effective. The one he had now, the same he used in the battle, was more of a spare, and it was generic in its qualities, so it would work equally well for all. The blade he took from Mage now was fine-tuned for him, and at once when he gripped the handle, he could feel a difference. All Elvin and Iumenta blades would feel natural in his hand, but once when Mage had allowed Legon to use his fenna, the weapon felt off to him. Its physical makeup wasn't the problem; it was the magical makeup that was different. It felt foreign to him. With this new blade, he understood fully why fenna were built to each fighter's needs.

"It is named Tento, unless you would like a different name for it," Mage explained.

Most soldiers named the sword they used. This was the case for all three races. Mage's fenna was named Wrath, which was odd since most Elvin blades were named in the Elves' tongue, but Mage liked the word, and from what Legon could see, it was fitting.

"What does that mean?" Legon asked.

"Attack."

He pulled the long sword from the deep purple sheath, taking in its mirror-like appearance. Embossed near the hilt was his crest. Just next to that, but much smaller, was the house crest. The handle felt perfect in his hand. The handle's wood was grown to look like it was wrapped in white and black silk, the fine gold bars twisting along like they were decoration rather than a conductor for magic. The guard and pommel were gleaming platinum.

"It looks more like art than a weapon," he said. Mage smiled in agreement. "They all do. Wait until you have used it before saying if you like it or not. This is why we ended early," he said evenly.

Legon was incredulous. "That was early? How was I supposed to fight more?"

"Un Prosa, when you are tired is when you grow the most. It is my job to protect you, and part of that job is teaching you how to protect yourself." They walked out to the terrace, and Legon asked a question he had been thinking about ever since they had left the training room. "Today when you used the Binon on me... why didn't the Iumenta I fought use that? I haven't seen any Venefica use anything like that, for that matter."

"Yes, in the type of combat you were in, it would not have been advisable. The vast majority of Venefica have not attained Binon, but even those who have can't use it in battle most of the time. Today you saw how powerful a fenna can be, but that attack drained me of a lot of power. In truth, I can only attack like that four or five times before I'm exhausted. Then I must rest for a while. In a fight like the one you were in, I might use that attack two or three times, but then I will hold off until my energy has recovered some."

"Recovered?"

"Yes, like when you exert yourself physically. The same is for magic. But like your muscles, you can train yourself to have higher endurance with magic and also spurts of power. But in combat, you must also delegate energy to wards that protect your soldiers and the spells that make them stronger," Mage explained.

"So that Iumenta couldn't use Binon on me even if they knew how, is that what you're saying?"

"Most likely. He might have made one last attempt to kill you, like you did defending Iselin. However, you defeated him before he was able to try, so we will never know."

Legon spent most of the rest of the day learning everything he could about fenna and looking forward to trying out Tento as soon as he could.

SALTY AIR FILLED EMMA'S NOSE AS SHE LOOKED DOWN ON A small harbor town. She didn't remember its name. All she knew was that they were going to meet a ship here. She couldn't see the ocean, as it was obscured by buildings, but she could smell it.

"It's different, isn't it?" Arkin asked the group.

"I've never been to the sea, but I've heard that it is beautiful," Laura said.

"We lived near the coast until I was twelve," Edis said, breathing deeply and seeming to relax.

They made their way through the teeming streets. The sun was high in the sky, and the day was unusually hot for this time of year. The humidity and heat were making Emma's hair and clothes stick to her, and she thought back longingly to the aridness of Salmont. As they made their way through the town, the smell of fish in the sun assaulted her, and she wondered how people could live in a place like this.

Arkin sensed her thought and explained. "We are heading to the part of the bay where all the fishing boats land. All the markets are there as well. The rest of the city doesn't smell this way," he said in her mind.

Sure enough, there was a gap in the buildings, and Emma caught her first glimpse of the sea. Her mouth parted slightly as she took in the sparkling bay. Gulls flew overhead, swooping down onto the ships as they came in. A breeze drifted off the water, cutting the scent of fish. She followed Arkin as he made his way down one of the docks. He stopped at one of the boats that appeared empty. They all dismounted, Emma making her way to the edge of the dock and looking down the gap between the bobbing ships and the structure. Water was lapping against the thick moss-covered beams that supported the dock.

"Good day, can I help you?" a gruff voice said.

She started and looked up in time to see Arkin shake the hand of a scruffy-looking man. "Hello, we are here for a tour of the bay. Could you help us?"

The man paused, looking Arkin over, still holding his hand. Finally, he let go and turned to yell at someone somewhere below deck. "Kevin, get up here! We have a job."

A tall, lanky boy who was presumably Kevin came above deck, running his hand through shaggy black hair. "What's that, boss?" he asked.

"Captain," the older man corrected. "Take these horses to the stable," he said meaningfully.

"The stables? But weren't we..." he trailed off, taking in Emma and her companions, and then he jumped like he'd been shocked. "Right, right, the stable. Got ya, boss."

Kevin scuttled onto the dock, yelling for a few nearby hands to come help him. Edis and Laura didn't protest, and neither did Arkin, but the whole thing felt a bit odd to Emma.

Arkin spoke over the mental network. "This is Mick. He is going to take us out to the Elvin ship." She noticed a new presence in her mind, and then the same gruff voice as before. "Get on board and go below deck. Your horses will be sent via the regular means of smuggling."

Emma did as she was told and stepped over the rail of the ship onto the shifting deck. She made her way below deck into the musty hold. She was assailed by the smell of fish and brine. Her nose crinkled, and she tasted the salt on the back of her tongue. She found a pile of nets to sit on and waited for Arkin to show up. Soon she was joined by Laura and Edis, who both seemed to dislike the space as much as she did.

Edis spoke. "Maybe we'll get used to it over the next few weeks. I can't imagine it will take too long to get to the Pawdin Empire."

Laura nodded her head in agreement, but Emma thought otherwise. After her encounter with the Elvin house, she was pretty sure the Elf ship would be nothing like the one they were on right now. Soon enough, she felt movement, and she knew they were shoving off and on their way out to sea.

After an hour, Arkin came below deck and told them they could come up. Emma was grateful to be out on the main deck of the ship. The fresh sea air was welcome after the musk of the hold. Pelicans played in the spray from the ship's bow, and she had to admit that it was peaceful. She was alone, overlooking the railing when she felt Arkin beside her.

He looked uncomfortable. "Emma, it's been a long few weeks, and we haven't had any time to talk, and I don't want to bring up painful memories, but I think you have the right to know about Kovos' last few months."

Was she ready for this? Was she going to be able to handle hearing about her love? She thought that she was and nodded for him to speak. Arkin explained how Kovos was doing everything he could to prepare himself for her. Her chest tightened when she learned about how Elves connected so deeply that they died when their spouse did and that Kovos had wanted that with her. But they wouldn't have that; they never would; that future had been stolen from her.

After Arkin was done, she took a moment to collect herself. "Is there anything else?" she asked.

Arkin frowned. "No. Just know you were the last thing he thought about before he engaged the Iumenta."

Hours passed, and night fell as Emma leaned against the rail of the ship, letting its rocking motion lull her mind. The moon rose high overhead, and the stars appeared. She gazed up at the twinkling dots, thinking of everything she'd lost.

"Are you up there?" she asked the stars.

"They are," said a voice next to her.

Emma started a bit at the boy from earlier in the day. "Oh, I'm sorry," she breathed. "I didn't see you there."

"Yeah, the sea and the sky have that effect. It's easy to lose yourself out here; you have to be careful," he said.

Emma's smile was more out of politeness than anything else. She didn't care to talk to anyone right now. "Well, that's why we have you and your father," she said.

The boy smiled warmly. "The captain isn't my father, but I wasn't talking about the ship getting lost; I'm talking about you."

"And how's that?"

"I've seen that face. You've lost people close to you, haven't you?"

Emma's cheeks flushed. "Yes, my parents and my husband," she supplied.

The boy nodded his head knowingly. "You can get lost out here, Emma; keep your wits about you. And they're up there watching you, waiting for you to come home when it's time." He walked off, back below the deck of the ship, and she thought she heard him say something about a gold dragon. She wasn't sure what she believed, but as she looked to the heavens, her eyes fixed on the bright unmoving star that appeared almost a year ago. Arkin had told her about that star and what it meant, and she couldn't help but feel a chill run down her spine.

CHAPTER 16
RIPTIDE

"Eyes and hearts tell lies. The truth is almost never what we see."
— *Teachings of the Restored Queen*

Emma wrapped her arms around herself as the chill morning air bit at her. She hadn't gone below deck all night, and she was feeling stiff. The horizon was just starting to turn pink when she caught a glimmer of something silver shining in the distance. As the light increased and the ship came closer, a figure loomed before her; a ship rose from the water directly ahead. There was a call from behind her, and she looked to see Mick signaling with a flag. As they drew in, she saw that this ship was not like the ships she had seen in the harbor. Its long, smooth shape was elegant, its beauty apparent even from afar. But there was something off as well.

"What is it?" she asked softly, not expecting a response, so she was startled to hear Arkin speak. "It's the Propero from House Evindass."

She looked with awe as the Propero came into view. She could see its colors flying boldly. At first, she thought it was a little reckless of them, but as she thought about it, she figured an Elvin ship was going to stand out regardless, so why not flaunt it? There was activity on the deck, and she could tell that something was terribly wrong.

Once alongside, Captain Mick came up and was about to speak when there was a blur from the Propero. A red-haired Elf landed lightly on the deck of the ship Emma was on, and without an introduction, started to speak urgently. "Captain, get your crew and passengers on board immediately. There is an Impa frigate inbound; you won't have time to get away. Where are you keeping your belongings?"

"Below deck, I'll show you," said the Captain, and then he yelled at the boy whose name Emma still didn't know, "This is our port of harbor; you know what to do!"

The boy's eyes flashed in alarm, and he ran off below deck. The red-haired Elf said something in Elvish and followed the Captain. Edis and Laura were on deck now.

"What is going..." Edis started, but stopped as several more Elves landed on the deck, all jabbering in Elvish. They all wore robes of the deepest purple, and Emma's mind went back to what little Arkin had told them about the Elves. *These are members of the house guard,* she thought.

One of them, with straight, long blonde hair, approached her. The many red flecks in his pale blue eyes glinted in the light, and she inhaled in fear, knowing what he was. Without so much as a word, the Elf reached out and scooped her up in his arms. Before she could assemble her thoughts, he took a few quick steps and jumped into the air. They arched across the space between the ships and landed on the deck of the Propero. She heard a yelp from Laura, and soon she and Edis were on board the ship as well, being carried by other Elves. Her bags flew on deck, and then the redhead was back with Mick and the boy.

The deck of the ship was a blur of Elves as they lowered sails and readied the ship. Arkin grabbed her arm. "Come on, we need to get to safety." As her gaze swept out over the sea, she saw oars extend, and the ship began to move. Arkin tugged, and she moved with him in shock, unable to think. The last thing she saw before going below deck was another ship in the distance racing toward them, its hull white and shining, bearing down on them.

It was hard to move down into the ship as it lurched forward. There was a deafening sound, and Arkin wrapped his arms around Emma and slammed into the wall, yelling, "IMPACT!"

There was a crack like thunder, and then another and another. There were other sounds too that she couldn't make out.

"ARKIN, WHAT IS IT?" Edis yelled. He was clutching Laura to the wall, just like Arkin was doing to Emma.

"That sound means we are getting fired on, and that thunder is the ship's wards taking hits."

ARKIN PASSED EMMA OFF TO MICK AND MADE HIS WAY BACK up to the deck. He wasn't powerful, but still, the thought of doing nothing while the crew of the Propero took on the Iumenta was unacceptable to him. As he made it back on the deck, his eyes swept out to sea just as a glowing yellow bolt from a ballista exploded against a wall of brown, the crack from the ward making his ears ring. The Propero was not returning fire but instead retreating as fast as it could out to open sea and away.

The redhead was at his side. "Is everything okay?" he asked.

"What can I do?"

"Class two, right?" the Elf asked.

Arkin nodded, and the Elf spoke again. "Opes can use you; follow me."

They made their way to the stern of the ship, where several Elves stood shooting balls of magic into the sea. One, presumably Opes, turned to them. "We are freezing the water to slow them down. We do not need to get into a battle with that ship." Arkin didn't need any more explanation than that. They needed to leave the area—that was obvious. With the number of magic users on the Propero and with the more advanced Elvin ship, they could easily defeat the Iumenta attack. But if that ship was not alone, if it was part of a carrier battle group, the number of Ascended that a carrier would contain would make it certain suicide for the Propero.

"What's to keep them from calling in our location and heading?" Arkin asked as he took his place at the rail.

"We've jammed the ability to tell the course and the location. They can still notify other ships, but with our current speed, it will be difficult for anyone to plot an interception course. Now make as big of blocks of ice as you can, please," Opes said, not unkindly.

Arkin did as he was asked, having no desire to question the battle tactics of a house guard. Magic of many different colors launched into the turning water, creating giant blocks of ice that would sink a ship. He knew this wouldn't do much to the Iumenta frigate, but it would force them to slow down. Already the gap between the ships was opening. The frigate didn't have a prayer of catching the Propero, even without the ice. Arkin looked as the frigate reached Mick's ship, not even changing course. It nicked the bow of the small ship. The little ship's bow exploded, and the rest of the ship twisted sideways in the water, sending debris in all directions. The frigate wasn't even slowed down. They were out of range for the ballista now, and that was a good thing. The Iumenta ship started to make its way through the field of impromptu icebergs. Iumenta Venefica on board sent magic into the water, breaking up the ice, but it had worked. Sooner than Arkin would have thought possible, the frigate was just a dot on the horizon as the Propero cut through the waves.

"Thank you for the help," Opes said in his breathy voice. "If you don't mind, I would like to debrief you once you get Prosa's family settled."

"Of course," he paused, and then asked, "What was that ship doing out here? We are way past normal patrol routes."

Opes looked back out to sea as if to confirm something. "We are, but that ship's flag wasn't that of the Cona Empire; it was Impa from up north. The way it was moving leads me to think they knew we were here."

"Then why just one ship?"

"That I don't know. It's possible the Impa fleet wasn't positive of our location. Who knows? But the way it was moving straight for a kill tells me it was on its own, and that is almost more disturbing."

Arkin didn't pursue the subject. Opes had the same amount of information as Arkin, so they couldn't do more than speculate. Arkin made his way back to the others and found them settling into bunks in their cabins. Edis looked up, worried. "Is it over?"

"Yes, I don't think we will have any more problems."

Then, Edis demanded angrily, "You pull us out of our house, and we've been attacked by robbers and now the Iumenta. What else is going to happen, Arkin?"

Arkin tried to remember that they had been through a lot and attempted to calm them. "Nothing else is going to happen, Edis. You and your family are safe. The whole of the land is dotted with bands of robbers, and well, as for the ship..." He wasn't sure what to say. "To be honest, that was a surprise to everyone."

Arkin did what he could to try to comfort them, but it was mostly in vain. They had left their homes, been attacked, and now were on a ship that was fleeing the Iumenta. "I need to be debriefed by Opes. If you need anything, just ask one of the crew, and they will get whatever you need."

"Do we have to stay in here?" Emma asked.

Arkin was about to say no but realized that he wasn't in charge anymore and reached out with his mind until he found Opes. "No, you can go anywhere on the ship, though I would ask you to stay off the main bridge." They nodded, and Arkin left.

On the bridge, he found Opes and several other Elves looking down at a large flat crystal display that showed the location of the Propero and every other vessel in the area.

Opes looked up and smiled briefly. "Arkin, I am sorry to be so unpleasant today. You could say this wasn't how we had planned this meeting. Would you like some Poti?"

"That would be welcome, thank you. It has been an interesting day, to say the least."

Opes handed Arkin the drink and went right to business, asking about their trip and the conditions in the Empire. He found out that the ship that attacked them was from one of the other provinces in the Impa Empire, which was odd. The Impa fleet did not patrol Cona waters unless absolutely needed, and even then, they were never far from the coastline. The Cona and Impa fleets' main job was to protect the coast from attack, not to search out and destroy the enemy. That they were in these waters was strange, let alone that they seemed to know where the one Elvin ship was. After a few hours of talking, they decided to call it a night. It was early evening, but everyone needed a break. Arkin went to his cabin and decided to get some sleep before figuring out what to do next.

EMMA ROLLED OVER IN HER BUNK. THE MATTRESS SHE WAS on was the most comfortable bed she'd ever slept on, but she was still having a hard time sleeping. She could feel the ship moving, rising up and down, but she wasn't sick—a result of the ship's magical qualities. It was a little unnerving. The last boat they were on creaked and made all kinds of noise, but not the Propero. Even her house made sounds at night, but now it was dead silent. She couldn't even hear the ocean outside. She gave up on sleep and decided to go on deck.

The cold night air was invigorating, and she made her way to the rail. There were a few Elves up on watch who greeted her. They were all beautiful and moved with grace. They were a little intimidating but polite. She leaned against the rail of the ship, listening to the water. She closed her eyes and let herself drift. When her eyes opened again, there was a predawn light that broke her heart. She closed her eyes tight, trying vainly to keep tears from escaping.

"The dawn is a hard time," said an airy voice.

She looked to her right and felt her gut clench in fear.

Opes examined her with his watery blue eyes, cold and appraising. The small amount of light glinted off a red fleck in his eye, and a chill ran up Emma's spine. His face, carved like stone, softened. "You are afraid of me."

He wasn't asking, but she answered anyway. "I'm sorry."

Again his face hardened, and she spoke. "Please don't be angry, I..."

"Was attacked by an Iumenta Ascended, I know. Please don't take my sour mood as a reflection on yourself, but rather my distaste for the filth that give immortals a bad name."

He knew. Of course he knew. Arkin had told them everything, hadn't he? He had been debriefed. The man next to her now probably knew everything about her. A thought came to mind. "You said that dawn is hard."

"Yes."

"Why did you say that?"

Opes frowned and took a place next to her, gently holding the rail of the ship. "I come out in the mornings at dawn. It holds memories for me." He seemed to struggle. "You see, I too have lost someone because of the Iumenta."

She looked over at him. "In the War of Generations?" she asked, trying not to sound too curious. She knew almost nothing about the war, but here was someone who may have lived during it, for all she knew.

"Yes." He looked over at her, reading the look on her face, and smiled. "I'm that old. It was my wife. She was killed."

Before Emma could stop herself, she asked, "But I thought Elves die when their spouse does?"

"Oh, we do, but that kind of connection takes a few decades. My wife and I were connected enough for me to want to die, even now for me to wish for death just so we could be together. But instead, I had to settle for a piece of myself dying instead."

His explanation was sobering. The war was two thousand years ago, and still he wasn't free from the grief.

"He would stay the night at my house. My family didn't know, of course, but he would leave about this time of the morning. It was the best and worst part of my day—the best because we had the whole night to ourselves and the worst because he was leaving." Then choking, she added, "The last time I saw him was at a time like this, leaving my house. Never to return."

Opes moved his hand on top of hers and gently squeezed, not a gesture of attempted empathy or sorrow, but one of understanding, one that said 'I know.' She looked at the Elf, who had a few minutes ago seemed terrifying to her because of what he was, but now, taking in his eyes shining with emotion, she saw that he was more like her than anyone she'd ever met.

"I'm sorry for fearing you before, and thank you for bringing me on board and protecting us," she said.

There was a blur of red fire on her other side, and she yelped, jumping out of the way and bumping into Opes, who steadied her with ease. She pressed her back into Opes, moving out of the way of a flaming ruby raccoon in front of her. Its glowing eyes seemed to bore through her.

"Sorry, Emma, this is my familiar," Opes started.

She spun to look at him. "What?"

"He's made of magic; he's a familiar. They are connected to their masters, and when he sensed my emotions, he came to investigate. Forgive me; he won't harm you."

She turned back to the little creature that was making its way to her on the rail. It leaned out and sniffed her. Tentatively, she reached out and patted its head and then scratched its ears. "He's kind of cute," she said, and then the raccoon jumped at her, and she caught it. "Whoa, hey there, you're not so bad," she said, petting it and then turning to Opes. "I'm sorry..."

He laughed. "Don't be; by all means, keep him company—keep him out of trouble, and just so you know—you can always contact a Venefica with their familiar."

Opes wandered off, leaving Emma with whatever this thing's name was. The creature was warm in her arms, just like a real animal would be, and it was playing with her necklace. "Do you like that? Kovos gave it to me." The raccoon looked up at her with more intelligence in its eyes than any animal she'd ever seen, and she wondered just how linked it was to Opes.

EDIS SPENT MOST OF HIS TIME ON THE PROPERO relaxing and learning everything he could about the ship, its crew, and the Elves. At first, the ship reminded him of that house they'd found Legon in as a baby, but the ship was smooth and streamlined. It was organic, but it also exuded the perfect balance of death and elegance. Presently, he was enjoying a hot cup of something, leaning over the stern of the ship. They were almost to Seeon, and he was surprisingly nervous to see his children. Legon would be different, this he knew; but what of Sasha?

He'd always protected his little girl, and she had been through a lot since he had last crushed her in his arms.

Thin arms wrapped around his waist, and he pulled them tight around him. "How are you, love?" he asked.

Laura rested her head against his shoulder. "I'm ready to get off this ship. It's amazing, but I want to see our children."

He turned to face her, bringing her in close and kissing her forehead. "I know. I want to see them too. Do you think we will like the capital?"

"Do we have a choice?" she asked with a chuckle.

They didn't have a choice. The Human lands were no longer safe for them. They would be in danger nearly all the time outside of the Pawdin Empire, and while they could live wherever they liked, why would they pick any place other than where their children were?

Arkin came up to them. "We will be there soon. Opes and the crew apologize, but they do not have any clothes for you other than the ones you brought. I suppose we should have picked some up in Manton when we dropped off Mick."

Laura spoke. "What do you mean? What's wrong with what we have?"

"Nothing, it's just that they are hot, and also the Elves dress differently than we do. You do not have to wear their attire, but, well, you will see."

Edis didn't know what to make of that but had more important things on his mind. He spotted Emma along one of the side rails with that red raccoon that didn't seem to leave her side. She was with Opes, and he was pointing to something. They went down to join them.

As soon as they were close, Emma said, "Edis, Laura, look, they are farming. They are growing food under the water. Isn't that amazing?"

Edis looked out to where she was pointing, and sure enough, there were several Elves in small boats with others in the water going under and coming back up with what looked like fruit. Opes yelled something in Elvish, and one of the Elves threw several things at the ship. Three blurs arched across the sky, and in quick succession, Opes caught them without a sound.

"Peach?" he asked, holding them out.

"You grow them underwater?" Edis asked, taking one.

Opes just smiled, waiting for them to take a bite. Edis was a little unsure. There was an orchard in Salmont, and they grew peaches the old-fashioned way. He didn't think this water one would be the same— he was right. When he bit in, his mouth filled with juice, and he heard Laura give a little groan, as did Emma. His mouth filled with the most delicious peach he'd ever tasted.

"I'm going to assume you like them, based on the groans of delight from all of you. We can control plants perfectly, so we make the fruit just the way it needs to be. With the sea, we can make better plants, and the fruit tends to have more juice."

LAURA FINISHED THE PEACH AND DECIDED THAT EVEN IF they were never allowed to leave the capital, so long as she got peaches, she'd be fine with that. Looking over the side of the ship, the city was coming into shape. Along the shore were trees that didn't look right; they were too big and not natural looking. As they got closer and she could see more than the shape, she saw that they were buildings. She could make out terraces, doors, and windows. They were fascinating, and she wanted to examine them more. Then, as they rounded a corner, the ship entered a large harbor, and her mouth fell open.

Seeon stretched out in all its bewildering glory before her. The hillside was painted in every color of autumn, with bright dots of color from flowers that had no business being in bloom this time of the year, and all of the buildings were covered in them. The sight of it almost broke her heart. The harbor was full of ships, some like the Propero but many far more breathtaking. Before this, she'd thought she'd never seen anything more beautiful than the Propero, and now she understood that it was truly a warship.

"They are so different," Emma said, looking up.

Laura followed her gaze, and her mouth fell open again as she saw the glittering forms of Dragons over the city. She realized what Emma meant. Laura had seen a Dragon when she was finishing her certifications in Salez. Those were not like the ones she saw now; these seemed to glow like dreams coming to life.

The ship was pulling up to the dock. There were Elves in the same dark purple as Opes and his men, spread out along the dock. After the ship was tied down, they disembarked onto the dock. She'd gotten used to the constant movement of the Propero, and it felt odd to be on stable ground again. As they walked, Opes was in front, and members of the house guard flanked them. But she wasn't noticing much; she was looking for her children.

At the end of the dock, they came to a group of Elves. Everyone was dressed exquisitely, and Laura understood what Arkin meant about clothing. In the center of the group were three people. One was a blonde whose beauty was stunning even from afar, her lavender dress accenting her perfect form. Next to her was a man in a white and purple robe. He was an Elf, and he too was incredible. Next to him was a beautiful girl in a purple dress and thin white robe. The girl smiled, and Laura's heart skipped as she realized she was looking at her daughter, which meant that next to her... "Legon..." she said, trailing off. He smiled.

She wanted to run, wanted to race to her children and hold them, but she resisted, knowing they were public figures and she didn't want to break any protocol. They were at a stop now, and she could see the three people smiling warmly.

Opes spoke, "Un Prosa, as promised, your family."

Before Opes could go on, Sasha rushed forward to her mother. Laura opened her arms just in time to catch her daughter. She squeezed her tight, letting herself relax now that she knew her children were safe.

"I'm so happy to see you! Did you enjoy the Propero?" Sasha asked.

"It was wonderful! Look at you, dear; you look amazing!"

Sasha beamed at her and then turned to Edis, who scooped her up in one of his bear hugs. Laura turned to the Elf in front of her. "Legon, you look... look so..."

He smiled and hugged her. "I look different, I know." She didn't respond but ran her hands down his face, not quite believing he was real. The blonde was there now, looking at Laura in a way that made her feel like this woman had known her for years. Legon spoke, "This is my fiancée, Iselin."

Laura took in her soon-to-be daughter-in-law. "It is very nice to meet you, Iselin."

EMMA STOOD, STILL NOT SURE WHAT TO DO. THEY WERE almost to Legon, Sasha, and Legon's soon-to-be wife, Iselin. The emotions of the day were strong, and she couldn't decide how she felt. On one hand, she was sad, still mourning, and worried about the reception she would receive from the Elves. But on the other hand, she was happy for Legon's family. She was scared to talk to Sasha. What should she say?

"Sasha…" Emma started, but was cut off as Sasha hugged her. "It's all right," she whispered into her ear.

"But I'm so sorry, Sasha," she said, choking, and then Legon was there, and Sasha gave him a meaningful look.

"Hello, Em, it's been a while," he said in a smooth tone.

"Legon, thank you, and I'm sorry for…" She didn't know what she was sorry for, and she needed to control herself.

Legon leaned in and wrapped his arms around her. She felt his mind, vast and alien to her. There was an immense power she couldn't describe. The power and his mind reached into her. She felt all of her pain brought forward, and with a flick of the power, she felt the pain swept away, tossed aside. In its place, she felt Legon and his love, and then unexpectedly, she felt what must have been Sasha and her love as well. Her knees buckled, and she leaned into Legon's arms as she let all of the pain leave her from the time Kovos had left Salmont up until this second. She stood up and away from Legon, seeing compassion on his face as he said, "Welcome home."

CHAPTER 17
SETTLING IN

L aura snuggled up to Edis in the large bed that was now theirs. She wasn't too hot or cold. The bed heated and cooled based on the occupant, and she had never slept as well as she did now that she was in the capital. She turned over, looking out the window as the sun made its way up the sky, lighting the harbor. She was excited. She and Sasha were to deliver a baby this morning. She wasn't sure how you could time something like a baby, but she wasn't going to question anything. She got up and ready for the day, and made her way across the massive palace until she arrived at the designated room.

When she entered, there were people already there. A blonde Elf sat in something that looked like a chair, her belly swollen with pregnancy. Next to her, chatting with Sasha, was a brown-haired Elf who turned to look at her as she entered.

"Good morning, you must be Laura. This is my wife Elsy, and I am

Toonok." He beamed, striding across the room to grasp her hand. Elsy waved and smiled.

Laura was taken aback. She'd never seen people so calm right before a baby was about to be born. She turned to her daughter. "Okay, what do you want me to do?" This too felt odd. Sasha had helped her deliver many a baby, but Laura wasn't sure if Sasha was ready to do it on her own yet. But still...

Sasha pointed to a table with a box on it. "Will you get those for me, please, and we can start."

Laura did as she was told and picked up a light wooden box, handing it to Sasha. Laura could see that Elsy had her feet in some kind of strap, which looked uncomfortable. If she had to be there for any amount of time... Laura wasn't going to say anything, but she was definitely bothered by the total lack of concern that everyone, including Sasha, was showing.

Sasha plopped herself down on a stool and moved in closer to Elsy. She pulled out a crystal from the box. "Elsy, are you ready?"

"Yes, please. My parents are coming this afternoon to see the baby, and I don't want to rush."

She didn't want to rush? Were these people all mad? Laura had to say something. "Elsy, Toonok, I'm not sure what you think is going to happen here, but delivering a baby is a lot of work and dangerous. Elsy, I'm sorry, but you will need to rest, and who knows when this baby will come... I understand this is your first child..." She was cut off by Elsy and Toonok laughing.

Elsy spoke, "Thank you, but this is number twenty for us. We have been together for almost 4,000 years. With magic, I assure you there will be no problems today. Trust us."

Before Laura could even try to get her head around that, Sasha cut in. "Things are different here. Look, see this crystal I'm holding?" She asked, holding up a little clear crystal and then going on. "This will make it so that Elsy feels no pain. There are a series of crystals I will use that will heal any wounds the mother or baby might receive, and other crystals with spells that will even pull the baby out. Then we will place the baby on that tray you saw next to the box of crystals. From there, spells will clean the baby, check its vital signs, and determine its health.

Elsy and Toonok will be ready to leave with the newest member of their family in about twenty minutes from now."

Sasha didn't wait for a response but just started working. Laura had to admit she was of no use. She couldn't even speak most of the time; she was in so much shock. Toonok even asked if she needed anything. As Sasha had promised, in no time at all, Laura was handing a darling little boy wrapped in cloth to Elsy, who was beaming with delight. Toonok leaned in and kissed the baby and then his wife. "Thank you so much, Un Prose, this was very kind of you."

"Anytime; I love this. Babies are so cute. You have to bring him to visit."

Elsy was up and holding the baby again. "We will, you can count on it, and thank you, Laura, for your help and concern." With that, the family left, leaving Laura alone with Sasha.

The latter placed her arm around her mother. "So, what would you say to some breakfast?"

EMMA WALKED BRISKLY DOWN THE HALL, HER SHOES MAKING a staccato noise against the hard floors. She was, in effect, Sasha's assistant, a position Sasha attempted to argue but lost. Emma was going to the guest suites of the palace to make sure everyone had everything they needed. In a week, Legon and Iselin would be married. As a result, Keither, Sara, Barnin, Ankle, and Sara's friend Samantha had all arrived on one of the house ships last night. It was Emma's job to make sure they were comfortable and were otherwise able to enjoy themselves. As she had been upon arriving in Seeon, the others were overwhelmed by the city. Emma was now an expert on all things Seeon, or at least she thought she was. She knew where all the good places to eat were and where some of the more entertaining spots in town were, so that would have to be good enough.

Emma walked into a combined living room to find the group waiting for her. Barnin eyed her, raising an eyebrow. "What's with the purple, Em? Don't you have other-colored dresses?"

She stopped and looked down at herself. Her dress today was light and came up to her knees. It would be perfect for the day. "It's the house colors, and I'm house staff. Is your lot fed and watered?"

They said they were, and she nodded, thankful she didn't need to worry about that. "All right, we are going to go meet Legon and Sasha at the training field, and from there we can decide what you would all like to do. Did everyone sleep well?"

"Are we in an Elf building?" Sara asked with a chuckle.

Barnin laughed. "I don't know. I had a hard time sleeping, Sam, how about... ouch!" He stopped talking when Samantha, or Sam, hit him. Emma had figured they were together, but had a love-hate relationship, the likes of which she'd never seen.

Ankle tried not to laugh, and this earned Barnin another smack, or rather punch, on the arm. "Ouch, woman. Don't make me put you in your place," he said, rubbing his arm.

Sam puffed up. "Put me in my what? Did you just go there? I will smother you in your sleep!"

"Don't be like that, baby," Barnin said, putting his arm around Sam. She tried to hit it away, but he jabbed her side, and she laughed. "Don't tickle me, jerk face." Then Emma turned her attention away as Sam and Barnin were moving from hate to love.

SARA WAS HAPPY FOR SAM. SHE AND BARNIN WERE A GOOD fit, and they were funny to be around, but if she was being honest, the constant flirting and fighting just so they could make up was about to make her vomit.

They made their way to the training grounds to find Legon and Iselin in her dragon form in the middle of a large arena-type area. Legon had his fenna out and was doing his darnedest to try and hit Ise. She, in turn, was snapping and clawing at him. They made it to where Laura and Edis were standing with Arkin, Sydin, and Sasha.

"Is she going to kill him?" Laura asked in horror.

"Oh no, don't worry, they both have blocking spells. This is good for both of them. With their connection, they can see what the other is doing. Normally this kind of fight wouldn't happen. Any Elf Venefica is no match for an Ascended," Sydin said.

Iselin roared and snapped at Legon. He sidestepped and swung up with the fenna, grazing Ise's neck as she backed away. The fight progressed quickly, and Sara was having a hard time focusing on what Legon was doing. He was so fast. He was darting around trying to outmaneuver Ise, which seemed to be working rather well. Legon made it onto her back and was trying to hold onto one of her spikes as she bit at him. Laura looked like she was about to have a heart attack. Legon was having a hard time keeping his footing, and Ise jerked around, sending Legon sailing to the ground. He hit with a thud and was trying to get up when one of Ise's huge clawed feet slammed him back down to the ground. Now, even Edis, who had been cheering up to this point, looked worried. Legon was looking up at his soon-to-be wife and yelled, "Don't you dare!"

Iselin craned her head down to Legon's face and licked his whole head. There was a collective "Eww" from the watching group. Legon was attempting to move Ise's foot off himself while laughing. She licked him a few more times like a cat would her kittens, then her form shifted, and she was back to the breathtaking blonde. She was still on Legon, but now in one of her pink silk dresses, startling him in a suggestive way. They kissed in earnest this time, and Legon tickled her. They rolled around on the ground, the pair apparently unconcerned with any onlookers.

"Gross, get a room, you two!" Sasha shouted playfully. Iselin flicked her hand out, and a solid pink dome of magic formed, covering the couple. Sasha laughed.

Laura didn't look impressed. "They are getting married in a week; you would think they could hold it together," she sniffed.

"Attaboy," Edis said with pride, and then "Ouch!"

Laura scowled at her husband. "Nice, Edis, real nice. 'Attaboy.' So mature."

"What? They are about to get married. You remember what that was like, right? Don't you remember when we... ouch!"

She was pointing now. "No." She jabbed her finger at him again and walked off.

Sara tried not to giggle out loud. Keither was next to her. "Do you want to take a walk in the palace gardens?" he asked.

She connected and asked the others if they wanted to come, but Barnin answered for everyone, saying they had something to do. He gave Keither a look as they left. Sara thought she knew what was coming as they made their way to the gardens. She looked back over at Keither. He'd changed; there was no denying that. He'd lost a lot of weight and was doing everything he could to train both mind and body. He still was a horrid fighter; that hadn't changed, but in a way, she liked that. Keither was at the top of all of his classes and was a master at planning. He would never command armies—that wasn't his passion—though he scored high in every strategy test he took.

Sara and Keither stayed connected most of the time. It was just simpler, and while he tried to hide how he felt, she still knew. She thought about what she would say to him now if he brought that up. Would she say yes to him?

The gardens were gorgeous, with the trees turning every shade of autumn, but because the Elves controlled the place, all of the spring flowers were still in bloom. The contrast worked. Keither led her to a rail at the edge of the rooftop garden that looked out into the harbor. He leaned against it, and she noticed there was sweat on his brow.

"Sara... I think you know how I feel, and I..."

"Thought this would be the opportune time to ask me?" she poked. There was a flash of emotion on his face. "You did think so, didn't you?" She accused.

"Well, it's before a wedding. I picked the Elves' garden, and maybe put in a request for some changes to it so we could be surrounded by your favorite flowers," Keither explained.

He looked like he could go on, and she cut him off, looking around and noticing that there were lots of her favorites. "Wow, you really did put in effort, didn't you? Did you think it would take that much?"

She looked at him and thought. She knew him, knew the change, and she knew that he would never let her down or hurt her intentionally. She bit her lip, thinking. He was talking, but she wasn't paying attention. He'd be using some logical argument that would just make her want to say no. "We can try being together; how's that?" she asked, reaching out and taking his hand, which was cold and clammy, but his face was jubilant.

———

LEGON WALKED HAND IN HAND WITH ISE UP TO WHERE SARA and Keither stood, Keither's arm around Sara. Legon stopped next to Keither, whose heart was still racing. Legon placed a hand on his shoulder, and Keither started a bit.

"Sorry, I forget you can't hear as well as we do," Legon said.

"Don't you scare Sasha all the time?" Sara asked.

"They are too connected, and her guard is never far," Iselin supplied, and then went on. "Do you like our city?" she said, sweeping her hand out to the glittering harbor.

"It's amazing," Keither said. "Thank you for having us."

"You are welcome anytime you like," Legon said. "So, I hear that you both are doing well, and that if you would like, you can deploy. Is that something that you want?"

Keither and Sara, while Humans, were not part of the Cona Republic, nor were they citizens of the Pawdin Empire. Only Sasha could claim that. Rather, Sara and Keither were under political asylum under the protection of House Evindass. This meant that the Human and Elf factions could not take command of them; only House Evindass could.

"We'd like to stay together. I have been working in local hospitals," Sara said.

"And I've been invited to sit in on some strategy sessions and organize some refugee camps and the like," Keither said, and then paused. "But I would like to seek higher-level training, if that would be okay with you?" Then, turning to Sara, "Unless you don't want to go?" She squeezed his arm and was about to speak when Ise cut them off.

"Answer in your minds; it keeps you more connected," she said warmly.

Legon waited for a moment, and when Keither seemed to relax and the back of his neck reddened, Legon thought he knew Sara's answer. "All of your instructors have spoken rather highly of you, Keither. There is no higher level in Manton. You will have to move here for six or so months."

Keither looked a little crestfallen, not understanding Legon's invitation. "Does living in the palace for six months sound that bad to you?"

"You mean I could study here? No Human has ever attended an Elvin school before."

"That's not true," Iselin said. "There have been a few, but less since the Iumenta began to infect Humanity. We couldn't risk a spy, but you two are far from being spies. It will be nice to have you around."

Legon felt Sydin's mind. "We are about ready."

He thanked Sydin and spoke out loud to the group. "Iselin and I have a meeting. Keither, I would like you to attend for part of it, if you don't mind. Sara, Sasha is planning on spending the afternoon with you and your friend Samantha, if that is okay with you."

They didn't object and all made their way back into the palace. Legon led them down a hall until they reached a large set of double doors. "This is the war room," he said.

Sasha and Emma walked up with Arkin, Barnin, Ankle, and Sam in tow. "Boys, you have fun. Come on, ladies," she said, pulling Sara and Sam along. Sam looked overwhelmed and not keen on the idea of being away from Barnin, but Legon was sure that she would be well cared for in Sasha's capable hands. The doors opened, and Legon entered with the others. Around the large crystal table were Sydin and the rest of Legon's military advisors, along with some from a few of the other great houses. As the doors closed, the table glowed white and projected a three-dimensional map of Airmelia just above its surface. It was a mark of Barnin and Ankle's training that they didn't make a sound. As for Keither, he would have seen one of these during his training.

"May I ask what it takes to power this thing?" Ankle asked.

Sydin responded. "While the image may seem complex, the projection of a map isn't extremely difficult, but it's nothing to the magic it takes to run all of the other things this map does. The spells it requires are immense. You are only seeing the top of the crystal. The remainder extends three floors down. There are only about twenty of these outside of those in the Dragon Domes."

Legon adjusted the map with his mind, moving it in close around the border. "Barnin, we get reports, but you've been on the ground. What can you tell us?"

Barnin moved closer with Ankle and then spoke, pointing along the border. "As we thought, for the first few weeks we didn't get any resistance, but as time passed, the Empire tightened the area up." He circled an area around the Precipice. "This area here we hit the hardest, so there are high amounts of military around there now."

"Are you still doing a lot of damage?" Sydin asked.

Ankle spoke up, a little defensive. "We can't all go in anymore. That size of a group attracts attention. We have to be careful, but yes, we are still doing what we can."

"Perfect work, good job. How is the refugee situation? I understand it's been a problem," Legon said. He didn't want Ankle and Barnin to think that they were failing in any way, shape, or form, but they couldn't know the whole picture.

Keither spoke this time. "At first, people stopped crossing the border, but after a few months, the Empire started openly allowing large groups of people to pass. In the beginning, command thought they were trying to strain resources, but it became apparent that they were using the large groups of people to smuggle soldiers into the Republic."

"Is this still a problem?" Iselin asked.

Keither adjusted the map to show a small valley. "We are using this as a staging area for refugees. They come in and are processed. With help from the Pawdin Empire, food, water, clothing, and shelter were a non-issue."

"But it wasn't always that way," Legon said. He wanted Keither to take credit where it was due, and he was due some serious credit.

"Yeah, well, I asked to help, and I was the only one on the strategy committee that was part of the refugee area. Anyway, that valley," he pointed. "It does have spring water, but food and shelter were a problem. Like most things in the Cornis Mountains, it's difficult to supply, and with the number of people moving in and out, it would have been impossible. But I asked the Pawdin Empire for some assistance, and we found ways to use Elvin technology to bring food up the mountain, along with medical supplies. I also asked the Elves to grow shelters, and they grew the windmill used to power a gondola system."

There were nods from others in the room, and Legon was pleased. Keither made it sound easy, but what he had done was a bit of a miracle. He had found a way of shipping food for thousands downriver from the Pawdin lands and then have it carried hundreds of feet up the side of a mountain. Legon decided to comment on what he had done. "Keither, you make this sound small, but in reality, what you did has saved lives. By using this valley, the Cona army has been able to find insurgents and still care for sick and homeless people without putting a burden on the rest of their country. Furthermore, if this could not have happened, the Cona Republic would have been forced to turn people away—people who would have been killed or starved. It is for this reason that you will be allowed to study in Seeon."

Legon knew that the other houses would not be overly thrilled about Keither being allowed to study in the capital. In the past, only those who had shown considerable potential were allowed in. Keither needed to be understood as one of those people so that he would not be viewed as someone given favors by House Evindass.

Barnin continued his report, and when he was done, he, Keither, and Ankle left, leaving Arkin. "We know how well you've been doing," Sydin said wryly.

Arkin smiled. "Yes, well, it helps that the Cona lands were closer to breaking than we thought. As ordered, we have toned down our work."

"That's good, and right before the invasion, we will have to turn it back up. The ratio of Elf to Iumenta Ascended is still not where we need it to be, nor will it be for many years to come. The Iumenta showed that they too are willing to change tactics. The refugees were sign enough of that."

"It should be noted that about a week ago, groups of people just stopped crossing the border," Iselin pointed out.

"Yes, I suspect that once they realized they weren't getting anything out of using refugees, they just started killing anyone who came too close to the border," Legon said bitterly. "Opes, do we know anything more about the ship that attacked you?"

Opes shook his head. "No, Un Prosa, we don't; but based on the fact that it wasn't Hoelaria, I would say that we can assume that the Impa Provinces are doing some intelligence work of their own."

Unlike the Elves, the Iumenta did not have a house-based system, but rather the country was broken down into Provinces. Everything was owned by the government, and everyone started at the bottom of society. It was only with age that one rose in society. Hoelaria was an exception to this rule. She had somehow taken control of the smallest province in the Impa lands, but the one that bordered with Humanity. Her takeover of the Cona lands gained her Province enough land and resource holdings to actually take over the Impa government. The Pawdin Empire didn't know much about how it happened, but from all accounts, it was a project she'd started working on shortly after the War of Generations. It took her 600 years to gain control over her little province and another 1,300 to fully control the Impa government.

"Do you think there is some trouble inside the Impa Empire?" Sydin asked.

"Could be, but more likely if they thought they had sensitive information, they may not have wanted any form of their business to even be around Human ears; it's hard to tell."

They continued talking for hours about what might or might not be going on in the Impa lands. They also discussed tactics for starting a sea campaign. Legon was exhausted by the time he left for the day. He and Iselin went to the dining hall to see that most of their guests were still sitting around having drinks and talking. It was nice to see them enjoying themselves.

Sasha walked over to them. "How'd it go?" she asked, and then proceeded to view all of Legon's memories, bringing them into her mind. "That's good to know, thank you," she said, not wanting to say more around other people.

Legon and Iselin plopped down, and an Elf brought them each a plate of food.

"How do they know what you want to eat?" Sam asked, looking at the plates of food and then instantly backpedaled. "Oh, sorry, Un Prosa, I mean, ah..."

Legon laughed. "Sam, right?" She nodded. "Sasha is connected to me, and when we got out of the meeting, she rummaged around our heads and told the kitchen what we wanted. Don't worry about formality around us; it really isn't our style. So, how's Barnin treating you?"

Sam looked elated that Legon knew her name, but Barnin didn't let her answer. "I'm the greatest man she's been with; what do you think?" he said sarcastically.

Sasha leaned into Sam and wrapped her arm around her shoulder. "Oh dear, you're young; don't settle. Hold out for someone better, all right?" Sam laughed, and Legon added in, "Yeah, really, if you think this is the best you can do..."

"Screw you, and screw you," Barnin said, pointing to Legon and Sasha in turn and then to Iselin. "You too, Sparkles. I know you and Legon are connected, so you get at least half credit for him now."

"Sparkles?" Iselin asked, trying to sound offended.

"Yeah, Sparkles, when you're a lizard and then that junk is in your eyes... Sparkles."

"I will eat you," Iselin threatened.

And that was the end of civil conversation for the rest of the night.

CHAPTER 18
WED

"It has been said that the Everser Vald was an unstoppable, driven man, but to those that knew him in those days, they saw a man of joy with a great and terrible purpose."
— Excerpts from The Diary of the Adopted Sister

Sasha couldn't remember having more fun. The week leading up to the wedding was beyond busy, but she was enjoying herself. Legon, like most men, cared not at all about most of the wedding. He just wanted to know where to show up, when he was to show up, and what he was to wear. Sasha told Legon to turn around in a circle.

"Sash, this is ridiculous. Why can't we just have a small ceremony with family and friends, and then Ise and I can leave so we can consummate our marriage?" he asked, winking.

She scowled. "That's nice. I'm glad to see you have your priorities in line," then she muttered, "Consummate, honestly."

Legon tried a different tack. "Ise doesn't want a big production either..."

Sasha huffed. "You are the head of a great house. You have to do it. And also, who said weddings are for the bride and groom? Weddings are for the rest of us to celebrate that our loved ones aren't defective and were able to find someone and turn into normal people. Now go put on the black one."

Legon got serious. "Not defective?" he said, leaning over to kiss her forehead before going to change.

She was thankful that he left the room to change. She hadn't even picked up on what she was saying when she was giving him a hard time about the wedding. But she had to ask: did she believe that? Did she believe that those who stayed alone were 'defective?' Was Emma defective? No, she had someone who was taken from her. What about Arkin? There seemed to be something with him and that Stacy girl he worked with. Keither and Sara were together... was she the defective one? In the Cona Empire, she knew that she was, and was told that she was, but what about now? She couldn't leave the Pawdin Empire; she had too much to do, but what Elf would take her? She thought about it for a while and absentmindedly rubbed a bruise on her hip from where she had fallen that morning at the onset of an episode.

Legon stepped back into the room and read her face and thoughts, coming over next to her, wrapping his arms around her and resting his chin on the top of her head. "Never think that, Sash. You're too good for all of them anyway. Whatever happened to that Edling guy? Do you still keep in contact with him?"

"Ed... Edling?" she muttered. He'd remembered him? "Not really. I talk to his father. We have been working on some crystals..."

Legon chuckled. "Sash, I don't mean about rocks. Do you talk to him? He had a thing for you."

"No, he didn't. I thought he might, but I'm sure it wasn't anything."

She felt Legon tense a little and then relax and chuckle again. "Well, he did have a thing for you, I promise."

She looked up at him dubiously. He didn't need further prodding. "Would you be very angry if I had him looked into..."

"You had him what?" she said, half-agitated and surprised.

Legon backed away, trying to make peace. "So maybe I was still a little overprotective, ya know, and even though I knew we would know if he was a bad guy as soon as you two connected, I thought, 'Hey, why not make sure?' So I may have had some of the house guard do a little digging and..."

"You had them spy on him!" There was no more surprise, just agitation and extreme embarrassment now.

"Whoa there, don't freak out. He didn't know, but they asked around and... some other things, and anyway, he did talk about you and he definitely had a thing for you, so let's not focus on me, but on the fact that he likes you."

LEGON WAS A LITTLE AMAZED AT HOW MANY OCTAVES Sasha's voice could go up when she was mad at him. To be truthful, he wasn't sure Humans could even hear anything that high-pitched. He had it coming, that was for sure; he was out of line for doing what he did, but it was fun and useful. He made a mental note to talk to Edling's father and try to get him to bring his son back to the capital.

Iselin's voice popped into Legon's head. "What is she on about? I've never seen her upset before."

"I told her about having Edling spied on."

Iselin laughed. "Fair enough. It's kind of funny, isn't it? Why did you tell her anyway?"

"She needed to hear that someone wants her. She needs to know she's not 'defective.' Now she knows, and like you said, it's funny when she's this mad—watch this."

Legon reached forward like the lash of a snake and flicked the end of her nose. "That's enough, peanut; calm down now."

Sasha went speechless with rage and then, after a moment, she deflated. "You are such a jerk!"

Iselin's voice was back. "Really, that's all it takes?" Legon responded to her, "Yeah, she has to just get it out of her system, and she hates to have her nose flicked. It's like it burns all the anger out of her."

"Are you still mad, Sash?" Legon asked.

She scowled. "Yes; you owe me. Just for that, I'm going to add on to your wedding reception," she said, sticking out her tongue and walking off.

"Oh, come on," Legon groaned.

Iselin was not so amused now. "What? Why do I get punished? You were the creep who had her boyfriend followed! Dang it, Legon!"

Sasha made good on her promise, and even though the wedding was the next day, he saw a revised schedule, prolonging the reception. The guests were happy, at least.

The day of his wedding, Legon woke up, showered, and dressed. Unlike Iselin, who had been up for hours by now getting ready, this was turning out to be a fairly normal morning for Legon. He sat on the terrace eating breakfast with his father.

"Men really do have it easy, don't we?" he asked his father.

Edis smiled. "Yes, we do. Other than taking a little extra time to shave, our wedding day grooming doesn't take much effort. So tell me, your clothes have a hole over your tattoo; what's that about?"

Legon sipped his juice. "Humans use rings as part of the ceremony, but Elves do not. Instead, the one performing the ceremony is a Venefica. When he pronounces us Perpetuo, he will change our tattoos. The empty dot in mine will take on Iselin's mark, and her tattoo will take on mine. The patterns will appear to continue indefinitely, like our love."

Edis was silent for a moment. "And why is it Perpetuo?"

"Because we are married for time and all eternity. You see, we believe that by melding our minds in the way we do, we are actually binding our souls as well. That is why when one dies, so does the other."

"But I thought that was because part of your mind dies?" Edis asked.

Legon took a moment to try and organize his response. "Yes, that is the technical term, but over great distances, Elves cannot network their minds, and they don't die then. Also, even if an Elf is too far away to connect to their spouse, if their spouse dies, they do too. How could that be if the soul wasn't connected? At least, that's what many Elves believe."

This was an odd conversation to be having. His father never talked about religion. It wasn't that they didn't have beliefs, but rather that the conversation just didn't come up all that often.

"What do you believe, son?" Edis asked.

"I don't know, but I have faith that it's true. I hope that after today, Iselin and I will be together forever." And he did. Maybe it was Iselin rubbing off on him, but for the first time in his life, he could say that he had faith.

Edis looked happier than Legon had ever seen him. "You will, son, you will," he said, a little choked up.

"Are you okay?" Legon asked.

Edis nodded and uncharacteristically dabbed his eyes. "I never thought you'd have this day, Legon. I always thought you'd have to take care of your sister. I always just wanted you two to be happy together, you know. And when you left..."

"You thought you'd lost us," Legon finished.

Edis only nodded.

Before they could say more, Sydin walked out onto the terrace. "It's time."

"We'd better not be late," Edis said.

Sydin gestured for them to follow and then turned back and pointed to the sky. "Legon, you see the guard is flying cap today over the ceremony. You should know we are not worried about any attack, but should you and Iselin have any plans of flying off and ditching the rest of us right after you're Perpetuod, the guard will make sure you make it back to the reception," Sydin said with a smile.

Dang it, Legon thought. He opened the connection with Iselin. "What is it?" she asked. He told her what the guard was to do if they left, and she took a moment. "That's not fair! Both Sydin and Opes did that very same thing. How dare they corner us!"

"Legon, stop bothering Ise. So help me, I'll fly up there myself. You two are going to have a good time; don't be difficult," Sydin ordered.

EMMA MADE HER WAY ALONG A COBBLED PATH THAT LED TO the grove where the wedding was to be held. Her escort was Ankle. He was nice enough but looked uncomfortable being around all of the finery that was the Pawdin Empire. One advantage was that he was rather tall, which meant she could wear whatever shoes she liked. This was rare for her, and while she thought she would probably regret six-inch heels once the dancing started, she was happy right now. They slowed as they reached the back of the line going into the grove. She hadn't been allowed in to see it. Sasha wanted the venue's decorations to be a surprise. Emma and Ankle made it to the archway that led inside the grove. The grove had been surrounded by a large hedge that obscured the view inside. The hedge made a wall of pink and lavender flowers that rose ten or fifteen feet high. A member of the house guard nodded, and they entered.

"Wow," Ankle said.

"Wow" didn't really cover it. Sasha had the grove grown for the occasion, and the Elves did not disappoint. It was a large, flat, oval-shaped space with a perfectly manicured lawn. White chairs with soft seats were lined up in front of a raised platform and altar. Surrounding everything were Aspen trees, but not any normal Aspen trees. Their trunks were perfect, without blemish, and seemed to have a silver hue to them. The leaves were autumn gold and had been enhanced to slightly shine. The leaves had bright silver edges to them. If this and all the many flowers that littered the area weren't enough, there were crystals in the trees making the canopy sparkle, giving the place a dream-like appearance.

They made their way to the third row, and Emma found her seat. Almost all of the guests were seated. Emma didn't know many of them, but from all of the white she was seeing, she could gather that all of the heads of house were in attendance. She turned to Ankle. "All twelve heads of the great houses are here today," she whispered to him.

Ankle tensed and looked around. "Whoa, I mean, I guess it makes sense, but we better not trip or make ourselves look like fools. I don't want to go home and tell people that."

Trip? She hadn't thought about that. She looked down at her shoes and cursed herself. There was nothing to be done now. Maybe Opes could help her out with a little magic...

She looked up to the platform where Legon, the groomsmen, and

Opes, who was officiating, were standing. Keither was the best man. Standing next to him was Barnin, then Edis, Sydin, and Arkin. All were dressed in purple. It was tradition that the groomsmen wore colors that matched the color of the tattoo of the groom, and the bridesmaids did the same. Legon was in all black, accented with a white shirt and a high collar. Music near the entrance started to play. Emma turned in her seat, looking back to see an orchestra she hadn't even noticed.

Sasha was, of course, the maid of honor. It had been she who poked and prodded Ise and Legon into courting, so she'd earned it. She was in a pink gown that looked incredible on her. She moved with grace down the aisle, oozing with satisfaction at her handiwork. Sasha was followed by Iselin's sisters, who also looked radiant. Then it was time for Ise to walk down the aisle. Everyone stood as her father escorted her along. He was tall with brown hair and hazel eyes and wore a grin that was probably a permanent feature on his face. Iselin was amazing, covered in white lace. Her gown was large and puffed out with a long train. Lace covered her arms down to her hands and wrapped around her neck up to her chin. Emma was confused. The Elves, while not immodest, didn't hide their form or skin with any of their attire, but here today the bride and groom were all but covered with cloth. It wasn't until Iselin passed and Legon took her hand and they turned to Opes that she saw it. On both their backs were openings that revealed their tattoos. On Legon, the hole in the garment was surrounded by pink fabric, and on Ise, the hole was surrounded by lavender.

"What's with the backs?" Ankle asked.

Emma whispered back, "Today is about Iselin and Legon being married. If you notice, on each of them, the predominant feature in their attire is their mark, and today, as both those marks will be changing, it is the focal point... I think."

Everyone sat. As Opes began his remarks, he spoke about the power of love and the responsibility of marriage. His remarks were not long. Unlike Human marriages, there were no vows exchanged and no elaborate rituals performed. Instead, the audience was asked to ponder the meaning of this union and how they could best support the new couple. There was a flash of light from the altar, and Legon and Iselin's tattoos were changed.

LEGON WATCHED AS ISELIN WALKED TO HIM, HER FATHER holding her slightly back. She looked stunning, and he used every memory technique he knew to ensure that he would never forget today. To his right stood Keither, standing as proxy for Kovos. Legon could see that today was affecting Keither as well. His position was a reminder of Kovos and his sacrifice. Today he would do his brother's memory proud.

Teenki and Iselin approached, and Legon took Iselin's hand. They stood side by side, their hands hot in each other's. Slightly turned to each other, Legon was able to make out Iselin's elaborate hair, piled high on her head, and the lace dress, but it was her eyes that he couldn't help but notice. They were the same blue-green that had transfixed him when they first met, the ones he saw every time his eyes closed. Now they would be the last thing he would see each night and the first each day.

"Stop, you're going to make me cry," she said into his mind, but it was hardly a command or even a request. She was just as happy as he was.

Opes was talking about something, but he wasn't sure what it was. Elves kept weddings short with the bride and groom being mentally connected. They almost never paid attention to the words that were being spoken. So common was this that Opes had to jab their minds when it was time for them to have their tattoos changed.

Legon refocused as Opes spoke. "And now, in the name of the White Dragon, I Perpetuo you, Iselin and Legon, for time and for all eternity." There was a flash of light, and Legon felt his tattoo change.

Legon looked into his wife's eyes, which were glassy and shiny, then he leaned forward, and they kissed. It wasn't long or passionate; it was a soft and caring kiss that said from both, "You are more important than anything else in this world." Then the guests clapped, and the orchestra started to play. Legon was soon to learn that the reverie and reserve that was the norm for his race was done for the day.

Once the main event was done, the bride and groom were swamped with guests congratulating them. Legon felt time blur as they were approached by each head of house, his family, and Iselin's family, and the procession of all their friends. Before he knew it, the sun was setting, and the grove was being lit with magical lights in the trees. People began to dance and eat, and Legon and Iselin were pulled onto the dance floor for their first dance.

Everyone cleared off so they could have it to themselves, and Ise leaned into Legon. "This has been a lot more fun than I thought, but I'm a little tired," she said into his ear.

"I know what you mean, but I'm glad we didn't sneak off."

"And our families are so happy. I don't think I've seen anyone cry so much in one day as your mother."

Legon chuckled. "Yeah, she's like that at weddings, but to be honest with you, everything has been a blur since our marks were changed."

The song had changed, and people were now on the dance floor. Ise let go of Legon and smiled.

"Thank you," Sasha said, taking Iselin's place.

Sasha beamed up at Legon. "So you're pretty proud of yourself, aren't you?" he asked.

She shrugged in a non-committal way. "Well, with us being connected and all, it was pretty easy to find the right one for you."

Legon laughed. "Really? What about all the girls you tried to set me up with before?"

She was unfazed. "They were merely to show you just how perfect you and Ise are together. Think of them as a point of reference."

"Excuse me, Un Prose, but may I cut in?" a sweet voice said.

Legon turned to see Edling, with his mother standing next to them. Sasha's face flushed a bit, and the woman spoke again. "May I have a dance with the new groom?"

"Of course," Legon said.

Edling's mother went on. "Edling, dear. You and your friend here should catch up. Why don't you two dance together?" She said, giving Edling a not-so-subtle nudge. Sasha went on her own accord, but Legon saw her give him a stern look.

"Thank you for that," Legon said, taking the sable-haired woman in his arms and starting to twirl.

"No; thank you, Un Prosa. He won't stop jabbering about her, but he doesn't have the nerve to do anything about it—it's a start."

"It doesn't bother you that she's Human?" Legon asked.

"No. I suppose it should, her being mortal and all, but it may not go anywhere. If it does go somewhere, then they were meant to be, right?" she asked. Legon nodded.

Before long, Opes came back up to Legon with Iselin in tow. It was time for them to leave. As was the tradition, an Ascended would fly the new couple to wherever it was they were going for their honeymoon. Even though Iselin was Ascended, the gesture was a gift to the new couple, so Opes would be taking them to the Golden City. The City was named such because it was grown entirely out of Aspen trees and was kept in a perpetual state of autumn. It was this city that inspired Sasha's grove today.

The guests cleared off the floor, and Opes transformed into a giant red dragon. Iselin and Legon used Opes's leg as a step and sat sidesaddle on his shoulders. Legon felt a sticking spell, and Opes launched into the sky. As they flew away from Seeon, Legon wrapped his arms around Iselin, and they looked off into the horizon.

CHAPTER 19

REFLECT AND PREPARE

"What is it that controls the future? Is it the past? I would say so. Without the past, we have no point of reference to move from."
— Articles of the Mahann

Keither sat on the edge of the bed, running his finger along the intricate flames of the sword. His mind reviewed the three years since his brother's death. What would Kovos think of him now? Everyone else's opinion had changed. He'd gone to school with the Elves, married Sara, and was even relatively fit. He patted his belly—well, maybe not fit. He still could not fight to save his life and had some social issues, but he'd moved up fast in rank, earning the title of Supply Commander. When the invasion happened, he would be one of the lead people in taking care of supply routes and rebuilding efforts. A soft hand rubbed his back.

"What are you doing up so early?" Sara asked groggily.

"Today is the day it happened."

Lethargy left her, and she sat behind him, wrapping her arms around his shoulders. "Are you okay?"

Keither turned his head, giving Sara a kiss. "Yeah, I'm just looking back at everything, you know?"

She nodded.

The morning was uneventful. Keither always cleared his schedule on this day. Sara and he would spend the evening with Keither's family. Well, with his parents, anyway. No one had heard from his other brother in a few years. There was no reason to think that anything was amiss, but there wasn't much in the way of communication with people in the Cona Empire. Legon and Sasha's plan had worked. The Cona lands were all but shattering under their own weight. Keither sighed. The invasion would happen within a few years. The Cona Republic and Pawdin Empire were not leaving anything to chance. They would not invade until they knew they would have a clear victory. While he hated to think of people suffering, Keither agreed with this. The war would not be won with forces of the Cona Republic. While more trained than the average Cona Empire soldiers, the Republic was vastly outnumbered. This meant that the Elves would have to carry the standard of the resistance across Airmelia. The Iumenta forces had to be weakened in order for this to work. If they were equal to the Elves, then all would be lost. If the Iumenta's strength was that of the Elves, then the Elves would be forced to take on their equals along with the Human military of the Cona Empire—a war the Elves could not win. But the Iumenta were not as strong as the Elves, not anymore, and the Cona Empire itself was beginning to crumble. Sometimes Keither wondered if the Elves and Cona Republic would have anything to conquer in the next few years.

Legon and Sydin walked down the road that led to the harbor. Today they were going to inspect the state of the house fleet. A majority of ships were out to sea, but much of the fleet was anchored in the harbor. Also, several ships were under construction, including a new carrier. Each of the Great Houses laid claim to some military prowess. Naval power was not the claim of House Evindass; that honor belonged to House Insa. Their navy was large and powerful, bringing the Impa forces to their knees in the War of Generations. Their navy was almost the entire focus of the House military. When the invasion came, it would be House Insa that would command the Elvin fleet. House Floren would be handling any construction and food needed as they focused on plant growth. House Coreen would lead the ground forces. If the Pawdin Empire had a set of Great Houses that were more powerful than the rest, they would be Evindass, Coreen, Floren, and Insa. Evindass was all about magic. Evindass had the most Venefica and Ascended. They also were the primary suppliers of crystals and crystal development. It would be Evindass that would control the magic users in the war, putting them in charge of securing the air.

Legon stood, looking up the bow of the massive carrier sitting in dry dock. This one and her two sister ships would be released into the water within a month. There were others too, some coming out from storage, but many new vessels were under construction.

"Where does the fleet stand?" Legon asked.

"When these are done, we will have ten carrier battle groups. This is the largest our fleet has been since the War of Generations. With the other houses, the Pawdin fleet will be able to secure the coast," Sydin said with pride.

Legon knew they were going to need every ship. The Cona fleet would be large, if not mostly Human and ineffectual. The learning houses for magic were going seven days a week now, with Venefica coming from everywhere to prepare themselves for the coming war. High above Seeon, Ascended after Ascended jumped in and out of the city's airspace as all came in for advanced training and conditioning. The Pawdin military had taken a backseat since the War of Generations, but now everyone was trying to re-hone their skills. Legon toured the rest of the fleet with Sydin until after lunch and then returned back to the palace.

SASHA WAS IN THE GOLDEN CITY SPEAKING AT A conference. They had made headway. At first, her orders to look into Iumenta crystals were met with polite tolerance, but not anymore. She hadn't been the one to make any significant discoveries, but her team, taking her lead, looked into combining known Iumenta techniques with that of the Elves, and they had several successes. It was about six months into the whole experiment when they started seeing results, but a year ago the team had had a major breakthrough. They were able to create crystals far more advanced than the ones the Pawdin Empire currently used, and maybe in a few decades they would be able to surpass that of the Iumenta.

Sasha was sitting outside the hall where she was speaking, taking a break before she had to go in and speak again.

"Long day?" Emma asked.

Sasha smiled at her. She was thankful to have Emma around. "Yes, but good. I'm glad to see the rest of the country take what we are doing seriously. I don't think we will make any real advancement before the war, but our current crystals are still more powerful."

"But you've made strides, and that's what matters, right?" Emma asked.

"Yes, and I think in the long run it will be helpful. I just wish there was more we could do to assist our country before..."

Emma rubbed her hand up and down Sasha's back. "We won't go to war for a while still, probably not even another year or two."

This was true. Even though it appeared as though they were about to go to war, it was far from the case. Legon was due to tour the house fleet that day, but Evindass was far ahead in their preparations than many of the other houses, and the Iumenta still had too many dragons. While Emma wasn't completely in the loop, Sasha was. From the current state, the optimal time for attack wouldn't be for a year and a half. However, there was the chance that the Cona Empire would try to attack before they lost their advantage. It was unlikely, but the Great Houses were prepared for it. It would be difficult for the Cona forces to attack the Pawdin border, as it was protected by the Mahj Line, but the Cona Republic was a different story. The Cona Empire had the forces on the border capable of an attack, which put the Cona Republic and House Paldin in the position of making sure the Precipice was able to hold its own. The Cona lands could also be invaded by sea, which put

House Insa in the situation of having to be ready to repel a naval invasion without much notice.

Sasha answered Emma's implied question. "Yes, this is true. The
new carriers will be assisting House Insa. They will need a significant
magical advantage if they are to stop a possible Impa or Cona naval invasion without the aid of the rest of the Pawdin fleet."

A mental nudge told her it was time to go back into the conference.

LEGON WAS IN THE PRACTICE ARENA WITH MAGE. THEY
were working on a technique with the fenna and using a familiar. Legon's
familiar, Bill, was in his fully released form and looked like a lion. Mage's
fox was also released and the same size as Bill. The two sets of combatants
circled one another. He felt the magic course out of his body and into the
blade as he moved, syncing his mind with Bill's. In this form, the familiar
had an aggressive edge to him. He wanted to fight and was looking
forward to it, but he was also being smart. Bill, in essence, lived in Legon's
mind; therefore, he reacted in the same manner Legon did to each situation. Venefica and familiars were forces to be reckoned with when they
were in tune with one another, a skill Mage had learned a millennia ago.

The golden fox barreled forward, rushing Bill, and at the last second,
he leaped to the side at Legon, who swung his fenna Tento up,
deflecting the fox. The cutting spell in the Tento caused the familiar to
shift its form, giving Legon a moment to attack Mage, who was warding
off Bill. Bill took over the fight with Mage's familiar, leaving the two
class fives to each other. Mage grinned, loving the challenge that Legon
posed. Most heads of house, while decent fighters, did not put in the
effort that Legon did. As a result, he was more skilled than most, even
though the other heads had thousands of years on him. Legon did not
make it a secret that when the war started, he would be in the thick of
battle with the rest of his house's forces. This attitude gained the head of
House Evindass many loyal followers throughout the different military
units. Mage sent fire at Legon, which he deflected with Tento. He sent a
pain spell at Mage, causing a glow of gold magic to form around him.

Legon was a biological Venefica, which, while not the most effective in combat, gave him a few choice spells at which he was adept.

Mage jumped back and growled, "Binon." His fenna exploded with a thick cord of golden fire. Legon raised Tento, calling, "Binon." A rush of lavender burst from Tento, creating a wall that stopped Mage's attack. Legon felt the power drain from him as he released Binon. Choosing to attack, he slashed Tento across his body, keeping the magic in close to the flame. It made contact with Mage's fenna with a loud crack like thunder. Legon felt more drained. This was the drawback to being a biologic. While he could heal a large group with Binon or grow something, stopping Mage's elemental attack required Legon to use either an element or pure power to stop the onslaught.

"Good, Un Prosa; now let's see if you can stay at Binon for more than one attack."

ISELIN SQUINTED INTO THE SUNLIGHT, TRYING TO SPOT HIM. He was out here, she knew it; but she was having a hard time finding him. Class sevens, while large, were rather proficient at hiding themselves when they wanted to. She wove her way through the misted peaks of the mountains. Above her was the too-bright sun, below her jagged peaks, and in between; unnatural mist and clouds. The temptation to use magic was overwhelming, but if she did that, the game exercise would be over.

Sydin's voice rang in her mind. "No, no Ise, no magic, tsk tsk," he chided.

She didn't respond. That also was against the rules. That's when she saw it—just a glimpse of green, and she knew she had him. Iselin caught a thermal and rode it, stalking her prey from on high. Like her, he would be blinded by the glare. His tail slipped through the mist, and she saw the hint of a green trail. Magic was energy; energy that people could see when powerful spells were used, but those who were Ascended were more attuned to it; the stronger Venefica you were, the more you could see. Magic left its mark wherever it was, and if you paid attention, you could see and feel it. This was the point of the exercise, to teach her how to more fully notice magic. An Ascended was magic incarnate, which meant they left a mark on the world. Furthermore, immortals could sense the electrical impulses that living things used. It was weak, but it was there. For a dragon, this was more so, but she had to focus on it.

She closed her eyes, letting other senses take over. She was flying as silently as she could, using the thermals and the wind as much as possible, but she could still hear Ampus' wings thudding. It was just trying to pin down the location of the sound that was so difficult in these peaks. She focused, feeling the air and listening so she didn't smack into the side of a peak. She paid close attention to her sense of impulses and sense of magic. She groped around her until she found it. He was right under her. She folded her wings to her side, going into a dive and opening her eyes. As the mist rushed by her, she felt his magic. When she focused on him, it was distinct; she could almost see him in her mind as she felt the impulses going to his muscles. Her wings opened just at the right moment, and she glided in behind him. His massive form flew in front of her; he was completely unaware she was there.

"Got ya," she said to all the minds around her.

Ampus snapped his head back to look behind him and he growled, "What? How did you do that? I was using every concealment spell I know." This she had assumed. The rules were different for everyone. In an exercise, each Ascended had something specific they were there to learn. Ampus' was obviously concealment.

Sydin's voice rang out. "Very good, Iselin. Ampus, you did well, too. It took her a long time to find you. So what did we learn?"

"That magic isn't everything, and that sometimes it can be a hindrance," Iselin said, put out. She hated not using magic, but the point was well taken. Ampus had been using powerful concealment spells. These would hide him from most any seeking spell. He was a class seven, and a large one at that. There wouldn't be any out there more powerful than he. But these were the spells that would get him caught. Had he used passive magic or had he hidden the impulses in his muscles and focused on using the terrain, mist, and sun, Ise would have never found him.

Ampus and Sydin were quiet as she thought. Sydin was satisfied and Ampus impressed. Sydin spoke, "Iselin is known for being a prodigy with magic, and she is so good at it—to a fault—in that she relies on it too much. As for you, Ampus, you are large for a class seven and extremely powerful. You don't use stealth at all; you use your brute strength and your physical size to dominate an opponent. And because of the vast magical power your sheer size affords you, you expect to be protected from a magical attack. Ise, had you used magic, Ampus would have found you, and in single combat, he would have defeated you. Ampus, she was able to sneak up on you, even though she has nowhere near the magical strength you possess. Had she gotten close enough, she could have come right down on your back and killed you with a bite to the base of your neck and head." This was true. While a class six and seven were closer in magical power than, say, a class four and five, a class seven was about 20 percent larger in physical size. Most of the time, if a six took down a seven, they were either extremely skilled or they had been lucky and killed the seven within the first few moments of a fight.

They made their way back to Seeon, coming in as the sun was setting.

"Would you care to join us tonight, Ampus?" Iselin asked. "Or you, Sydin?"

"My wife and I have plans, but thank you, Ise," Sydin said.

"I would love to; thank you," Ampus replied.

Iselin liked Ampus. They knew each other from when they both first ascended. Ampus was from House Metlum, which specialized in all things metal. Ampus did his house proud. He was an elemental and was adept at working with metals. As they approached the palace, Iselin could feel Legon. He was just getting out of the shower after spending much of the afternoon training. He was happy to feel her coming home.

"We have company for dinner, love," she said.

———

Legon watched as Iselin and Ampus approached. A few years ago, he would have never connected the difference between the size of dragons and their class. Ise came in first, shifting as she landed on the terrace, followed by Ampus. As always, Legon grinned broadly when Ise walked up to him and wrapped her arms around his neck. He leaned down and kissed her, feeling like he always did—that he had married up.

"How was your day?" he asked.

Iselin rolled her eyes. "You didn't marry up." She kissed him again. "Today was good. I think I got what Sydin's been harping on about." Then she turned in Legon's arms to look at Ampus. "And I beat him," she said, pointing, "so that always makes for a good day."

Ampus gave her a look and smiled. "I felt sorry for you; you've never beaten me before." He directed his words to Legon. "And we all know how the pink fury gets when she doesn't have her way," he said with a wink.

Legon laughed. "Pink fury, I like that. Ouch!" He moved to grab Ise's hand so she couldn't pinch him again. "Woman, don't make me angry," he said, this time seeing her thought and blocking the pinch.

"Woman, huh? Don't you mean dragon..."

"Just wrap your arms around her before she tries to change," Ampus said.

Iselin spun. "You did not just tell him that!"

"What?" Legon asked.

Ampus laughed. "How did you hide that for so long? Legon, this is something most people don't know about the Ascended—we need a little space to change. If you're in the way, she can't shift. It takes a lot of power. That's why the first time someone changes, it can have such drastic effects."

Iselin could read Legon's joy and how intrigued he was at this new information. She answered his unspoken question. "Do you remember when you changed into an Elf?" He nodded, and she went on. "You changed Sasha and Sara when that happened, which seemed odd to us at the time, but it shouldn't have been. It made sense, really. It was just that Human to Elf transformations are so rare that we don't know much about them. When an Elf or Iumenta ascends for the first time, their magic is raw and powerful. Like you, they can change those who are too close to them, be it with a mental link or physically." Ise more than had his attention now. "You ascend when you use powerful magic; we know that much. Most times this does not happen in dire circumstances. Someone will be training on, say, the Binon, and will push themselves far enough to ascend. Some of us have even felt that we were going to ascend and then focused on making the transformation happen."

"All right, I get it, but why doesn't it affect everyone you're connected to?"

Ampus answered, his gray eyes knowing. "In the situations Ise talked about, we aren't as engaged with our significant others. In combat, it's different. There have been cases in which an Elf and their spouse will be fighting in close proximity and fully mentally connected, when one partner will ascend for the first time. The effect can be amazing. Someone who was a non-magic user before can become a class five with the possibility to ascend, depending on how powerful their spouse was."

Legon stopped them there. "What do you mean, how powerful the spouse was?"

Iselin responded. "In all of the cases that we have seen, the most significant changes occurred when a class seven ascends. Their bodies are altered so that the magic classes have actually changed people, and even some with disabilities have been cured. We don't fully understand it. That being said, never in our documented histories has anyone been that close and connected when a class eight ascends."

Ampus went on. "The rules of magic are absolute, like gravity, but the rules for Ascended have always seemed different, and when it first happens, just like when you changed, there seem to be no rules at all. We have no idea why this phenomenon occurs, the spontaneity of ascension, but it corresponds to when the White and Black Dragon disappeared from this plane. They used magic so strong that it created the Elves and Iumenta."

They were walking to the dining room now, and Legon was deep in thought. It made some sense. It explained so much that had happened to him and what he had seen when he changed. The topic changed shortly after they started eating, but Legon made a mental note to ask Ise more later.

SASHA OPENED HER EYES TO MIST. *SO I'M GOING TO HAVE ONE of these tonight,* she thought. She got up and started to walk along the familiar path to where she assumed Iselin and Legon would be. She was right. They were standing in front of the tree that had dominated these dreams for the last few years.

"How was your evening?" Sasha asked.

"Fine, you're still in the Golden City, right?" Iselin verified.

"For another week, yes. The city is too far away for us to have a strong link. I guess that confirms this isn't a dream," she pointed out.

She looked up the white bark with its many winding pink, purple, and ruby lines. Over the last few years, the lines on the bark had changed. Before Legon and Iselin were married, the pink line wasn't as intertwined with the red and purple ones. Over the years, that had changed. Now all three colors were more and more tightly knit, almost blending into one line in some sections.

"What do you think we'll see tonight?" Legon asked.

His question was answered by the tree. The colored lines started to glow, which was new. They grew brighter and brighter, starting to undulate, connecting together. The whole tree itself shone bright, and finally, with a brilliant flash of light, all of the lines merged into one glistening golden thread that wove up the tree.

"Look," Iselin said, pointing.

The tree's canopy was bursting with butterflies. Some were bright pink with lavender veins in their wings, while others were large and purple with pink veins. But the odd ones were the red ones. Their wings were a reflective red, and their wings were huge in comparison to their bodies. It was amazing they could move their wings at all. One descended, and Sasha held up her hand, the butterfly landing on her index finger. Its scarlet wings fluttered to keep it on its perch. Sasha looked closely, seeing that the tiny body of the butterfly was entirely purple.

CHAPTER 20
INSIGHT

"Fear is the greatest of all smoke screens. When we see it, we don't see what is causing the fear."
— Diary of the Perfectos Compatioa

Arkin stretched out in bed, trying not to disturb Stacy. She sighed, "It's too early. Go back to sleep."

"It's not early. I'll go make breakfast."

She opened one eye and looked out the window, then turned her head into the pillow. "It is too early; there isn't even any light out. What is it with old people getting up so early?"

Arkin thought about making a comment but decided against it. *And I'm not old*, he told himself. He made his way to the kitchen and started preparing something for them to eat for breakfast. His days and nights were starting to coalesce into one. Their mission was getting harder and harder. The Iumenta were being forced to crack down, implementing curfews and martial law. The reports coming in from other cities were the same, and as for the countryside...

Stacy walked into the kitchen in just a button-up shirt. This was an added bonus to the mission. In all his life, Arkin had never had anyone, not when he was growing up or before he moved to Salmont. After Legon's mother and father were killed, he didn't even think about being married or having someone to call his own. Stacy was young—too young—but like him, she hadn't let people into her life; it was too dangerous. It was this situation that brought about their love. That aside, he was still thankful for the opportunity.

"What are you thinking about?" she asked.

"Why you're with me," he replied.

She pressed her lips together. "You think it's because with the work we do, my choices are limited?" She paused to read him. "Well, that may have been why we got together, but I'd be willing to bet that neither one of us would change that now," she said warmly, then added, "We should step a bit more lightly; the noose is tightening."

Every other conversation came back to how far they could go with the mission. He wasn't sure. Stacy wasn't a coward by any stretch, but she was right to be worried. Arkin felt worried too. Before, he only had himself to keep alive. He cared about his people, but at the end of the day, if things got too hot, he could leave without a backward glance. That was how he had always worked, but now he had her. He couldn't jump ship so easily, nor could she.

"I don't think local law enforcement has what it takes to track us down, and I'm not sure the Iumenta are aware of us, or if they are, they can't know what we are doing," he said.

Stacy sat down in one of the rickety table chairs. "Can't know what? That there is a clandestine group in the Cona Empire trying to bring it down from the inside?" She shook her head. "Oh, they know; don't you kid yourself about that. The question is, how much do they know? And who do they suspect?"

Arkin set a plate of eggs down on the table in front of Stacy, sitting in a chair of his own, taking up the other half of the table. They ate in silence, both thinking. As always, he wished she would let him in her mind, but she wouldn't. Well, she did, but not all the way. He wondered what had happened to her to make her so unwilling to connect with someone.

"What are your plans for the day?" she asked after a bit.

"I'm going to the shop and to work for a while, and then get ready for tonight. You?"

She shrugged. "I have a few things to do around town, but that's about it. I need a few odds and ends for tonight. Where do you want to meet?"

"The ministry next to the north fortress. I want to poke around in there."

"What are you looking for? That building is a little close to all the Iumenta Ascendeds, if you ask me."

Arkin shook his head. "I'm getting odd reports from other towns, something about the North and... and..." he huffed, "and I don't know; we keep hearing more about these men in the black cloth. There has to be something to it, but I don't know what."

Stacy rolled her eyes, as he figured she would. "They are just playing mind games with the resistance; nothing sinister is going on. The Iumenta are losing control of the south; why mess around with things up north?"

That might be the case, but Arkin wasn't all that convinced. He left their apartment and went on with his day, working in the shop and otherwise wasting time until he could go to his real job. He couldn't figure out what was wrong with Stacy. It wasn't that she had lost her backbone; she just didn't like when the conversation turned to the northern lands. Tom came in, bringing Arkin lunch.

"What's on your mind?" Tom asked.

Arkin stopped eating to explain what was going on with Stacy. He normally didn't confide in people, but Tom had earned his trust.

"She's scared," Tom said matter-of-factly.

Arkin raised an eyebrow. "Stacy, scared? Of what?"

Tom shook his head. "Look, Stacy is a resilient one, I'll give her that; but everyone has their limits. Plus, have you ever thought that maybe she's from the North? After all, what do we know about her?"

Arkin thought. "Well, not much, but the same could be said for all of us."

Tom nodded. "Yeah, I know that, but I'm just saying that while Stacy may be great at everything she does, she's bound to have limits.

Maybe she doesn't want to think there is anything wrong up North, and that's why she's being difficult. That's all I'm sayin.'"

Arkin thought Tom was probably right, and in truth, he didn't really know anything about Stacy's past. He trusted her more than anyone in his now vast organization, but they didn't talk about the days before their own personal war began. Arkin had things he wasn't going to share with her, and he knew that went both ways. He decided that after tonight he wouldn't make her do anything to investigate the North anymore—that was, if tonight turned anything up.

As the sun was setting, Arkin made his way to the east side of town, getting some tea at a shop across from the building they were going to break into. He felt Stacy's mind and told her where to meet him. The teashop he waited in was stuffy, so when Stacy opened the door, there was a gust of cool air. She plunked down across from him.

"You look like you've had a hard one," Arkin said, seeing her disheveled appearance.

She pulled a ribbon out of a pocket and tied her long dark hair back, then before answering him, she took his tea and sipped it. "You don't even want to know, and I do not want to talk about it."

He waited for it.

She set the cup down with a clink. "Okay, just this," she said, raising her hands in frustration. "Is it really that hard to tie a horse? Really? So, since for once I didn't have all that much to do today, I said to myself, 'Stacy, go see if Jenny wants to go out,' right? Not a lot to ask. Well, Jenny had an errand to run, and I was willing to go with her." Arkin nodded, knowing better than to stop her once she started. She went on. "So we had to go to this little shop, right, and when we were there, some idiot comes in to pick something up. So he's got his cart outside and whatever, but he is rude to everyone around and didn't even bother to tie his horse up. I don't know, maybe in the country they don't tie them up. Well anyway, an Ascended flew overhead because it's Salez, so the horse FREAKS out, I mean full-on tantrum. It has a cart behind it, so that makes it freak out more. Anyway, long story short, the storefront is obliterated. So, I'm thinking Jenny and I can leave because it's pretty obvious what happened. NO, that's right, I said no. Some peacekeeper comes along to sort things out and made us stand around all afternoon going over what happened." She huffed and took one long pull from Arkin's tea, finishing it off. "And why haven't you offered me tea or anything? I've had a hard day!"

Why hadn't he what? It wasn't worth it. Arkin apologized and ordered tea for her. After a few cups, she seemed to calm down. He decided that it was probably safe to broach the subject for tonight. He poked her mind, and she looked at him and then sighed, speaking in her head. "Sorry."

"It's all right; you had a hard day. Do you want to pass tonight?"

"No, I'll be fine. I want to get back at that peacekeeper. I'm gonna get his address so I can mess with him."

"You know what they say about revenge?" Arkin said wryly.

"Yeah, dig two graves: one for the person you're getting revenge on, and the other for the guy who tried to tell you to drop it," she thought acidly.

He tried not to smirk; people in the teashop would think he was a loon. "Fair enough, let's have something to eat and then go over to the building. I've had this place cased out; no one stays late."

After dinner, Stacy and Arkin made their way across the street and into a small alley. Arkin looked up the side of the rough wall to a window high overhead.

"So what do we need to look for, exactly?" Stacy asked in a whisper.

"Anything that seems out of the ordinary, really; but it will likely show in the paperwork."

"What will show in the paperwork? You know what; it doesn't matter. Let's go."

Arkin looked down at his hands and let the energy flow to them. "Caulo." There was a slight green glow that faded. Stacy did the same. Arkin reached up, placing a hand on the wall, feeling it stick at his will. He started his ascent with Stacy right behind him. Right underneath the window, he placed his right hand in his jacket pocket and pulled out a mirror on a thin metal rod, holding it up to the window. There didn't appear to be anybody in there. He lifted himself to the window and checked for spells that might be protecting the building. There were a few in place.

"They have this place protected," he said across the network.

Stacy wasn't surprised. "It is a government building. What is there?"

"Looks like some basic wards to stop people from breaking in and vandalizing the place. They don't look like anything that would block a Venefica." He paused, feeling with his mind and energy. "Wait, here's one. It's a detection ward. I'm not sure how it alerts security." He groped around more. "And there is a blocking ward too. If we try to disable the detection spell..."

"We will be blocked by the other ward, which will in turn set off the detection ward. Peachy."

Arkin thought for a moment. "A detection spell is looking for a certain level of magic, so in theory, we should be able to hit them at the same time."

"Wait—how does that work? If you attack that blocking ward, you're gonna set the detection off," she said, concerned.

"Let's see, if it's a simple blocking spell... if I'm right, these aren't complex spells, and the blocking ward won't be able to handle more than one person at a time, so if I attack it..."

"I should be able to disable the detection spell before it picks you up. Got ya," she said, unconvinced but resigned.

Arkin put just a little energy behind his breaking spell, and just a heartbeat later, Stacy hit the detection ward with all her might. Arkin felt resistance, but he didn't push more.

"I CAN'T FEEL THE OTHER WARD; I GOT BLOCKED!" Stacy yelled in his mind.

"What?" Arkin readied himself to fight or escape. If Stacy was blocked with the amount of power she had put behind her attack, there was no way the detection ward hadn't found them. "We need to move." Arkin was about to drop to the ground but stopped at a snicker. He looked down at Stacy, who was red in the face, tears streaming down her cheeks.

"You should have seen your face; don't worry, the ward is gone. Good idea," she giggled.

Arkin gritted his teeth but didn't give her the satisfaction of making a remark. He reached out, disabling the other wards and protecting the window. He opened it. The window wasn't even locked, which, when he thought about it, made sense. The wards were the lock. Climbing in behind him, Stacy was all business now. They moved like ghosts in the darkness from room to room until Arkin found the records cache he was looking for.

He opened a cabinet, rummaging inside. Stacy whispered to him, "I still don't know what to look for."

"I told you; anything that seems off."

She huffed. "It's a big city, Arkin; I'm sure there is a lot that is 'off.' I mean, after all, we are half of what is making this city non-functioning. I need more to go on here."

Arkin's mind rushed. *What would tip us off?* he thought. Then it came to him. "They need a workforce."

"A what? You aren't making sense."

Arkin moved across the room. "Salez is a hub for those going into the care. Everyone who goes from this Province has to be processed in Salez. If you are doing something you don't want people to know about, use slave labor."

"Or Iumenta..." Stacy pointed out.

"When have the Iumenta done their own lifting?" He stopped. "We need to find the record rooms for those who go into the care."

Arkin walked out of the room into the hall with Stacy hot on his heels. She was babbling about something, but he wasn't paying attention. He found a door labeled "The Care" and opened it. The room was vast, with shelves of records from those in the care. The Empire documented everything, so if something was amiss, it would show up here. He looked around for almost an hour with a nervous Stacy standing guard. Finally, he found something. "Stacy, look at this."

She came in and looked at the papers he had laid out. He started pointing. "Look at how many people they are sending to the North."

She looked. "It's wrong, I know, but I don't see anything unusual about it."

"But it is. Look, not only has the number of people going into the care gone up, but the demographic is what's odd. Look, many of these people have the same physical attributes and talents. Why are so many people with the same skills and abilities all going to one city up North?"

She looked even more uncomfortable, and Arkin thought he'd hit a nerve somehow. "Arkin," she said in a growl, "I want to leave now."

He looked over at her. Her face was covered in sweat, her eyes wide.

"We can go," he said, not knowing what had come over her and not wanting to push it. If there was one thing he'd learned over the years, it was that everyone had a breaking point. Sometimes those breaking points didn't make any sense. You just didn't want to be on a mission when they were met. He cleaned up the papers, making a mental note to go back to the building later. He'd have to figure out how to get past the wards.

Once outside the building, they walked at a good pace and kept to the shadows. Salez had a curfew in place, but he didn't think they would run into any trouble.

Over the next few weeks, Arkin spent almost every evening checking out the records. He didn't tell Stacy where he was going, and she didn't ask. He never found out what was wrong with her, but once back to her regular duties, she seemed to go back to normal. Finally, one night he caught a break. As he read, he couldn't believe what he had stumbled upon.

LEGON GLIDED DOWN THE HALL WITH ISELIN AND SASHA close in tow. They entered the large war room to see Sydin and Opes already waiting for them there.

"This is unusual," Legon commented.

From the center of the room came Arkin's amplified voice. "Yes, I'm aware of that. Please forgive me for not using the normal channels."

"That's fine; what is it?" Opes asked.

"I have been looking into activity from up North, as I've reported. Well, I've found something," Arkin said.

Legon listened carefully as Arkin spoke. "I found some oddities in the care records; things just didn't make sense to me. There were more people than ever before going into the care and an even higher number going up north. It might not have made much of a difference if the normal types of people were going up north. Normally, maid types and services go north, with military types and hard labor going south. Given, much hard labor goes north, but that's unimportant. Those going to the North have the same physical, mental, and skill profiles, and they are all going to a border town up there, which makes me think they are going into one of the Iumenta Provinces.

"Before you interrupt, there is more. Many are being sent to one town, like I said; some go to a few other places, but the common thread was that they are all part of something called 'Mors'..."

Legon stopped listening. He knew that name—not just its meaning; it was the word for death—but there was more to it. Something sinister in his memory. He thought hard, thinking back until he heard a gravelly voice speaking in Elvish, and the word "Mors" jumped out. The man speaking had gray skin and yellow eyes. "When have I been around an Iumenta that I wasn't trying to kill?" he said out loud.

The room went silent. "What's that, Legon?" Sasha asked.

"I've heard that word spoken by an Iumenta, but it was a long time ago, and I can't place it."

"How can that be? I thought you had a perfect memory," Arkin said.

"I do have a perfect memory, but it's like it's not mine..." Then it came to him. "Sara!"

SARA LEANED INTO KEITHER'S WARMTH. THEY WERE spending the day with his family. Brack and Margaret were rattling on about the street they lived on, what Misses so-and-so was doing, and so on. The couple had settled into Manton well. Brack was working at a foundry as the foreman, and Margaret was enjoying herself. There was a knock at the door, and Brack rose to answer it.

"So, Margaret, I hear you're becoming famous in this area for your cakes," Sara winked.

Margaret laughed. "Flattery is always the key, my dear. Would you like so—Brack, what is it?"

Brack came back into the room with a tall man.

"Tuneal?" Keither said, surprised.

The raven-haired Elf gave them a slight nod. "Sara, Keither, it is good to see you again. Keither, I take it this is your mother, Margaret."

Tuneal held out his hand and shook Margaret's hand. Her face was turning pink.

"Please sit down; what brings you by?" Keither said.

"I am most sorry to be so rude as to decline visiting for a while, but it's business that brings me here today." He turned to Sara. "Sara, if you would be so kind, your presence is needed at the dome."

Her presence was needed at the dome? What was going on? Keither looked concerned, and from his thoughts, she could tell he had no idea what this was about either.

"Tuneal, what is going on?" she asked.

Tuneal's face softened. "Sara, we just need to find out some information about when you were in Salez. I am sorry, but we cannot risk an insecure connection to Seeon."

So they were going to be talking to the capital, were they, and it needed to be secure. She huffed, resigned. "Okay, I will pack some stuff up."

"That won't be necessary; we will be flying. I'm sure you will be back before dinner."

"Flying? This is important, isn't it?"

He nodded and looked at Keither. "If you would like..."

"Don't worry about it; I don't need to know." He looked at Sara. "Unless you need me there?" he asked. Her time in Salez never came up. It didn't bother her so much. Legon had taken care of that when he freed her, but they weren't pleasant memories. This was something that Legon and Sasha knew; therefore, if they were asking her to remember that time in her life, then they needed something badly.

She left the two-story house and walked next to Tuneal down the white-paved street. Her steps were the only ones that could be heard. Tuneal walked with quiet grace. People on the street would glance in their direction as they walked, but Tuneal didn't seem to notice. He just walked briskly to a large field where children would go to play.

Tuneal turned his green eyes to her. "I assume in Seeon you flew?" he asked.

"Yes, Ise would take us. It was scary, but fun, too."

He nodded, the blue flecks in his eyes glinting, and he stepped away from her, motioning for her to stay put. He turned back to her, and his form changed in front of her eyes. People in the area gasped as the giant blue dragon grew out of the man. Sara realized that most, if not all, of the people in the area, while they had seen dragons, had never seen anyone Ascend. After living in Seeon, she now could see the difference in size. It was obvious that Tuneal was a class seven, and a powerful one at that.

He lowered his head to her level. "Do you mind?"

"Not at all," she said as a mist of blue surrounded her, picking her up and placing her on his back, sticking her in place. She leaned against his neck as he reared up to take flight. The sun was obscured as his wings lifted into the sky. He dove upwards with a jump, driving his massive blue wings down, pushing them up in the air. Sara felt a sticking spell keep her on his back, and the wind buffeted her. This was different from being on Iselin. Tuneal was larger and more powerful. If she was being honest, it was smoother with Tuneal as well. She was connected with his mind, and he commented, "Sevens are larger, and therefore we seem smoother. It's just because wind currents don't affect us as much."

They soared through the azure sky, looking down on the white-capped Cornis Mountains. The air was cold this high up, but Tuneal placed a spell around Sara, heating the air. As time passed, she found the rhythmic thudding of his wings to be relaxing. Soon enough, she could see the Dragon Dome on the horizon.

They descended, seeming to almost hit the mountains. As they approached the opening to the dome, she felt a little nervous. Logically, she knew the opening was more than big enough for even a class eight, but from a distance, it was just a small hole in the top of a hill. They glided close, and Sara was tempted to shut her eyes. The small hole didn't appear to be growing, but right as they got to it, the opening seemed to expand to let them in. They came down to the hangar floor and touched down lightly.

"The opening always looks like that; it's the angle we come in at— it's deceiving."

She chuckled. "I'd say!"

They made their way to a conference room that had a large crystal table in the center of it. Upon entering, Tuneal shut the door behind them. "We are here," he said.

Legon's voice came over the crystal. "Hello, Sara; I hope all is well, and that we didn't pull you from anything important."

"We are good. What is going on, Legon?" she asked, getting right down to business.

"When you were in Salez, your owner spoke about something called 'Mors.' Do you remember that?"

She blanched, and her voice caught a bit. "Ummm, yes, I do sadly, don't you? You have my memories, don't you?"

"I have the memories of your pain; yes, and you connect this word with pain, but the word itself never hurt you, so I can't place it."

She took a moment. "The owner would talk in Elvish to other Iumenta, and sometimes he sent us to the regular barracks, but other times," she paused so that she could stay in control of her shaking voice, "they sent us to the others." Her voice caught, and she went on. "We knew when it was going to happen because he would say something about Mors. It always seemed to bother him, like he was having to make a sacrifice."

"Sara, I'm sorry, but can you tell us more? I know this is hard for you. If you would prefer, I can ask everyone else to leave us alone," Legon said. "Please, just a little more, just enough for my memory to connect the dots, then I promise we won't talk of this again."

She nodded. "They did stuff to us. They had no feeling whatsoever. A few of the girls died..." she choked. "They would—"

Legon stopped her. "I am so sorry, Sara; are you talking about where Peg and Jean were killed?" he asked, and she could tell from the tone of his voice that he was remembering it now.

"Yes, that's the place."

"Okay, Sara, you're done now. I am sorry."

"Do you need more?" she asked, torn between not wanting to remember and a need to help.

"No, now that I know what place you're talking about, when you say Mors, I will be able to remember back from the memories I took from you. With your permission, I will show some of your memories to my advisors so that they fully understand what happened."

"Okay, that's fine; are they going to play on the crystal?" she asked, not sure if she wanted to know.

"Yes, but you don't hav—"

"I'll do it," she said, cutting off Legon. She didn't want those memories, but they were hers. If Legon's staff needed to understand what took place, then they were to fully understand. "They are my memories; I should do it."

"Are you sure?" Legon asked.

In response, her mind reached out to the crystal as images and sounds flashed across it for everyone to see. She couldn't show them everything, but she was able to fill almost an hour of time, including how Peg and Jean were killed. When the images and sounds stopped, no one spoke. Legon thanked her in a shaky voice, and the connection with Seeon was cut off. An ashen-faced Tuneal walked Sara to his apartment and made her some hot chocolate.

"This will help," he said soothingly. "Sara, I don't know everything that happened to you, but now I know enough, and what you went through must have been horrific. How do you live after that?" he asked.

She took a moment. "What you saw today was by far the worst of it, not to say that my time in the care was pleasant by any stretch, but... every time I thought I was going to break and lose it, my owner would have me do something else. Not at first. He broke us at first, but once we would do what we were told, he tried to keep us from going mad. Not out of some sense of caring, but rather I think he figured that if we lost our minds, we wouldn't make him as much money," she explained.

"That sounds like something an Iumenta would do, but how do you make it through your days now with those memories?"

To this, she laughed a bit. "Sorry, it's not funny; just a little unbelievable to me is all. When Legon took those memories, that's really what he did. I can relive them if I choose to, but he freed me from them. Now, in many ways, they don't feel like my memories anymore, more like a nightmare. Also, if I am being honest, Keither loves me with the purest intent. My past has no effect on how he sees me, and when I'm in his mind, I have nothing to fear or to be sad about. That is how I can live my life without fear."

Sasha hated hearing the pain in Sara's voice, and even worse was seeing her memories. The brutality of Peg and Jean's rape and subsequent deaths was almost unreal. It was as if they were being attacked by animals and not men. Iselin turned green and started to cry. Sydin looked like he could kill someone, and Opes' face was blank. "Going to kill them all," he muttered. For her part, Sasha felt like Iselin, wanting to vomit. She vowed to herself that she would never let Sara suffer like that again.

Legon shook himself. "I think we can see that these aren't regular men that are in the care. They have been brainwashed or something."

"Opes, what are you thinking?" Sydin said.

Opes clenched his fist and spoke in a low, deadly voice. "I think the Impa Empire has re-instituted its training programs, but with a twist."

"What programs?" Iselin said.

Sydin looked confused for a moment, and then somber. "I think you may be right, old friend." He spoke to the rest of the room, "One of the big contentions with the Impa and Pawdin Empires prior to the War of Generations was that the Impa Empire was trying to train Humanity. They were looking for slaves. One province was known for it—"

"That's it!" Opes interrupted.

Everyone looked at him as if he'd gone mad, but he went on. "The ship that attacked us on our way back from picking up your family was from the Oris Province."

"The Impa naval province?" Sasha asked.

Opes explained. "Yes, but remember the Impa Navy was more of an afterthought. Even when they had lands that bordered the ocean, they rarely ventured out to the sea. The Oris were most famous for their work on training Humans and their schools of thought on how to handle what they called 'ape issues.' It would make sense that they would be involved. They would be up where all of the people from the care are going."

"I've heard enough," Legon said. "We need to send people to go and take a look. I want to know what town it is that people are being sent to, and what part of the Impa Empire we think they are headed to, if any." He directed his words to Sydin. "Send Barnin, Ankle, and Heath. We have to have people we can trust, but tell them not to go too deep into Impa land. I would like to have them back."

Sasha wasn't happy about Barnin putting himself in harm's way, but Legon was right; there wasn't any other way. Now they would have to wait. It would take Barnin some time to get that far north, but Sasha suspected that in the meantime, Legon and the rest of the house were going to be busy.

CHAPTER 21

WIND AND BRUSH

"True horror is not what nature inflicts, but rather what we do to our own."
— An Island of Sorrow (Author Unknown)

B arnin made his way up the side of the dome with Ankle and Heath. This wasn't going to be a good day; he could tell. Humans never went into the dome, and if they did, it was because security was an issue or they were invited to some social gathering. Since Legon wasn't in town, he was pretty sure it was the former.

"What do you think it is, Sir?" Ankle asked.

Barnin shrugged. "I honestly couldn't tell you, but we'll find out."

They were met at the top of the dome by an Elf with long brown hair that matched her flowing dress. She smiled slightly as they made their way to her. Barnin was accustomed to Elves; he'd been around plenty of them, but Heath... Barnin looked over at him and watched his face turn as red as his hair when she greeted them.

"Hello—you must be Barnin, Ankle, and Heath," she said, her voice like music.

Heath looked elated that she knew his name, while Ankle appeared a little miffed that she knew his nickname.

"That's us; you know our names, so I assume you know why we are here," Barnin said.

"Yes, right this way; please let me know if you need anything while you are here," she said, leading them into the dome.

This was Heath's first time inside the Dragon Dome, so he was a little shocked upon seeing the hangar floor. Whoever this woman was who was guiding them, she patiently answered all of Heath's questions as they walked to command.

"Are you a Venefica?" Heath asked.

"No, I'm not. You are a class one, correct?" she asked.

"Yes, I am; how did you know that?" Heath replied.

Barnin rolled his eyes. "Heath, come on buddy, we are here by invitation. I had to submit both your names for whatever mission we are going on. I'm sure whoever this is has been given information on all of us so she can make our time here more pleasant."

"That is correct, and my name is Leena," she said.

Turning to Heath, Barnin added, "And you're a magic user, so if we were a threat, I'd bet you'd be the first one to go."

Heath balked. "Come on, she's not a Venefica—"

"No; he is correct, Heath. While the chances of you being a threat are almost nonexistent, if your group was a problem, you would be the first I'd kill," Leena said, as if she were talking about the weather. "But since you are being brought in for a special mission, I'd say you are trustworthy." She looked back and winked at Heath.

Barnin was sure Heath was hyperventilating by this point, but he tried to push it from his mind because Leena had hit the nail right on the head. They were here for a special mission, which most likely meant it was going to be dangerous. *Wonderful,* Barnin thought. They entered a conference room, and Leena asked if anyone wanted anything to drink.

"Poti for all of us, please," Barnin said.

She left to get the drinks. When she returned, Tuneal was with her. "Thank you, Leena," he said, dismissing her.

Barnin moved his chair closer to the large conference table, waiting for Tuneal to begin.

"Thank you for coming. I will get right to the point. First, everything said today and in the mission is to be kept secret. This mission is voluntary only. It will be dangerous and difficult. You will run a high risk of capture or death. If you don't want to be part of it, please leave now." Tuneal paused as all three men took a drink. "Very good. We have reason to believe that the Iumenta have started a training program for Humans. Before you ask questions, let me explain. In the War of Generations, the Impa tried to turn Humans into perfect slaves.

"They did this by brainwashing them. We think they have a new program like that now, and we think this is where the Dark Warriors have been coming from.

"We need to find out more information. Unfortunately, we cannot send Elves to gather more information due to the difficulty for us to blend in. You three are to go north. You will be going to a town called Mors up there. From there, you are to find out what the Iumenta are up to and what type of threat Mors may pose, if any. It is probable that you will have to venture into the Impa lands. Heath, this is why you are to come.

"You will train here in the dome for the next three days. You will then travel by ship up north to your drop point. Any questions?"

Ankle raised his hand. "Yes, Sir. How are we getting to shore?"

Tuneal smiled. "That is a good question, and the answer is you won't be going to shore. The Iumenta have their pants around their ankles right now. They are patrolling the south with much diligence, but up north, outside of the Impa lands, that is not the case. One of our most highly trained Ascended will be flying you inland under the cover of darkness. You will be at a high altitude so that folks on the ground cannot see you. Once over your insertion area, you will free fall to the earth. You will each have a belt with a crystal that will stop you once you get close to the ground. By the looks on your faces, I can tell this is new to you. This was something that was done frequently during the War of Generations; do not worry. Once you drop off, the Ascended will clear the area and tap into the jump crystal on the ship you came in on. They will jump from the area, and no one will be the wiser."

Barnin wasn't all that convinced that the mission would go as smoothly as Tuneal said it would, but it didn't really matter. Getting them there was the Elves' problem.

After some of the most intense training Barnin had ever received, they boarded a ship and made their way north. He had always wondered why the Elves and Iumenta didn't jump more until he saw the crystal.

Jump crystals were normally only on carriers, and even then rarely active. The ship they were on now, while not a carrier, had been fitted with a jump crystal for this mission. To save weight, the ship had been stripped of most everything else. The crystal was in the main hold, and it was massive. Furthermore, unless connected to a constant source of energy, it would lose power quickly.

"So, how does this work again?" Ankle asked, looking at the crystal.

A raven-haired Ascended glided up next to them. "Ascended can communicate over long distances. Once we leave the ship, we will head out to sea as fast as we can. The connection I will share with the others will be faint by the time I drop you off. Once you are on the ground, I will clear the area, and then the jump crystal will be activated. Under normal circumstances, there are two crystals—one at the end point and one at the beginning. The one on the ship will have to function at full power for me to make it back. Once connected, the ship will put the crystal at full power, and I will have five or six seconds to lock onto the ship's position and jump."

"How common is this?" Heath asked.

Umbra smiled. "There aren't many of us who are capable of this. We are part of a single squad that can handle a mission like this. You see, there are many of us that can make the jump. It was common in the War, but slipping into enemy territory and back without detection is difficult. I was dispatched here from House Coreen for this assignment."

That made Barnin curious. "Can you tell us more? How old are you? How many are in the squad?"

"That's a lot." She smiled. "There are eight of us. We are all class sevens and black when Ascended. We have all turned our horns, claws, spikes, and teeth black as well. We use magic to keep our scales from sparkling. In short, on a dark night, not even an Elf or Iumenta can see us when we are high overhead. We train for centuries in the art of stealth and speed. Don't worry, you'll see." She winked again. Barnin never thought he'd see the day when he met a cocky Elf, but he was pretty sure he just had.

Finally, the night of the drop came. Barnin, Heath, and Ankle clothed themselves in regular attire with rucksacks, so they appeared to be trappers. Before going on deck, they all put on the belts that would stop them before hitting the ground, and black cloaks with cloth masks. On deck, the sun was almost gone. Umbra was in her Ascended form. Barnin looked her over. Everything was black on black like she had promised, but unlike a regular dragon, there was nothing reflective on her. Her massive form almost slipped into the dark background of the sea.

Barnin climbed onto Umbra's back, wrapping a strap around one of her back spikes. He lay flat down the length of her back, with Heath lying behind him and Ankle on the other side. There was still room for maybe six or seven other people, if situated right.

Once everyone was situated, Umbra spoke in their minds. "Make sure your strap is connected. I can only use minimum magic, so I can't stick you to me. It's going to be a long flight, so I hope you all went to the bathroom," she thought, with a playful edge at the end.

Barnin rolled his eyes. "We're ready, let's go."

He was excited. They'd been on so many dragons back at the dome in preparation for this mission, but now they were in a combat situation. Umbra unfolded her wings and leapt off the edge of the ship. This takeoff was different than any other Barnin had experienced. Umbra shot forward with increasing speed and power. He felt the harness holding him to her dig into his back as she propelled herself at greater and greater speeds. After she stopped accelerating, her wings made almost no sound at all. They were silent wraiths soaring over the black water.

The night air bit at him, growing colder as the night wore on. There was a new moon and cloud cover, so Barnin couldn't see the water at all, but the sound of waves hitting a shore caught his attention. He looked up. The outline of mountains rising from the water was barely visible. Umbra zigzagged left to right as they reached the coast, and Barnin realized with a bit of a start that she was avoiding rocks. Umbra hugged the ground, and as Barnin's sight focused in the dark, he started to see just how close they were to treetops and hills. Still, Umbra rushed forward at an incredible velocity. She never seemed strained by their weight or by the sheer energy required for this type of flight. After several hours of being jostled around, the excitement was starting to wear off. Umbra was using just a bit of magic to keep them from getting motion sickness, but it was cold, and they hadn't moved in hours. Barnin was stiff, and his teeth were chattering. Finally, something changed.

"I am going to go high now in preparation for dropping you," she said in their minds.

The drop zone was near the city, and worse, it was near Iumenta-populated areas, which meant that Umbra had to fly at a high altitude in order not to be discovered. This meant that they would be jumping off of her at a high altitude, free-falling to just a few hundred feet before the crystals in the belts slowed them.

Umbra started her ascent. It was steep, and the air grew even more frigid as they climbed. They could see city lights in the distance. As they went higher, the towns and city lights flickered. Even frozen as he was, Barnin had to admit it was beautiful seeing the world at night from this height. Soon, Umbra leveled off and resumed her rapid forward pace. Another hour later, and Barnin didn't think he would ever feel his body again. Ankle and Heath felt the same, but Umbra was unaffected by the cold. Barnin had a limited mental link with Umbra but picked up on something uneasy in her mind. "What is it?" he asked.

She was slow to respond. "Something doesn't look normal to me. I've been this far north many times before the Iumenta took over, but there don't seem to be as many towns," she said.

Barnin looked around, seeing seas of light. "There are a lot, if you ask me."

"To the southeast, yes, there are. With my eyes, I can even see the faint glow of the capital in the distance, but northwest there should be more..." Her tone changed. "We are almost there; get ready," she said to them, changing the subject.

All of the cold and discomfort vanished as they got ready. Unfastening their straps, they slowly worked their way down Umbra's back to her tail and waited. Time seemed to stop as they held onto Umbra's back.

"GO!" she commanded.

Barnin let go, feeling gravity do the rest. Air rushed by him as he fell toward the ground. Buffeted by wind, his cloak flapped violently, and the cold wind burned his skin. The black landscape rushed up to meet him. His vision turned black as the crystal's wards enveloped him, slowing him until he hovered in the air for just a moment, and then WHAM, he hit the ground. There was a splash near him, and Heath's grunt as he thudded to earth.

"Dang it," Ankle said in a whisper. "Hit a ditch."

"Shhh," Barnin said. "Mental."

Ankle's voice was in his head. "Sorry, Sir, where are you?"

Barnin clicked his tongue, and the others came to him.

"We need to move northeast." He pointed to his right. "There is a town just over that hill. We need to avoid it if we can. We are two days out from the border. We need to move out." Heath and Ankle did as they were told. They made their way through the brush and woods in the area, moving toward their objective.

Legon sighed in relief as he read the report that Umbra had made it back to the ship safely and that the drop had gone as planned. Barnin just had to keep himself alive for a few days, and then he could make his way back to the south. He would meet up with Arkin in Salez, but first, Heath would have to relay what they found through Arkin's vast network of people.

Legon walked back into the bedroom, crawling into bed next to Iselin's sleeping form. Pulling her in close, he shut his eyes, willing there to be nothing in the world but the two of them. There was no way that he could fall asleep. His last remaining childhood friend was deep in enemy territory, and he wondered if he would have another broken-hearted widow to care for.

"They'll make it out," Iselin said in a sleepy whisper.

Legon kissed her shoulder. "I hope so, love; how did you sleep?"

She rolled over, so they were facing each other. He gave her a long kiss. "I slept fine, but I could use some help waking up..." she said suggestively, molding her body to his.

Legon chuckled a bit. "I suppose I could help with that."

———

BARNIN DECIDED THAT HE LIKED THE SOUTH A WHOLE LOT better than the north. The two-day journey to the border wasn't a hard one. They ran into a few people but were passed off as trappers or hunters. There was little in the way of security in the North. But where the northern lands lacked people trying to kill them, it made up for it with cold weather.

"It was cold where you grew up, right, Sir?" Heath asked.

"Not like this. Salmont had some nasty winters, but it was all snow and we were inside..." A gust of blistering cold wind made the point for him. It was spring, and he understood that weather wasn't always peachy in the spring, but the frost at night was a killer.

"I still can't get over how little people seem to suspect us up here," Ankle mused.

"Well, why would they?" Heath said. "They aren't being invaded, and let's face it; who would be stupid enough to come up here and cause trouble?"

"Good point," Ankle said.

"We aren't going to cause trouble. We're going to get information so that later the resistance can cause trouble. If you remember, the south was like this too, until tensions rose," Barnin pointed out.

Ankle laughed softly. "That's right, things were real shiny back when we first started picking a fight."

"We didn't pick a fight," Heath said, annoyed.

"Yeah, yeah, but I wish we had picked it," Ankle retorted.

"Don't worry, we'll finish it; now look alive," Barnin said.

They were cresting a small hill. The scent of smoke from many fires filled the air. Barnin got down on his belly, popping his head over to view what lay below them. Taking out his seeing eyeglass, he looked down at what was thought to be a town but was actually more of a depot.

"That's why we can't find the name of a town, and we just have a project name of Mors to work with," he said.

Heath and Ankle had glasses of their own. Ankle spoke, "No fixed buildings. How much you wanna bet they move this thing every few months?"

"You want me to call it in, Sir?" Heath asked, but Barnin told him not to.

He was eyeing the large grouping of burlap tents. There were just as many Iumenta as there were Humans—well, free Humans. It was obvious who was in their care. They were in long strings of chains that linked them by their necks. They looked cold and tired. A group was at the far north of the camp with another group of Iumenta. They looked as though they were about to leave.

"Hey, look up there," Barnin said, pointing. "There are no Human guards going with them." They watched as the group moved out and up the base of the mountains. They were at the base of a large range that was similar to the Cornis Mountains, though not as hostile. "They know these mountains, but rough terrain isn't new to us. Let's stay above them and keep out of sight. They don't look to have any camping gear, so they can't be going far."

"Right, Sir, I'll take point," Ankle said, moving off.

They kept on the group for most of the day. It was hard not to try to kill the Iumenta. They moved the people quickly, not letting them stop for food, water, or even to relieve themselves. If someone fell, the rest of the group was forced to drag them until an Iumenta noticed. One woman fell a few times, her hands bloody from where she had cut herself. She looked about nineteen or so, with short brown hair and disheveled clothes. An Iumenta walked up to her the third time she dropped. As she struggled to stand, he pulled out a fenrra and cut off her head. Her body fell, and the chain connecting her to the rest of the group slackened, no longer dragging her along. None of the people made a sound as they stepped over her body. Obviously, this wasn't the first time they had seen such a thing.

Heath grabbed Ankle. "Let me go," Ankle said angrily.

Barnin turned. "Shhh, shut up, what are you doing?"

Ankle's face was red. "Sir, it's a death march. We can't just..."

"Can't what? You want to go and get killed? Who will that save?" he said. "Look, this is what we do. We find out what's going on and we leave as fast as we can, then we call it in." He put his hand on Ankle's shoulder. "We'll come back, and when we do, we'll kill them all, right?"

Ankle looked down. "Sorry, Sir, it's just, it's just not what I'm here for, ya know. I signed on to save people, not watch them die." He sat down hard. "I know why we are here. I'm sorry, Sir, it won't happen again."

Barnin slugged Ankle in the shoulder. Ankle looked up, confused. "Why did ya..."

"Don't do it again, but don't apologize. Never apologize for wanting to help people."

They didn't talk for the rest of the afternoon. As dusk approached, they saw a valley. As they approached it, still high in the mountains, Barnin's mouth dropped open as he saw the sea of buildings below.

CHAPTER 22

MORS

"Sometimes even the best of men need motivation to act, and other times acting is needed for motivation."
— Atavus Imperata House Evindass, Secunum Renovatie

Barnin took in the large camp, city, or whatever it was, laid out in the valley below them. Trails of smoke curled up into the air, turning the setting sun red. The group they had been following was approaching a tall wired fence and gate. Barnin used the seeing glass to look at those entering.

"The gate looks fortified, but not heavily guarded. Hmmm, I wonder why that is," Barnin wondered aloud.

Ankle was on his right, surveying the place. "Something seems odd about the way it's laid out and built, ya know what I mean?"

Heath spoke up. "Yeah, it's like a prison camp, but then other parts of it look like a military base."

Barnin interjected, pointing to a clump of buildings. "And other parts look almost like the school in Salez and Bailaya." He thought more. "What if it's all of those things? The Elves thought this was some kind of training center, right? So what if that's what all this is? Maybe you come in a slave and come out brainwashed and trained."

"I don't know, sir, it seems like a bit of a stretch if you ask me," Heath said.

Well, that was why they were here, wasn't it? Barnin decided that the best plan was to spend a day watching, and then if they thought they could, they would enter the camp. But he needed more information before walking into death.

"Heath, can you tell anything about this place? Any magic?"

Heath agreed, shutting his eyes. Barnin watched his face, calm as he used his abilities to look around. He wasn't surprised to see it darken. He figured the place was pretty fortified. After an hour, or what felt like it, Heath's eyes opened, looking confused.

"What is it?" Ankle asked.

"That's just it, nothing. There isn't much in the way of defense, if anything at all. The only place I am seeing any magic is in the center of the camp," he said, pointing to a group of stone buildings that were by far the nicest in the camp. "I would guess by the way those buildings look, that's where the Iumenta live, but the rest of the camp has nothing. In fact, I can't even find other magic users, or at least any trace of them..."

Barnin was instantly worried. "How much can be hidden from you?"

Heath shook his head. "I wouldn't think much by this point. I've had practice at finding wards and other magic users, but I'm not seeing anything."

Barnin took his time. "I don't like it. We will rest here for the night and then tomorrow figure out what to do. We can't stay unnoticed for more than a few days at the max, so we need to find out what we can in the next two days, and then get out."

ANKLE HUDDLED AGAINST A ROCK, TRYING TO KEEP OUT OF the wind. The air was freezing as the sun set, but it could have been that he just wasn't acclimated to colder areas. Heath set a detection ward, so there was no need to keep a watch, but Ankle couldn't sleep. His mind kept replaying the scene of that woman getting killed over and over. He'd signed on as soon as he was old enough to join the military; two years were expected of every young man in the Cona Republic, but he signed on before he was required to. He thought he'd be a hero, but it didn't feel that way.

He thought about what it must have been like growing up in the Cona Empire, thought about the constant threat of being made a slave. Before today, he'd always thought that those in the Republic lived in unrealistic fear, but now he wasn't sure.

He peeked over one of the big jagged rocks they were hiding behind. The camp was still in full swing, the lights from the many fires burning bright in the night. At night, it was easier to see the layout of the camp. The lights from windows and streets showed that the buildings were in a spiral that moved inward. It was an odd way to design a town, and Ankle wondered if it had a purpose.

By the time the sky was lighting before dawn, they were moving. Today was simple: figure out if there was an obvious routine and also try to figure out the lay of the land. If possible, they would try to enter the camp that evening or the next day, but that was a big if. They had separated, and Ankle was next to the east entrance of the camp when dawn broke. Hiding, he scanned the horizon with his seeing glass.

There was movement by the entrance. He peered at a well-organized formation of figures. They were small, and he needed his seeing glass. He squinted in the eyepiece, trying to figure out what he was seeing. *There's no way*, he thought, looking again. "What is going on here..."

BARNIN WATCHED WHAT HE THOUGHT WAS A TRAINING yard. In it was a group of men. He thought they were part of the group they'd followed the day before, but he wasn't positive. They were in a group, listening to an Iumenta speak. He wasn't sure what was being said, but the men in the group were looking at each other.

The Iumenta waved his arm, and the group of men seemed to be having a hard time. They looked agitated, a few moving off to the walls of the training area. The Iumenta looked to be yelling now, and more Iumenta came into the training area with whips. Barnin couldn't tell what was going on. The group of men was moving to the side of the training area, but he couldn't tell why they were moving. Without warning, one of the figures with a whip pulled out a sword and killed one of the men. Everyone ran to the edges.

He looked at the people on the edges. They were eyeing a group of Iumenta that were bringing in weapons, piling them in the center of the space. People were looking at each other again, and the speaker was back. Pointing at the body in the center of the training field, he said something. To Barnin's amazement, almost everyone ran to the center and grabbed one of the many swords, spears, and maces in the center. Still, what was going on didn't register until the men started killing each other.

Heath used magic to magnify the seeing glass's view. He looked down on groups of women being shepherded into different buildings. There were also a few men moving around the area as well. Heath continued looking around. There was something else that was off with the scene. Many of the women had bulging bellies. With the sheer number of them, he'd assumed that they were fat, or that there was something wrong with the seeing glass, but as one of the women cradled her belly, a chill ran down his spine.

Barnin sat at the meeting spot waiting for Heath and Ankle. His gut hurt, but thankfully there wasn't anything left to throw up. Heath was the first back, his face ashen. Before they could talk, Ankle was back. He wore a look of pure hatred. No one spoke as they read each other's faces.

"Report," Barnin said hoarsely.

Ankle started angrily. "They are training children as soldiers. I saw about 200 of them today doing drills and running in formation." He paused. "Sick part is they were performing at the same level as professional soldiers." He made a fist. "When did children start going into the care?" He spat.

"I don't think they were taken into the care," Heath said. "What I found were large amounts of women—all pregnant. From what I could see, they are running a breeding facility. I wondered why, and now I guess I understand..."

"They're doing what?" Ankle said. "Sir, what's wrong? Doesn't this bother you?"

Barnin pinched the bridge of his nose. "I should be surprised, but I'm not." He explained what he had seen, how he'd watched slaves fighting to the death until the last man was left standing. How he'd seen teenagers killing grown men and women, how he'd seen what they did to some of the women before they died. By the end, Ankle's anger was replaced with fear, and Heath... well, Heath looked like he was going to cry. Both the men next to him had been through hell on the battlefield. They'd seen horrible things, but no one was unaffected by what was going on in Mors.

"You know it's going to be worse when we break in and look into records and dig around, right?" Barnin said. They didn't say anything. "We need to hold it together until tomorrow night, and then we will get out of here." The thought of breaking into the Mors camp bothered him.

"When are we going, sir?" Heath asked.

"The camp is just as active at night, but I think we need the cover of darkness. We need to go now." He tried to take a drink of water. "Take a few to collect yourselves, but then we move out. Remember, the sooner we get back, the sooner we can come back and free these people."

They were going to go in the west entrance near the spot Heath had been observing during the day. From what they had seen that day, the Iumenta were managing the camp, but it was Human forces who were running the day-to-day activity, including security. If they were lucky, the Iumenta spent the night in the complex in the center of the camp. If they weren't lucky, well, Barnin wasn't thinking about that.

Moving like a wraith, Barnin came up to the fence surrounding the camp. Making their way north, they looked for a weak spot in the fence.

When they were unable to find one, Heath had to use magic to part the wire without cutting it. It took a while to make it through the fence. The barbed wires crisscrossed in many places, but finally, they made it in. The dirt street was rough with frozen mud, and there was a horrible odor. Ahead of them were lines of squat buildings made of wood. He couldn't see any light coming from them, so he assumed the occupants were asleep. They stayed low, trying not to make a sound in the crunchy frozen mud. Ever since Barnin was a kid, he would hold his breath when he was sneaking about, and once he made it to one of the buildings, he pressed his back against the wall and let out a breath. When he inhaled, the air caught in his chest, and he almost wretched. In all his life, he'd never smelled such a thing. It was a mixture of death, excrement, and every other kind of filth there was. Heath and Ankle were holding cloth to their mouths and noses, but it didn't appear to be helping.

There were sounds too: whispers inside the walls, moans, and coughing. The night was bitterly cold, and Barnin examined the wall, seeing that it was barely worthy of the name. Gaps were predominant. Had there been any light inside the building, they would have been able to see inside. Barnin resisted trying to peek inside; he didn't want to know. He motioned for them to keep moving.

Their destination was a four-story stone building further up. Based on the dilapidated barracks it was surrounded by, they figured the stone building was of some importance.

There weren't many guards in this part of the camp. They only had to hide from a few on their way to the building. But that wasn't altogether surprising; the barracks, huts, or whatever they were had large doors that were bolted shut. No one was getting out.

The stone building wasn't relatively well-sealed, but with Heath around and no wards to protect it, picking the lock was easy. Ankle closed the door behind them. The entrance hall was still warm. As they made their way down the wooden floors, they were able to breathe. Sconces along the wall held plants and herbs that covered up the stench from outside.

"We need to try to get an idea of what is going on in here. I want to know how long this place has been here, and how many people have been through here," Barnin whispered.

"Do you think they'll have those kinds of records?" Heath asked.

Barnin nodded. "The Iumenta document everything. Plus, this place doesn't smell, which leads me to believe that the people who work in here aren't the dregs of society. They may be Iumenta."

The first floor was relatively basic: dining area, conference room, etc. They split up for the top three floors. Barnin took the second, Heath the third, and Ankle the fourth. Heath kept a network going. If anyone found records, they were to contact Heath, who was the only one who had a working knowledge of Elvish.

HEATH WAS THE ONE TO HIT PAYDIRT ON THE THIRD FLOOR. He found a room of files. By the time Barnin and Ankle had searched the other floor, Heath had barely started.

"What is it?" Barnin asked.

They had been right to think Iumenta worked here—everything was in Elvish. Heath explained, "Most of the records listed those who have come in, how many children they have had and by whom. It gives if they are alive and a glut of other information, but we knew that. I'm trying to find the oldest records or yearly reports."

"So look for paper with numbers?" Ankle said.

"Yes."

Not long after, Heath was waved over by Ankle. "Hey, I think I found something."

He had; there was a file of annual reports. "This is it." Heath read the file's name for them. "This is the commission of the Mors facility. It's dated February 3, 1941 A.G. This place has been in this location for almost sixty years.

"But there is more. The commission talks about revising from the original charter in August 11223 P.B..." he trailed off.

"What does P.B. mean?" Barnin asked.

"We don't use A.G., P.B., or P.A. when recording time. The Immortals use these to separate periods. For example, P.A. means Prius Ascension. It marks the time before Immortals existed. P.B. is Prius Bellum, and A.G. is after the War of Generations."

"So you're saying this place was here way back before the war?" Ankle asked.

"Looks like it. The War of Generations started in 11239 P.B., but the thing is, the name of the head of this place hasn't changed. The same Iumenta was in charge of the camp then and now," Heath explained.

"Right, so this creep has had a couple of thousand years to figure out what he wants to do. That's all we need. If this place doesn't pose a threat, I don't know what does. Who knows how many of those Dark Warriors they've grown?"

They did their best to put everything back as it was when they found it. Barnin felt a sense of relief knowing that they were going to be leaving this nightmare of a camp. At the same time, he wasn't looking forward to traipsing across all of Airmelia. From their high-up vantage point, they'd been able to figure out the guards' patrols and were going to head out of the camp another way. Once again, they were assaulted by the thick scent. Heading along some buildings, they came across something none of them expected. Against the wall of a building were stacks of cages with figures inside. They made their way up to them carefully, morbid curiosity getting the best of them.

The people inside the few occupied cages looked to be mostly dead or asleep. The cages were four by four and stacked two high and made of iron bars. The women inside were no more than skeletons of people. Barnin could see the shivering form of one on the bottom row. Something was dripping on her from the presumably dead body above her. He looked in the top cage in front of him, Ankle by his side.

The woman inside looked dead. Never had Barnin seen someone so thin. He could see every bone protruding through her blotched and damaged skin. Clumps of hair were missing, and what hair was left on her waxy skull was thin. Her clothing was dirty and tattered. Barnin leaned in, ignoring the smell. He couldn't imagine what suffering this woman had faced before death. The skin of her face was no more than a wax cover over her skull. Her eyes were closed sockets, and Barnin hoped she was now at peace.

Her eyelids snapped open. With a gasp, he realized she was alive. Hazel eyes trembled back and forth, looking them over. Barnin's heart slowed as he gazed at the girl. "My name is Barnin. Who are you?"

Her voice was hoarse and shook. "Rachel."

Barnin could see her shaking; from the cold or fear, he couldn't tell. "Hello Rachel, what are you doing in here?" he asked, trying to sound calm.

She looked confused. "This is where I live." She didn't know they weren't part of the Mors camp. Barnin could tell that she was on the verge of death and likely had been for some time.

Barnin was about to speak when Heath interrupted. "Someone's coming..."

Ankle moved quickly to where Heath pointed, hugging the corner of the buildings. Rachel still looked confused. Stopping was stupid. She had seen them. If they ran, she could report them. If they stayed, they would have to deal with the guard, whose death would not go unnoticed. Ankle looked back, and Barnin signaled to him. Both he and Heath tried to hide in the shadows as they heard footsteps. Barnin turned to Rachel and put a finger to his mouth.

A single guard rounded the corner, and Barnin stepped into view. The man saw him and started forward, passing Ankle without seeing him. Ankle grabbed the man's head from behind him, covering his mouth and lifting his chin in one motion, slitting his throat with his right hand. Rachel didn't scream but looked wide-eyed as Ankle quietly lowered the body to the ground.

"That's our cue to leave," Barnin said. "Leave him there; we need to get out fast."

Ankle trotted up to them and nodded at Rachel. Barnin looked at her. "Okay?"

Ankle quickly unlocked the cage, and Rachel pushed herself back. "I won't tell I..."

"Shhhh, we're going to get you out of here. Can you walk?" Ankle said, reaching out a hand.

She hesitated for only a moment and then reached out a skeletal hand and took Ankle's. He helped her out of the cage. She didn't have shoes, of course. "They are in a locker..."

"We don't have time," Heath hissed.

Ankle looked at her. "Don't scream." He knelt down and plucked her up in his arms. At a jog, they made their way to the fence. Heath made short work of it, and soon they were out of the camp. Rachel was looking back at the facility as if she was having a dream, and Ankle ran with her up the side of the mountain.

After a ways, they had to stop and catch their breath. "Rachel," Barnin said, "I need to ask you some questions." She looked at him, waiting. "Do the Iumenta come around a lot, or do you ever see dragons?"

She answered right away. "Yes, the Iumenta will be there in the morning, and once a week a dragon comes. It's pale green and huge."

"Once a week?"

She looked scared now and took a moment. "Yes, it just appears in the air over the center of the camp. It's so scary."

Heath swore. "They have a jump crystal here. Rachel, when will the dragon be back?"

She thought for a while. "I think today."

With that, break time was over.

HEATH WAS EXHAUSTED BY MORNING. THEY HAD BEEN moving all night long, but he still wasn't able to contact anyone. Shortly after they left, there was the sound of bells from the Mors camp. Rachel told them that was the alarm.

"Sir, by now they have to be searching outside the camp. We aren't going to make it to any populated area," Ankle said, panting. Rachel was in bad shape and smelled something foul. Heath didn't know how Ankle was able to stand it.

"Heath, we need to get you close enough to call this in. We probably aren't going to make it out of this alive," Barnin said.

"I don't know, sir. Umbra said that there is a backup plan to get us out. By now, the jump crystal in the ship should be charged. If we can contact them, she might be able to evacuate us," Heath said, trying to sound optimistic, and they had good reason to be. Rachel would be a glut of information about Mors. On the trip last night, she said she had been there for over four years.

By noon, they were close enough for Heath to call in. They found a small alcove in the mountain to hide in, and he reached out.

He felt Umbra and tried to get her attention. "Umbra, we need help; we found something," he relayed all of what they had seen to her and everything that happened.

"You idiots, you were found!" she said. "Sit tight. I can be there within five hours. There is no way the Iumenta won't be on your trail." She was angry but understood.

"Five hours. We need to sit tight," he told the others.

"She's coming in the day?" Barnin said.

"Yeah, she thinks the Iumenta will be coming."

Rachel shivered a bit in Ankle's arms.

———

UMBRA HAD BEEN CORRECT. WHEN BARNIN FIGURED FOUR hours had passed, he saw small dots on the horizon. He couldn't make them out with the seeing glass yet, but they were moving fast, too fast for Humans.

"How are they following us?" Ankle asked.

"They can smell me..." Rachel said. "I remember when I came there how strong it was... I should leave you."

"No, you're not," Barnin said. "Heath, I don't know if they can use magic, but you need to buy us time."

There was a yellow flick of wards, and Heath sent spells to rocks nearby them. "I will blow up the rocks when they get here. It might kill a few; I don't know."

Barnin watched as five Iumenta crested the hill, moving like mountain goats. The terrain did nothing to slow them. Barnin remembered with a chill that this was their homeland. When they were still a hundred yards away, there was a boom as a large stone exploded, sending shards in every direction. One of the Iumenta was down, another wounded on the ground, and the others were disoriented. Barnin and Ankle stood and fired arrows at them. Still confused from the blast, one of the Iumenta was caught off guard, and Ankle's arrow killed him.

Barnin's arrow was dodged, and now the two unharmed Iumenta were pulling out fenrra.

"Heath!" Barnin yelled.

He shot bolts of magic at the two Iumenta, causing them to take cover. More rock blew, filling the air with dust. Arrows glanced off Heath's wards. There was a THUD in the distance.

"Heath, tell me that's Umbra," Barnin said.

Umbra's voice came in their heads, urgent. "What did you do? An Ascended is in the area. Get out in the open; I'm almost there!"

"Move out!" Barnin ordered.

They ran to the nearby cliff's edge. They could see Umbra weaving between rocks below them. Rachel shrieked. Ankle wrapped his arms around her. "Elf, Elf, she's an Elf!"

Black mist pulled them off the rocks and down to her back as she passed by. Barnin felt himself stick to her back as wind tore at his clothes. There was a flash of light from where they had been. Umbra rose in the sky as a bolt of pale green shot by them.

Umbra swore in their minds and started to weave as more magic came their way. He felt her mind connecting with the jump crystal. Her wings folded, and time stopped. Barnin turned his head to look back. In the air behind them was the largest dragon he'd ever seen. Magic shot from it right at them. Barnin heard in Umbra's head, *Jump.* There was black, and then nothingness.

The world returned in a flash, and his lungs filled with sea air. The Elvin ship waited below them.

CHAPTER 23

RACHEL'S STORY

"It was not his will to vanquish the masses of evil that made us follow him,
but his love of the one that compelled us to follow."
— Excerpts from The Diary of the Adopted Sister

As they descended, the ship was a buzz of activity. Sails were being raised, and Elves were running across the deck. Barnin felt a slight jar as Umbra touched down. He slid down her side, landing heavily on his feet with Heath next to him. On her other side, Ankle was catching an unconscious Rachel.

"MEDIC!" Ankle yelled.

Barnin turned to see Umbra back in her Elf form, running up to one of the many approaching Elves. "I need a line into Seeon now!" She was speaking to the Captain, who seemed dumbstruck. "Forgive me, but I just confirmed there is a class eight Iumenta Ascended."

The deck went still. Even Ankle took his attention away from Rachel. Before anyone could say anything, the ship's doctor ran on deck. "Who's hurt?" he called.

Ankle started over to him. "I don't know what happened, doc; she passed out when she saw Umbra."

Barnin heard Umbra and the captain leave the deck, presumably heading for the bridge. The silver-haired doctor was looking Rachel over. Ankle looked back at Barnin and Heath.

"Stay with her; we'll bring in your gear," Barnin said.

ANKLE WAS THANKFUL HE DIDN'T HAVE TO LEAVE RACHEL. "Can you help, doc?"

"She's lucky to be alive, but I think she just passed out from stress. Let's get her inside."

"I'm not sure after what she's been through if 'lucky' is the word I'd use, but lead the way."

He could barely feel her weight in his arms; she was so thin. As they went below deck, Ankle watched the expressions of the Elves they passed. Many turned, sniffing, and then once their eyes rested on the frail body in his arms, shock crossed their faces. Sometimes that shock was replaced by anger or sorrow. He could hear them whispering in Elvish. He wondered what they thought.

The doctor opened the door to a smallish room with several cots, motioning for Ankle to take his pick. "Her name is Rachel," he said. He laid her down, and the doctor began examining her without a word.

Rachel stirred, but before her eyes could open, the doctor placed his hand over her chest, and there was a magenta glow. "Sleep, young one, sleep." Her chest rose and fell softly, and she almost looked peaceful. "It was reckless saving her," the doctor said softly.

"We couldn't, I couldn't just leave her there," Ankle said, his voice thick. "I couldn't live with..." he stopped, having a hard time speaking.

The doctor looked up and placed his hand on Ankle's arm. "That wasn't a reprimand, son. You aren't stupid. You wouldn't have been picked for this mission if you were. You knew that saving this girl would likely get you killed, but you did it anyway. You're a good man."

"I didn't even think about that."

The Elf nodded. "Then I apologize. You're a far better person than I gave you credit for." He looked Ankle over. "I need you and your men down here."

"We didn't get hurt," Ankle said.

"But you may have been exposed to some nasty things while in there. If Rachel here is any indication, I'd say disease runs rampant where she's from."

"Will she be okay?" Ankle asked, worried.

"Yes, she needs a lot of care, and I will keep her sedated for several days, but I think she will recover. I will see if I can bring her back to Seeon or at least to the Precipice's dome."

Ankle left the room to collect Barnin and Heath.

LEGON GRITTED HIS TEETH. "THANK YOU, UMBRA; I'M GLAD you made it out alive."

"You're welcome, Un Prosa," Umbra's voice sounded in the war room.

Sydin spoke, "May I ask why you were so close to their position?"

"Yes, sir, we had planned on staying in the area for a few days to transmit Barnin's team's report. I figured since I was up there, I may as well do some looking around."

Sydin smiled a bit. "Did you find anything?"

"No, sir, nothing."

"Well, that's good, isn't it?"

"Sorry, I meant that literally. There was nothing up there, not alive anyway. Many of the known Human towns and cities I flew over were ghost towns. There was no one there. Sir, if I may, I think there is something worse going on than we thought... if you saw this Rachel girl, Sir... Sir, in all my years, I've never seen anyone like this, and Barnin and his men... the looks on their faces, and the smell..." She was shaken up.

No one seemed to know what to say. Umbra wasn't affected by anything; nothing shook her. Iselin spoke, "Umbra, you did a good job; now you get home safe, okay?"

"Yes, Un Prose," was the quiet reply.

The connection was closed. Sasha had placed her hand on Legon's when she'd heard the report of Rachel's condition. Her nails dug into his skin. He pried them off, and her eyes closed. "I want her here," she said. Legon looked at Sydin, and he sent the order to the ship to bring Rachel to Seeon.

BARNIN WALKED ON DECK AFTER SEEING THE SHIP'S DOCTOR. Heath was in his rack. The doctor had given him a sleeping draft. Barnin had refused his, and Ankle was glued to Rachel's side. Barnin had never seen him act like this before, but he didn't blame him. The sea air was cold, and mist from the waves peppered his face as he walked to the hunched form of Umbra at the rail.

Her eyes were puffy, and she looked defeated. Barnin put his hand on her shoulder and squeezed. "Thanks for saving our backsides today. I owe you."

She forced a smile and looked at him, her eyes filling with tears. "We didn't know," she whispered.

He realized what she meant. "I know. How could you have?"

"Tell me; I've only seen Rachel. Tell me what I didn't see." Umbra pleaded.

Barnin relayed the story of their trip to the Mors lands, and then what they'd seen at the camp. About how long it had been going on, how they found Rachel, everything. "You said there was a class eight?"

She wiped her eyes. "Yes, it must have just jumped in. It takes a lot of power to jump any real distance. If it hadn't just jumped, we would have died."

Barnin felt goosebumps. "You couldn't have gotten away or hurt it or anything?"

She chuckled. "No; even if I wasn't planning on jumping, it takes several class sevens to bring down an eight. That's why I was so frantic when we landed. But an eight is small in comparison with Mors. When you've been an Ascended as long as I have, you can tell when someone is new. It shows in the way they fly, in the way they use magic, everything; it's like a child almost. I don't think we will have to worry about that eight for some time to come. I don't see the Impa wasting him."

"It's a him, huh? I guess I didn't look at the plumbing when he was trying to kill me."

This time she laughed, for real. "Shut it."

The Captain came up to them then. "Umbra, you have been ordered to take Rachel with you to the capital. Once we are in range, you will fly to Manton and jump to Seeon. Barnin, we will drop you and your men off in Manton before we make our way back home," he said, and then left.

"Sasha was in the room when you gave your report, wasn't she?" Barnin asked.

"Yes, Un Prose, Sasha was there; why?"

Barnin relaxed. "Sasha is the most caring person to ever live. She'll do whatever it takes to make sure that Rachel never suffers again." He was proud. Sasha was the closest thing to a sister he had.

A few days later, Rachel woke up. The doctor had patched her up well and wasn't letting anyone question her. Barnin was fine with that. He didn't really want to know what it was like living in Mors. He'd seen enough to give him nightmares for the rest of his life. Ankle was still not leaving her side. Barnin was sure that if given his way, Ankle would never leave her. Something inside of him had changed when they watched that woman get killed.

UMBRA WAS GETTING READY TO LEAVE. THEY WERE CLOSE TO Manton, and then she and Rachel would depart for Seeon. Rachel wasn't looking much better than she had when they'd picked her up. She was still thin and bony. The doctor said she would recover, but that it would take a long time. Ankle was having a hard time with the idea of leaving her, and the Captain contacted Seeon to see if they could send Rachel to the Precipice dome instead, so Ankle could be close to her. It was decided that Rachel was too much of an asset and that she needed to be in Seeon, although Legon had requested that Ankle come with her so he could give a firsthand report.

It was early in the morning, and most of the ship was asleep. When Umbra got on deck, Barnin and Heath were talking to Ankle. "You make sure they know everything we do. Heath, can you give him our memories?" Barnin was saying. Umbra was surprised that Barnin didn't protest that Ankle was leaving. When she had asked him, he just said that Ankle had earned it.

"I have the memories, Barnin. Heath sent them to me when he made his report," Umbra said.

"That's what I'm worried about. Heath isn't all that bright, and then to you..." Barnin said, shrugging at Umbra and Heath. The latter gave him a rude hand gesture.

"You know I can eat you, right?" Umbra said, coming up to them.

Barnin smirked. "Anytime, baby, anytime," he said.

"I bet Sam will love to hear that," Heath retorted.

"Heath, so help me, I will tell the new replacements that you like to share bedrolls," Barnin threatened, and then looking at Umbra. "And what's with the threats? Iselin has threatened to eat me like fifteen times too."

She pursed her lips. "I really don't know; it's not like anything about you is appetizing in any way," she said suggestively.

Umbra turned at the sound of other footsteps. Rachel was coming on deck. She was moving around fine, but her bony form always made Umbra think she was going to break somehow. The ship's doctor had cleaned her up and given her new clothes. Color was starting to return to her face, but she still looked much the same as she had the day Umbra had first seen her. Rachel made her way to Ankle's side, standing close to him. She turned her hazel eyes to Umbra. "Thank you for taking me today," she said timidly, and looking at Ankle, "You're still coming, right?"

It was good Ankle was coming with them. While Rachel was getting better physically, she was nowhere near ready to be on her own again mentally. She looked at Ankle as if he was her personal hero, and in truth, he was. Umbra couldn't imagine taking that away from anybody.

Umbra ascended, getting ready to leave. Many Ascended preferred being in this form rather than Elvin, but she didn't have a preference. There were times when each was nice. She looked down at Rachel and Ankle as they were getting ready. Unlike last time, they would be able to ride on her shoulders, which would be far more comfortable. Still, Rachel didn't have any padding. She'd be sitting right on bone.

Ankle touched Umbra's mind. "I have a pad here; do you mind?"

"Good thinking; I will stick it to me and her to it," Umbra said.

Soon her two passengers were secured to her, and she was ready to leave. Umbra looked back at the wide-eyed Rachel and sent soothing emotions at her. She seemed to calm. Normally after a person's mind has been touched, it was difficult to influence their thoughts unless they were open to it. Surprisingly, Rachel was. Umbra figured all the girl had seen was fear for who knows how long, and she probably relished the feelings of peace and happiness Umbra sent her.

Umbra turned to the sea and launched herself into the air. The cold didn't affect a dragon, but the warm, moist air felt good on her wings nonetheless. She rose up in the sky, making her way to the dome. Now that Rachel was comfortable with her, she almost seemed to enjoy it. Being in Rachel's mind, Umbra could feel just how foreign happiness was for this girl. She didn't seem to feel comfortable smiling, as if it was something entirely new. This tore at Umbra. Seeing someone in the state Rachel was in, she couldn't help but feel compassion for her. Ankle had her tucked in close to him. There was one who hated flying, but if that was the price to protect Rachel, it looked like one he would pay. Umbra could understand Ankle. His attachment to Rachel was stronger than what Umbra felt, but she knew that like Ankle, she too would do anything to keep this girl from suffering again.

The morning fog was still burning off the sea, but as they grew closer to the coast, they started to see ships. Most of them looked military, sailing in formation.

"Looks like your navy is getting ready for the war," Umbra said.

Ankle's tone was grim. "We figured it would happen in the next few months. Manton has been getting ready for some time now. These ships have been here for a while, doing maneuvers and such," he explained.

"War? What war?" Rachel asked.

Umbra decided to answer her. "Yes, between the free Human lands and the Cona Empire, and of course the Pawdin or Elvin Empire and the Impa or Iumenta. It has been coming for some time now, Rachel, but do not worry; you will be safe."

They were over the Cornis Mountains now. Umbra was taking a direct line to the dome, so they would not be passing over Manton, but they did see the many camps of soldiers as they passed overhead.

They were almost to the jump site, and Umbra disconnected with Rachel and Ankle, feeling out for the crystal. Power welled up in her as she prepared to make the jump. She connected with the crystal and checked to make sure she was clear. Power extended out to her talons and wing tips, and she closed her eyes. 5... 4... letting herself slip into the jump 3... confirming Rachel and Ankle were secure 2... folding her wings 1... opening her eyes to the spot of light... *JUMP*... the rush of energy and then nothingness for a heartbeat. Umbra unfolded her wings and breathed in the sweet air of Seeon.

LEGON WAITED AT THE EAST ENTRANCE OF THE PALACE FOR Umbra to land. With him were Sasha, Laura, Iselin, Sydin, Opes, and a host of medical staff, along with the normal guard. Umbra's dark form glided to them, touching down lightly. Ankle, and who Legon presumed to be Rachel, dismounted. Rachel was thinner than Legon thought possible, and from what he'd been told, she'd gained weight on their trip.

Legon gave the medical staff the go-ahead to take care of Rachel. Four Elves walked over, flanking her in case she fell. Rachel was still too far away for non-Humans to see just how poor of a shape she was in. When they got close, Legon heard Sasha and Laura gasp.

"What happened to her?" Laura asked, her voice low and disbelieving.

"Mors happened," Legon said in a low voice, and then to Ankle and Rachel, "Ankle, thank you for coming." He walked up to Rachel, who was looking down and uncomfortable. Legon lifted her face, looking into her eyes. "Rachel, my name is Legon. I am the head of this house. I know that you have been through a lot. Would you like me to make you feel a bit better?" he asked. She nodded, unsure. "Thank you; please relax your mind."

Power welled up in him as he delved into Rachel's mind. He felt more pain and misery than he had ever thought possible, but there it was. He didn't look for specific memories; her pain was too vast, but he was able to give her a reprieve. The suffering and fear were like poison. It took all of his will to try to manage it. It was a testament to his magical minor that he didn't lose his mind. Still, he wasn't scratching the surface. Umbra's thoughts joined Legon's, lending him strength, and then there were Iselin, and Sasha, Opes, and Sydin. Umbra introduced Ankle's mind. Soon Legon had a sea of support, and he held Rachel's torment at bay, allowing her to fill with the compassion from those in the network. Too soon, Legon had to pull away.

Drained, he opened his eyes and looked down at Rachel's calm expression. He placed his hands on her small frame and leaned in to her ear. "I know you're hurting again, but remember, there is hope." She nodded slightly.

Legon moved back. "Thank you all. Rachel, you have had a long day. Please allow us to show you to your quarters. Ankle, Umbra, please forgive me, but we would like to debrief you immediately."

SASHA WALKED NEXT TO LEGON AS THEY MADE THEIR WAY TO the war room. She was having a hard time believing what she had just seen. Even her guard seemed shaken. Entering the war room, she tried to push Rachel from her mind. Ankle and Umbra entered the room behind them, Umbra in her Elvin form. The table in the center of the room lit up.

"Umbra, why don't you begin?" Opes said.

Umbra explained her entrance into the Cona Empire and her drop of Barnin's unit. "The day I retrieved the team, I was doing some basic reconnaissance work. I was trying to figure out Impa routes into the Cona lands, bridges, towns, and other key areas."

"Did you find anything of value?" Sydin asked.

She shook her head. "I'm not sure, Sir. There were towns and the like, but from what I could tell, many of them were empty."

"Empty?" Iselin asked.

"Yes, Un Prose, empty. The towns were ghost towns. I think I may have found seven or eight. I was going to make another pass and see if I could figure out why they were abandoned, but I was called away by Heath.

"I made my way to where Barnin and his men were. When I was close, I became aware of another Ascended. They were not doing much to hide themselves, and based on my encounter, I would say they are young."

"This was the class eight?" Opes verified.

"Yes, he was a class eight. There is no denying it."

The room was quiet for some time. The news that there was an eight was not good. Thanks to the efforts of the last few years, the Elves should have a significantly higher number of dragons than the Iumenta, but this was still a problem. One eight could take down several sevens, and...

"How do we know there aren't more?" Legon asked.

Sydin frowned. "We don't. From what we've seen, we still have more Ascended." He didn't sound overly confident.

Legon pinched the bridge of his nose. "I guess it's a moot point anyway. Ankle?"

Ankle launched into a detailed account of what they had seen. The crystal in the war room could project someone's memories on the display, and they watched Ankle's, Barnin's, and Heath's memories. "As you can see, the people in the breeding program are kept separate from the others, almost like livestock. We don't know where Rachel fits into this. We didn't talk about that on the way back.

"You can also see here that they are training children from birth. Once again, we didn't get much in the way of detailed information. Sorry, Sir."

Sasha was disgusted and didn't care to be part of the conversation anymore. Her mind reached out to her mother. "Is Rachel settled in?" she asked.

"Yes, she is, but I dare say she'd rather be with you guys," her mother said, flustered.

Sasha was confused. "Why is that? Is everything okay?"

"She is insisting that she is well enough to talk. Honestly, I think she feels guilty that she is now safe and all of those other people are not."

Sasha considered this. "Is she well enough?"

"Yes, I suppose so."

Sasha turned her attention back to the room. Everyone was talking theories about what all Mors could hold when she interrupted. "My mother says that Rachel is insistent that she speaks with us. She is well enough. I think we should let her talk."

Legon nodded his head. "Very well. If she's able and willing, let's have her."

"Mother, please bring Rachel to the war room."

———

LEGON WAITED PATIENTLY FOR RACHEL TO ARRIVE. WHEN she entered the room, she didn't seem to need support. The tall wooden door shut behind her. Nervous eyes curtained in thin hair swept the room. Her outline against the dark wood of the door made Legon pause. She looked like a corpse come to life from a nightmare. What hair she had was only in patches on her head. Her skin was almost translucent and pale against the door.

"Rachel, thank you for doing this. Would you like to take a seat?"

"Yes, thank you. Un Prosa, correct?" she verified.

Legon smiled warmly. "Legon is fine," he said, bringing two chairs to the center of the room. She sat across from him, the rest of the room standing out of the way so as not to intimidate her. "Rachel, we have many questions for you about Mors, but please do not feel like you have to answer them all today. If you feel ill or tired..."

An odd look crossed Rachel's face. It was one of mingled pain and anger. "Thank you, but I have felt sick long enough. I would like to tell you my story, and then from there you could maybe ask me questions?"

"Very well. Would you like some water or Poti?" he offered.

"Thank you, whatever you are having, and please forgive my tone. I assure you my anger is not directed toward you. I suppose you know how grateful I am..."

Legon poured her a glass of Poti. "We only took your pain, and there is no need for apology. That being said, knowing your pain, I have a fairly good idea how grateful you are. Now, please tell us your story."

Rachel took a breath and launched in. "I was sixteen. I lived in a town up north. It was spring, and we started hearing things... started hearing of people going missing... not into the care though. There seemed to be more of those, but just random people. Anyway, we started to see Iumenta at dusk on the outskirts of town. It was... unnerving, to say the least. That's when people started to disappear from our town. We were all frightened.

"One night, they came," she shivered. "Humans, in black. They killed most of the town, dragged off the bodies. Those of us who survived were in the center of town. Some Iumenta came and asked around. There were only ten of us, so it didn't take long. I told them that my mother was a wet nurse, and that I had helped her out. It was that skill that saved my life...

"We were taken to Mors and held in a large stone room. We were chained to the wall. An Iumenta came and used magic to put a mark on the back of my neck. They did the same with my friend Pamela... the people from our town were there as a treat for the men who performed the best taking our town... Pamela and I were not to be touched, but we were to watch, to see what awaited us.

"There were five of them. They first unlocked one of the men from the town... they had whips and sharp tools. I've never seen so much blood in my life, never heard someone scream like he did. It took him over an hour to die...

"They took one of the women next. They ravaged her and then killed her in much the same way." She shuddered and looked up, glassy-eyed. "They made us watch everyone die. They made us watch. They broke us without laying a hand on us." She took a drink. "That was the beginning. Pamela was a breeder. I was to help with the pregnant women and in the nurseries. This gave me the benefit of not always having to be in the breeding area, but that also meant I learned more about the camp.

"Breeders are fed and sheltered. I was given some food too, but we stayed in the cages. It was a long road of work and starvation that would be my death. Anyway, how the camp works is straightforward actually. If you are in the care and you are female, you are a breeder. If you are a male, you fight to the death. Whoever lives is then made a breeder. They only want the strong. The men will impregnate ten or so women, and then they are used to teach the children how to kill.

"Not all of the breeding is done with those in the care; most of the girls there breed with those that were born in the camp. In fact, many of the women breeders were born in Mors. The lifetime of hardship seems to make them more resilient.

"Other than that, you saw what happens. They are trained from the time they can walk. If a baby is not perfect, it is destroyed. If a mother miscarries too often, she will be killed. There are more specifics, but I think I am at my limit for today," she finished.

UMBRA LOOKED AROUND THE ROOM, OBSERVING FACES. Rachel was looking tired again; Iselin was green, Sydin was shaking his head muttering. Opes was enraged, a vein in his temple pulsing. Sasha looked the model of compassion as she stared at Rachel. Her brother Legon was different. Umbra saw the hate in his eyes. She saw the fury of the Everser Vald kindled against the Iumenta.

Legon spoke. "Umbra, Ankle, please take Rachel to her room and make sure she gets the rest she needs."

They left the room without a sound, breathing out a sigh when the doors thumped shut.

Rachel slept most of the day, but Ankle and Umbra did not leave her side. All that night they stayed with her. In the morning, Laura came in with the Captain of the ship that had taken them to the North.

Rachel was up. "Thank you all for the kindness. Laura, where are Legon and Sasha?"

Laura pursed her lips. "I don't know. They are busy, but I'm sure they will come by and visit."

At that moment, Opes entered the room, erect and formal, his eyes puffy and red. By his appearance, Umbra assumed that they'd spent the night meeting in the war room. She stood at attention, as did the ship's Captain. Taking their cue, Ankle did the same.

Opes stood next to the bed and glanced at Rachel, his face softened in sadness for the briefest moment, and then he was back to business.

"Umbra, you are to take Ankle back to Manton. After that, your squad is to go north to the town of Noris and scout the countryside and coast. Look for enemy entrapments and note any place that will make a viable beachhead. Captain, you are to remove the jump crystal from your ship and report in to fleet command for immediate deployment."

Rachel looked worried. "Opes, what's going on?"

His face again softened just a bit looking at her. "The Pawdin Empire is going to war." He turned and left the room. As the door closed, Umbra heard the city-wide announcement telling all military units to report for deployment and announcing that the Empire was now in a state of war.

CHAPTER 24
GOING OFF TO WAR

"People often think that mercy stays justice's hand, but what they fail to see is that oftentimes, it is mercy that turns justice loose on the wicked."
— *Diary of the Perfectos Compatioa*

Sasha looked up from the journal she was reading when she heard the door to her study close. In the entrance, Edling stood nervously, playing with the hem of his blue shirt.

"Hello, Edling, how are you?" Sasha asked.

Sasha adored Edling. She'd had a crush on him for years, one that her guard and his family were sure he shared, but he never acted on his feelings. She didn't honestly see a relationship ever developing between them. After all, she was aging, while he was not. *On the bright side, the scenery won't change at least,* she thought.

"I was wondering if you had a moment. I know you're busy and all," he said, still acting oddly.

"Sure. Do you want to sit down?"

It didn't look like he was sure, but he sat anyway. *What is going on?* she thought. He seemed to be collecting his thoughts. "Look." He stopped. "I've heard that you will be going with your brother... off to war," he explained, "and... and I just wanted to talk to you before you, um, ya know, go running off into battle."

"All right; what's up?" She tried to sound bright.

Up to this point, Edling had been uncharacteristically looking down and fidgeting, but he looked up at her now, a look of fear and determination on his face. "I love you," he stated.

He what? "Sorry, you what?" she asked, confused.

He wasn't looking as determined now. "I love you. Look, I know that I'm an Elf and that you probably want someone you can grow old with. But for the last few years, you're all I can think about. I told myself that I would lose interest and that it wasn't a good idea. The fact is, you are going off to war, and well, I might not see you again..."

"Really? You want to be with me?" she asked. "I mean, my brother and guard and, well, your parents said you liked me, but I didn't think anything would ever happen..."

He looked up and said, "My parents?" then shook his head. "It doesn't matter. Yes, I want to be with you; I have since the first time we met."

"This whole time?" He nodded, and she laughed. "This is too perfect," she laughed.

He looked confused. "I'm sorry..."

She laughed again. "Don't be sorry. I'm crazy about you; it's just... it's just that we have both felt this way for years and never did anything about it."

He smiled. "Seems pretty stupid, doesn't it?"

"Yes, it does," she agreed. "I'm taking off the rest of the day," she announced.

"Are you sure you can?" Edling asked.

She laughed again. "Nope, I'm swamped, but if my past experiences with the Iumenta are any indication of the future, I don't want to risk losing any happiness before I die."

"Way to be positive," he said dryly.

It was late in the day, and Legon and Iselin were just finishing up dinner when Sasha came bounding into the dining room. "Edling loves me, and we spent the day together, and we kissed, and it was so much fun," she gushed. And then stopped at the looks she was getting.

Legon chuckled. "About time; I was wondering what he was waiting for."

Iselin gave him a look. "Sash, that's great! I'm so happy for you," then looking back to Legon, "You can't rush love."

Legon smiled up at Sasha. He was so happy that he was having a hard time containing himself. Connected as they were, she could sense that. "Legon, someone wants me... can you believe it?"

His voice was thick. "He has always wanted you, but I'm happy you know now too." Why had it taken so long for her to see that there were those who did want her? Legon didn't know. Maybe if she had, something between her and Edling would have happened a long time ago, though it was unlikely. She was mortal, and he wasn't, but that didn't matter now. All that mattered was his sister finally realizing she was someone worth loving.

Sara looked down at the map that had been resting on her living room table for the better part of a week. She looked at her husband. "Why Noris? And why by sea?"

Keither walked over next to her to look down at the map. He pointed to the town of Noris on the map. It was on the north side of the Kayloose's inlet to the sea.

"You need to keep in mind how the Cona Empire is laid out and also that at one point, Noris was more centrally located." His finger traced the Kayloose. "The first thing to understand is that east of the Kayloose is where almost seventy percent of the Cona Empire's food comes from. This land is wide plains, but it gets a good amount of rain, and there are many lakes and rivers. Most of the people in these areas live in villages or co-ops. Food goes in one of a few directions: either north to the Iumenta or northland lands, south to Coreum, or west. The vast majority of it ends up at the Kayloose. The river has lots of cities, towns, and villages along its banks. I assume you noticed that in Salez, the river is much wider and slower than, say, by the town of Kayloose."

Sara said she had, and Keither went on. "And it becomes more so. It's deep enough and slow enough that it's littered with barges. These barges move food along the river to Noris."

"Yes, I know, but why Noris?"

Again he pointed at the map, this time to Salmont. "We grew up in the Laetuc Mountain Range. It goes north into the Impa lands. These mountains split the northern part of the Empire. Around the capital, they are more like hills, but then they become higher and more densely forested north of that. Salmont was also in a high-density area. We were the only town in that part of the mountains. There are a few other little valleys that people live in, but needless to say, you can't transport goods through those mountains. South of the Laetuc, the landscape turns into rolling hills. You can move goods across it, but not as effectively as with the barges. Also, intelligence reports show that transportation along land routes is getting nearly impossible without spending a significant amount on security.

"So you see, Noris is the best option. If not, you have to send goods north and then back along the coast, and with almost eighty percent of the population living along the coast..."

She got it. "If you take Noris, you destroy supply lines."

"Right. Furthermore, if I know the Elves, they are going to play to their strengths and use their Navy to wreak havoc along the coastline, so no going to the sea for food. The coast will be where most of the fighting takes place, and up the Kayloose River. The Cona Empire will have no choice but to move goods across land, and in order to do that, they will have to pull men from the front line to ensure said goods, like food, make it to their desired destination."

Sara could see it now. Cities would be under siege but wouldn't be able to last long knowing that there was no support coming. On the flip side, once a city was taken, the resistance would be able to ship food in from the sea.

"Won't Noris be hard to take?" she asked.

"Yes, knowing its importance and seeing an attack coming, the

Cona Empire has the vast majority of its fleet anchored there right now. The Human resistance has no chance of defeating that fleet, so the Pawdin Empire will be taking care of most of that. We will mostly be sending transport ships and providing bodies to go ashore once they clear the path."

UMBRA HUGGED THE GROUND, TAKING THE WESTERN EDGE of the formation. It was overcast tonight, which was making for great cover. On the northern side of the town of Noris were high cliffs that fell straight to the ocean. The other side of the Kayloose was hills. Not that it mattered—the river was close to two miles wide at this point.

"Spread out. Look for anything that we can hit that will help out the landing parties," she ordered.

The other seven dragons spaced themselves out, covering as much land as possible as they glided over. Spells looking for everything—wards, concealed bunkers, and personnel—were activated, but they tried not to use too much magic; stealth was key. There were tons of Ascended in the area, which Umbra had to admit added a little excitement. Here she was gathering information, and the filth would sometimes fly right overhead and never see a thing. Noris itself wasn't all that big, but it was connected with several other towns. She wrapped around the cluster of towns, looking at the harbor. It was inside the river, and rock banks protected it. That way would not work for landing parties. To the north of the town, there was a stretch of beach where some of the smaller fishing boats would come ashore with their catches. The water was deep enough that the landing vessels could run themselves aground and drop off their passengers.

The beach wasn't all that far from the town's wall. Umbra eyed the large wall around the city. Just inside that wall were ballistae, trebuchets, catapults, and all other manner of defenses. With that wall in the way, they would take heavy casualties trying to enter the city. Everyone would be sitting wide open on the beach. Even if the Ascended that were going to take part in the fight managed to take control of the skies before landing parties made it... Making another pass, she looked at the gate. It was there to allow the fishermen into the town, and it had a wide opening. Towers were on either side of it, but if that gate were to be open...

An idea came to her. "Okay, it will be light soon; we're out of here," she said, preparing to rendezvous with her squad. She was anxious to get back to base.

BARNIN WAS DOING A LAST CHECK OF HIS GEAR, WITH A sullen Samantha sitting on a chair watching him. He glanced at her. "Are you angry with me?"

She scoffed. "At you? You're doing what you're supposed to. I'm mad at this war."

He breathed out. "We have to do this. If you saw..."

She waved her hand. "Not angry at our side; I'm angry that we have to go to war at all. I wish the Elves would have killed the Iumenta off two thousand years ago and saved us some trouble. Or that Humanity would have been smart enough to not let the Iumenta take over in the first place," she said angrily.

"I know, babe." His hands tightened. Never before had he felt this way before going into combat. He knew it was because this time he would be gone for a long time, and he wasn't sure if he was going to come back. "Look, after this is, after this is over, I promise that we can find some quiet place and, and never have to think about this again."

Sam looked up at him. "You promise you're coming back?"

He nodded, but that wasn't going to cut it. He could see. "Yes, I promise."

"Good. If you don't, I'm going to raise you from the dead and kill you again," she threatened.

There was a knock at the door. He went to answer it. Ankle stood outside. "Sir, we have new orders. We are going to be on a special assignment."

LEGON FINISHED UP THE LAST THING HE HAD TO DO BEFORE leaving. He walked out to the terrace, gazing down at the bay, its water sparkling. Most of the house fleet was already on its way to meet up with the main force. Only a handful of ships remained. Iselin, from behind him, wound her arms around his waist, placing her head on his shoulder.

"Do you think we will see it again?" she asked.

He turned his head. "What, the bay? Yeah, I do." He squeezed her hands, pulling her arms tighter around him. "I am planning on standing here with you, looking out on this bay for many thousands of years to come," he said, kissing her cheek.

Someone cleared their throat behind them. Legon looked to see Emma. "Emma, what can I do for you?" he asked.

"Um, well," she seemed to gain her confidence. "I want to go. I want to go with Sasha. I promised that no matter what, if I ever saw her again, that I would never leave her side. Well, now she is about to go off to war, and I have no intention of backing out on that. We both know what she'll say, so I was wondering if maybe you could kind of order me along."

"Are you sure?" Legon asked. She nodded her head in the affirmative. "It's your funeral," he said.

Emma blanched. "You think we are gonna die?"

Legon laughed. "Yes, I'd say so, but I don't think it will be the Empire that kills us. Sash is going to have both our heads."

Emma smiled. "Don't worry, I can take her. I'll protect you." She winked and walked off.

Legon was right, of course, and a few hours later, a haggard Sasha approached him. Her face was still pale from the episode she'd had that afternoon. "What did you do?" she spat.

"Sash, relax; you're going to give yourself another one."

That was the wrong thing to say. "I'm going to what? Don't you even try that. Why did you tell, or I should say order Emma to come? Do you want her to die?"

"Look, she will be with us, first of all, and I'm not planning on us dying. Also, she has the right to go if she wants. She's lost in this too, and she may not be able to do much, but I dare say assisting you will at least comfort her. Furthermore, you aren't going to the front line after we land, so she'll be safe with you."

Sasha scowled. Her emotions told him he was winning. She wasn't happy but couldn't find a way to make an argument otherwise. "Are you ready to go?" she asked, changing the subject.

"Yes, Ise is already at the docks," he breathed out. "You know, if you stayed here, so would Emma."

Her face softened. "Not a chance."

"That's what I thought. Can you try to see that it's like that for Emma?"

She sighed. "Yes. That's why I'm not going to fight you anymore."

They made their way down to the docks. Emma was already there waiting for them. She wasn't going to be left behind. Also present were Laura and Edis. Legon's mind flashed back to when they left Salmont, to the hopeless look in his mother's eyes and the fear on his father's face.

Before he could say anything, his mother came up and hugged him, kissing his cheek. "I am so proud of you, but come back to me."

"I will."

His father shook his hand, holding back his emotions. "We've spent some time with that Rachel girl, and we've learned some things. This might not be the best farewell, but you're my son, and you're to change this land, so..." he straightened up, "come back to us with your head held high in victory." Iselin was with them, and Edis looked over at her. "And you just come back, sweetness," he added, giving her a wink.

Legon beamed, promising that he would not come back until the job was done. As the ship left port, Legon was filled with a great sense of terrible purpose. His frame almost shook with it, as if fate had been saving this day for him.

The coast faded away, and Legon turned to look at the fleet that was waiting for them.

The sun was setting when Legon sat down at a desk on the ship. A memory from what felt like a thousand years ago bloomed in his mind. He thought of the first time he addressed his people. That day he felt sick with fear that he would make a mistake, that the people wouldn't like him and think him a fool. That was not the case now. Long ago, Legon shed his fear of the masses. Today it wasn't that he was to deliver a message that made his mouth drier than any desert; it was the message itself, its significance. A marble-sized crystal hovered in front of his lips, glowing blue. It would carry his words to all of the resistance. His mind ran with the inflections he would use to move people, the pauses to make the listeners think, and the words—words that were formal and stately—nothing like day-to-day communication.

He took a deep breath. "Today we stand as if at the edge of a great cliff. Behind us is nothingness, a land of waste and sorrow. Below us, the jagged rocks of life, of possible failure and death. But also there is water, a stream that if we but travel down it, we will find ourselves free. We have stood at this cliff's edge long enough. We have looked to the jagged rocks and held ourselves back, but no longer. We find ourselves compelled to act. We find the edge of the cliff breaking away. If we stand fast, we will slip to the rocks below. If we jump, we will land in the river.

"This land has been ravaged by cruelty and hate. It has been soaked through by the blood of the innocent. It is their blood that cries out this night. It cries out against those that hurt, maim, and make afraid. It cries out for justice. It cries out for mercy. Are we to stand fast and have our hands stained with this blood? Are we to ignore the demands of justice? Or are we to put ourselves in harm's way? And are we to stop the pain and sorrow of the innocent? This I say to you: this is what I, what we intend to do. As we jump from this cliff's edge, we hurtle ourselves into the unknown. Some of us, perhaps all of us, will find the rocks. But even if all of us should perish in this struggle, I say happy day; for it is better that we die fighting wickedness than turn away from that which is right.

"I ask now, what is it that you will do? Will you jump with me? Will you fight with me? Will you become a force that will sweep over this land and cleanse it of the plague that is now so fully engulfing it? Will you go in harm's way? I know you will. I know this people, and I know your hearts, and that is why it is my honor to fight alongside you, and even if needed, to die alongside you. Over the coming months and years, we will face many trials, some that will seem to us to be unbearable. But if we exercise our faith in what is right, we will rise above our trials. We will beat back our foes. We stand as a light on the horizon. We must burn bright if we are to push back the darkness, if we are to bring the innocent out of the dark and into the light. This is our mission, our fate, and our purpose, and in this purpose, we will not fail." The crystal stopped glowing.

Legon stood and walked out of the tiny office he was in. Iselin, Sasha, and Emma were waiting on the other side of the door. "How did I do?" he asked.

SASHA STOOD ON DECK, EMMA NEXT TO HER. IT WAS EARLY IN the morning; the air was cool.

"You need to try to calm down," Emma said.

Sasha knew she was right. She always had more episodes when she was under stress. This morning had been no different, except today she could not afford to be sick. It hadn't taken them long to meet up with the Human fleet from Manton, and now they were on the dawn of the largest invasion in two thousand years. No, she could not afford to be sick today.

"I'll be fine, thank you, Emma." She turned to her. "You have been an amazing friend to me over the years. I love you like a sister, you know that, right?"

Emma nodded. "You too," then, "What's it like?"

"What's what like?" Sasha asked.

Emma shrugged. "Battle."

Sasha stiffened. "It's going to be the most horrific thing you have ever seen. After today, you will not look at the world the same way again." She didn't want to scare Emma, but she wasn't going to shelter her either.

EMMA TRIED TO TAKE SASHA'S WORDS TO HEART. HER EYES cast around the fleet, seeing the ships advance along like an unstoppable force. She then looked to the horizon, seeing a line of dots that would soon become ships, and she wondered which was more powerful, an unstoppable force or an immovable object? An alarm sounded, telling them to prepare for battle.

CHAPTER 25
CRIMSON TIDE

"The altar of freedom and peace is soaked in blood, that of the good and the evil. This is a simple truth. The question becomes, if your blood was to grace the altar, which would it be? Good or Evil?"
— *The Great Defeat, Secunum Renovatie*

Legon watched as Sasha and Emma made their way quickly back from the prow. Ahead lay the largest fleet the Cona Empire had ever commissioned. Above it flew ranks of Ascended, leaching light from the sky, hanging like a dark cloud over the Cona fleet. In the distance were the high sea cliffs of Noris. Iselin's mental touch was warm, a soft farewell. The only true fear he had was the knowledge that if one of them should die, they hadn't been connected long enough for the other to die as well.

Mage stood next to him, his fox familiar sitting next to Bill, Legon's familiar. Legon rested his hand on the pommel of Tento, his Fenna.

"Are you ready?" Mage asked.

Connected to Legon, Bill stood in answer and paced back and forth on deck. The ships were taking shape on the horizon. He heard a call from Sydin, and the fifty Elvin Ascended broke away from the fleet. The battle was starting.

Legon looked up, watching the V-shaped formations pass, their armor reflecting back the light of the waves. Across the expanse, the Iumenta were doing likewise. The Iumenta were outnumbered, but not as much as Legon would have liked. So captivated was he by the approaching conflict in the sky that at first he didn't notice the ship starting to accelerate. When he did, he turned his attention back to what lay ahead for him.

The rest of the guard was on deck now and all moved closer to the prow of the ship. The familiars wailed as they turned. Bill's form shifted; his teeth grew as his body grew and swelled. The fiery fur along his neck flared into a mane. Legon patted the shoulder of the lion next to him.

Legon's eyes flicked up, hearing the roars of many dragons. Bolts of magic shot from the Elf and Iumenta dragons, streaking across the sky. Wards flashed, and the air crackled with sound. Still closer they drew; more and more magic was flying until finally the two forces collided with each other.

Legon tore his eyes from the fight in time to see hundreds of ballista bolts being fired from the Pawdin fleet. Across from him, one of the few Iumenta ships fired, sending a brilliant blue bolt hurling toward them. There was a crack as it collided with the green wards of the ship. The Cona fleet did not fare as well. It appeared that only the Iumenta ship was being protected with magic.

Wards flicked over him as everyone in the group placed stop-all wards on each other, preventing anyone from being injured by crossfire. He gripped Tento and pulled the blade from its sheath. Wind blew in his hair as they raced to the Iumenta ship.

"It is unlikely that there are any other ships in this battle that have this many powerful Venefica on board. That will make us a strong tool, but also a high-priority target," Mage said.

Legon crouched to leap. *Just a hundred yards or so now.* The smooth ceramic hull of the Impa ship slid through the water at them, unafraid of its wooden counterpart. Right before the ships hit, Legon and his

guard jumped. The ships met with a crunch. Legon's forward movement kept him and his guard hurtling through the air toward the other
ship. The Iumenta were doing the same.

The air filled with the sound of metal and stone grinding together.
Legon used magic to lift himself higher as he rocketed toward an
Iumenta. He lifted himself, bringing his knee to the filth's head. The
Iumenta raised two fenrra to deflect Legon's knee. At the last moment,
Legon forced himself down and swung Tento at the Iumenta's unpro-
tected abdomen. With a squelch and gurgled scream, the blade cut the
Iumenta in half.

Bill was on the deck of the Iumenta ship before Legon, with two
other familiars. They were all fighting the same gray bear. The animal's
fiery fur was rent and then re-formed almost instantly. Legon turned his
attention to the aft of the ship as he ran across the deck. The sheer
number of Venefica in Legon's guard was easily overwhelming the
Iumenta.

Legon knelt, dodging a blow, and spun, facing a silver-haired
Iumenta, its yellow eyes full of hate burning against the gray skin of its
face. The Iumenta gritted its teeth, giving it an even more wolf-like
appearance. Tento collided with the thick, flat blade of the Iumenta's
fenna. Grey light oozed from him. *So this is the bear's Venefica,* he
thought. Legon gritted his teeth and lashed out. Every attack met opposition. The Iumenta countered with a spell that surrounded Legon with
mist. *He's a Biologic like me!* The mist was poison. Quickly, Legon held
his breath but felt one of his wards being slightly tested. The Iumenta's
eyes bulged. Biologics were rare and not extremely effective in combat in
general, but they had a few tricks up their sleeves.

Legon took the Iumenta's surprise as an opportunity. Power flowed
out of his hand down the length of the blade, altering the wards for
Biologic attacks. A grey flash arched from the Iumenta. Legon blocked
it with ease, not feeling a drain on his own power. He had been right to
assume that his opponent would use more Biologic spells.

Legon countered with a convulsing spell of his own. It was deflected
by the other fenna. Again he attacked, but this time with a simple
breaking spell. It was unaffected by the fenna and cracked against the

Iumenta's own wards. As the Iumenta's wards failed, he raised his blade to block Legon, who caught the eye of one of his guard.

"NOW!" he yelled. The Iumenta's head turned just in time to have a ball of emerald fire engulf him.

Iselin left Legon with a warm touch and refocused on the task at hand. Sydin was in command of the Pawdin Empire's Ascended. They flew in V formations in the direction of similar Impa formations. The order came to separate from the fleet. The air was a strobe of wards as everyone put stop-all spells in place for their own magic on the other Ascended. Her wings spread up as she accelerated. Her armor felt constricting.

The ships were behind them now. Hers was one of the lead formations. Iselin locked eyes with a brown Ascended across the void. Their mission was simple: first, break the line and open a gap so that the others could make it to the coast, and then, kill everything.

It was so hard not to fly faster; she wanted to rip and tear. In this form, she was more animalistic, and all she wanted to do now was let that side of her take over, but she couldn't. She needed to stay focused. A guttural roar ripped from her as Sydin told them to attack. A pink orb of energy left her, hurling itself at the brown Ascended. It, in turn, was sending something her way. She dipped in the air, letting the spell fly by harmlessly. The second blast hit her left wing, rending the air with a crack. *Fool me once...* she thought, sending four quick spells as the gap closed.

The brown Ascended tried to avoid them but only made himself off-kilter. Iselin slammed into him, feeling her chest plates dig into her scales. With a growl, she bit down on his shoulder. Her mouth filled with the salty tang of blood. Her sides burned as the brown Ascended raked his claws down her ribs. The cuts healed almost as fast as they were being inflicted. Even her bite was gone now. Their tails thrashed as they tried to cut each other with the blades attached to them. Bands of energy lashed out from each dragon, twisting and curling in the air.

He snapped at her neck, catching the showy armor and ripping it off. The chainmail on his left flank was dangling in the air. Hers was also all but gone, leaving only the real armor. They separated, trying to gain altitude. The sky was filled with magic as the dragons fought.

Sydin's voice rang out. "Break the line! Break the line!"

Right, she was to break the line. She shouldered the brown Ascended, forcing it sideways. This earned her a tail blade to the thigh. Too late, she tried to block it, as it sliced through the muscle, hitting bone. She screamed with pain, but it soon faded as wards healed the wound. The next time he attacked with his tail, Iselin blocked it with the thick metal on the bottom of her feet.

Again she rammed into him, driving him where she wanted to go. A gap was opening in the Iumenta line, and they seemed to notice what was going on. The brown and others were trying to reform the line, but it was too late.

There was the sound of crunching wood, and a bolt from a ballista passed by them. Iselin looked down, seeing that the fleets had met. She caught a glimpse of the few Iumenta ships colliding with Elvin ships and stopping fast. But for the most part, it was looking to be a slaughter. Most of the enemy ships were Human. The ships shattered like glass as the Elvin ships rammed them. Men jumped overboard, trying to avoid arrows.

The air below them filled with flaming missiles fired from ballistae on the Pawdin ships. The dragons tried to keep above the line of fire. Iselin refocused on her job and tried to ignore the scene below.

BARNIN SETTLED HIMSELF ON UMBRA'S BACK YET AGAIN. JUST on the other side of the spikes that ran the length of her back was Josher, behind him Heath and three other men. Barnin had four behind him, each clinging to a spike. It wasn't going to be a comfortable trip. They were packed closely together on her back, each man's head at about armpit level for the one in front of him. Barnin felt a sticking spell suck him into place, and he let go of the spike he was holding.

His unit was spread over three dragons, each carrying ten guys. Barnin's unit was the only Human unit that was a part of this mission.

There were ten dragons in all, three carrying Barnin's men and the other seven carrying Elves. They were going to fly to the beach ahead of landing parties. The dragons would come in close to the ground and use magic to place them behind the town walls of Noris, close to the gates. From there, it was a simple plan: open the gates. With Umbra and others wreaking havoc, opening the gates shouldn't be overly difficult. The hard part was making it to Noris. Between them and the town was the Cona fleet and a lot of Iumenta dragons.

Josher, who had come a long way since joining Barnin's unit, looked like he was thinking rather hard. "What's on your mind?" Barnin asked.

"Sir, let me get this straight. Just in case, ya know, I didn't understand what you've been telling us in every briefing for, I don't know, a week. So we," he motioned to everyone on Umbra's back, "we are supposed to ride Umbra here to Noris, and then open the front doors and say to our buddies, 'Let's level this place.' But to do that, we are going to fly over the Cona fleet and hope that the other Elvin dragons have opened a hole for our little group here to fly through. And during that time, the Iumenta ships are going to be shooting spells and bolts and all that fun stuff at us."

"That's about the gist of it, yeah," Barnin said, smirking.

Josher craned his neck, looking around the deck of the carrier.

"What are you doing?" Barnin asked.

Josher turned back to him. "I'm trying to check out one of those Elf skirts before we leave. Since we're gonna die, I want to look at one last beautiful woman before it all ends, ya know?"

All of the men on Umbra laughed, and she twisted her neck to look at Josher.

"What, am I not good enough for you?" she teased.

Josher grinned up at her. "Don't worry, hon, you can eat me any time you want," he said with a wink.

Umbra rolled her eyes, and Barnin felt as if he was going to be chucked off her back when she laughed.

A horn sounded on the ship, and everyone became serious. It was time for them to leave. Barnin looked up the length of Umbra's neck, noting all of the dings and scratches on her armor. Today she was only wearing the bare minimum for speed. Barnin went over a mental inventory of his own armor, trying not to think about what would happen if he fell. The spell sticking him to Umbra was strong, but if it failed, he would plunge into the water wrapped in metal and sink to the bottom like a rock.

The carrier they were on was in the back of the formation. He watched in awe as the rest of the dragons took off, covered in gleaming metal. They would wait until the main body of Ascended were on their way before taking off themselves. There was no smoke in the distance or the sound of spells and wards colliding, so he figured the fleets hadn't engaged each other yet.

Umbra unfurled her wings and coiled to take flight. Barnin felt the man next to him tense, never having been on a dragon before. Barnin closed his eyes and felt himself hurled into the sky. When he opened them again, the sea air stung a bit. He looked down at the fleet of carriers sweeping behind him. Umbra was flying lead for her squad, which had been joined by two other dragons that acted as replacements. The ten black dragons slid through the azure sky, their wings rising and falling in unison.

They circled the carrier fleet, waiting for their time to go. In the distance, Barnin heard the sound of thunder, and he looked to see the horizon lighting up with magic. He wondered how people were faring. Was Legon fighting anyone? Surely, he thought, Iselin was. She'd have been in one of the lead formations.

Umbra touched his mind. "The main fleet has engaged the Cona Empire. The ships with landing parties are attempting to skirt around the fighting; they will be free of the main battle soon." She paused and went on. "In the air, we are winning. The Impa line will break soon. When it does, we will start our approach. They will have figured out by now what we are planning on doing. They may let the line break to get us in close.

"The landing ships have broken away; we will have to make our approach soon, even if the line doesn't break," she continued.

A few minutes later, Barnin heard her roar, and she turned in the sky, angling toward the fight. Barnin turned back to his men. "This is it! Keep your head in the game and try not to lose focus. Things are going to get bumpy until we hit land."

Umbra was facing the coast, forcing her wings down as fast as she could. Barnin felt the air buffet him as she sped up.

KEITHER FINISHED CHECKING TO MAKE SURE THEIR LANDING ship was packed. He would be going in the third wave, but he wasn't going to wait until the last moment to prepare. He heard grinding metal above him but didn't bother to look up. The ship he was on was making its way around the Cona fleet, without much in the way of resistance. The Pawdin fleet was holding the Human and Iumenta forces at bay. Above, the dragons were paying almost no attention to the ships below.

"Why don't the dragons care about us, and why is Umbra going through that fight?" Sara asked, looking up.

Keither followed her gaze. "It's a different fight. Dragons can move faster than ships, so Barnin and his group can't just skirt around like us. They need a direct line."

As he watched the sky, he saw a hole form in the Iumenta formation. He looked west, seeing the all-black Ascended streak through the sky, headed for the hole in the formation. They weaved through the air, avoiding magic and weapons shot from ships. His attention was pulled by a messenger.

"Sir, wave one has broken away and is preparing to drop lines. They will be on shore in twenty minutes," he said and ran off.

BARNIN'S BREATH BECAME SHORTER AND SHORTER THE closer they came to the fighting horde of dragons. There was so much light and sound he felt like he was going to get sick. Umbra was focusing completely on what lay ahead. If anything went amiss with Barnin and his men, she'd have no idea.

There was a hole in the group of dragons, and Umbra made for it. Barnin was jarred as she pitched and rolled. He looked down, seeing an Elvin ship collide with a Human one. The Humans jumped from the decks to be pulled down to the bottom of the sea by their armor. Some didn't jump but rather were crushed by the ships.

Time was slowing as he took in the skies around him. Light flashed, making little spots pop in his eyes. He thought he saw Ise, but wasn't sure.

"HANG ON!" he yelled to his men.

As if in response, Umbra turned in the air, rolling over like a corkscrew. An emerald ball passed by. Barnin looked behind them to one of the dragons with Elves on its back. Their armor caught in the day and magic light. A small object that looked like a package floated between Umbra and the rest of her squad. Barnin focused on it, wondering what it was. There was a flash of light and *BOOM*. Barnin saw the black of Umbra's wards.

"Hang on, we are over the Iumenta; there will be flak," Umbra said and then disconnected.

Flak? Barnin wondered as he watched several more packages. They blew up like the first one. This time he saw little trails of something small in the air. Umbra shook with the concussion of the explosion, then the ballista bolts started whizzing by them.

It was hell in the sky. Barnin felt as though he was going to vomit, so rapid were Umbra's rolls and turns in the air. One of the other dragons carrying Elves was next to them now. Barnin turned, looking at the figures on the dragon's back. They didn't seem shaken or surprised by the happenings. Suddenly, a red Iumenta dragon broke past the Elvin Ascended. Barnin tried to yell a warning to the Elves as if it would change anything, but it couldn't. He watched helplessly as the red dragon's tail, encased in a blade, slashed down the line of men. Blood and innards hung in space. He couldn't tear his eyes away from it...

His head hit one of Umbra's spines as she turned in the air. Barnin felt her whole body tremble as she roared, spewing black fire. As he looked, his face turned warm with the glow of flames, one the jet black of Umbra's fire mingling with the bright blue of an Iumenta dragon.

The Blue Iumenta Dragon slammed into Umbra, knocking the wind out of Barnin. Dots swam in his vision as they fell back. The dragons cartwheeled in the air, biting and clawing at each other. Barnin moved out of the way as one of the Iumenta's paws reached around

Umbra's shoulder, trying to get purchase. Barnin jerked away as one of the dragon's blade-extended talons made contact with Umbra's spine armor. The bladed extension to the beast's natural claws added another two feet, and they were sharper than any knife or sword Barnin had ever used. The talon squealed along the armor and back up Umbra's shoulder. It dug into her scales, spraying Barnin with blood. He gasped, worried that she was injured, but once the claw was gone, her body knitted together almost instantly. Fear gripped him. In his current position, he was all but useless. He couldn't even draw his sword. *What could you do to a dragon with a broadsword?* a voice in his head asked. In truth, there was nothing. He was just along for the ride.

Barnin was hyper-aware. Umbra's back was facing down, and he took in the ships below them. They were over an Iumenta one, its gray form gliding in the water. On the deck, they could see Iumenta running about, pointing ballistae up at them. They fired. The tips of the bolts glowed magenta.

Barnin turned his head to Heath. "What's with the glow?"

"They have crystals in the tips. When they make contact with a ward, they try and break it. Most should glance off Umbra, but if they make direct contact..."

There was a crack as if to bring the message home. A flash of magenta and black blinded him. The bolt's point glowed hot as it skidded across one of Umbra's wards. Above the tip, Barnin noticed what looked like spikes, but it passed too quickly. There were more cracks, and he looked down her tail, which was pointed at the ship. Magenta strikes ran up her sides, some making it through her wards to clatter up her body, trying to get purchase. Barnin and his men dodged the best they could. One flashed bright and buried itself at the base of Umbra's tail. There was an almost instant flash of black, ejecting the projectile with much blood and tissue. It wasn't a moment too soon. The bolt exploded, sending shimmering trails up her back, and one glowed yellow. The yellow bolt zipped over to Heath. Barnin, craning his neck, looked at him and Josher on the other side of Umbra.

Caught in Heath's hand was a three-inch spike that looked like the head of a spear. Barnin stared at the spike as Josher yelled, "If one of those went off inside her wards, we'd all bite it in a matter of—AHHH-HHHHHHHHHH!" he screamed.

Barnin jerked his head up to see Josher. The dragon that Umbra was fighting had his paw around her again, but this time one of its claws pierced more than Umbra. It was going through the center of Josher's back. The paw raked back along Umbra's shoulder, slicing straight up Josher through his back, out between his neck and shoulder. It had cut right through to Umbra. Blood sprayed out of him, and his screams gurgled. Barnin could see his ribs and shoulder blade, but they were soon covered as blood poured out of Josher, covering Heath and the men below him.

"HEATH! STOP THE BLEEDING!" he yelled, trying to reach over to the man.

Yellow fire burned the wounds closed, but there was still too much blood. Josher was out but still coughing, vomiting blood. "HE'S GOING TO DROWN!" Heath yelled. There was nothing they could do. Magic was flashing everywhere, and it was all he could do to stay focused as Josher drowned in his own blood. Umbra could save him, but her mind was closed so she could fight. "Hang on, buddy, we are almost through, then Umbra will fix ya up," he said. Heath was trying to stop the bleeding and keep Josher's one good lung clear. Finally, Josher stopped convulsing. Heath was still working on him. Barnin reached over, feeling sick, to grab Heath's hand. "He's gone, he's gone. Save your strength."

Laura sat next to Edis, clenching her glass. Across from her was the still small Rachel, her thin hair draped around her face. In the center of the table, holding their collective attention, was a crystal. There was a crystal in every house today. Through the crystal, they heard the sound of a man speaking in Elvish. Laura didn't know a lot of the language, so they had a translator with them, a bronze-haired woman.

"The fleet has engaged the Cona forces. There is no word on the

Ascended yet, or on the Human landing parties," the woman said in her melodic voice.

Edis took Laura's hand and then reached over to the bronze-haired woman, taking hers. Laura took Rachel's as well. The girl was under so much stress. *Please let them come back home*, she thought to herself.

"The Ascended are fighting now," the Elf said tensely.

"Is your husband one of them?" Rachel asked.

She looked up and nodded. Laura could see the Elf's face grow pale. Could she feel her love from this far away? "What is your name?"

"Ina."

"Can you sense him?" Laura asked.

She shook her head. "But if... if he gets killed, I will know. And so will you." Then she cut off. "The fleet is pressing in now. It won't be long until landing parties will be able to make their run for the coast."

Time took forever. Laura's fingers were numb. Everyone was crushing each other's hands as they hoped that their loved ones would come back home. Finally, more news came. "They are about to start landing. This is good; that means that we are win..." she stopped and looked odd. "NO!" she gasped. Ina gagged, and Laura saw the most heartbreaking look of pain cross the girl's face as their eyes met. Ina slumped, falling off her seat and hitting the ground.

"What is happening to her?" Rachel screeched.

More Elves were there, reaching down to Ina. Her head lolled. Laura looked into dead-looking eyes and understood. "Her husband passed, didn't he?" One of the Elves just looked up. Laura sat down hard. "She's gone?"

"Yes, I'm afraid so," one of them said.

Edis wrapped his arm around Laura, and they reached out to Rachel, bringing her in close.

FROM THEIR CLIFFSIDE VIEW, ARKIN AND STACY LOOKED down at Noris. Dragons were dropping men next to the gates and then turning to attack the city defenses. Landing boats were paddling toward the beach as balls of fire launched from behind the city walls.

"Will Noris fall, you think?" Stacy asked.

Arkin turned to her. "Yes, the fighting with the Ascended has moved south. They won't be able to defend the city, and out at sea, it looks as though the Pawdin fleet has won. Elvin ships will land soon, and with them, Noris will fall."

She huffed. "Will you be able to get Un Prosa, Legon, to talk to you?" she asked.

"Yes, what we need to do is too important, and the cover of the invasion will be perfect. Good work, dear; you saved a lot of lives today."

She smiled up at him. "I know I did."

LEGON TOOK A DRINK AND BIT OFF THE END OF A POWER pack. Behind them was what remained of the Cona fleet. It was making its way north, most likely in an attempt to regroup. There hadn't been much of an Impa showing in this fight, which didn't surprise him. While the Impa ships were powerful, they took a long time to construct and repair. They were costly, and even after all this time, the Impa ships were not to the same standards as the Pawdin fleet. He knew that this was not the case for the Impa Dragon Domes, which he was not looking forward to. There was one between them and the capital city of Bailaya, but he wasn't going to think about that right now. Right now, the only thing holding his attention was Noris. Smoke was rising high in the air. The Ascended were still fighting, but it was away from the city and to the south. The Iumenta were being driven deeper and deeper into Cona land.

The dragon-borne landing teams had done their job getting the city gates open, and now Human and Elvin forces were storming the city. If all went well, the city would be secure by midnight.

Sasha and Emma walked up next to him. Sasha spoke. "Sad, isn't it?" she said.

"I suppose so. It depends on how you look at it," Legon replied.

"And how is that?" Emma asked.

Legon shrugged. "Today is a sad day. These people will not yet see themselves as being freed, but as time goes on, as they rebuild, they will see a higher quality of life. That being said, the people of Noris will not forget this day. It will rather be the next generation that will see today as a blessing."

Emma placed her hands on the rail. "A tragedy for the living, but a victory for the unborn," she said.

"That is a good way of putting it," Sasha said, and then turned to Legon. "Arkin has contacted us. He needs to meet us on the beach. Emma and I are coming," she said, as if to close the subject.

Legon thought about fighting her but decided against it. "Fine, but you're both wearing store crystals. Did he say what he wanted?"

Sasha seemed satisfied. "No, he said it was important, though. I don't think he wanted to tie up communications. Emma and I will have stores, but I don't think they will be necessary. We are meeting Arkin on the north beach. The whole area is nothing but cliffs. Mage said that Ascended have already cleared that area. It was a poor area to set up a defense."

"Yes, it is. The mountains are a defense in and of themselves, and we couldn't have used that route even if we wanted to. When we looked at this place, all we saw up there was a monastery of sorts. Noris butts up to a cliff. We would have had to rappel into the city."

Emma looked concerned. "But won't there be guerilla forces in that area?"

Legon shook his head. "A few, yes. I'm sure the Ascended took them out, but you have to remember that the terrain is difficult. The trails wind around and are single-track most of the way. Umbra and her team took a good look at it. There aren't any usable escape routes for the city there. They only had a few options, and we made sure they stayed open." He ate another power pack. "Okay, we will make landfall in just a moment. Let's get ready."

———

KEITHER AND SARA GOT OUT OF THE LANDING BOAT. THE fighting had all moved into the city, so they were able to take their time. The beach was littered with bodies, some Human and others Elves. Many were still in the water, washing up to shore from the sea battle. He looked to where an Elvin and Iumenta dragon lay dead in the shallows. Their bodies no longer leaching or emitting light, they sat mutilated and draining, turning the tide crimson. The whole of the beach was reddened by the blood as far as he could see.

"Crimson tide," he said.

"What's that?" Sara asked.

Keither cleared his throat. "That is what today will be known as—Crimson Tide, the day the sea turned to death."

She took his hand, and they slowly made their way up the beach to the city wall.

CHAPTER 26

ASCENSION

"Faith is believing in something without ever seeing it. Knowledge is seeing faith come to fruition."
— Confessions of Love, The First Wife

Iselin circled over the harbor of Noris. She was tired but not ready to go back to the carriers yet. The fighting for the day was done; Noris was captured. Once the Iumenta realized they'd lost the town, they retreated up the Kayloose. Most of their Ascended were flying tight cover over the area southwest of Noris, but the town and surrounding area had a wide berth. She was connected with her husband, as always, but not strictly paying attention. He was doing what he had to, and so was she. Legon did seem happy to her—something about Arkin, she thought.

Sydin spoke in her mind. "Iselin, Legon and Sasha have met up with Arkin and one of his top people; her name is Stacy."

"Yes, I've heard of her."

"Apparently, Arkin has a contact with vital information about the invasion, but this contact wants to meet a ranking official and can't risk a lot of attention. Legon, of course, offered to go and do that."

She didn't really care for this plan. "Where are they going? Do you want me to try to talk him out of it?"

"They are going into the mountains to the north of town. There are no Ascended in the area, and we don't believe there will be any resistance. Mage is going with them. Arkin and Stacy are there too. That's two class fives and three class twos with Legon, and Mage's familiars. I don't see there being a problem."

She had to agree. "Plus, Arkin has more than proven our trust. Okay, I will act as if I am flying patrol in the area. If they run into trouble, I can pull all of them out, and I'll send Cat too."

Sydin agreed with her, and she broke off from what she was doing. This little plan had the makings of a perfect storm, but Arkin was Arkin, and with no Ascended in the area, even if there was a trap...

Arkin looked up as Iselin passed overhead, a little pink ball detaching from her to form into a saber-toothed tiger next to him. Cat nudged Arkin's shoulder, and he looked back down the path.

"She flying cover?" Arkin asked.

Legon responded, "Yes, it will look like a patrol. Don't worry. Now stop stalling, old man; let's get up this hill," he said with a smile.

That was easy for an elf to say. The side of the hill they were scaling was steep and unforgiving. Arkin's legs and lungs burned with the effort, but he pushed on. Just ahead of him was Stacy. Normally, Arkin assumed she would be making comments about him staring at her backside, but even she was breathing heavily.

Stacy stopped to take a breath and looked back at Legon and Mage. "Aren't you two winded at all?" she asked.

Mage just smiled, and Emma spoke breathily. "Try living with them," she huffed out, reaching for her water skin.

"Right. My man is over that ridge," Stacy winced. "You lot go to the monastery on the cliff. Arkin and I will meet you there."

Mage frowned. "Why aren't we going to meet him directly?"

Stacy shook her head. "Couldn't risk it. If he was being watched or if someone got to him before we did... while the chances of that were small, I didn't want to risk it. Legon and Sasha are heads of house, after all." She looked up the hill. "Of course, when I made these plans, I was just looking at maps of the area, and now that I've about killed myself, well, ya know what they say about hindsight, right?"

"We'll meet you there; don't worry," Legon said and started back up the hill.

Arkin and Stacy broke off, and Arkin had to admit he was thankful that while the others still had a sizeable climb ahead of them, he would be moving sideways for a while. It didn't take long to get to an open area. To his left and up the hill, he could see the monastery.

"Okay, where now?" he asked.

Stacy pointed to his left. "Over there."

Arkin passed her, headed where she pointed, and flinched. "Ouch," he said, turning. Something had bitten him. Arkin stumbled back, feeling weak in the knees. Stacy hadn't moved yet. She was just watching him. Arkin fell over, breathing hard.

Stacy, who normally looked so happy and lighthearted, wore a stony expression as she walked up to him. "Stop struggling. The more you fight it, the faster it will kill."

The faster it would what?

"You're confused," she said, amused. "Let me help," she said as four figures emerged. They were in black and wearing cloth over their faces. Stacy turned to them. "Stay put; I'm not ready yet," she said in a cold commanding tone and then looked back at Arkin. "Sorry, they are bred for killing, not for manners. Where was I? Oh yes, your confusion. Let's see, I will have to make this fast. You do not have long, and I'm sure you have figured out that you cannot communicate with your mind or use magic. We were on to you from the moment you went and talked to your aunt and uncle. We have been watching, obviously.

"You were all so pleased with yourself for finding Mors, weren't you? Thought you had finally cracked the northern mystery. Well, you haven't. Didn't you ever wonder why there were no magic users at Mors? Did you ever think that maybe there was another place for them?" She leaned down and whispered, "There is, and I'm from it.

These animals behind me are just that—animals—but they are not from where I'm from. You see, Humanity is a tool; well, most of us are, but there are a few of us that have potential as more than just labor, like Venefica. I'll keep this short; I can see that you're having a hard time. You never looked into my past, so you never really understood me, but you depended on our mental link to give you all of the information you needed. Here is the problem—we were never fully connected, were we? Not even you would be willing to do that, not in our line of work. Truth be told, I don't even feel emotion, but I fake it well, don't I?"

Arkin couldn't believe what he was hearing right now. But he couldn't move, and he felt himself dying. She went on. "Here is what is going to happen. Right now, there are two dragons and about six Iumenta Venefica headed to meet the heads of House Evindass. They will kill them." Arkin didn't want to believe it. He didn't want to know that it was him who had let this happen. "These men here are going to mess me up pretty bad. I'll be found, and when I am, I will spin the tale of your end. You were—well, I suppose still are—the most trusted Human to the Elves, and I am your mate. Tattered and torn as I will be, and emotional too, who better to put in charge of your organization? They will give me everything you have passed on, and I in turn will pass it to my commanding officers. A lot like that time you picked up those people from Salmont."

Arkin managed a whisper. "That was you?"

She nodded. "Yes, it was. We knew that the ship wouldn't be able to cause any real damage, but it proved your trust in me, didn't it?" She ran the back of her hand along his cheek. "But I don't want you to think that this had anything to do with our relationship. I don't really feel anything, not just for you, but in general. That being said, did you really think someone as young, beautiful, and smart as I am would fall for someone like you?" She looked up, hearing something. "The Ascended are coming, so I have to go now, but do try to enjoy your last few moments alive, and know that once again, House Evindass is headless because of you."

Arkin felt as though a hole was being ripped in his chest. It had all been a lie; nothing was real. He had killed them and all of his people— all of the people in the Empire who would be affected by his actions.

How many were going to die because of him? Sickeningly, what tore at him the most was that when he moved his eyes to see the men stabbing and beating Stacy, part of him wanted to protect her. At least for him, the love had been real, and now, even knowing what she was, he couldn't help but want to save her. His breathing was becoming more and more labored. His eyes rolled up into his head as little spots formed in his vision. He twitched a few times, and then Arkin moved no more.

Iselin made her way through the cloud that was covering the tops of the cliffs. She couldn't see anything, but she was still managing just fine. There didn't appear to be anyone in the area, or at least not that she could find. She closed her eyes, just feeling her way around, when she noticed that something seemed off to her. She couldn't feel Arkin or Stacy anymore.

"Legon, is Arkin with you?" she asked.

"No, they went off to go find his contact. Why?"

"I can't feel him or her."

Legon took a moment. "Maybe they had to close their minds when they talked to him. You know, like when he called in to talk to the Elves," he offered.

She was over the sea now, but still close to the monastery. She decided to fly over it and see if she saw anything. She'd be silent if Arkin's contact was skittish. He wouldn't even see her.

Emma was thankful to be at the meeting place. She wasn't all that into climbing up giant hills for secret meetings in a war zone. Mage was walking around in a circle around her, Legon, and Sasha. The three familiars were doing likewise, all in their large forms: Legon's lion, Iselin's saber-tooth, and Mage's huge fox.

Sasha wrapped an arm around her. "How are ya?" she asked.

Emma responded honestly. "I don't think this is a great idea. I know you guys think the world of Arkin, childhood mentor and all, but something seems off to me."

Sasha frowned. "We saw into his mind. He is confident in Stacy. I think he trusts her more than he trusts us, to be honest with you."

"That's what I mean. I don't know; just chalk it up to me not being used to combat, is all," Emma said dismissively. She heard a thud. "What is..."

"It's Iselin. She is just flying over the area," Legon said.

Emma looked behind her. Just a short distance away was a sheer cliff that led to the sea. If she was being honest with herself, that was where her nervousness was coming from. Emma hated high places, and high places that dropped to jagged rocks and surf that pounded you into said rocks...

"LEGON!" Mage yelled.

Emma turned to look away from where the cliffs were to a patch of trees where twelve figures made their way out. Legon and Mage drew their fenna as the three fire animals moved to the front.

Six Iumenta with fenna stepped into their little clearing, accompanied by six familiars. Emma started to move back, but was stopped by Sasha's mind.

"Emma, stay close. Iselin is on her way, but if this gets bad, it's going to take all of us to hold them."

How was Emma going to hold anybody? She couldn't use magic. All she had was a store crystal that Legon and Mage would be using. Where was Iselin? She would be able to pull them out without issue. The thudding of her wings was close now. The Iumenta must have heard it too because they were looking up to the sky where she was coming from.

As Iselin came into view, two things happened. The first was that Emma heard the roar of three dragons—one from Iselin and another from two other dragons that were coming from the same direction the Iumenta had. The second was that the other dragons were leaching what little light there was in the sky. There was a blot of emerald from one of the Iumenta dragons that hit Emma and her group, but it didn't hurt them. Instead, she saw the pink of one of Iselin's wards flash and break. In the next moment, Iselin and the two dragons collided in the air.

Wind buffeted the top of the hill as the dragons fought. Emma watched in horror as the two Iumenta dragons forced Iselin away and over the sea. Light filled the clearing, and Emma felt heat. She turned to see that the other Iumenta were now attacking.

Emma couldn't do anything. She watched as Legon, Mage, and Sasha tried to hold off the Iumenta. The familiars were trying to hold the Iumenta familiars at bay but were not having much success. Mage and Legon were doing everything they could to defend the group. Sasha was working on offense but wasn't getting anywhere. She sent a jet of ruby to the feet of the Iumenta, freezing the ground. One of them slipped and fell. Legon took the opportunity and sent a shredding spell at the downed Iumenta. His arm ripped to pieces, sending blood everywhere, but the other Iumenta seemed unaffected by their injured comrade.

Mage yelled, "BINON!" His fenna burst with odd flames, and he sent them whipping out at the Iumenta. Emma thought she could hear the dragons fighting, but she wasn't positive. She turned then to look into the eyes of a silver-haired Iumenta, its blade raised and a ball of blue coming toward her.

This was how it was going to end. This was how she was going to die. Mage stepped in its path, blocking the magic with his fenna. There was a boom, and Mage crashed into Emma, sending both of them flying back into some trees. Emma landed hard, feeling her leg give way. She screamed and clenched her broken limb. She looked to Mage, whose head was resting on a rock. He was knocked out. Now Legon and Sasha would be alone. Emma watched helplessly.

She watched as the familiars were keeping close to Legon and Sasha, trying to hold off the Iumenta. Emma watched as a ribbon of red magic lashed out and struck Sasha, sending her to the ground. Emma saw that Sasha's chest had been slashed open and was bleeding badly. She was screaming and moaning with pain.

"No!" Emma gasped.

She pulled herself along the ground, but she was so far away, and Legon was all on his own and starting to take damage. They weren't going to make it.

LEGON FELT SASHA'S INJURY AS IF IT WERE HIS OWN. HE WAS holding their attackers off with sheer force alone. The two stores were all but gone, and soon he would be overwhelmed. He felt himself losing power. His healing spells weren't even doing anything anymore. Mage was gone, and he could sense that Iselin was about to collapse. She couldn't take on two fresh Ascended after fighting all day.

He was trying to think of a way out of the situation, but there wasn't one. His whole body was shaking with the force of his desire to save those he loved. He glanced down at Sasha. She was pale and bleeding badly. If she wasn't healed soon, she would die. There was nothing to be done. Legon looked into the eyes of one of his foes to see the ball of yellow coming at his head.

Bright white light consumed his field of view. He couldn't see anything, and he wondered if this was part of the attack. Tento was no longer in his hand, and he couldn't feel any of the small injuries he had sustained. He was dead. That's what this must be. Maybe he would see his deceased relatives. Wasn't that what was supposed to happen? The light was too bright for that; it hurt his eyes.

He fell to his hands, digging them into the soft dirt. He looked up. There was a figure in the light, just above him. He squinted, seeing two blue circles come into view. They focused into eyes. Around them were white diamonds that shimmered, creating light. They looked like scales that ran down to a nose, and a mouth with pearl teeth and a dragon's head with horns made of solid gold. Then, with a shift in his vision, the rest of the White Dragon came into view. And he realized that it wasn't that the dragon had come down to his level, but rather that he was taller. He felt the dirt with his fingers again—no; not fingers, but talons.

"Am I dead?" Legon asked.

The dragon chuckled and responded in a deep voice that touched Legon at his core. "Far from it, my child. Though had I not interceded, you would have been."

"Why did you save me?" Legon asked, and why did he think he even had the right to address the White Dragon?

"Because you know that you are mine, and that you have nothing to fear from me. That is why you feel no fear. I saved you because you still have much to do. You are the Everser Vald, if you'll recall."

Yes, yes, he did know that he was supposed to be that. The dragon went on. "You have done well."

Legon felt shame creep in. "How come I saw your brother so much?"

"He would have liked to have you, yes; but you were always mine. How could you not be with Sasha at your side? Now, enough; our time is short here. Know this: you have my support." And with that, the dragon leaned in and touched his nose to Legon's. He felt more power than he thought possible rush into his body. He felt everything—his wings, his tail, his whole being—course with energy.

The light dimmed, and Legon was back in the real world again. On all sides of him were enemies, but enemies that now looked scared. He felt Sasha's pain and felt her dying. Rage filled him as he looked at the Iumenta. As naturally as taking a breath, Legon opened his mouth and roared, sending a torrent of lavender flames to engulf the Iumenta. Energy rushed up his throat and felt wonderful. He stopped the fire, seeing only burning trees in its wake.

He was standing over Sasha. He moved and craned his head down over her. His heart tore with each beat. She was pale. Blood no longer ran from her body, and her breath was almost nonexistent. Her body all but dry. Even now, if the wound was healed, it was too late. Great tears rolled down Legon's nose, and his mind reached out to hers.

SASHA WAS IN PAIN—SO MUCH PAIN. SHE COULD FEEL HER life running out of her, and she welcomed it, anything to stop the hurting. There was a bright light from Legon, and then standing in his place was a giant purple dragon. It was larger than any she'd ever seen. It roared and burned the men that had attacked them. It was looking at her now. Her mind was fuzzy. She knew she didn't have long. The dragon's beautiful eyes filled with pearly tears that ran down its nose.

Legon's mind pulled at hers. First to go was her physical pain. When the tears hit her, they stopped the pain, and she felt calm. His mind pulled all of the sadness she'd ever felt away. All the worry and sorrow of her life was gone. No more was even the memory of a dull day. All she felt was joy. This was not such a bad fate, she thought. Her body was even feeling it. She felt more alive than she ever had before. She wanted to laugh. How odd it was that this was the best moment of her life. Her eyes filled with the most wonderful tears of joy as she looked into her brother's eyes. As the image faded, she rejoiced in the knowledge that never again would she suffer an episode. With that wonderful thought, she closed her eyes.

ABOUT THE AUTHOR

Nicholas Taylor is a fantasy and science fiction author. He was born in 1981 in Denver, Colorado, where he lives with his wife and family. Nicholas was an imaginative child who enjoyed writing stories and daydreaming about new worlds and places from a young age.

In his twenties, Nicholas rekindled a love for reading and consuming fantasy and science fiction. The culmination was his decision to write a novel in the winter of 2007. That first novel was Legon Awakening, which ran as a weekly podcast and was later released in print, digital, and audio editions that thousands have enjoyed.

Nicholas enjoys writing fiction that pulls readers into immersive worlds with likable and relatable characters. He strives to draw the reader into the scene with the characters, allowing them to explore magical realms or distant planets.

For more about Nicholas Taylor
Visit:
www.NicholasTaylor.co

www.ingramcontent.com/pod-product-compliance
Lightning Source LLC
Chambersburg PA
CBHW030921260626
47169CB00002B/350